- 8 AUG 2023
2 1 AUG 2023   2 2 MAR 2024
2 4 AUG 2023   2 6 APR 2024
1 2 OCT 2023
3 0 OCT 2023
2 2 DEC 2023
LP
Langley Park
2/24
0 5 MAR 2024

Adults, Wellbeing and Health
Libraries, Learning and Culture

Please return or renew this item by the last date shown.
Fines will be charged if the book is kept after this date.
Thank you for using *your* library.

i

THE POACHER'S POCKET

First published in Great Britain as a soft back originated in 2023.

Copyright © 2023 Michael K Foster
The moral right of this author has been asserted.

All rights reserved.

All characters and events in this book, other than those clearly in the public domain, are fictitious and any resemblance to real persons, living or dead, is purely coincidental.

No part of this publication may be reproduced, stored in a retrieval system, or transmitted, in any form or by any means, without the prior permission in writing of the publisher, nor be otherwise circulated in any form of binding or cover other than that in which it is published and without a similar condition including this condition being imposed on the subsequent purchaser.

Typeset in Bookman (*Body*) & Sears Tower *(Titles)*
Editing, design, typesetting & publishing by Remobooks

ISBN: 13: **978-1-9161210-5-8**

Cover images by ©Robert Barnes
www.storyography.co.uk/contact

MICHAEL K. FOSTER

For my beloved wife Pauline.

Acknowledgements

All my DCI Mason and David Carlisle novels are works of fiction based in the Northeast of England. There are so many people without whose help and support it would have been difficult, if not impossible, to write with any sense of authenticity. Suffering from dyslexia as I do, my grateful thanks go out to the late Rita Day and my dear late wife Pauline, whose belief and inspiration never waned.

I am indebted to Detective Constable Maurice Waugh, a former member of the Yorkshire Ripper Squad, and Ken Stewart, a former member of South Shields CID. Their technical assistance of how the police tackle serious crime has allowed me a better understanding of what takes place. Their efforts have helped me enormously.

To single out a few other names who helped on the technical side, I would like to thank Robert Barnes and Lynn Oakes for their encouragement and unqualified support in developing the initial cover graphics. Finally, I would express my heartfelt appreciation to the Beta reader team: Daniel Inman, Suzanne Lane, Brenda Forster, and Maria Jones without whose help this book would never have made the bookshelf.

Michael K Foster
www.michaelkfoster.com

MICHAEL K. FOSTER

By Michael K Foster
DCI Jack Mason Crime Thriller series

THE WHARF BUTCHER
SATAN'S BECKONING
THE SUITCASE MAN
CHAMELEON
THE POACHER'S POCKET

Novellas
DS Jack Mason the early years

HACKNEY CENTRAL

THE POACHER'S POCKET

Chapter One

Amsterdam, November 2017

Running short of ideas and desperate to get away, Shaun Quinn was now within earshot of the church of Our Gracious Lady Amsterdam. Not too long ago, he felt safe. Not anymore. The rules of engagement had changed, and to be caught out in the open meant certain death. Exhausted, he stood for a moment and gathered his bearings. Close to the bridge, at the corner with the jeweller's shop on Rozenstraat, he could see the glare from his sunglasses. Short in stature, athletic looking, there was absolute stillness in his body.

Quinn froze.

His mind in turmoil; with any luck he would soon reach his target, but the dangers were enormous. He knew that. It was a big risk, and there was no other option. Now turned thirty-five, married with two young children, Quinn had his father's looks, but not his strong rugged features. His hair was thin and wispy on top, and yet his eyebrows were thick and bushy. Dressed in a thin cotton shirt, black denim jeans and trainers, he could easily be mistaken for a tourist. He wasn't, of course.

Stationary for some moments, he pushed hard on the door, and it opened.

The church had a musky smell; it hung in the back of his throat and caused him to swallow. Cursing the pain in his leg, he felt for his iPhone and then realised he'd lost it scrambling over a wall. Isolated, and with no other means of making contact, a feeling of helplessness washed over him. Sure, it would all die down as time passed, but how to protect his sanity from the terrible things he'd witnessed was the dilemma. Murder or not, this had been a violent attack: a potent mixture of fear and untold brutality.

Fear rarely troubled him, but the house of God could be a creepy place to a non-believer. As his eyes adjusted to the dark, candles shimmered in heavy silver holders casting long spectral shadows in every direction. Beyond, close to a side aisle, he heard a door latch click and a short, overweight figure emerged. A sad looking man with a pockmarked face and receding grey hair swept back at the sides. He walked with a limp, his waxed-like appearance glistening in soft flickering sunlight as he approached. There was hesitation in his eyes, uncertainty, as if not knowing what to expect.

'You wish to speak with someone?' asked the priest.

'Forgive me, but I am here to see Father Jagaar.'

'What is the purpose of your visit?'

He spoke in gravelly broken English, more Italian than Dutch.

'We had arranged to meet here. I was given his name.'

'I see.'

Quinn hesitated as the priest opened his hands, his cassock making a swishing sound as he went. He appeared unruffled, calm, which threw Quinn off balance. One thing he'd learned over the years was never underestimate your adversary. You kept alive that way. Stayed out of trouble.

'May I speak with him please?'

'You already are my son.'

Quinn stared at him bemused.

'Would you join me in prayer?' asked the priest.

Time was precious to Quinn, and prayers were the last thing on his mind. Lured into a false sense of security, he felt the rail flex as he knelt on a hassock directly in front of the pulpit. Unsettled, a deep silence befell them, but the expression on the priest's face never faltered. Offset to his right, Quinn noticed the statue of Christ. Arms outstretched, nails protruding through upturned palms, he shuddered at the thought. If nothing else, it was a stark reminder of just how low mankind could stoop.

'Who sent you?' asked Father Jagaar.

'A man called Judas.'

'Ah, Judas—'

The priest's voice crackled with uncertainty. It reached into the darkest corners of Quinn's mind. *Act normal,* he told himself. *You're lucky to be alive.*

The priest turned as he spoke. 'How long have you been running from these people?'

Quinn shook his head as if to answer, but the words got stuck in his throat.

'You say Judas sent you.'

'Yes. He did, Father.'

Fear clawed at Quinn's skin at the mere mention of the man's name. Now desperate to be away from here, he tried to think more clearly. And yet, the church of Our Gracious Lady Amsterdam offered him the only protection he so desperately craved. He'd seen terrible things. Unimaginable things. Things that no man should ever witness.

'You have something for me?' asked the priest.

'Forgive me, Father.'

Anxious, Quinn reached into his rucksack and pulled out a small paper package. *Don't rush it,* he kept telling himself.

As he let his mind drift, he thought about his family and what they might be doing right now. It was Friday, and the kids would be at school just like every other day of the week. His wife Freda would be working as a care assistant at one of her outreach patients' homes. Freda loved helping people in their hour of need, and her thoughtfulness never went unnoticed.

He handed the priest the brown paper package, and he took it.

'This one is different from the rest. Do you know what it is?'

'No Father, but the seal is intact.'

The priest wagged a finger at him. 'This man. The one who gave it to you. How would you describe him?'

Quinn lowered his eyes as if trying not to betray his lies.

'It was dark, and I did not get a clear view of him.'

'Your mind is much troubled, my son. Unless you can help me, how can I help you?'

An awkward exchange of glances befell them.

The air felt heavy and sweet. It was then that Quinn remembered something. Something he'd dreaded, something to do with concentration camps in occupied former Yugoslavia. At one such camp in a village called Jasenovac, as many as 800,000 people were slaughtered. Croatian clergymen had served as guards and even as executioners at the camp. It wasn't looking good suddenly, and despite his need to stay calm, he caught the irritation in the priest's eyes and wondered if he saw it in his own. *To hell*, he thought. If he couldn't trust a man of God, who else could he trust?

'This man you talk of, the one they call Judas. What can you tell me about him?'

Quinn stiffened.

Not a religious man, the kaleidoscope of colours filtering through the stained-glass leaded windows had caused him to hallucinate. This wasn't right. The priest was asking too many questions and casting doubt in an already troubled mind. Was this the right church? Was this the person he was meant to meet? Panic gripped him, and he desperately tried to steady himself. Soon it would be dark, and the city would take on a different guise.

'What am I to do with this?' asked the priest.

Quinn instinctively brushed his comment aside, as if to command his attention.

'Until I return, you're to guard it with your life.'

'And when is this?'

'Those are your only instructions.'

Unable to contain his composure, Quinn turned towards the vestry door.

'No, no, no,' Father Jagaar called out. 'This will not do. I—'

Then silence.

Only the sound of Quinn's fading footsteps and the slamming of the vestry door could be heard. Whoever these people were, they wouldn't think twice about killing him. Of that Quinn was certain.

Chapter Two

Three hours into their shift, and paramedics Dan Bakker and Tess Vries were on their second cup of coffee when the call came through from the Ambulance Service Control Room. In what had been a quiet night, Tess had been working on her Christmas shopping list and trying to conjure up new gift ideas. Not anymore.

As Dan tapped the call acknowledgement button and waited for the satnav to automatically upload, it suddenly sprang to life. Next, he switched on the vehicle's blue spinner lights and eased the Mercedes E class ambulance out of the Expat Medical Centre parking bay. Marked as a Category One, the government target response times in the Netherlands EMS decreed an ambulance must be at the scene of any emergency within fifteen minutes of the call being received. Dan loved the thrill of the chase. It gave him a buzz like no other.

Joining the steady stream of traffic heading west, he glanced at the GPS again. Directed to the Bovenkerk district, a journey time of eleven minutes, his foot hit the accelerator hard. This was their second emergency callout that evening, but this felt different. Having stopped breathing, they were now racing to the aid of a twenty-two-year-old student who had collapsed on the kitchen floor.

'It's still coming up gender unknown,' said Tess.

'Who called it in?'

'A distraught friend according to the operator. They are still in contact with the caller, and relaying instructions as to what they should do.'

'Is the patient still breathing, do we know?'

'Let's hope so.'

'Sounds like a drugs overdose.'

Tess shook her head and sighed. 'More likely than not this time of night.'

Speed was paramount in these situations, as the lack of oxygen to the brain could cause all kinds of life-threatening concerns. Common causes of breathing trouble were a drug overdose, asthma, lung disease, choking, cardiac arrest, or an allergic reaction that caused tongue, throat, or airway passages to swell. The list seemed endless and being a paramedic could be highly rewarding at times. But there were drawbacks, as Tess had all too often found out. Apart from the physical, mental, and emotional demands, decades of low pay and disabling injuries incurred through the work had turned many a person away from the service. Tess loved her job, and although the good times far outstripped the bad, she still had concerns. Married with six-year-old twins, her husband Kurt had been her bedrock over the years. Never once had he complained about the unsociable hours or having to look after the children at short notice. If Tess was happy, so was Kurt. Theirs was a solid relationship built on trust and belief, with never a bad word said between them.

Tess stared through the windscreen as the traffic ahead pulled over. Some didn't bother, the unscrupulous arseholes who didn't give a dam about society or its rules. But that was the way of the modern world. People nowadays were thick-skinned, void of feelings and trapped in their own self-centred insular bubbles.

'How are you finding the new car?' Tess asked casually.

Dan glanced into the rear mirror and smiled. 'Fine, the kids think it's cool.'

'What about Freda, what does she think?'

'Convincing her we made the right decision is proving rather more difficult.'

'What made you go for a Ford? I thought your minds were set on a Peugeot?'

'The exchange rates the garage were offering were unbelievable, as were the finance repayments.' Dan smiled as he turned to face Tess. 'I couldn't walk away in the end. It was as simple as that.'

'Sounds like a good deal.'

'It was.'

Tess laughed. 'The last heap of crap you drove around in was forever breaking down as I remember. You obviously made the right decision.'

Dan grinned as he checked the computer screen for new messages.

They were travelling at speed along Beneluxbaan and fast approaching their first turn off. No two callouts were ever the same according to Dan, and you never knew what state the patient would be in on arrival. An experienced team, they'd seen it all. Homicide, suicide, head on collisions, and even the odd shootings or two. Some callouts could be much worse; their first together had been a total nightmare. A young lad smacked out of his mind on cocaine who had thrown himself in front of a bus after an argument with his girlfriend.

Tess could still visualise the firefighters scraping his body parts from under the bus and shovelling them into a black canvas body bag. Not the prettiest incident to experience. Not on your first day, it wasn't. As a large group of curious onlookers watched Tess perform her duties, all she could do was to grin and bear it.

It was a professional thing. It went with the uniform.

Disturbing events always came at a cost, and for months Tess had suffered a form of post-traumatic stress disorder. Apart from the anxiety attacks, she had difficulties sleeping. Thankfully, her husband Kert had managed to help her through it, and six years on, she'd become hardened to grizzly sights that spilled onto the streets of Amsterdam. It was all in a day's work, and she loved her job.

The moment Dan pulled into Nicolas Beetslaan; they were met by a quartet of blue spinner lights.

'They've beaten us again,' said Dan, pulling up behind a marked police car and staring out through the windscreen.

'Let's hope the patient is still alive.'

Twelve minutes and thirteen seconds from first receiving the call. Not bad, thought Dan. Well within the government target response time, he relayed their arrival back to the emergency call centre. Tess, meanwhile, had flung open the rear ambulance doors in readiness to receive their patient.

She needn't have bothered.

With a face like thunder, the officer in charge of proceedings walked purposefully towards them. Something was afoot, and whatever it was they were about to find out.

Chapter Three

Inspector Eva Jansen slid from the front seat of her unmarked police car and took in a lung full of air. A petite brunette with brown eyes, her eight years with the Dutch National Crime Squad had taught her many things. Above all, never rush into a case. Earlier that morning, having taken command of an undercover sting operation involving missing shipping containers at Amsterdam's port, she was feeling the strain. In what had been a dramatic car-smuggling sting involving dozens of armed officers, they'd made ten arrests, seized forty high-end stolen vehicles, and caused havoc with local shipping movement. Not all raids were usually this successful. Anything involving international crime syndicates was typically classed as high risk. Even so, the nasty piece of dirt with a four-million-euro luxury apartment in Pieter de Hoochstraat had annoyingly given her the slip. Jansen was furious. Allowing these people to spend the rest of their miserable days in the freedom and lifestyle they were accustomed to, wasn't her style of policing.

Stopped at the police cordon tape, the inspector was surprised to see so many officers in attendance. A few she knew. Others she'd never seen before. Local enforcement officers, the self-opinionated desk cretins keen to make a name for themselves.

Pocketing her warrant card, Jansen slipped on her disposable white over suit and moved towards a row of modern two-storey terraced houses. Forensics had beaten her to it. Even so, there was something unnatural about all the morbid activity in such a quiet corner of the city. This was a respectable community, unlike many of the rundown dumps she'd been accustomed to working in lately.

'Morning, ma'am.'

'What have we got, Peter?' she asked, turning to the bulky figure of Peter van der Vleuten the acting scene of crime officer.

The SOCO pointed a latex-gloved finger at the house opposite as he spoke. 'We've another corpse on our hands, ma'am. He's male, late thirties, medium build, and around one hundred and eighty centimetres. His throat's been cut, and he's been savagely beaten about the head. It's a weird one, as he comes with a note pinned to his chest.'

The inspector looked at him sharply. 'Note. What kind of note?'

'The kind that says – "*Big Mistake!*"'

'A bit presumptuous, don't you think?'

'Let's hope it's not another disgruntled housewife trying to make a statement, as we've seen plenty of those over the years.'

'I wish it were that simple, Peter.'

It wasn't a pretty sight. The body lay slumped against the back wall. Mouth agape, head lolled to one side, the eyes wide open. Blood spatter everywhere, the main carotid artery had been severed, and the blood loss substantial.

Holding back the disdain, Jansen checked her surroundings. The living room was small and had an austere, unlived feel. Bare walls, low ceiling, and a large casement window overlooking the main street. Jansen could see the adjoining area had been cordoned off, but this room was the centre of attention.

'What do we know about him?' she asked.

'Not a lot if I'm honest, ma'am. There's no wallet, phone, or personal effects, and he's stripped of all identification. The flat keys are missing, and there's no signs of forced entry.'

'Whoever killed him obviously knew what they were doing.'

'A professional job?'

Jansen peered out of the window wondering who he was, what kind of person, and why he had ended up like this. One thing for certain, over the following hours and days she would need to drop everything else for this investigation. She would get to know many details about this man. Who his friends and family were, where he worked, and what he got up to in the middle of the night. Nothing would escape her attention, and she would know more about him when he was dead, than anyone when he had been alive.

'Who owns the property?' she asked, after jotting down notes.

'A local business investor, ma'am. We've already made contact, and he's on his way.'

'Good man. What else do we know about the victim?'

'According to the duty surgeon, a Dr Bakker, the victim's been dead around three hours. Nothing cast in stone, but Bakker believes he was attacked from behind when his throat was cut.'

'Has anyone contacted the coroner's office?'

'Yes, ma'am. It's all in hand.'

'Dr Bakker's a good man,' Jansen acknowledged. 'Let's see what the post-mortem throws up before we go making assumptions.'

The inspector adjusted her face mask and pointed at the upturned coffee table. 'He obviously put up a fight.'

'We believe so, but we're still uncertain as to how many people engaged in the attack. More than one, I suspect.' Vleuten pointed to the windows and doors. 'We've checked every entry into the property and there's no signs of forced access. He was obviously expecting them. That said, anything of interest will be bagged, tagged, and taken away for further forensic examination.'

Jansen gave Vleuten a nod of approval. 'His visitors were his killers. If not, they had a key.'

'It's possible.'

'What about this so-called friend – the one who called it in. What has he said to us if anything?'

'No one's seen hide or hair of him.'

Jansen drew back.

'Don't tell me we have another anonymous caller on our hands?'

'I'm afraid so.'

'I thought he was in attendance when the first responders arrived?'

'No, ma'am. Whoever he was, he legged it the moment he saw the first police vehicle arrive.'

'Let's get a trace on the call, Peter. Find out what is going on.'

A thin-faced forensic officer, also present in the room, turned to face them.

'It's already in hand.'

'Good. As soon as you hear anything, you're to let me know,' Jansen replied.

'Will do, ma'am.'

Blood everywhere, floor, ceiling, and walls: signs of a desperate struggle. Surely someone must have seen or heard something. As her eyes explored the room, she sucked in the air and stared at the body again. The victim appeared well dressed. Nice suit, expensive shoes, not the type of person to go looking for trouble in the dead of night. Jansen had attended some serious crime scenes in her time, but this one felt weird. Their key witness was missing, they had no ID on the victim, and the flat didn't look lived in.

Her stare hardened.

'I get the impression this place has been stripped clean.'

The SOCO nodded. 'It's strange you should say that. There's nothing in the fridge, and the bed hasn't been slept in for weeks.'

'Which begs the question what was our victim doing here?'

'A set up, perhaps.'

Jansen sighed. 'Premeditated murder, or an arranged killing. Even so, why here?'

'Goodness knows. This is a respectable area, ma'am. People around here lead insular lives and aren't the type to live in each other's pockets.'

Jansen stared at the victim's spooky face. DNA would be the most reliable route to take. If a struggle had taken place, there would be plenty of cross-fibre contamination.

'What about CCTV coverage?'

'I was wondering when you'd ask,' Vleuten replied.

'Well?'

'There's a team out working on it.'

Jansen made a quick back-calculation.

'Estimated time of death was three hours ago, you say?'

'Yes, according to Dr Bakker.'

'With any luck a pathologist's examination might tell us more. But that takes time, and time is a luxury we can ill afford.'

The SOCO whistled through clenched teeth.

'We should ask ourselves who the note was aimed at. If not the police, is there a more sinister motive behind all of this?'

Somewhere in another room the inspector heard the distinct whirr of a SOC camera lens opening up and caught the flash in the hallway. For some unknown reason she was overcome with uncertainty. This wasn't as straightforward as she first thought. Whoever was responsible must have had good reason to kill this man. But what could that reason be?

Outside on the street, Jansen was surprised to see so many senior police officers in attendance. It was then she spotted Commissioner Ruud Cruyff. Not the easiest man in the world to get on with, Cruyff had an abrupt manner and always stank of garlic.

Her phone rang, and she answered it.

The owner of the property had arrived and was demanding to speak to the person in charge. Conscious of prying eyes, she pocketed her phone and moved purposely towards the police cordon tape.

'Ah, Inspector Jansen.'

She turned at the tone of Cruyff's grating voice and tried to avoid eye contact.

'Good morning, sir.'

'Do you have a minute?'

Jansen cringed. Cruyff was the last person she'd want to speak with at the beginning of a case. Removing her facemask, she fluttered her long eyelashes, and put on her bravest smile.

'How can I be of help, sir?

Chapter Four

Gateshead, England

From his third-floor office window at Gateshead Police Station, a red brick building on High West Street next to the Magistrates Court, Chief Inspector Jack Mason stood pondering. It was Thursday and nearing the first anniversary of his ex-wife's tragic passing. He'd planned to visit her graveside but was still trying to get his head around the idea. Brenda hadn't stood a chance according to the road traffic investigation team yet driving conditions had been perfect that day. Killed outright in a nine-vehicle pileup on the M25 in Essex, she'd died at the wheel leaving her family distraught. Not the best way to end a life, he thought. Four dead, five in hospital including two children under the age of ten. If there was comfort to be had, a Polish lorry driver was now serving a seven-year prison sentence for causing death by dangerous driving.

His mind made up, he would spend the weekend at his eldest daughter's house, then drive to Golder's Green the following morning.

The A1M was a nightmare these days. Mile upon mile of roadworks, a 50mph average speed limit in place, and cameras over the whole distance. Still, his eldest daughter lived within easy walking distance of the garden of remembrance so there wouldn't be a problem with parking.

Thinking back, his hadn't been the best marriage break-up in the book, and his ex-wife could be a vindictive sod when the mood took her. Although many years had passed, the divorce settlement had been a nightmare, and his ex-wife's legal team had taken him for every penny they could lay their hands on.

He recalled his mother's words after his father had walked out on them. *"There's good in everyone,"* she would say. His mother was right, of course. This was a time for forgiveness, being there for his daughters when they needed him most.

Still deep in thought, Mason munched on a Greggs sausage roll and took another swig of his coffee. These past few months had been manic. Crime rates had shot through the roof, and getting time off work was like trying to draw teeth. Something had to give; if not it would all end in disaster.

Mason picked up a thick green folder which had lain on his desk for weeks. He thumbed through the pages. It had been ages since they'd last made an arrest. Operation

Woodpecker was wallowing in a sea of procedural red tape, and sorely testing his patience. Ever since the reorganisation, the chief constable had taken on a more active role in proceedings which meant more meetings and less leg work as far as Mason was concerned. Rumour had it that the long-awaited raid on the Riley twin's warehouse was about to be given the green light. He doubted the raid would ever take place. County lines were the scourge of society, but the Riley twins' ability to move freely around the streets of Gateshead sickened him. Neither had an ounce of empathy for the havoc they were causing in the community, nor the damage they were inflicting on vulnerable young children. All the Riley twins ever cared about was lining their pockets with illicit drugs money and sod the rest of society. The sooner those two cretons were behind bars the easier he'd sleep at night.

His desk phone warbled, and he recognised the Netherlands land code.

'Good morning, Chief Inspector,' said Eva Jansen, from the Dutch national crime squad. 'How are things over in sunny Gateshead this morning?'

'Could be better,' Mason replied, with a half-hearted laugh. 'Did you receive the information I sent you regarding the Terrence Baxter case?'

'Yes, I did, and can't thank you enough.'

'Only too pleased to help.'

THE POACHER'S POCKET

They had never met, but Inspector Jansen seemed keen and business-like in her approach. Information was a police officer's lifeblood; without it you were working in the dark. He'd always felt at ease sharing his hard-fought knowledge with fellow police officers, as it often led to solving crimes. The mechanics of a murder investigation could be overwhelming at times but failing to get a conviction more daunting.

'How much do you know about Baxter's involvement in the diamond trade?' Jansen asked.

'In what respect?'

'His dealings here in Amsterdam.'

'I presume this is in connection with the body you recently discovered?'

'Yes, it is.'

Mason's chair creaked as he shuffled a few papers around on an untidy desk.

'Just for the record, the Baxter case was wound down several months ago and the officers involved have since moved to other duties.'

'Any reason, Chief Inspector?'

'Sure. Six months ago, Terrence Baxter was killed in a terrorist attack after stepping into the arrivals lounge at Istanbul's Airport.'

'That certainly wasn't in any of the files you sent me. A terrorist attack you say?'

Mason raised an eyebrow curious as to Jansen's train of thought.

'Baxter was killed outright according to eyewitness accounts. Never saw it coming. Nobody did.'

'What happened exactly?'

'According to the Turkish authorities, a terrorist splinter group entered the airport's terminal building and started indiscriminately shooting at anyone in sight. Dozens of innocent people were killed. From what I recall, one of the terrorists detonated the suicide vest he was wearing. Baxter was caught in the blast.'

'Goodness,' Jansen gasped.

'I know. A simple case of wrong place, wrong time I'm afraid.'

'Tell me,' said Jansen, 'How was his body identified?'

Mason gulped a huge mouthful of coffee before speaking.

'With so many people coming from various parts of the globe, they carried out a DVI, a disaster victim identification. Many of the bodies were beyond visual recognition, and the Turkish authorities had a major job in trying to pull everything together. No doubt fingerprints, dental records, and DNA recognition would have been used in the identification process. But I guess you're familiar with that.'

'Is that how Baxter was identified?'

'God knows. I suspect many were named through flight passenger lists and matching them against unclaimed luggage. It would have been sheer mayhem.' Mason stiffened. 'Why? Is there a problem?'

'There could be.'

Intrigued, Mason peered out of the window and onto the carpark below. There was something unsettling in Jenson's tone; he was struggling to come to terms with.

'May I ask what this is about?'

'New evidence has come to light.'

'Don't tell me you've uncovered the terrorist cell responsible?'

'You wish—'

'What then?'

Jansen remained silent for some seconds.

'Humour me a bit longer and I'll explain. Terrence Baxter. What can you tell me about him? His associates?'

'Baxter kept to himself as I remember. Most of the goods he handled were stolen to order, broken up, and moved on at a later stage. That's how Baxter liked to operate. He knew people, important people, and spent a lot of his time wheeling and dealing around Europe.'

'He also spent some time in prison according to the reports you sent me.'

'Yes, he did. Three years in Frankland if I'm not mistaken. But that was ten years ago.'

'I was thinking more recently.'

Mason put his mug down, irritated by her persistence.

'If you must know, up until the Istanbul incident Baxter was under round-the-clock surveillance. He wasn't the nicest person in the world to deal with, and we didn't mourn his death.'

'Round the clock surveillance regarding what?' she asked.

'A high-end jewellery heist he was supposedly involved in, but it never came to anything.'

'And what was Baxter's involvement, exactly?'

Curbing his frustrations, Mason said. 'We believe he had links to the Turkish Mafia. Which is always a good pointer as to which side of the law you're sitting on.'

'Hence his Turkish connections.'

'Like I say, a matter of wrong place, wrong time.'

He thought she'd finished, but she hadn't.

'One further question, if I may. At the time of his death, what type of people was Baxter dealing with? Were they seasoned criminals or wealthy clients investing in stolen gemstones?'

'I'm not comfortable with your line of questioning if I'm honest,' Mason replied. 'Is this in connection with the Bovenkerk flat investigation?'

'Yes. It is.'

The chief inspector took another swig of his coffee and placed the mug back down on the desk. 'All leads went cold after Baxter's death. As for the stolen gemstones, we've had little or no success in their recovery. Not that we've stopped looking.'

The line went quiet. A moment of hesitation.

'I know this may sound difficult to believe, but we suspect your case may have links to an international diamond smuggling ring.'

Mason's ears pricked up. 'Really! What makes you say that?'

'According to the latest lab reports, DNA samples recovered from the Bovenkerk flat are a hundred percent match to Terrence Baxter.'

Mason nearly choked on his coffee.

Impossible, he thought. Either the Dutch authorities had made a grave mistake, or someone had tampered with the evidence.

Jansen told him more before she hung up. Not a lot, but enough. Mason felt the hairs on the back of his neck prickle. The mere mention of Terrence Baxter's remarkable reawakening had sent shivers down his spine. If what she was telling him was true, then how come so many people had got it wrong? People in high office; people who never made mistakes. He sighed. What the hell was she on about? The dead never came back to life unless they hadn't been dead in the first place.

Chapter Five

Five feet-nine, with powerful shoulders and a large moon-like face, Jack Mason was old-school. Having risen through the ranks throughout the years, he never took no for an answer. Behind the narrow-lipped smile was an unbending ruthless streak. A pessimist by nature, digging up the past always gave him the heebie-jeebies. This was a seedy world the Dutch police were dealing with. That much he was certain.

Reaching for his notebook, he began to ponder his options. If this was Terrence Baxter's body, they'd discovered in an Amsterdam flat, then the Turkish authorities had a lot to answer for. It didn't make sense. None of it did. Besides, why would a killer make every effort to avoid detection and yet, audaciously pin a warning note to the victim's chest? Surely there'd been a mix up – people don't come back from the dead. Not when they'd been blown apart by a terrorist bomb, they didn't.

THE POACHER'S POCKET

Now deep in thought, Mason logged onto his computer. Opening old case files was one thing, but the repercussions of a wrongful verdict could be pure dynamite. No doubt the chief constable would not be happy with this latest development, especially when he'd personally been involved in the case.

Stay well-clear, he mused.

Twenty minutes later, Jack Mason addressed the assembled team regarding a large shipment of drugs about to hit the streets of Gateshead. Intelligence gathering had finally paid dividends and they were close to nailing the architects behind a huge drug operation. Things were moving along nicely.

Joined by a member of the national crime intelligence service, a dark-haired woman in her late forties, she was flanked by two fellow officer's intent on busting the gang. It was a strong turnout, and Mason was beginning to feel upbeat about what had been a long and complex operation involving five million pounds worth of high-quality cocaine.

Despite a lack of forensic evidence, he'd managed to persuade the powers in charge to give the go-ahead. It was never going to be easy, Mason knew that. The puppet masters behind the drug syndicate, the Riley twins, were two of the vilest villains in the West End of Newcastle. Surrounded by a pack of unscrupulous lawyers prepared to bend the law, the ops team were having to deal with corrupt council chambers only too willing to turn a blind eye to the twin's immoral activities. Determined to crack the case once and for all, Mason was feeling upbeat.

He stared at the whiteboard and tried to get his head around it. Once they'd broken the supply chain, it would be a matter of rounding up the distribution networks, along with the gang's trusty lieutenants. These were the cruellest shits in the organisation, responsible for meting out punishment to anyone who stepped out of line. His biggest headache, apart from the seizure of drugs itself, would be trying to hold the various pieces of the jigsaw puzzle together. One loose tongue, and the gang masters would vanish without trace.

First, he took the team through the county lines, and how the suspects had been identified through tracking dedicated phone lines known as deal lines. Disclosing more evidence, the chief inspector then took them through known safehouses including images taken by undercover officers who had infiltrated the supply chain. Next, he pointed to a second whiteboard full of offender mugshots. Not the sort of people to be messed with, it was a rogues gallery of 'Who's Who' in the seedier side of drugs trafficking. Brutal people, with little or no scruples in exploiting young children and subjecting them to extreme physical and sexual violence.

'Where are we with the latest drug shipments?' the Chief Inspector asked, as he pointed to a large coastal map pinned to the back wall.

'I can tell you,' said Maria Delaware, a smartly dressed port authorities customs officer in her early fifties who had sat quietly throughout, 'that for the past two months, Border Force have been monitoring shipping movements around the Northeast coastline.' She pointed to the map with the tip of her pen. 'We now know that significant quantities of high-quality drugs are shipped into the River Tyne under the cover of darkness. Having infiltrated their supply chain, we also know that regular shipments of drugs are smuggled into North Shields' Fish Quay via a rogue fishing trawler. The difficulty is, without spooking the perpetrators, we are unable to get close.'

'Do we know who they are?' asked Mason.

'We do,' said Delaware confidently.

He nodded for the custom officer to continue.

'Our prime suspect is this man,' said Delaware, tapping the rogues' gallery with the back of her hand. 'Leon Docherty. The co-owner and skipper of *Ocean Swell*, a thirty-one-meter Panama Class trawler currently sitting in the Port of Rotterdam and preparing to set out to sea on another drug run. Most won't know that Docherty is sole supplier to the Riley organisation. We have the fruits of the Rotterdam police's dogged intelligence work, which tells us that the *Ocean Swell* is to rendezvous with a French trawler named *Gloire* just off the Danish coast.'

The bulky figure of Sergeant Collins from digital forensics shuffled awkwardly in his seat. 'Is this where the drugs will change hands?'

'I was coming to that,' Delaware smiled. She pointed to the map. 'A final date has yet to be finalised. Having shadowed *Ocean Swell* on previous drug runs, there's every possibility that to coincide with the high tide on the Tyne, which is in the early hours of Saturday morning, the next drug transfer will take place on Friday night.'

'If I'm reading you correctly,' said one of the firearms officers, 'how will we know that she'll be carrying drugs?'

'We don't, but our sources confirm there's a ninety-five percent chance.'

Mason nodded approvingly.

'I'm no gambling man, but those odds excite me.'

'Why don't we impound her before she lands?' Detective Sergeant Savage said, in a strong Geordie accent.

'That's not going to happen, Rob,' Mason replied. 'Looking at previous shipments we know the Riley twins always check their merchandise before money changes hands.'

'Good point,' Savage acknowledged with a nod.

'With five-million pounds of hard drugs at stake, these people trust no one,' another officer chirped in cynically.

Mason ran through the possible risks in his head. Any sniff that a police raid was about to take place and the gang would scatter like rats leaving a sinking ship. No, he thought. They would need to stay vigilant. This was a brutal gang that wouldn't think twice about using extreme violence.

'Okay,' Mason said, thoughtfully. 'That leaves us with two possibilities. Either a drug transaction will take place in the early hours of Saturday morning at the Fish Quay, or once the trawler has landed, the drugs will be taken to the Riley's warehouse and away from prying eyes. That seems the most likely option.'

'There is a third possibility,' said Maria Delaware, staring across at Mason.

'Which is?'

'We believe the drugs may be packed into false-bottomed boxes and sold at the fish auction.'

DS Savage gave a thin smile. 'Blimey, who would have thought of that.'

Mason nodded as he did a quick mental calculation. Delaware had raised a good point, but not all boxes would be loaded with drugs. It would be down to a chosen few. Which ones? Thinking this through, he figured that someone at the North Shields Fish Quay must be involved in the gangs underhand tactics. Either way, it was a clever ploy of which he was now mindful.

As the meeting ended, Mason called in at the canteen to pick up a bacon butty. Having skipped breakfast that morning, he felt as though he hadn't eaten in days. Now thinking about his partner Barbara Lockwood and what she might be up to, he pulled out his iPhone and punched in the magic number. Never in a million years had he dreamt he would ever fall in love again. Not after such a messy divorce. And yet here he was, back in the love stakes and living the dream. Barbara, three years younger than him, was different. More mature, more understanding, and less demanding than any woman he knew and had met over the past few years.

'Hello, my love. How's your day going?' his partner asked, in her usual chirpy voice.

'Not a lot happening actually.'

'Really?'

He took a bite of his bacon butty, swallowed quickly, and said, 'I was wondering if you fancied eating out tonight. Somewhere nice.'

'Anywhere special in mind?'

'It's just that—'

Mason's brain felt sluggish after another hard slog meeting. Like most senior police officers he knew, staying connected with family and loved ones was a crucial part of maintaining a solid relationship. Too many marriages had failed owing to long hours of separation over the years, including his own disastrous breakup. It was every police officer's nightmare, and there was no easy answer other than to stay in regular contact.

Mason was lucky, of course. Barbara was very understanding about the long, unsociable working hours.

'Trouble at the mill?' she asked.

'What makes you say that?'

'I can always tell when you're under pressure, Jack. I've known you long enough.'

'True. It's not that easy, I'm afraid.'

'You need a holiday, my love. You've said so yourself often enough.'

Blimey, he thought. Chance would be a fine thing and far too many problems were cropping up.

'You're right,' he replied, coyly.

'Why don't we spend a few days in Scotland?'

'Let's talk about it over dinner,' Mason replied, 'How does seven o'clock sound?'

'Oh. So, you do have a table booked?'

'Well – err,' he hesitated. 'What about our favourite Italian restaurant down on the Quayside?'

'That's absolutely perfect.'

'Seven it is then.'

Mason ended the call and strolled back to his office. Having started with a clear diary that morning, it was beginning to fill up. Deep down he knew Barbara was right. Once the Riley twins were behind bars, he would seriously consider taking time off. Not now, though, as he had far more pressing challenges on his mind.

His phone rang, and he checked the display.

God, he thought. It was turning into another one of those days.

Chapter Six

Jack Mason sat in silence inside the office of his area commander, Superintendent Albert Gregory. It was a large oval room on the fourth floor overlooking Gateshead city centre. As part of the reorganisational structure the whole building had been given a make-over, and everything seemed much airier and brighter. The office walls had been painted in muted pastel shades of blue, complimented by thick, heavy-duty matching cerulean carpets. Gone were the drab industrial brown floor tiles, along with Gregory's large imposing desk which always screamed of authoritarian gone mad.

Hands cupping a glass of water, the superintendent looked strained. A dapper man, with grey swept-back hair and thin on top, Mason's boss was a stickler for detail. Close to retirement, Gregory seldom ventured out of his office these days. An insular police officer, they'd had their fair share of run-ins over the years, which undoubtedly had done nothing to enhance his promotion prospects. The DCI had always regarded Gregory as a bit of a dickhead.

Never one for putting his neck on the line, he'd risen through the ranks on the back of other people's efforts. It was a classic case of autocratic prejudice, twenty-five years spent crawling his way to the top using any means possible. Mason despised devious sycophants with a vengeance, it wasn't his style of policing.

'I take it you've read the latest report regarding our old friend, Terrence Baxter?'

Mason nodded, 'Yes sir, I have.'

'What's your take on it, Chief Inspector?'

'There's not a lot I can add if I'm honest. I suspect it's a case of mistaken identity.'

Gregory shuffled awkwardly and looked at him with his habitual nervous smile.

'From what I recall the Turkish authorities did tend to rush into things.'

'Even so, there's no easy answer to dealing with such devastating carnage.'

Gregory shook his head. 'I wonder what the Home Office will make of it?'

'Not a lot I would imagine.'

What puzzled Mason more than anything was the savage nature of the murder. Surely, the Dutch police had made a grave mistake. The moment the press got a whiff of it all hell would be let lose. Media gatherings, press interviews, police appeals, the list seemed endless. It had been years since he'd last worn his uniform, not since the passing of an old colleague in 'C' Division. He had piled on the weight since then and doubted it would fit anymore. Everything was a tight squeeze these days, and apart from the effects of an overindulgent lifestyle, there was little else he could do other than give up the junk food and go on a diet. Not a good prospect, he mused.

He opened his notebook in readiness.

There was no getting away from it. DNA samples found at the Bovenkerk flat were a hundred percent match according to forensics. How had Baxter survived a terrorist attack to live out another six months? And yes, he could think of a dozen people who'd want Baxter dead, as dead he now was according to the Dutch authorities.

God what a mess!

Gregory lifted his head as he spoke. 'I am informed you've recently been in contact with the Dutch National Crime Squad. Is it true?'

'That's correct, sir. An Inspector Jansen asked me for information regarding Terrence Baxter's criminal background. Knowing the national crime squad were involved, I emailed her some details.'

'Did she say why she wanted this information?'

'Just that she was engaged in a murder investigation in the Bovenkerk district.'

'I see,' Gregory replied, shifting in his seat. His boss was floundering, trying to pick his brains in his usual condescending manner.

'Did Jansen mention why Terrence Baxter was of particular interest to them?'

'Not really. The inspector was more interested in Baxter's associates, his criminal friends, the usual background details required to run a murder investigation. Knowing Baxter had been dead six months, I never gave it a second thought.'

'What about **Operation Wizard**. Did you mention anything about that?'

'No, sir. I did not.'

The superintendent took some notes as he spoke. 'I don't usually get hot under the collar over such matters, but there are a lot of inconsistencies in the forensic report. The Dutch authorities may have a murder investigation on their hands, but I'm far from happy about the way they are handling the case. This Inspector Jansen you've been dealing with, what else can you tell me about her?'

'As far as I can tell, she's efficient, amicable, and extremely thorough in the way she goes about her business.'

'If you ask me, she's a bit of a loose cannon. Either that, or she thinks you're an easy touch.'

Mason bit his lip.

'Surely there's been a mistake.'

'There may well be, but it appears Inspector Jansen has led you up the garden path on this one.'

'Really. And here's me thinking I was doing her a favour.'

Gregory swung to face him. 'The problem I'm faced with is the Dutch tabloids are full of it. God knows where this will end up once our media get their hands on the story.'

'Sounds like the shit is about to hit the fan.'

'It already has,' Gregory replied. 'I've already had the Chief Constable on the blower, and he's far from happy at the way this case is developing. He wants you to take a closer look at Operation Wizard.'

Mason reflected on this.

'There could be a simple explanation, of course.'

'If you can think of one, I'd love to hear it.'

Mason shook his head.

'Our biggest concern is that this gets blown out of proportion,' Gregory stated. 'What if this turns out to be another gangland killing?'

The fool always assumes it's a gangland killing, Mason thought. Resolved to prove him wrong, he nodded in agreeance pushing it to the back of his mind.

'You may not be aware of this, but fingerprints lifted from the Bovenkerk flat implicate a fellow British police officer in Baxter's murder.'

'Blimey!' Mason gasped. 'She never mentioned that.'

Gregory looked at him. 'I'm surprised, Chief Inspector. You're usually one step ahead of the game at this stage, and quick to express your opinions, might I add.'

Mason drew back. 'What in hell's name is going on?'

'For whatever reasons you supplied information to this Inspector Jansen, in future you need to start asking her a few pertinent questions. It's not looking good. There's an awful lot resting on these latest DNA findings, and some disturbing parallels with Operation Wizard.'

'Yes, sir.'

Sharing information about a known criminal was one thing, but never would he have imagined Inspector Jansen would be withholding vital information from him. Anger flared in Jack Mason. He'd been hoodwinked into believing he was assisting her in a difficult murder enquiry, when all the time it involved a British police officer.

This wasn't good, he thought grimly. The fact that Terrence Baxter had survived the Istanbul terrorist attack only to be killed in Amsterdam, puzzled him. Either someone had made a grave error, or they were tampering with the evidence. It didn't add up, but he was still keeping an open mind as to the credibility of the latest DNA findings.

'Having talked to my counterpart at the Met, what I'm about to tell you is strictly confidential.' Gregory looked down at his notes. 'The UK police officer implicated in Terrence Baxter's murder, is called Ellis Walker.'

'Never heard of him,' Mason replied.

Reaching over, the AC showed him a series of images of a casually dressed man standing in front of a Series 2 BMW. 'His real name is Shaun Quinn. He's one of ours, and prior to his transfer to 'L' Division he worked for digital forensics for a number of years.'

Mason drew back in his seat. 'What? He's a spook.'

'I thought that might interest you.'

'If I'm not mistaken, we've been down this avenue before.'

Gregory answered with a smile that Mason found impossible to read. Things were heading in the wrong direction, and he'd already been singled out for his collaboration with the Dutch police. Mason felt he was being sucked into something more sinister.

'May I ask what this officer was doing in Amsterdam around the time of Baxter's murder?'

Gregory's face darkened. 'Did Inspector Jansen mention anything about this to you?'

'No. She did not.'

The Area Commander stroked his chin, then tapped a large bundle of case files that were lying on his desk in front of him. 'Nine months ago, the Metropolitan Police received a tip off that Terrence Baxter was involved in one of the most audacious robberies of the century. It was the breakthrough the authorities had been waiting for. What nobody knew, not even counterintelligence, was that millions of dollars' worth of uncut diamonds were about to be stolen from the cargo hold of a Lufthansa jetliner. Where or when the raid was to take place was apparently only known to those at the top of the crime organisation.' The AC gestured as if to make a point. 'Once counterintelligence got a sniff of it, their network of undercover agents went in search of these people. Their biggest fear, and rightfully so, was that the crime was funding a terrorist organisation with known links to Pakistan.'

'Hence Baxter's knowledge in shifting uncut diamonds.'

'Indeed.'

'So, where does Shaun Quinn aka Ellis Walker fit in all of this?'

'I was coming to that,' said Gregory, rolling his eyes. 'Ten months ago, Quinn was seconded to the Serious Crime Division as part of an elaborate undercover operation aimed at weeding out the mastermind behind a series of violent diamond robberies that were taking place throughout Europe. It was all very hush-hush. Quinn's task was to infiltrate the gang's core operations. It was a significant risk but working with the Home Office and Florida's State Governor's team, they concocted a plausible story that would allow Quinn to be locked up in Liverpool Prison.

Mason's grin broadened. 'Why Liverpool? If Quinn was a plant, then what was the reasoning behind his being there?'

Gregory looked surprised at Mason's directness.

'The simple answer is, counterintelligence had reason to believe that someone inside the prison had connections to the diamond smuggling gang, and Ellis Walker's expertise in armed robbery might be extremely useful to them.'

'A bit over the top don't you think?'

'If it was, then most of the inmates at the prison fell for it. The thing was, nobody had heard of Ellis Walker in the UK criminal fraternity, but a violent trumped-up criminal record in the US had obviously preceded him.'

'Ah. A sprat to catch a mackerel?'

Gregory smiled, which Mason took to be a show of exuberance. As ever, once into his stride, the area commander was keen to elaborate.

'The criminal underworld is usually good at sniffing out rotten apples; how come they haven't picked up on Walker's story?'

'True,' Gregory nodded, 'but in Walker's case, counterintelligence had been conspiring with the head of the US Corrections Department to add credibility to the story. The real Ellis Walker had been given parole on medical grounds after he was diagnosed with terminal cancer. Within weeks of his release, he had passed away. Along with his criminal records. In other words, Shaun Quinn's new identity, Ellis Walker, was watertight.'

So much for the technical explanations, Mason thought. But he doubted Walker's alibi was watertight. People at the top of an international crime syndicate had ways of finding things out. As more of the story unfolded, Mason considered his options.

'As I recall, the Schiphol diamond heist was a brilliant piece of planning. Who in their rightful mind would think of breaking into a secure establishment such as an international airport?'

'Someone obviously did,' Gregory countered.

'Let's face it, sir. Protected by dozens of layers of security including armed police, trip sensors, close circuit TV: these people had balls.' Mason paused, then continued, 'You mentioned counterintelligence were close to establishing who the mastermind was. Do we have a name?'

Gregory pursed his lips. 'No, unfortunately. Even if they did, I doubt that kind of information would be given to us.'

'How much was actually stolen?'

'In the region of fifty-million dollars. It could be a lot more.'

'Crikey, that's a shedload of diamonds,' Mason gasped.

'And that's where Terrence Baxter came into it – disposing of the gang's ill-gotten gains. There were others involved, including our old friend Edward Coleman, but we're merely scratching the tip of the iceberg at this stage.'

'So, what happened to the diamonds?' asked Mason.

'No one knows for sure.'

'I take it Baxter's visits to Turkey must play a crucial part in this?'

'We believe so.'

Mason felt a sharp, sinking sensation.

'You mentioned Edward Coleman. What was his involvement in all of this?'

'Ah! Edward Coleman,' said Gregory, the tone of his voice faltering. 'There have been some interesting new developments regarding Coleman's status, which I'm not at liberty to discuss. But rest assured, we have our fingers on the pulse.'

'That doesn't surprise me. Anything involving major crime usually has Coleman's stamp all over it.' Mason rallied, certain there was more. 'So, what was our man Shaun Quinn doing in Amsterdam at the time of Baxter's death? I thought he was operating as a plant in Liverpool prison, or am I missing something here?'

Gregory nodded.

'To cut a long story short, Ellis Walker is now working for Ed Coleman.'

Mason could hardly believe his ears.

'What!' he gasped.

'It's a well-kept secret, but it took me by surprise too.'

'Too right. No one has ever managed to get close to the man.'

'Up until now,' Gregory countered. 'Our friends at the Met have obviously found a chink in Coleman's armour and are exploiting it to their advantage.'

Mason felt a tremor of excitement. This case had stepped up a notch and he was eager to find out more.

'Tell me,' said Mason. 'How did Ellis Walker become involved with a notorious gangster like Ed Coleman?'

Gregory tapped the case files with his pen. 'After the charges against him were dropped on trumped up technical grounds of mis identity, Walker was allowed to walk free from prison. But he kept active, and shortly after his release he was introduced to one of Coleman's close associates at a charity function. Coleman was so impressed with Walker's criminal credentials, he decided to take him on.'

'Was this in connection with the Schiphol diamond robbery?'

'We believe so.'

Mason drew back in his seat. 'Who's leading the investigation?'

'The Met is, but it's all part of a wider national strategy involving Central Intelligence.'

'Special Branch no doubt?'

'No. This is being run by Specialist Crime Directorate 7.'

Mason blew through his cheeks. 'God. This must be big.'

'It is,' Gregory confirmed.

'And our Dutch counterparts, what is their involvement in all of this?'

'They now have a murder investigation on their hands, and one with possible links to the Schiphol Airport diamond heist.' Gregory paused for effect. 'From what we can gather, Dutch Intelligence are keeping their own police at arm's length for fear of recriminations. We know they've interviewed dozens of airport staff, but nothing has come of it.'

Mason sat quietly.

'I'm missing something here. If Baxter was alive up until a few weeks ago, then where has he been all this time?'

'Good question. The chief constable wants you to link up with your counterpart in Amsterdam, take on a more active role. Now the British Consulate General is involved, he's worried about a backlash.' Gregory paused, then said: 'There's a meeting at Police Headquarters at ten-thirty.'

Not one for getting involved at this stage of his career, Gregory had unwittingly been dragged into the thick of things. No doubt he'd be offloading much of his responsibility at the first opportunity. That's how the sly old sod worked.

'One other thing,' Mason said, closing his notebook. 'What about my current involvement in Operation Woodpecker? I'm expecting a large consignment of drugs to arrive in the Tyne in the early hours of Saturday morning. The shipping forecast looks good, and I'm told that once the trawler *Ocean Swell* links up with its French counterpart *Gloire*, it's to be kept under the watchful eye of Border Force.'

'Leave that with me, Chief Inspector. This case is far more important than any Riley twin. As far as the chief constables concerned, he's keen you take on a more active role. Boots on the ground if you get my drift.'

Too damn right, Mason thought. A notorious criminal lay dead: another was up to his neck in a diamond heist, and an undercover officer had mysteriously gone off the radar.

Mason fidgeted uneasily.

'And team selection? Anyone in mind?'

'I'll leave that entirely to you, Chief Inspector.'

Mason smiled. At least something was going in his favour. Then the penny dropped. No wonder Gregory was keen to nip this in the bud. Get it wrong and the entire operation would come crashing down on top of him. Not for the first time in his career he'd been handed the poison chalice, but it was time to bite the bullet and do what he did best – ruffle a few feathers.

Chapter Seven

Back in his office, Mason googled, "diamond theft." It didn't add up. None of this did. If the chief constable's aim were to reopen Operation Wizard, there had to be more to this than his Dutch counterpart was letting on. If not, then why was everyone running around like headless chickens? It had been years since he'd handled an old case and digging up the past wasn't his style of policing. The past was full of bad omens; any thoughts of chasing halfway around Europe looking for answers to a brutal murder, didn't exactly enamour him. Whoever was behind the armed robbery would be watching them, Mason was sure.

He surfed the Internet, this time putting in "Schiphol diamond heist" into his search. Tucked away in the smaller print, he found what he was looking for. According to the security report's, the gang had bypassed the airport's sophisticated protection system by disrupting the electricity supply and tapping into a power relay close to the control room. Dressed as airport security and armed with

Walther P99 semi-automatic pistols, the gang had entered the airport through a gate in the perimeter fence. It was a well-thought-out plan. Watertight. Using three yellow vehicles disguised as airport security trucks, the gang had driven in convoy straight up to the Lufthansa aircraft where the uncut diamonds had been transferred from a Brinks armoured van. Not one person had challenged them according to the report, and airport security staff hadn't been alerted. With split precision timing, and barely a fifteen-minute window before the plane moved to take off, the gang had managed to overpower ground staff and work with military precision in offloading fifty-million dollars' worth of uncut diamonds.

He sat back and thought about it. Not for long. The operation was so finely tuned, that passengers were unaware of what was taking place. When the alarm was eventually raised, police rushed to the scene and roads to the airport had been immediately controlled by roadblocks. It was all in vain. The gang had vanished without trace leaving airport security chiefs with an awful lot of explaining to do.

He made a mental note of what had taken place, then analysed each of the elements to create a bigger picture. Who could mastermind such a daring operation? Who were the people involved? He knew from experience there would be plenty of contenders who would have given their right arm to have taken part in the raid. But were they capable? No, he thought. This had the hallmarks of an international crime gang, faceless villains with contacts in every corner of the globe.

When tea and biscuits arrived, Mason realised he'd missed lunch. It was pub time, and he was really looking forward to a pint. Not today though. With so many unanswered questions, he would need to devise a plan. This was no ordinary crime. This was pure dynamite. He also knew that prior to the raid Dutch Intelligence believed the gang had been watching the airport's security for months. The problem was uncut diamonds were virtually impossible to trace. He knew that. There was no simple explanation, just a catalogue of uncertainty that would suck on resources and stretch them to the limits.

For once Gregory was right, the post-mortem was key. Apart from confirming it was Baxter who had died in the Bovenkerk flat, Mason felt something more sinister was lurking beneath the surface. He pocketed his notebook and pondered his options.

His immediate thoughts were to run it past his friend, profiler David Carlisle. The man was a mine of information. An excellent choice at getting into other people's minds. He dialled the number and waited for the connection.

'How are things with you, my friend?' said Mason, by way of introduction.

'Could be better. Not heard from you in a while.'

'You should know me by now. Never a dull moment.'

The profiler laughed. 'You always did have a nose for sniffing out trouble, Jack.' The line went quiet for a moment. 'On a more sober note, did you manage to visit your ex-wife's graveside?'

'Why do you ask?'

'The last time we spoke you were still undecided.'

An image flashed in Mason's head.

'Yes, I did. I stopped overnight at my daughter's house and drove to the garden of remembrance the following morning. Peace of mind and all that.'

'I'm glad you made it. How's the grandson? Still keeping you occupied?'

It was Mason's turn to laugh. 'I'd almost forgotten how demanding little people can be. I was knackered by the time I got home.'

Mason sensed hesitation.

'What can I do for you, Jack?'

'How's the workload at the moment?'

'Plenty of it, just not my cup of tea. Why, is there a problem?'

'I may have a proposition to put to you.'

'Really! Regarding what?'

'It involves an old friend of ours.'

'Less of the old,' Carlisle jested. 'What's on your mind?'

'New evidence has come to light concerning Terrence Baxter, and there's talk of reopening Operation Wizard.'

'I thought the case was closed.'

'That's what everyone thought.'

Mason dug deep as he relayed his story to Carlisle. His dealings with Inspector Jansen and the Dutch National Crime Squad, the Bovenkerk flat incident, and fingerprints found at the crime scene. By the time he had finished he felt he'd done enough to whet his friend's appetite. It was never going to be easy for Mason. Carlisle had a sharp, analytical mind and would want to know the bigger picture. This was why he preferred to eschew Carlisle's expertise unless the case specifically involved criminal profiling.

'What are your thoughts?'

'Sounds a bit fishy to me. Someone has made a massive blunder, I suspect. What makes them think it was Terrence Baxter's body they found in the Bovenkerk flat?'

Mason sucked the air. Carlisle was thorough and could be darn right frustrating at times. But he was good at his job, and if anyone could climb into a predator's mind, it was him.

'Here's my problem,' said Mason, still grappling to curtail his emotions. 'The Dutch authorities have more than enough DNA evidence to convince a thousand juries that Baxter had survived the terrorist attack. I've done a few checks, and there's no disputing the fact.'

The profiler rallied. 'That is an interesting assumption.'

'Good. I take it you're interested.'

'Could be.' A pause. 'This Inspector Jansen you've been dealing with, what can you tell me about her? What kind of person is she?'

Mason's phone rang, but he ignored it.

'Where do I begin?'

'Well, if you were her first port of call, it was an incredibly shrewd move don't you think?'

'Not really, Interpol were guilty of that.'

'In what way?' asked Carlisle.

'Once they'd confirmed the murder victim's DNA matched Terrence Baxter's, that's when they put her onto me.'

'Have the two of you met?'

'Not yet, we haven't. She's no push over, I can assure you.'

'I didn't say she was. I was merely thinking along the lines of you jumping to conclusions. There's a lot of inconsistencies in the narrative, and no two stories sound the same.'

Mason drew back, trying his best to remain calm.

'So, what's your take on the case?'

'Tread carefully, Jack. If this is a cold case you are working on, you could be treading on dead men's graves. I know how the system works, and these investigations are always fraught with danger. Never take sweets from a stranger my old man used to tell me, and it's stuck with me ever since.'

Terrific, Mason thought.

'I take it you're not interested?'

'Could be. Then again, what sort of role did you have in mind for me?'

'Past case history, and your uncanny knowledge of what makes people tick.'

Carlisle laughed. 'Sounds like you definitely need a profiler.'

'It had crossed my mind,' Mason chuckled.

'The undercover police officer who's gone missing. What more can you tell me about him?' asked Carlisle.

'I've been looking into his history and there's involvement in the Irish troubles. Brought up in the backstreets of Belfast, Walker had quite a reputation. Well educated, his ambition of becoming a solicitor were dashed when he failed to gain the necessary 'A' level grades. Having turned his hand to journalism at the age of twenty-two, he worked for several Irish newspapers before joining the local Gardai as an intelligence officer. Counter-terrorist operations, bandit country, places you and I would not dare go.'

'He's well-schooled, by the sounds.'

'Like I say, counterintelligence aren't daft, they've obviously done their homework.'

The profiler remained silent for some moments, and then said, 'What if Walker didn't kill Terrence Baxter. What then?'

Mason slumped back in his seat. 'Thinking outside the box, are we?'

'Just trying to get my head around the case. If Edward Coleman's involved, that gives you another headache.'

They chewed over the facts. About Operation Wizard and Baxter's history with Newcastle gangsters. Outwardly reserved, Carlisle had never fully got over his wife's tragic death; it had left him totally devastated. The scars ran deep, and he could not forgive himself for not being there when she needed him. The profiler's biggest drawback, if Mason could think of one, were the disruptive mood swings. Even so, he was a likeable person. Above all else, Carlisle's reputation for understanding the working of the criminal mind was second to none. He was the best.

'Why don't you accompany me to Amsterdam?' Mason asked outright, 'Get a feel for the case. There's a flight out in the morning.'

'Hang on a minute! I'm not that desperate to drop everything.'

Mason rolled his eyes as he tried another tack.

'The tone of your voice tells me otherwise. Besides, it will be like old times again.'

'I don't like the sound of that either.'

'Really?'

'I know how your mind operates. Tell me,' Carlisle said. 'What terms of reference were you considering?'

'Jesus, this is a murder investigation involving a missing police officer not a game show. The same as before I would imagine.'

'Good,' said Carlisle, with more than a touch of cynicism. 'We understand each other perfectly.'

Mason snapped his thoughts back to the matter in hand. The profiler was right, there were dozens of loose ends, and now Edward Coleman's name had been thrown into the mix, nothing could be ruled out.

Chapter Eight

There were four of them sitting around the table at Gateshead police station that afternoon: Jack Mason, Detective Sergeant Rob Savage, Detective Sue Carrington, and the profiler David Carlisle. Things were moving at pace, and whilst the area commander had gathered his support team in MIR-1, the chief constable had informed his counterpart in Amsterdam that his officers would soon be joining them.

Mason took another bite of his cheese sandwich as he ran back over Inspector Jansen's latest report. It was Monday, and they were still awaiting blood sample results from the Netherlands forensic lab. Once they had those, he could set the wheels in motion.

'It seems to me,' Mason said first, 'that our best course of action is to establish a possible motive.'

'Why would we want to do that?' replied Savage, in his gruff Geordie accent.

'If Ellis Walker's last known movements puts him inside the Bovenkerk flat, then what was he doing there? I'll admit I'm no clairvoyant, but blood sample results will go a long way to proving or disproving he murdered Terrence Baxter.'

'I thought that was down to Inspector Jansen's team to determine?' said Savage.

'It is. If Ellis Walker and Baxter were in a fight, I'd expect to find DNA contamination evidence on the victim's clothing.'

The sergeant screwed his face up at Mason's response. 'If they were in a fight, we'd have known about that before now, surely.'

He watched as the detective took another swig from a can of coke and flopped back in his seat. The sergeant was right, of course. It felt as though the Dutch police were moving at a snail's pace. Savage wasn't a specialist at anything, more a jack of all trades which suited the chief inspector down to the ground.

'These things take time' Mason said, trying to defuse the situation, 'but you're right. For one reason or another, Inspector Jansen is keeping her cards close to her chest. I suspect she's worried about the press and trying to keep a lid on things.'

The smile slid from the sergeant's face. He looked puzzled.

'How the hell did Baxter manage to survive a terrorist attack?'

'I'm hoping the Turkish authorities might tell us more on that.'

'Yeah, but they have a lot of explaining to do.'

'So do a lot of people,' Mason shrugged.

Carrington pursed her Cupid-bow lips as she turned to Mason.

'Why Amsterdam, boss? He had to be there for a reason.'

'Diamonds, Sue. It's as simple as that.'

Carrington looked up. 'Just because Walker's fingerprints were found in the Bovenkerk flat doesn't mean he murdered Terrence Baxter.'

'That's my point,' Savage interrupted, 'though it still puts him at the crime scene.'

Mason bit his lip.

He watched as Carrington flicked through her case files, stopping at the desired place. 'According to the Dutch coroner's report,' she said in a quiet voice, 'the cause of death was massive blood loss after the victim's carotid artery had been severed.'

'Any other injuries?' asked Savage.

It was Mason's turn to intervene, and there was sharpness in his tone. 'Had you read the report, you'd have known Baxter received a massive blow to the right side of the head, along the suture line midpoint between the frontal and parietal bones. He was struck with such force he suffered multiple skull fractures.'

'Which begs the question,' said Savage, shaking his head, 'did more than one person participate in the attack?'

'There had to be,' Carrington concurred, pointing at her notes. 'According to the coroner's report, apart from extensive stab wounds to the arms and upper body, he was beaten around the head with a heavy metal object.'

Beneath the angelic charm, Carrington was tough and certainly no push over; one of the requisites of Mason's team selection. She was intelligent, incredibly quick witted, and had a slightly wry sense of humour. The solution to solving some crimes lay in a solid team foundation. The detective was not only business-like in her approach, but she could also manage demanding situations.

'This Inspector Jansen who's leading the investigation,' said Savage, looking across at them. 'She's a shrewd cookie by the sounds.'

'What makes you say that?' asked Mason.

'Let's face it, we are still lacking information.'

'What's bothering you, Rob?'

Turning to the chief inspector, the sergeant said, 'I am not liking it, boss. Either Jansen's a control freak or she doesn't want us getting involved in the case.'

'Let's not put obstacles in our way,' Mason replied, 'as we need to be seen working together on this one.'

David Carlisle who had sat quietly during the meeting, was keen to draw their attention back to the Schiphol airport heist and Ellis

THE POACHER'S POCKET

Walker's involvement. 'What about the diamond robbery itself. What do we know about that?'

Mason explained, 'With so many uncut stones slushing around in the system today, a lot of the cutting and polishing is done in India and China. Billions of dollars are changing hands, and it's hard to keep track of their movement.'

Savage's brow corrugated. Around six-foot one, he had a thin-set face, fair complexion, and fair hair.

'I thought Belgium and Holland were the main diamond centres of the world.'

'Not anymore.'

'Bloody hell. No wonder Baxter was engaged in that side of the business.'

'Nothing is sacrosanct,' Mason replied stoically, 'Even you should know that.'

Carrington tapped the end of her pencil on the table. 'If this was a gangland execution, I can think of a dozen motives behind Baxter's killing.'

'Me too,' Savage agreed.

'Who owns the flat and why were both parties drawn to it?' questioned Carlisle. 'There may be a simple explanation, of course, and it doesn't necessary mean they were both in the flat at the same time.'

'Only Walker can tell us that,' Mason replied.

'So where do we start looking for him?' asked Savage despairingly.

The room fell silent again.

'It's my guess Walker is still in Amsterdam,' Mason said, pointing at the crime board. 'He'd obviously gone there on Ed Coleman's instructions.'

'Yeah, but nobody knows where he is.'

Mason put his pen down and rubbed tired eyes. 'Which means there are two possible lines of enquiry open to us, as Walker cannot be in two places at once. Either he's hunkered down in Amsterdam, or he's made his way back to Liverpool.'

'Hang on a minute,' said Savage. 'If he's back in Liverpool, why hasn't he touched base with central control?'

Carlisle was quick to react, 'Since we know little about Baxter's movements after the terrorist attack, someone obviously did. Baxter's murder was premeditated, I'm convinced of that. If not, then why pin a note to his chest?'

'Good point,' Mason agreed, 'there's obviously a third party involved here.'

Savage stared across at them as he spoke. 'Like whom?'

'Ed Coleman isn't exclusive. There is more than one Mister Big in Amsterdam.'

Savage gave Mason a curious look. 'What, you think Baxter may have overstepped the mark at some point?'

'Who knows what went on in the flat that night? But this killing was definitely pre-planned.' Mason then drew their attention to the undercover officer's photograph. 'The trouble we're faced with is everyone will be out looking for Walker. The Dutch police, Ed Coleman, and anyone involved in the Schiphol diamond robbery. Walker's key in all of this.'

'If he'd arranged to meet Baxter at the flat, then whoever the third party is, they must have followed him.' Savage drew back in his seat. 'What if Walker's cover story has been blown?'

'Rob raises a good point,' Carrington agreed.

Mason swore he could hear cogs rotating inside the profiler's head. It was hard to determine at times whether his friend was a pure genius, or just swimming around in the cesspool of life like the rest of them.

'If Walker's covers been blown, then he's already a dead man,' the profiler argued.

Mason twisted in his seat.

'Okay. Let's not get carried away here.'

'Think about it,' Carlisle persisted, 'if we leave it to the Dutch police to go after Ellis Walker, it will add credibility to his undercover story. In the meantime, we simply keep an eye on the airports and ferry terminals and wait for him to show up.'

'What if he's already back in Liverpool?' said Savage, playing devil's advocate.

'I'm not convinced he is,' Mason argued.

'Me neither,' Carrington agreed. 'The Dutch police aren't daft. Their borders will be in lockdown.'

Mason checked his notes. 'Okay, here are my thoughts. Walker is key, and we're all agreed on that. The trouble is, it's been seven days since he last reported in which is a heck of a long time to go off radar. Could Walker be in some sort of trouble?' Mason walked over to the incident board and tapped one of the photographs with the back of his hand. 'If a second robbery is in the planning, then who are the probable players?'

'That's a big ask,' Carrington insisted. 'Even counterintelligence don't know the answer to that.'

'But they must have their suspicions.'

Savage looked at Mason with concern.

'Why don't we come clean with the Dutch authorities, boss. Tell them who Walker really is?'

'It can't happen,' Mason insisted. 'It's our duty to protect Walker's identity at all costs. Now that counterintelligence have one of their agents inside Ed Coleman's camp, they'll want to keep it that way.' Mason turned to face them. 'Our mission is to find Ellis Walker and establish what's going on. As far as the Dutch police are concerned, they have a murder investigation on their hands and Walker's obviously a key suspect. We need to get to him first, do I make myself clear?'

Nods all around.

'Good.' Mason lowered his head in thought. 'Here's the plan. Before David and I fly off to Amsterdam, I'll talk to the operational director and see what information they have on Ellis Walker's last known movements. In the meantime, I want you Rob, and Sue here, to contact Merseyside Police. Do some ferreting around, suss out what they know about Edward Coleman's latest movements. Check with Border Control if you must. Establish if Walker is back in the country.'

Savage smiled. 'Sounds like we're finally heading in the right direction.'

'Let's keep it that way,' Mason said grimly.

Chapter Nine

De Wallen in Amsterdam was exactly as Jack Mason had imagined it. A warren of medieval alleys with dozens of one-room cabins rented by prostitutes. It brought a wry smile to his face. Behind typically illuminated red light district windows and glass doors, scantily dressed sex workers left little to the imagination. A major tourist attraction, the area was littered with sex shops, peep shows, dodgy theatres, and a well-stocked cannabis museum amongst other things. This was a seedy district to move around in. A criminal's pleasure ground.

Still waiting for DNA results, the chief inspector was keen to preserve Ellis Walker's identity. They weren't out of the woods yet. Far from it. If Walker did kill Terrence Baxter, he had a lot of explaining to do. But that would come later once they'd worked out his whereabouts. Keen to tap into Inspector Jansen's local knowledge without which they were having to work blind, it wasn't the best way to conduct a murder investigation.

Speculation ran rife, and the distinct lack of feedback from the Dutch police wasn't helping either. Mason hated time-wasting, and never felt comfortable around those in high office who kept a tight grip on events.

The chief inspector's wasn't a good situation to be in. The sooner he broke free from the bureaucratic shackles, the quicker he could get down to the task at hand. Finding Quinn. But a murder had been committed, and Mason fully understood the constraints surrounding it. Even so, after their visit to the Bovenkerk flat, he wasn't overly impressed by Inspector Jansen's weak explanations as to what had actually taken place that fateful night. Jansen was equivocal. Vague. As if conducting a crime-scene tourist experience. He would need to tread carefully in order to get to the truth.

They entered a dimly lit hallway leading to a long flight of wooden stairs. Junk mail cluttered the floor. Still leading the way, the inspector turned sharply to face them at the top of the stairs.

'This is where Terrence Baxter spent the last six weeks of his life.'

'Alone?' Mason asked.

'We believe so, and forensics found nothing to suggest otherwise.'

'How did you come by this information?' asked David Carlisle, staring directly into an open living room area.

'Neighbours spotted Baxter's picture in the local newspapers and informed us of his whereabouts,' she replied. 'After reaching an agreement with the paper's editor, we managed to keep a lid on things.'

'So, the press do have their benefits,' Mason smiled.

Jansen nodded. 'At a price.'

The living room was small, cramped, with barely enough space to move around in. A plasma television filled one corner, a worn sofa bed the other. The bathroom was beyond the kitchen, which looked more like an annexe than anything. It felt enclosed, claustrophobic, and badly in need of some tender love and attention. Linoleum covered the floors, and the wall decor looked tired and outdated. As his eyes toured the room, Mason saw nothing to suggest Baxter had ever lived here. Either forensics had stripped away his personal belongings, or someone had beaten them to it.

Mason picked up on the questioning.

'What do we know about Baxter's immediate neighbours?'

'This is a red-light district, so I'd imagine he felt at home here.'

'A villain amongst thieves, eh?'

The inspector's frown lines tightened as she held the door open.

'You could say that, yes.'

'Who owns the property?' asked Carlisle, turning to face her.

'He's Greek, and lives in Germany. But I doubt he had any connections to Baxter, nor his business associates for that matter.'

'Have you spoken with him yet?'

'Yes, we have.'

'And what did he say?'

'The flat was let through a local agency, and we know three months' rent was paid in advance but that's not unusual in the Netherlands.'

Mason eyed her with suspicion. 'So, who killed Baxter?'

'Our main suspect, not surprisingly, was Ellis Walker. However, the latest DNA results now tell us otherwise. Such a pity,' Jansen said, shaking her head. 'I would have put a week's salary on it being Walker, especially with his criminal background.'

Annoyed the inspector had withheld vital DNA results until now, Mason turned sharply to confront her. 'What gave you that impression?'

'Simple, Walker's fingerprints were all over the Bovenkerk flat and we naturally put two and two together.'

'But the real killer may have worn gloves.'

'We now believe he did.'

Mason stared out of the window and onto the street below. A popular tourist's attraction, the flat was directly above a tobacconist's shop. Not the sort of neighbourhood he'd want to police. De Wallen was littered with sleaze clubs, haze-filled coffee bars selling weed and smack. No doubt a haven for pimps, drug pushers, and the kind of people he had little time for. It was exactly as he imagined it. Fraught with danger, and full of violent crime. No, he thought. This would be a difficult case to crack.

'It's extremely cramped,' he said, as if to make a point.

'Yes, sleazy bijou does spring to mind.'

'It's definitely that,' Mason nodded, relieved in the knowledge that Ellis Walker was no longer her number one priority. 'Any idea as to what Baxter might have been up to whilst he was staying here?'

'Living the dream, I would imagine.'

'It would appear so.'

The inspector bit her bottom lip and frowned. 'Dare I suggest he was gay?'

'Not to my knowledge. Mind, he did spend a lot of time in prison, and we all know what goes on inside those places.'

Jansen stared at him oddly, clearly not amused by his humour.

The bed was made, but impossible to tell if it had been shared. A well-thumbed book lay on a bedside cabinet, along with a brass reading lamp that had seen better days. Mason felt uncomfortable here, as though he'd walked into a movie set starring Humphry Bogart.

They stood for a moment. Then Carlisle pointed to heavy traces of white forensic powder covering a pinewood chest of drawers. 'You people have been busy, find anything of interest?'

'Nothing out of the ordinary.'

'What about personal effects?'

Mason thought she hadn't heard the question.

'No. Nothing,' Jansen replied, vaguely. 'This place had been gone over with a fine toothcomb long before we arrived on the scene.'

Mason swung on his heels.

'Which suggests someone was watching the property before Baxter was killed.'

'There are many ambiguities surrounding Baxter's death, but unless the evidence tells us otherwise, we can only assume what he was doing here.'

'Yes, of course.'

Not here for sexual services, Mason's natural curiosity had suddenly got the better of him. And when in Rome. . . *Crikey*, he thought, how would Barbara react if she ever found out?

They moved back to the living room.

'So, you think his murder was planned?' quizzed Jansen.

'I know so. If not, then why pin a note to Baxter's chest?' Mason took stock. 'Let's face it, his body was stripped clean at the Bovenkerk crime scene, and now you're telling us his bolt hole has also been gone over with a fine toothcomb. It doesn't take a senior police officer to work that one out, Inspector.'

'You obviously know Baxter better than we do.'

Jansen was fishing, evading the questions and giving little away. But why?

Mason turned to face her at the head of the stairs. 'I keep thinking back to the SOCO pictures you sent me, the ones concerning the Bovenkerk flat. Baxter's body was lying slumped against the living room wall. He was well dressed. Nice suit. Expensive shoes.' He paused in thought. 'The thing was, Baxter had money and wasn't frightened of splashing it about. So why would he stay in a dump such as this? It doesn't make sense.'

'Those are the facts,' Jansen replied. 'But I must agree, there's an awful lot of ambiguities surrounding the case.'

'Who was Baxter running away from, do you think?'

'Good question,' she replied. 'It was as if he never existed.'

Mason felt the hairs on the back of his neck prickle. Jansen was right, everyone believed Baxter was long dead – blown apart in a terrorist attack six months ago.

She stared at Mason oddly. 'When I first entered the flat, I must admit it did take me by surprise. There are much better places to stop at.'

'Why Amsterdam? Why this district?'

'I can assure you that Terrence Baxter spent the last six weeks of his life here. Who he met and what he got up to is very much under investigation.'

Mason pocketed his notebook as he turned to face her. 'Let's not forget Baxter was confirmed dead after a terrorist attack in Istanbul.'

'I'm aware of that too.'

'People don't die twice, Inspector.' The profiler's voice was still resonating down the hallway when they reached the front door. 'If as you suggest, none of Ellis Walker's DNA was found on Baxter's body, then whose DNA did you find?'

'We're working on it. These things take time, Mr. Carlisle.'

Mason's patience suddenly snapped.

'The difficulty I'm having with that is, how did Terrence Baxter arrive at the Bovenkerk flat on the night he was killed. Did he drive there himself, arrive by taxi, or did someone simply drop him off at the door?'

Jansen carried a large bunch of keys in her hand, and the third one fitted. She turned to face them. 'CCTV footage shows he was dropped off outside the building. But there lies another problem, as the vehicle he arrived in was carrying false number plates and we are unable to trace the owner.'

'That's the first I've heard of it,' Mason groaned.

'Things are very fluid at the moment, and it's difficult to keep track.'

Mason showed his annoyance by tensing his shoulders. 'I'm not the person running this investigation, so I don't expect to be privy to every single piece of information. That said, if we're not getting regular updates then how do you expect us to help solve a murder crime?'

'I'll bear that in mind when I talk to my superiors, Chief Inspector.'

He could hear Jansen's intake of breath and the pregnant pause that followed. Something about her had changed. As though someone in high office had taken charge of the operation and Jansen was reading the autocue.

Not a good start, Mason thought.

'Thanks for the property tour,' he nodded. 'I understand your frustrations. And yes, protocol can be a pain in the arse.'

Jansen eyed him with suspicion.

'I'm glad you understand my predicament, Chief Inspector.'

'Sure, I often get it in the neck too. It's a senior officer's thing, the people at the top aren't streetwise like you and I and lack the basics of how the criminal mind operates.'

Jansen nodded in agreeance, before dropping the bundle of keys into a black leather shoulder bag. For a few moments she said nothing, then gazing into the distance as if focusing on something, she said, 'Here in the Netherlands information is something we don't give away freely. The chains of command are vastly different to that of the UK police, and the pace at which we operate much slower. You have my number, so perhaps we can meet up under different circumstances. Outside of office hours if you get my drift.'

'Thanks for your candour,' Mason grinned. 'I'll bear that in mind.'

Jansen walked towards her undercover vehicle, then turned sharply.

'I'll leave you two gentlemen to get on with it then.'

Chapter Ten

Twenty minutes later, they were sitting in Stone, a laid-back coffeeshop in the heart of Amsterdam's red-light district. It was the perfect experience to lift Jack Mason's spirits. It felt like heaven. The range of exotic coffee blends and hallucinogenic aromas wafting past his nostrils was intoxicating. It had been years since he'd last felt this relaxed. Rustic decor, comfortable bench seating, and an array of large, muted TV screens playing out all kinds of fascinating sport. This was undoubtedly a must go-to place. As he let his mind drift, all the pent-up tensions that had been building over the past few weeks were slowly leaving his body. Carlisle could not have chosen a better place had he tried. The ambience was awesome, sheer bliss.

Then the music started, and Mason nearly jumped out of his skin.

What the hell!

'I thought you said this was a sports bar?'

'It is.'

'I can hardly hear myself think, let alone speak.'

The profiler shrugged. 'There's a couple of pensioner seats outside.'

'Sod off. I like my music loud, but this is ridiculous.'

Packed with noisy revellers, it reminded Mason of a misspent youth when he was single and fancy free. Every Friday night he would go on a pub crawl with bawdy mates. After drinking themselves senseless, he would grab a cab home and wake up the following morning with the mother of all hangovers. Happy times, he mused. Now nearing forty-nine, those heady days were behind him, but he still loved a good drink.

They left Stone through an open side door and stepped into Ruysdaelkade – a long narrow street running alongside Boerenwetering Canal. It had brightened up a tad, and the rain that was forecast earlier was nowhere to be seen. With thoughts elsewhere, they found an empty bench overlooking the canal and settled down to chat.

Mason's only regret was that he hadn't been more forceful. Annoyed about the way Inspector Jansen had delivered her DNA results, he found her reticence odd. What was she thinking of when every scrap of information was vital to solving a murder investigation.

Carlisle shielded his eyes from the direct sunlight. 'If Ellis Walker is no longer her main suspect, then who is?'

'God knows! I get the impression she's fumbling around in the dark.'

'What else do we know about Ellis Walker? What's his background, Jack?'

Mason fell silent, pondering where to start.

'There's not a lot more to tell. After he left the Gardai, he worked in Manchester for a while – stacking supermarket shelves. Nothing taxing, but after years of involvement in Northern Ireland's sectarian troubles, I suspect he was trying to get away from it all.' Mason shuffled in his seat. 'After joining the Northumbria police, he married a solicitor's clerk straight out of university, and they moved into a two-up two-down semi-detached house near Forest Hall. They seemed happy enough.'

'Any kids?'

'Two. A boy, six, and a girl aged three.'

'How come he got involved with counterintelligence?'

'Walker worked as a computer analyst at the police headquarters in Ponteland. Backroom stuff – nerds work mainly. He was ideal material, a family man, low profile, and that's when they set about grooming him. It went against the grain in many respects. I suspect they had something on him. A ghost from the past perhaps. Who knows how these people operate.'

Carlisle cocked his head to one side. 'He's obviously good at what he does but moving to undercover is a big step change, especially for a family man.'

'Once he uncovers who the Schiphol mastermind is, they'll terminate his mission. That's how it usually works, an ever-changing cycle of new faces.'

'Not an easy role.'

'No, I suspect not.'

Carlisle looked up in surprise. 'What strikes me as odd is the lack of arrests, particularly with Special Branch running the show.'

'Our mission is to find Ellis Walker before the bad guys get to him.'

'On whose authority?'

'Specialist Crime Directorate 7.'

Carlisle blew through his teeth.

'Blimey, this is far bigger than I ever imagined.'

'I told you it was big, my friend.'

'I was merely thinking along the lines of Special Branch.'

Mason stared at the profiler. 'The question remains, was Ellis Walker responsible for Terrence Baxter's murder, and was he working under orders?'

'I doubt he'd go that far. Besides, Walker sounds like an honourable police officer from what you've told me so far.'

'So, who killed Baxter?'

Carlisle's frown lines corrugated. 'Knowing his background, I can think of a dozen people who'd want him dead.'

'Walker's key all right: finding him is a bigger challenge.'

'Surely counterintelligence must be tracking Walker's movements. Either through credit card transactions or phone contacts. It's not rocket science.'

'I would imagine Walker will be using a pay-as-you-go phone, and everything cash up front. Nothing is traceable that way. That's how Coleman likes to operate.'

Carlisle hunched his shoulders as he stared at a passing canal motorboat full of noisy sightseers. 'The question remains, where do we start looking for him?'

'That's your job. You're the bloody profiler...'

'I'm not a magician, Jack.'

Mason stared into the distance.

'Baxter and Walker were on the same page; I'm convinced of that. It's my guess their connection to the Bovenkerk flat had something to do with this diamond heist.'

'The man was a ghost agent. He had to be. Once the Turkish authorities declared him dead, they'd wiped the slate clean as far as his criminal record was concerned.' Carlisle's expression hardened. 'What about the Chinese? Do we know if Baxter ever visited the country?'

'According to the Home Office, he did. On several occasions. Uncut diamonds are a lucrative business in the right hands, but in the wrong hands it's a minefield.' Mason narrowed his eyes. 'It's all in the files. Weight, physical measurements, colour, and clarity. The problem is, once diamonds have been cut and polished into saleable commodities, they're extremely difficult to trace.'

'Worth killing for?'

Mason hunched his shoulders as he surveyed his surroundings.

'Don't look now but I think we're being followed.'

'Really?'

'The guy with the brown bomber jacket to your right. I clocked him earlier in De Wallen.'

'His face isn't familiar.'

Mason gave a little shrug as he weighed up his options. *Move now, and it might give the game away.* He decided to hold back. For now at least. The sun in their faces, they ambled back towards Stone coffee shop. Not fifty metres away, the man in the brown bomber jacket was trying not to arouse suspicion.

'Do you know what,' said Carlisle, with a serious look on his face. 'I get the impression you've conveniently overlooked that I'm not a police officer.'

'You were once upon a time.'

'So was Dixon of Dock Green.'

'God! That was a long time ago.'

'Exactly.'

Before reaching the next canal bridge, Carlisle ducked back into an alleyway leaving Mason to continue towards Stone. Levelling with him, the profiler immediately grabbed the suspect by the neck and spun him to ground in one quick flowing movement. The next thing the suspect felt, after looking up, was Jack Mason's size ten shoe pressing against his throat.

'Speak any English?' asked Mason menacingly.

The man garbled something inaudible.

'Okay,' Mason said, pressing his foot down harder, 'give me one good reason why I shouldn't break your fucking neck.'

'Police,' the man spluttered in broken English. 'I'm police—'

'I've heard that shit before,' Mason replied.

'Po—lice—' the suspect pleaded, his face turning a purple colour.

Mason eased his foot off the man's throat.

'What's all the fuss about, my friend?'

'Inspector Jansen, she told me to check you weren't being followed.'

'Did she now?'

THE POACHER'S POCKET

'Yes, Inspector.'

'It's Chief Inspector, actually.'

'Sorry, sir. I was simply following orders.'

Mason smiled with satisfaction as he dragged the suspect coughing and spluttering to his feet.

'Give Eva my kindest regards. Tell her close protection won't be necessary from now on. There's a good boy.'

The moment the officer walked sheepishly away; Mason burst out laughing.

Chapter Eleven

There it was again. That grating noise that tore through his entire body like a trillion-volt shock. He knew what it was, but still it didn't register. Unable to move, resistance seemed futile. Barely two hours had passed since they'd cut off his little finger. All because he wouldn't talk. One digit at a time the Poacher had warned. No mercy. This wasn't a trick of his imagination. This was the mother of all nightmares.

Never in a million years had Ellis Walker imagined that it would all end like this. Arms strapped to a chairback, ankles bound to the legs, he'd been trussed up like a chicken in a meat processing factory. Worse, his new prison was a pure cesspit of hell. Rectangular in shape, it had high vaulted ceilings, cold concrete floors, and was divided into two areas. Unable to move, the damn rats were everywhere. The slightest hint of provocation and they threatened to eat him alive. One rat in particular had already taken a chunk out of his leg, and the more he struggled to keep it at bay the more determined it seemed. He swore to get even one day.

Easing himself up, Walker stared at the saline drip now pumping all kinds of chemical shit into his veins. Theirs was a well-oiled routine, even down to the punishment they were meting out. Desperately craving a drink, his mouth felt on fire, and his head was still hurting from a terrible beating. Any thought of escape was pointless. His body was so weak he had reached the limit of his reserves.

'Who sent you?' the Poacher demanded.

At first, Walker thought he was imagining things. He could see shapes moving around, and patches of greater darkness. Where was he? Was he underground, or was this some sort of cellar they were holding him in? It was then he noticed the knife the Poacher was holding.

'. . . *let it all go,*' he urged. '*You don't have to suffer this shit.*'

'Your last chance,' the Poacher threatened. 'Who sent you?'

The officer winced.

'Tell me about the priest. What part did he play in all of this?'

The coldness of his breath caused Walker to flinch, as he waited for the blow that never came. As his tormentor's sinister grin broadened, the Poacher shuffled awkwardly towards the open dungeon door. How much more could he take? How much longer would the punishment go on? His mind running amok, fear ripped through Walker like never before. The mere thought of what this narcissistic bastard might do to him sent shock waves down his spine.

Drifting in and out of consciousness, Walker's thoughts turned to home. Was it sheer bad luck they had caught up with him? They'd certainly known where to find him. Barely a few more minutes and he would have been sitting in the comfort of the overnight ferry lounge and drinking his favourite tipple. The next thing he remembered, after the car's rear tyre had disintegrated, were the so-called good Samaritans pulling alongside him. At first, they were nice to him. Reassuring. All that changed the moment they stuck a needle into his arm. He thought he might escape them, make a dash for it. They were far too clever for that. Having bundled him into the back of a waiting Transit van, he knew the game was up.

It was raining the night they'd brought him here. He remembered that much. One of those cold damp miserable nights that could send a man's soul to purgatory. Dragged blindfolded into an upstairs room, they instantly set about him. Confused at first, he thought it was the diamonds they were after. It wasn't. It was something else, something far more important.

Now, losing the will to live, he stiffened.

This was serious shit they were pumping into his veins, and there was nothing he could do to stop the confusion in his head. He'd been in some terrible scrapes in his life, but nothing compared to this. And, if they ever found out he was working undercover, they'd finish it without hesitation.

He heard humming.

A soft, lyrical tune: the kind mothers sing to rock their children to sleep. He knew this vainglorious sadist who called himself the Poacher was evil, but he was surely off his fucking rocker.

There it was again.

Faint at first, but definitely getting louder.

He turned. Too scared to even open his eyes.

'We talk now,' the Poacher said, running his finger along a knife blade.

Walker screamed as his captor ripped the gag from his mouth. Then he felt a warm trickle of blood roll aimlessly down his chin.

'So, you do have a tongue?'

As in the dream, those large, staring eyes were watching him. He would need to stay strong, find a way through the barrier of pain if only for his wife and kids.

Eyes the size of goldfish bowls, the Poacher was drooling and making strange noises from the back of his throat. He moved in closer.

Much closer…

Chapter Twelve

Jack Mason was sitting in the hotel lobby relaxing and drinking coffee when his phone pinged. Expecting a return call from Barbara, he checked the display only to discover it was Inspector Eva Jansen.

'How can I help, Inspector?' Mason said.

'There's been a new development over at the DFDS ferry terminal and I thought I'd touch base,' she replied excitedly.

'Anything important?'

'It could be.'

'In relation to what exactly?' he asked.

The signal dropped out but quickly restored again.

'The port authorities are dealing with an abandoned vehicle. Naturally suspicious, they called in the army bomb disposal experts but found nothing untoward.'

He let it sink in before answering. 'What time was this?'

'The vehicle was declared abandoned around ten o'clock this morning, but the initial incident occurred much earlier.'

Mason looked at his watch. 'Bomb disposal, you say?'

'Yes. It's standard procedure in these situations as you never can tell.'

'No, I suppose not.'

The tone of Jansen's voice told him something more disturbing was about to unfold. He heard a police radio crackle in the background and guessed she was driving.

'The initial incident happened much earlier, you say?'

Jansen hesitated. 'Yes. I've not seen the CCTV footage, but on Monday evening around six thirty the driver of a red Ford Fiesta Ecoboost pulled over after a rear tyre blow-out. Within minutes, a white Transit van had drawn up alongside. When the occupants got out, a conversation followed and after overpowering the Fiesta driver, they bundled him into the back of the van.'

'That's almost three days ago,' Mason explained.

'I know.'

The chief inspector leaned forward in his seat and spoke. 'It sounds like a kidnapping to me.'

'We believe so. And that's what the video tapes are telling us.'

'What about eyewitness accounts?'

'This all happened so quickly, and nobody so far has come forward. The fact is the man they bundled into the back of the van bears a striking resemblance to Ellis Walker.'

Mason's brain raced.

A young couple sitting opposite looked up at him as he raised his voice. Anxious, he turned from them as he spoke. 'Why haven't the port authorities been in contact before now?'

'That's down to DFDS security, I'm afraid.'

'Where's the abandoned vehicle?'

Jansen sighed. 'It's been taken away for further examination.'

'And the Transit van, what happened to that?'

'It boarded the overnight ferry on Monday evening.'

'To where exactly?'

Jansen's voice wavered fractionally. 'North Shields.'

'Jesus!'

'I know, but that's as much as we know at the moment.'

'I'm grateful,' Mason said, surprised at her openness.

He stared at the couple opposite. Both were dressed casually. Was this the breakthrough he'd been waiting for, the one piece of the jigsaw puzzle that could open up a whole new line of enquiries? He was hoping so, and his gut feeling was telling him something good was about to come of it.

'Do we know who the vehicle belongs to?' he asked.

'We do. It's registered to a building company in Newcastle.'

'Newcastle?'

'That's what the vehicle records are telling us.'

'Where are you now, Inspector?'

Jansen laughed. 'Let's not rush things. Besides, this may have nothing to do with our murder enquiry.'

'Umm—'

'As soon as I have all the details, I'll call you back.'

The moment Jansen hung up Mason felt his body tense.

Don't rush it, he told himself. Stay calm. If this were Ellis Walker they'd bundled into the back of a Transit van, he'd already be back in England. No, he thought. He would need to see the video tapes first. Decide himself who this person was. Jotting down some notes, including the vehicle's registration number, he opted to give Rob Savage a call.

'What's up, boss?'

'Are you free to talk?' Mason asked.

Mason could hear music playing in the background, and pictured the sergeant holed up in some sleazy backstreet hotel in Liverpool's dockland with a young lady by his side.

'Sure. How's Amsterdam?' the sergeant asked in his familiar thick Geordie accent.

'Where are you now?'

'I'm with Sue Carrington and we're stuck in the greasy spoon cafe on the A1 services. It's a real dump. Right up your street, boss.'

'Cut the crap. What's going on? You're supposed to be in Liverpool.'

'Not according to the Merseyside police. Coleman's moved back to the Toon.'

The line went quiet.

'When did you discover this?'

'You sound surprised.'

'Too bloody right I am.'

The line fell silent. Then Savage said. 'A DI Wiggins informed us about Coleman at the start of the morning briefing, so we decided to head back north.' Savage sounded grumpy. 'Why, have we done summit wrong?'

'No. You did exactly as I told you – check Coleman's movements.'

'Cheers. For a moment I thought you'd gone off on one of your rants.'

Mason grinned. No diplomat, Savage had a way with words that could spark a nuclear war if you didn't know the man.

'Who else knows about this?'

'Nobody. I was going to ring you earlier, but we decided to head north first and see what was going on.'

'You did the right thing. I need you to check on a white Ford Transit van for me. Registration number. . .' Mason reeled off the details as he went. 'It boarded the overnight ferry on Monday evening and docked at the North Shields terminal early on Tuesday morning. We believe it's registered to a building company in Newcastle, so you may need to get Road Traffic involved.'

'What's so special about it?'

'It's been involved in a kidnapping, we believe.'

'Bugger me!'

Mason smiled at Savage's brashness as he went on to explain. 'I'm about to head off to Amsterdam police headquarters, so I need to be kept informed of any new developments.'

'Will do. Do you know who the victim is?'

'Inspector Jansen believes he bears a striking resemblance to Ellis Walker.'

'Shite. Has she twigged he's an undercover officer?'

'If she has, she hasn't let on about it.'

'Typical. If it is Walker, he could be in a shitload of trouble.'

Mason was quick to react. 'Let's see what the Amsterdam police have to say first.'

'What about this van. Do we stop and detain?'

'Not at this stage.' Mason thought hard. 'It's all a bit up in the air at the moment, but once I've seen the CCTV footage, I'll get back to you.'

'Roger that. In the meantime, I'll do some digging around. It shouldn't be too difficult to track this vehicle down. We'll put out an all-cars alert.'

'Good idea.'

Savage hung up.

Mason pondered this. Coleman's sudden appearance in Newcastle was too much of a coincidence in his view. Things were coming together, and it was time to rouse the profiler and work on a new plan.

Chapter Thirteen

The heavy downpour had stopped by the time they had reached police headquarters – a tall red brick building facing the Singelgracht in Amsterdam Centrum. After checking in at reception, they were taken to a side room and offered coffee and biscuits. Mason hadn't the foggiest idea where this new investigation was heading but felt its importance. If the Dutch police continued to withhold information, he could ask a few probing questions which might spark a reaction. That's how things seemed to operate around here, behind closed doors, and through the unassailable chain of command.

Inspector Jansen, dressed in a light grey suit with plain silk blouse and navy-blue-shoes, entered the room. Mason guessed she'd come from an important meeting. From what he had witnessed so far, the inspector dealt purely in facts and seldom deviated from the straight and narrow. In a way, she reminded him very much of Detective Carrington. An up-and-coming star in the team, who was keen to get things done.

'Sorry to keep you waiting,' Jansen smiled apologetically, 'but I've been held up with meetings.'

No stranger to theatrical entrances, it was Carlisle who spoke first.

'Any more news on the abandoned vehicle?'

The inspector dropped a large bundle of files on the table and took up a seat in front of them. Her posture was guarded, as if taken aback by the profiler's directness.

'Fingerprints found on the steering wheel of the red Ford Fiesta are a match to Ellis Walker.'

'Conclusive evidence?'

'It would appear so.'

Mason felt his jaw muscles tighten as he put his cup down and returned the profiler's glances. 'Sounds like Ellis Walker is up to his old tricks again.'

'No surprises there then,' Carlisle winked.

Jansen gave a little shake of the head before sliding the contents of a large brown envelope towards them as she spoke. 'These are the video stills we retrieved from DFDS surveillance cameras. They show a man being bundled into the back of a white Transit van. No doubt you people are better placed to confirm if it is Ellis Walker.'

Mason leaned over and picked up one of the stills.

'It certainly looks like him. Tell me, do we know who the other three men are?'

'No. Having checked with the port authorities we believe they are travelling on false documents. I've also spoken to UK Border Control. There's no record of Ellis Walker entering your country in the last three days.' She swung to face them. 'I find that odd.'

Carlisle was quick to react. 'In what way?'

'If Walker was smuggled into North Shields, how come it wasn't picked up by Border Force?'

'As far as I know, UK customs only carry out cursory vehicle checks.'

'Which means Ellis Walker could now be back in England.'

'It's more likely the case,' Mason acknowledged with a nod. 'Besides, it's impossible to check every vehicle. Not with the tight ferry turn-around times.'

Jansen checked her notes.

'At least that answers a few questions.'

'I would agree.'

The chief inspector would have preferred to have told her the truth about Ellis Walker, but that wasn't possible. Not under the current circumstances, it wasn't. If word ever got out that he was an undercover officer, his captors would kill him. Although Baxter's murder had all the hallmarks of a gangland execution, if this was the same people who had kidnapped Walker, it raised a whole new string of questions.

Inspector Jansen drummed the tabletop with her long, manicured fingernails. 'Having revisited the CCTV footage, I'm not convinced Walker put up much of a fight. He may have been drugged, of course.' She swung to face them. 'Is it possible to run these images through your national facial recognition database? Who knows, something of interest might pop up.'

'Yes, of course.'

Mason thought about this. Something didn't sit right, and he was struggling to know what. Concerned for Walker's safety, the only positives he could glean, was the officer was back on British soil.

'This changes everything,' Mason said, pointing down at the stills.

'No doubt you people will want to fly back to Newcastle.'

'We will. Whoever these people are, they've obviously crossed the channel for good reason.'

Jansen put her pen down and returned Mason's gaze. 'Those were my sentiments. If they'd wanted Walker dead, they would have done it here in Amsterdam.'

'Or thrown him overboard during the crossing,' the profiler added laconically.

Jansen pursed her lips and frowned. 'It's my guess that Walker knows something these people don't. If not, they'll be holding him to ransom.'

A short, slim woman in her late fifties, carrying a huge bundle of documents entered the room and placed them down on the table in front of Inspector Jansen. Carlisle was right. Never rush into a case until you had all the facts. They'd talked about it often enough, and the profiler's advice had saved him an awful lot of legwork over the years.

Jansen lifted her head as she thumbed through one of the documents. 'In which case I better inform my boss of your intentions.'

'Yes, of course.'

Mason drew back in his seat. If Baxter and Walker were in this together, these current developments did not bode well for the officer's safety. No doubt the streets of Newcastle would be awash with rumours, especially now that Coleman had returned to the city. As he chewed over the facts, he checked his voicemail for messages.

'Never a dull moment, eh?'

'No. I can agree with that.' Jansen gave a slight shake of the head as she stood. 'If there's no further questions, then I'll leave you two gentlemen to get on with it.'

'Thanks for all the help,' he smiled.

As she slid from the room, Mason decided to give Gregory a call. After all, he was the senior officer handling the case and he was keen to share some of the burden. Just how the port authorities would react, was anyone's guess.

But it wasn't looking good, and no doubt the Home Office would be onto it.

'What does your gut feeling tell you?' asked Carlisle, turning to face Mason.

'I don't have one at the minute.'

'That's unusual coming from you.'

Mason screwed his face up, uneasy about the outcome. 'This kidnapping won't go down well in the corridors of power. No doubt they'll be holding an inquest on our return.'

Carlisle gave a wry smile and then said, 'I was thinking more along the lines of Coleman's return to Newcastle. Something's afoot. I can sense it.'

'Why did he send Walker to Amsterdam, I wonder?'

'Who knows. That's why you're a copper, and I'm a profiler, my friend. I do the thinking, and it's your job to produce the answers.'

Oblivious to Carlisle's use of his own term of address, Mason closed his notebook and groaned inwardly.

What could possibly go wrong?

Chapter Fourteen

As the KLM Boeing 737-700 commenced its short descent towards Newcastle Airport, the chief inspector began to reflect on the past twenty-four hours' events. No matter how well you planned a diamond heist, there was always something to go wrong. Moreover, it would be virtually impossible to penetrate an airport's security system, not without triggering some sort of alarm. Considering the number of terrorist attacks around the world, these establishments were impregnable fortresses and nobody in their right mind would attempt such an undertaking. Unless they had someone working on the inside, and preferably in the control centre.

The plane wasn't full. A few in business class, but most were suntanned tourists returning from far flung corners of the globe. Mason fancied a holiday. A week in the sun and a pleasant hotel with an all-inclusive bar, and somewhere to relax at night with Barbara. There was little chance of that happening now.

Not at the speed the investigation was progressing.

The moment the plane banked over the Northeast coastline, the cabin stewards began their final landing checks. They'd made good time, and the short hop-on-and-off flight from Schiphol airport had taken them a little under fifty minutes. Uncertain as to what he was heading back to, Mason took a deep breath and considered his options. He would need to work out his day, prepare for his meeting with the area commander. Not looking forward to that, he dismissed the idea of a restrained approach as there were too many loose ends for his liking. Nothing was straightforward, and as two police forces strove to resolve the same challenges their investigations were becoming fragmented. If they didn't make a breakthrough soon, they'd lose the momentum.

As he moved towards the exit door, thoughts turned to security. Curious as to what type of checks the cabin crew conducted after the aircraft had landed, he decided to observe who did what, where and when. This was a fast turnaround flight, and time would be critical. There would be food and fuel to take on board, cabins to clean, and luggage to be stored in the hold. With so many different activities taking place, this was a perfect time to carry out a robbery, Mason thought.

'I never realised so much was involved in turning an aircraft around.'

'It's quite an operation,' Carlisle acknowledged.

'One thing I've noticed, most of the ground crew seem focused on their own little tasks.'

'There's obviously more to preparing an aircraft for take-off than meets the eye.'

'I couldn't agree more. We take too much for granted nowadays and yet our expectations are ridiculously high.'

The profiler laughed. 'Who reads the credit roll after watching a great movie?'

'Not many I would imagine.'

On nearing Border Control, Mason habitually checked his iPhone for messages. He was hoping Rob Savage might have some better news as to Coleman's whereabouts; if not, some feedback on the stolen white Transit van. Mason had lost count of the number of cases involving stolen vehicles he'd worked on, cases that often accounted for the most serious crimes. ANPR was his favourite technology for disrupting criminal gangs, both at local and regional level.

'Penny for your thoughts,' the profiler asked.

'I wonder what the Chief Constable has to say?'

'Funny you should ask that. I was thinking the same myself.'

It was never easy trying to gauge his colleague's thoughts, or his emotions come to think of it. The profiler's mind ran deep, and all too often he would turn inwards and hibernate for long periods. He was right about one thing, though. Never once had he watched a movie and sat through the credit roll.

***

The drive from the airport to Gateshead police station took just under thirty-minutes. Faced with a mountain of paperwork, Mason was hoping to debrief the team prior to his meeting with Superintendent Gregory. Coleman's sudden emergence on the scene had caused quite a stir. The gangster had form, including a nasty habit of keeping everyone guessing.

The front desk was busy. Fourteen overnight arrests, and the desk sergeant was grumbling about a suicide and a ninety-two-year-old granny whose finger had got stuck in the kitchen sink. Mason loved this city and felt an integral part of its make-up. These were his kind of people, down to earth Geordies, easy to get on with.

An hour and several cups of coffee later, Mason spread the CCTV stills out on the meeting room table in front of him. Staring at their faces, he waited for a reaction. He was hoping for positive feedback, something to get his teeth into. Sometimes a face would jump out at you, a known felon you'd come across on a past case.

Was this his lucky day?

'These images were taken at the Amsterdam port ferry terminal late Monday afternoon,' the chief inspector began. 'The guy in the black bomber jacket we believe is Ellis Walker. The other three perps are his captors. We've run each of them through the facial recognition system but with little success.'

Carrington raised an eyebrow as she stared down at her laptop.

'Have we tried Interpol?'

'We have, and the Dutch authorities believe these people could be part of an international crime syndicate.'

'They look Mediterranean to me,' said Savage, taking a closer look. 'Italian, don't you think?'

'Hired hands more like.'

'Could be. What did our counterparts in Amsterdam have to say?'

'Not a lot,' Mason replied.

'It's not that simple,' Carrington said, turning up the heat. 'I've logged over a hundred calls since the story broke, and every one of them needs to be followed up.'

Mason reached over and grabbed another biscuit. Hopefully, his meeting with the area commander wouldn't last long and he could squeeze in an extra couple of hours at home with Barbara. His trip to Amsterdam had flown by, but he'd missed her to bits. *God she was gorgeous.* He could not stop thinking about her warm body cuddled up to him.

Conscious he'd drifted, Mason turned to Savage.

'What about this van hire company in Benwell? Anything of interest turn up?'

'It was carrying false plates according to Hampshire police. The real one's sitting in the garage in Dover and still awaiting repairs. Involved in a head-on RTA with an Asda delivery truck, it's a write off according to the mechanics.'

'Shit!' Mason groaned. 'What about the Tyne Port Authority? Any actual CCTV coverage of it leaving the ferry terminal?'

'There were two sightings,' Carrington chipped in. 'One heading west along the coast road, the other was picked up at Gosforth as it moved north through High Street on Tuesday morning.'

Mason put his mug down. 'There must be more, surely. What about ANPR? If it was last seen heading north, it shouldn't be too difficult to track down.'

'It may have been torched,' Savage dutifully pointed out.

Mason looked at the sergeant hard. 'Any reports of that happening, Rob?'

'Not heard of any.'

'There's your answer then,' Mason replied, assertively.

Carrington lifted her head.

'These are no ordinary criminals we are dealing with, boss. Besides, Road Traffic are covering every inch of the city. If it's out there, they will find it.'

Mason glanced at the whiteboard.

'What's Ed Coleman been up to lately?'

Savage brought him up to speed on his findings, including their meetings with Merseyside Police. Opening a thick brown folder in front of him, the sergeant handed Mason a dozen photographs and ran through the salient points.

'Racehorses! What the hell is going on?'

'I thought that might bring a reaction,' Savage grinned.

'What's Coleman up to now?'

'Whatever it is, I'd wager it's not legit.'

Mason looked at Savage as the sergeant explained how Merseyside police had conducted an around the clock surveillance operation on the gangster's movements. By the time he'd finished, the chief inspector had calmed down.

'Sounds like this was a thorough operation.'

Savage ran his hand over his head, for once looking relieved.

'It was, and at one point Coleman spent some time over in Southern Ireland visiting a stud farm. A lot of money has been changing hands, and from what we can gather, he's bought himself a couple of thoroughbred racehorses.'

'Tell me you're joking.'

'No, boss. That's straight from the horse's mouth.'

Carrington burst out laughing as she leaned over to grab the last biscuit.

'Jesus. What else have you two been up to?'

'I believe he's serious about racing them,' Carrington replied.

'You're kidding.'

The detective's eyes narrowed still further. 'According to backroom staff, he's up to his neck in horse manure these days. Stable hands, trainers, veterinary papers, race entry forms, you name it; Coleman's involved in it.'

'What's going on, Sue?'

The young detective hunched her shoulders. 'According to Merseyside police, Coleman's been keeping his nose clean and it's all above board.'

'What a crock of shit,' Mason groaned. 'Ed Coleman wouldn't know where to begin with going straight. The man's as bent as a cucumber – believe me.'

'Well, that's how the Merseyside police see it,' said Savage, coming to Carrington's rescue.

'Racehorses aren't cheap, and neither are diamonds,' Mason replied. 'Put the two together and what have you got?'

Carrington looked at Mason quizzically.

'Perhaps we've overlooked something,' said Savage.

'Now here's my problem,' Mason said, trying to get to the crux of the matter. 'Ellis Walker is Coleman's sidekick. That's why he sent him to Amsterdam in the first place.'

'Are you suggesting this meeting with Baxter was pre-arranged?'

'I know so, Rob.'

The sergeant looked at him oddly. 'On what evidence?'

'If you can produce a better explanation, I'd love to hear it.'

Mason filled them in on Coleman's chequered past, his shady dealings in the diamond trade, and the type of clients he mixed with.

'There is a much simpler explanation,' said David Carlisle, who had sat quietly reading reports.

'Like what?' asked Mason.

The profiler pointed to the stills. 'These could be Baxter's killers.'

The room fell silent. Carlisle's theory was simple, and yet effective. Who were these total strangers dressed in grey suits? One short and stocky, another tall and slim, and a third with a neck full of gold bling.

Savage screwed his face up.

'Which means Ellis Walker and Baxter were intended targets.'

'It would appear so,' Carlisle agreed.

Mason asked a few more questions, then ended the briefing. Sometimes being in charge of a murder enquiry wasn't all it was cracked out to be. With nothing concrete to work on, it was time to hear what the area commander had to say. All things being equal, the meeting would be short, heated, with nothing constructive coming from it.

God what a prospect!

Chapter Fifteen

David Carlisle was eating breakfast cereal and watching TV when Benjamin the cat dropped another mole at his feet. One of its legs was missing, and half of its head had been chewed away. Ever since fitting the new cat flap, death was never far from his doorstep. And yet, in a strange way, he was proud of his companion's feline instincts. It's what cats did, they were primal predators and their senses geared to killing prey like mice, rats, and small birds. Benjamin was no different, but this time he had taken it to another level, and it was causing mayhem with neighbour's gardens.

As far as the murder case was concerned, three days spent trashing the streets of Amsterdam had left him totally drained. As the search for the stolen Transit van continued, his personal involvement in the case had reached an all-time low. Isolated, he was beginning to feel ignored. They were looking in all the wrong places, and too business-like in their approach. Something had to change or the whole case could implode on them. He knew from experience that Jack Mason was keen to get his hands on Ed Coleman. But there lay a problem. The Newcastle gangster was up to his old tricks again and his astute lawyer Sandy Witherspoon wasn't helping. The reasons to kill could be mind boggling at times, but there were plenty of willing contenders for wanting Terrence Baxter dead. The man had been a troublemaker.

Mindful of mistakes, Carlisle had begun to look at things differently. Abduction was one thing, but a police officer was in danger of losing his life. Being a profiler had its benefits, but it also had its drawbacks. People demanded answers, and if you didn't have any, that's when the real problems surfaced. The team were floundering, lost in a sea of confusion and unable to move forward in their quest to find Ellis Walker.

When Carlisle was a young boy, he'd often sit in his bedroom and mentally put the world to rights. It was a psychological mind game: his way of solving problems. How far was it to the moon? Where did space end and where did it begin? The demands on a young child's mind seemed endless but he'd always managed to find a solution. Not anymore. Age had crept up on him, and his brain wasn't the razor-sharp tool it once used to be. But that wasn't all. He'd often lose his glasses or forget where he'd put his phone down. And there were times, few thankfully, when he'd walk into a room and forget the reason why he'd gone there in the first place. How mad was that, and here he was trying to solve a complex murder when his memory was progressively failing him.

Pushing back the frustrations, the profiler put himself in the kidnapper's shoes. What made them tick? What was their motivation? The more he thought about it, the more bewildered he became. Bovenkerk was a quiet district where residents kept to themselves. Lulled into a false security, Baxter must have thought he was home and dry on the night he was murdered. A deal had been struck, and he was about to execute it, but these people had other ideas. He suspected a trap had been set, and they were lying in wait.

Hold on a minute, he thought.

Whoever rang the emergency services that night must have known Baxter was already dead. Surely? It had taken the ambulance all of fifteen minutes to reach the crime scene – barely enough time to strip a body and sanitise the flat. At least three people had been involved. One to distract Baxter, a second to deliver the fatal blows, and a third to keep a watchful eye over proceedings. It would be quick, over in minutes, which meant there was little or no chance of detection. But why pin a warning note to Baxter's chest? For whom was that intended?

The more he thought about it, the more perplexed he became. What had brought Baxter to the flat in the first place, and where was Ellis Walker at the time of his murder? There was no simple explanation, just a catalogue of events. Had Baxter overstepped the mark at some point? Enough to get himself killed. Walker's position was entirely different, of course, as he knew something his captors did not. Or so everyone believed.

But why?

This wasn't a revenge crime, nor was it the settling of old scores. Even so there was nothing complicated about Baxter's murder, it was simple yet effective. No guns, just brute force, along with an element of surprise. Baxter would have known he was dying, but did he know who his killers were? Carlisle doubted it. These had been professionals, faceless individuals sent to eliminate those who'd fallen foul of their organisation.

It was late morning when David Carlisle finally parked his Rover P4 100 at the back of Fowler Street in South Shields. In the cold light of day, his office wasn't the prettiest building in the neighbourhood. Tucked back above a carpet shop, it appeared more an afterthought than a private investigator's agency. Even the sign above the door looked tacky and outdated. He'd promised to smarten things up, attract better clients, but had never got round to doing it. Money was tight.

Now forty-seven, Carlisle's life had stagnated, and he was struggling to make ends meet. This wasn't the life he'd planned, nor the kind he'd imagined it to be. He'd been too caring, too sympathetic, and not forceful enough. Not like his counterparts who were busting a gut to extract huge sums of money out of their clients. You had to be ruthless in this game, heartless in your approach. He should never have gone into the business in the first place – should have made a decent career out of policing like the rest of his colleagues.

The moment his secretary Jane slid her long, elegant frame in through the office doorway his mind went blank.

'There's a DC Carrington here to see you.'

'Can you give me a few minutes, Jane?'

She smiled warmly. 'How was your trip to Amsterdam by the way?'

'Pretty boring if I'm honest.'

'Oh. I thought you were working in De Wallen? Isn't that a red-light district?'

'Ah-huh.'

'Sounds like a fun place to me,' Jane smiled.

As he let his mind drift, Carlisle tidied a cluttered desk and tried to look organised. His office was always full of bad vibes these days, as if something terrible was about to happen. Glancing down, he spotted the neatly folded newspaper and was drawn to a short article tucked away in the small print. When he saw it concerned a reliable mechanical mole trap guaranteed to free you of all garden pests, he burst out laughing.

'Was it something I said?' asked Carrington, as she poked her head in through the open doorway.

'Sorry Sue, I was a million miles away.'

'Care to share your thoughts?'

'What do you know about mole traps?' he asked.

She looked at him oddly. 'Nothing, why would I?'

'I was thinking of purchasing one, that's all. Never mind... How can I help?'

'DCI Mason wants you to do some digging around.'

'Oh. I thought he had forgotten about me.'

'What gave you that impression?' she asked, pulling up a seat opposite.

'I've not heard from him in a while.'

Carrington fluttered her long eyelashes as she spoke. 'There's been another sighting of this stolen white Transit van, and he's organising an overnight stakeout over at Ed Coleman's place.'

'Is this in connection with Ellis Walker's abduction?'

'He believes so. It sounds like a promising new lead.'

'Let's hope it's not another false alarm.'

The detective hesitated, then handed him a thin case file marked "HIGHLY CONFIDENTIAL."

'The chief inspector has asked me to show you this, and he's looking for your professional opinion.'

Carlisle read the content, scribbled down some action notes, then put his pen down. 'Is there anything in particular he's looking for?'

'Just an overall opinion,' Carrington replied.

'If this is true, then he needs to act swiftly.'

'That's what he thought you might say.'

'Really?'

They caught each other's eye.

'There is one other thing,' the young detective said, recovering the case file. 'He's asked if you would attend tomorrow's team briefing – ten-thirty in MIR-1.'

'Mason obviously feels strongly about this.'

She stood to leave.

'For everyone's sake let's hope this turns out to be the abductor's van.'

Carlisle did not press the matter further as he had a more challenging engagement to deal with that morning. But things were picking up, and now Ellis Walker was back on British soil, the rules of engagement had changed. The Dutch authorities had handled things badly as far as he was concerned, and if ever there was an opportunity to unravel the darkest inner secrets of these people's minds, it was now.

'See you in the morning then.'

'Always my pleasure, David.'

He caught the glimmer of a smile in Carrington's eye as she turned from the door. God, she was attractive. He was aroused by everything about her. Definitely his type, vivacious, full of vigour and fun. What he would not give to be back in her arms again. But that was another unfinished story, and one he was working on. It was all about timing, choosing the right moment. Even so, he'd not given up on the idea.

Not yet he hadn't.

Chapter Sixteen

One of the many things David Carlisle admired about South Shields, was its picture-postcard coastline. Located at the mouth of the Tyne, for centuries this whole stretch of river had been regarded as the port of Newcastle, and it wasn't until the mid-nineteenth century that North and South Shields were officially recognised as a port and separate entity from Newcastle. On a cloudless day he could think of nothing more exhilarating than to tread its golden sands and free his mind of the inner-city turmoil. It was a wonderful place to relax.

Close to the seafront and popular with young families, the coffee parlour had an almost futuristic look, reminiscent of a modern art gallery full of wacky paintings and bizarre sculptures. A well-stocked serving counter ran the full length of one wall, giving the place a homely atmosphere. Carlisle knew the owner, a man in his late sixties who also ran a wine shop a few blocks away and once played professional football for Charlton Athletic. It was that kind of establishment. Cheap and cheerful, an ideal meeting place.

Formalities over, Carlisle took a seat up opposite.

'How's business?' the profiler asked.

A stocky man, Derek Sharp had spent most of his life eking out a living on the fringe of society. Sharp's parents had died at an early age, forcing him to live with an aunt or face the childcare system. Carlisle liked the man he had been to school with; they had always stayed connected. A loner, a man with a shady past, rumour had it that Sharp had shot a local man dead in a bar fight over unpaid gambling debts. If nothing else, he'd certainly built himself a reputation.

'Business is fine. Getting paid is another,' his informant replied grumpily.

Carlisle chuckled, as he flexed the arms of his tubular seat.

'Same old problems, eh.'

'What's on your mind?'

'Information, Derek.'

'What kind of information?'

'What's Ed Coleman up to nowadays?'

His informant gave him a disparaging look, taking his time before answering. Despite his dealings with the criminal fraternity, Sharp had always managed to wriggle free of any charges the police had thrown at him. Nothing ever stuck. It was as if he were made of Teflon.

'Ed drove up from Liverpool on Tuesday night and hasn't been seen since.'

'A business venture?'

'Why the sudden interest in Ed Coleman?'

'Simply curious, that's all.'

His informant was testing the water. Checking for cracks in his storyline. It was a game he played, his way of keeping abreast of the situation. The man had a knack of catching people out, but Carlisle was equal to it.

'Rumour has it he's back at his mansion,' grinned Sharp.

'I smell a rat, Derek.'

'Yeah, but rat's like to congregate. . . they work better in numbers.'

Carlisle pondered this. Trying his best not to rush things.

'Talking about our four-legged friends, I've heard Coleman's recently purchased a couple of thoroughbred racehorses.'

'Who told you that crap?'

'You'd be surprised.'

Sharp shot him a dagger's look. 'What else have you heard?'

'A lot of money is changing hands. I'm talking of hundreds of thousands here. There's rumours that Ed's entering his horses at Newcastle's next race meeting.'

'You're joking.'

'Not this time,' Carlisle frowned. 'Why would someone go to all that trouble, and, more significantly, spend a shit load of cash on a couple of thoroughbred racehorses? What's going on, Derek?'

Sharp thought about this, then opened up about the gangster's shady dealings with local bookies and how he intended to get a foothold into the racing calendar. By the time he'd finished, Carlisle could think of a dozen racing scams hitting the headlines.

'Why racehorses, Derek? Coleman's more a diamonds man I would have thought.'

'Who says it's not legit?'

'What's he up to?'

Sharp's face fell. 'How would I know?'

Carlisle opened his hands wide as if to get a reaction. Whatever was going on behind closed doors his informant wasn't keen to reveal it.

'Racehorses and diamonds are not a good mix in the wrong hands.'

'Not heard anything.'

'Talking of diamonds,' said Carlisle, putting his drink down. 'I heard Terrence Baxter made a dramatic comeback a few weeks ago. The sad thing is, he ended up in Amsterdam with his throat cut.'

He caught the look of surprise in Sharp's glances.

'Hang on a minute! I thought Baxter was killed in a terrorist attack in Istanbul.'

'Apparently not.'

Bewildered, Sharp returned his stare. 'Don't shit me. You're making this up.'

'It's true. Like I say, it happened a few weeks ago.'

'What else have you heard?'

Carlisle leaned in closer. 'Some say Terrence Baxter was Ed Coleman's go-to man. They were partners in crime.'

'Who told you that shit?' Sharp retorted.

'They did business together, did they not?'

'Yeah, and they were never apart at one point.'

'Isn't it strange how these things turn full circle. One minute your alive, the next your dead. Mind, Baxter did have a nasty way of rubbing people up the wrong way.'

Sharp looked ruffled.

'Baxter wasn't liked. I know that much.'

Carlisle shook his head and chose his next words carefully. 'Some say he had a hand in the Schiphol diamond heist – moving stuff on through his network of international contacts.'

'Sounds about right.'

'The trouble was someone had it in for him.'

'You know me, Davy boy. Bling isn't my thing. Never was.'

'No. I guess not.' The profiler lowered his voice. 'If a lot of money is changing hands, then it can only mean one thing.'

'Like what?'

'Try money laundering.'

'How would I know,' said Sharp, staring into his cup. 'Sparklers don't interest me in the least. They're for the rich. Fancy people with influence.'

'Pity,' Carlisle replied, shaking his head. 'Rumour has it another diamond heist is in the making. Don't know when. Or where. But I heard it's in the making.'

His informant frowned.

'Same crew as before, I'd wager.'

'I've no idea, Derek. You tell me.'

'You know how it is,' said Sharp, 'some people just like to make their mouths go.'

'Which people are these?'

His informants demeanour changed suddenly. Less welcoming. More hostile. Sharp had been caught off guard and his only line of defence was attack. 'Take my advice, Davy boy. Steer well clear of Ed Coleman, he's nothing but grief.'

'Just asking. You don't have to answer.'

'And I'm not.'

They sat in silence, neither willing to yield ground. The mere mention of another diamond heist had unsettled Sharp. If there was any truth in the rumours, he knew he would never hear that coming from his informant's lips.

'This racehorse malarkey Coleman's currently involved in.'

'What about it?' asked Carlisle.

'Six months ago, Ed had a triple by-pass heart operation over in Switzerland.'

'Never heard that mentioned before. So, what's a man with a dodgy ticker doing getting involved with thoroughbred racehorses? I thought it was a stressful occupation.'

Sharp took his time before answering.

'After the operation, Ed spent some recovery time over in Ireland. He owns properties there. A place called Kinsale. Coleman was a sick man, living on borrowed time. His doctors only gave him a couple of months. That's how bad it was.'

'Ireland, you say?'

'Yeah. That's where the little green leprechauns live.'

Carlisle saw the funnier side. 'What's this to do with racehorses, Derek?'

'I was coming to that,' Sharp replied with a hint of a smile. 'There's a racing stables close to the village of Kinsale. That's where Ed got talking to one of the local trainers. A guy called Kerry Waterman. He's quite a celebrity in racing circles. They drank in the same pub together, became friends.'

'That must be a first. Coleman doesn't have friends.'

Sharp wiped the coffee froth from his lips as he turned to face him. 'Coleman was piling on the weight, and it wasn't good. The man was obese and warned by his physio that if he did not alter his lifestyle, he'd be dead within the year. Weeks later he was seen out riding with Kerry Waterman. It was the talk of the village as you can well imagine.'

'And why was that?'

His informant gave him another dirty look. 'You said yourself that gangsters and racehorses don't mix. It's a catastrophe waiting to happen.'

'Is Coleman's love for racehorses genuine, do you think?'

'Could be, especially if it stops him from having another heart attack.' Sharp grinned as he pushed back in his seat. 'Besides, who doesn't like racehorses?'

'Yeah, but they don't come cheap.'

'Ed's not short of a bob or two. That's for sure.'

Carlisle continued to press the matter. 'These racehorse's he's thinking of entering in race week. Do you think he'll go ahead with it, or is it just another smokescreen?'

'Who knows what goes on inside Coleman's head?'

'Something's not right, Derek.'

'What makes you say that?'

'Who's going to look after the racing side of the business?' quizzed Carlisle. 'There are vet fees to think about, stable hands, trainers, and a shit load of other things that need to be taken care of. It's not just about race day, there's more to it than that.'

'If Coleman's intentions are genuine, it's my guess this Kerry Waterman will take care of that for him. Ed's like that. He gets other people to do his dirty work.'

'Like shovelling horse shit?'

Sharp burst out laughing.

The profiler chewed over the facts; about Coleman's connection with Baxter in the diamond trade' and his newfound interest in racehorses. It didn't add up. None of it did. Talk of the gangster's underlying health problems wasn't helping either. Coleman was an out-and-out thug who wouldn't think twice about putting a gun to your head if he thought you were interfering. It was a fine balancing act and having decided not to bring Ellis Walker into their conversation, Carlisle stood to leave.

A blonde girl working the coffee machine glanced over and cocked her hip. She looked like a retired stripper or practising to be one, the profiler thought.

'It's been nice meeting up again, Davy boy.'

'Likewise, mate.'

Sharp eyed him up and down as if waiting for something. Information wasn't cheap, and his informant was waiting to be paid. Sharp by name and sharp by nature, the profiler groaned. Then again, not much went on in Tyneside without his colleague knowing. Being a private investigator meant you were able to operate on both sides of the fence. It was a game of cat and mouse. A game that Carlisle never grew tired of playing.

But some friendships turned sour, and you had to tread carefully. Toxic relationships could be deadly. He knew that too.

"Death can be fatal," he smiled.

Chapter Seventeen

Jack Mason lifted the binoculars and surveyed the area. Close to the village of Warkworth, three sides of the property were guarded by woodlands, a fourth by the River Coquet. A mile from the castle ruins and once the playground of the Lords Percy when wardens of the marshes played havoc along Scottish borders, the Newcastle gangster couldn't have chosen a more remote location. Completely isolated, it was one of those properties that was difficult to spot unless you knew of its existence.

Mason glanced at his watch. He was starving and in grumpy mood. Apart from a bar of chocolate, he'd not eaten in hours and could have murdered a full English breakfast. His mouth watering at the thought, he pictured the bacon sizzling in the pan and the sound of bread popping in the toaster. *God, he was hungry.*

Like most police officers, Mason detested stakeouts. Long hours spent whiling away time with little to show. His was a foolhardy idea, and not a single person had visited Coleman's property in the past twelve hours. Apart from a few headlights flickering in the night sky, there was nothing meaningful to report. And yes, a lot of questions would be asked of him, but he'd deal with that later.

Angry with himself, Mason wished he'd never thought of a stakeout in the first place. It was a drain on resources. Dozens of specialist police officers had covered every single blade of grass. By the time they had finished, nothing could move in or out of the property without his knowing.

Dressed in a green Thornhill jacket and waterproof trousers, DS Savage approached from a small coppice. There was a distinct nip in the air, and the solid groundcover from earlier that morning seemed to be breaking up with pockets of blue sky appearing in the gaps.

'Anything to report?' Mason asked eagerly.

The sergeant frowned. 'Not seen anything, boss. Mind, there's been activity around the stables about an hour ago – young stable hands watering horses. Apart from that, the place is deadly quiet.'

'What about this white Transit van that was spotted. Any more news on that?'

'Nah. Nothing.'

'Have you spoken to DC Carrington?'

Savage shrugged. 'Not seen Sue since yesterday evening. We should never have gone into radio silence in my opinion. It was a crap idea. It's bad enough trying to cover your own arse let alone knowing what's going on elsewhere.'

Mason turned his collar up and stared at the rugged landscape. His twenty-four-hour surveillance operation was a total disaster. Not a single sighting of the white Transit van and the longer it went on, the greater the danger Ellis Walker was in. Sometimes intelligence worked, this time clearly not. The trouble was, he didn't have enough boots on the ground to cover the whole area. Mason wondered sometimes, in his darker moments, if he was beginning to lose his grip. Apart from a few witness leads, they were no further forward today than they were last week.

Savage kicked the soil from under his feet and sighed.

'Summat will crop up. I'm convinced of it.'

'Let's hope you're right, Rob.'

Mason checked his phone. No messages. He knew from experience the minute he closed the operation down, things would kick off. It was Sod's Law. A coppers rotten luck.

What to do next?

'Why don't we get the tech boys involved?' asked Savage, grumpily. 'Plant a few hidden cameras and sound devices around the property.'

'Not now. The Transit van's our biggest hope. Find that and it may lead us to Ellis Walker. We just need a lucky break, that's all.'

The sergeant shook his head despondently. 'I'm not convinced Coleman has anything to do with this kidnapping if I'm honest. It's not his style.'

Mason turned sharply to confront the sergeant. 'A few days ago, you thought Ellis Walker was dead and changed your mind when you realised he'd been taken hostage. You cannot have it both ways, Rob. What if these people have rumbled his cover story? What then?'

'Let's hope they haven't for Walker's sake.'

'Too bloody right, and we know how Coleman reacts when made to look a fool.'

Savage stared into the distance.

'My gut feeling tells me someone else has their fingers on the pulse.'

'Like whom?'

'I've no idea, but it isn't Coleman.'

Mason considered this. Ever since leaving the North Shields ferry terminal the white Ford Transit van had eluded them. Captured on CCTV moving around the Warkworth area, it seemed too much of a coincidence not to be the same van.

Road Traffic wouldn't get it wrong. Surely not?

THE POACHER'S POCKET

The chief inspector stamped the ground to get some circulation back to his feet. Knowing that Savage had lost heart, Mason was beginning to question his own judgement. The trouble was, too many people were changing their minds and unsettling him. He would need to stay calm, think this through logically. If there was a simple explanation to all of this, Carlisle would know of it. His colleague would speak his mind; he wasn't bogged down by internal affairs or politics. That's why he'd hired him in the first place.

As he moved his position, Mason caught Carrington approaching along a narrow footpath at the top of a steep hill. Her hair blowing in the early morning breeze, she peered at him looking decidedly upbeat. Far from happy, he was looking for some better news.

'Anything to report?' he questioned.

'I've been talking to a couple of volunteer special constables,' the detective replied. 'There's a makeshift caravan site on the other side of the river about a mile from here.'

'Travelling people?'

'Could be. What is of interest, though, is that one of the constables swore he'd seen a long wheelbase Transit van parked by the riverbank yesterday morning.'

'What colour was it?'

'White.'

'Really?'

'I've told them to hang fire until I've talked to you.'

'Smart thinking, Sue.'

Mason would have preferred this kind of feedback at the beginning of the shift, but any information was better than nothing. Carrington was a good officer and had done the sensible thing. Any suspicious sightings were always worth following up. No matter how trivial they appeared.

He stood in the roadside, thinking.

'How many 'Specials' do we have at our disposal?' Mason asked.

'Six, boss. They're down by the riverbank and currently sitting in the back of a police van. I've told them to stay put and await further instructions.'

Mason took a deep breath and thought about his next move.

'Three of us should be enough, and we can always call on your officers as back up.'

'This will be a first,' Carrington smiled, 'I've never dealt with travellers before.'

'There's a first time for everything Sue, but don't get too close to them.'

She spun to face Mason. 'And why is that?'

'If one of them tries to kiss you, you're to make a run for it.'

'Why would they do that?'

'It means they wish to marry you.'

Savage laughed out loud.

'Nice one, boss. There's nothing like a good old Romani wedding.'

'Sod off,' Carrington retorted. 'It's not going to happen.'

The sergeant's grin broadened. 'I wouldn't put money on it, Sue.'

Chapter Eighteen

At the bottom of a long sweeping bend, Jack Mason could see horses tethered to a lengthy strip of grass full of buttercups. The Coquet ran swift here, broad, and shallow the colour of frothy beer. The scent of wild garlic filled the air and sunlight played through the treeline as clouds of midges danced over rolling waters. Mason was tired, and his body metabolisms were all over the place after a long arduous night spent on surveillance operations. He sat for a moment and assessed his surroundings. To his right, the treeline continued to follow the river, and the left was guarded by a narrow lane that ran at right angles to the river where the travellers were holed up.

Moving closer, one of the tethered horses lifted its head as if spooked by their presence. Seconds later they were joined by a uniformed Community Support Officer (SPO) who purposedly advanced from a footbridge not thirty metres away. Clipboard in hand, he gave their vehicle a cursory once over then stood back a pace before reciting a seemingly well-rehearsed speech.

'Morning,' the officer said, poking his head in through the vehicle's open window. 'May I ask the purpose of your visit here today?'

He looked ex-military, Mason thought. Shiny shoes, pressed uniform, and Windsor knotted tie. Reaching for his pocket, Mason flashed his warrant card towards the opening and the constable craned his neck.

'Sorry, sir. Just doing my duty.'

'Have you spotted a white Transit van in the vicinity lately?' asked Mason.

'There was one seen hanging around here yesterday afternoon, but it moved back into the Romani campsite.' The constable gave him a wry smile. 'Bloody travellers. The quicker they are off my patch the easier I'll sleep at night.'

'Causing you problems, Constable?'

'Not really, but you know what this lot get up to.'

Mason refrained from correcting him.

'How many travellers are in the camp?'

'Hard to say. Thirty, forty, could be more.'

Joined by Detectives Savage and Carrington, Mason gave out instructions and told the constable to stay put and guard the lane's entrance. His face was a picture, and Mason found it difficult to contain his laughter.

As they strode down the woodland lane, twigs snapped underfoot, and birds sang overhead. They were close, and Mason could hear dogs barking and children playing. He'd dealt with travellers before, many times, and knew how unpredictable they could be. The slightest provocation and things would turn ugly. He also knew most travellers' children never attended school, as the high exclusion rates forced many to stay away. There was a definite prejudice against Romani people these days, much of which had been fuelled by a myth that crime rates soared once they moved into the vicinity. And yet, according to recent reports, there was no evidence to suggest that offending was any higher amongst the travelling population. Just what the media had made it out to be.

As they came to a bend in the lane, the campsite opened up in front of them. Not more than a dozen caravans in total, well-spaced on firm unbroken ground. Set back to one corner of the clearing was an open campfire. Cooking pots hung in profusion over glowing embers, as smoke drifted lazily through the treeline into the hillside beyond. To his left Mason could see long lines of washing, and a small flee-ridden mongrel dog sat guarding them. Making its presence felt, it was keeping a beady eye on them, ready to pounce at the slightest provocation. It wasn't a large camp, and these people hadn't been here long either. Illegally, no doubt, which gave him an added air of authority.

A caravan door opened and a thickset man in his late forties with jet-black receding hairline approached them. Dressed in a blue chequered waistcoat, brown baggy trousers and white collarless shirt, there was purpose in his stride. Mason caught the demeanour of unfriendliness in the man's glances.

'Top of the morning to you,' the man announced, doggedly. 'What would you people be wanting here?'

'Police,' Mason replied, flashing his warrant card. 'I'm looking for a stolen white Ford Transit van. Seen in the vicinity during the early hours of Monday morning, we're here to follow it up.'

'And what might you be after?'

Mason banged on the van with the flat of his hand and a loud thud rang out. 'I'm particularly interested in this one.'

'And what is it you're wanting?'

He tensed as more travellers appeared. Some carrying sticks, all looking decidedly hostile. He chose his next words carefully. 'The van in question was stolen a month ago and we're checking every vehicle in the area.'

'I see,' the man replied, still maintaining eye contact.

'This won't take a minute,' Carrington confirmed, 'we just need to check the vehicles VIN.'

The man with the slick back hair shrugged as if none the wiser.

'Whose Vin?'

Mason smiled wryly. 'VIN is short for the Vehicle Identification Number.'

'So it is.'

'Whose vehicle is this?' asked Savage outright.

'It belongs to all of us.'

'No doubt it's taxed and insured,' Mason said firmly, 'and you have proof of ownership?'

'This is private land, mister. The van's classed as off road.'

Clever bastard, Mason thought. He'd obviously been questioned about this before.

'I take it you people have permission to stay on this land?'

'So, we do.'

'From whom, may I ask?'

The man gave him a withered look. 'The good Lord told us we could stay here.'

'Lord who?' Mason replied, sarcastically.

'If that'll be all, I'll be saying good day to you, so I will.'

The moment Savage lowered his phone, he turned to Mason. 'It's not legit, boss. The reg is down to a Vauxhall Vivaro, and it's carrying false plates.'

'Shit,' Mason cursed.

The man swung sharply to face them.

'Like I say, it's off road and that's the end of the matter.'

Mason took a step back.

'In which case you won't mind my officers taking a quick look for themselves.'

The man's face twitched then darkened as if fighting back his words. Obviously nicked, was this the kidnappers' van? Moving to one side, Mason peered in through the closed passenger window. Next, he tried the driver's door. It was locked. Curious, he walked to the rear of the vehicle and tried the doors. They were locked too.

Fast losing patience, he banged on the vehicle again.

'Who holds the keys?' he asked, in his best authoritative voice.

A crass thickset man in his mid-twenties stepped forward. Holding a hefty club in his hand, the angry look on his face told them he was more than willing to use it.

'I do, but I don't have them with me.'

'We need to look inside.' insisted Savage.

The young thug now turned his anger on the sergeant.

'Not without a search warrant, you're not.'

Mason took stock. This was beginning to turn ugly, and he didn't do ugly, especially after a twelve-hour shift. If these people thought they could get the better of him, they were wrong.

He turned sharply, as if in defeat. 'Okeydokey. If it's a search warrant you people want, I'll get you one.'

The crass man smiled smugly. This may have felt like a moral victory, but it was far from over. If these people were looking for trouble, they'd found it. He'd be back, only next time to tear the whole campsite apart.

On reaching the end of the lane, the three detectives caught the anxious look on their fellow officers faces. It was a tense moment, and they looked more than ready for battle.

'Right lads,' Mason shouted. 'Nothing moves in or out of here until I tell you otherwise. Nothing. Do I make myself clear?'

Nods of approval all round.

'What's happening, sir?' the senior officer announced.

Mason's face darkened. 'This is a crime scene. Until forensics are satisfied these people are not involved in a kidnapping, it's to remain that way.' He gave each of them a stern look then said, 'I'm particularly interested in a white Transit van that's carrying false number plates. You're to keep a beady eye on it and make sure it doesn't get torched. When I return, this place will be taken apart. Piece by piece.'

The senior officer tipped his peak cap as in salute.

'Leave it with me, Chief Inspector.'

THE POACHER'S POCKET

As Mason ambled towards his undercover vehicle, Carrington caught up with him.

'What happens now, boss?'

'Let's find a suitable pub where we can freshen up and get some breakfast. In the meantime, I'll get things rolling back at HQ. If Coleman is in anyway connected with these people, then we'll kill two birds with one stone.'

'And the Transit van?' asked Savage.

Mason's grin broadened.

'I have plans in mind for that.'

Chapter Nineteen

At first light the following morning, DCI Mason slid from the unmarked pool car and made for the long line of police vehicles parked close to the riverbank. The first phase of his operation in place, the whole area was now swarming with police. Eighty in total, and ready to go. The Romani campsite being the focus of attention that morning, it was a large turnout. As far as he could determine, the surrounding countryside had been sealed off and guards posted at every exit point. Nothing could move in or out, apart from SOCO's and Mason's close team. Not all had gone to plan. There were still a few loose ends to tie up before he could give the final order.

Pleased with his findings, Mason wasn't anticipating resistance. Not with this amount of force at his disposal. These operations were unpredictable, and there were women and children in the camp, young babies too. Many things could go wrong, but he was willing to take that risk for the sake of further progress. Once things had settled down from the initial impact of their unwelcomed return, he would widen his search beyond the woods. If this were the white Transit van used in Ellis Walker's kidnapping, there would be dozens of places to hide a person captive. Mason had prepared for that too. That's where the dog handler teams would come into their own.

The chief inspector walked up the steep incline to where the road skirted the Coquet and stood for a moment. Tucked back in the treeline, the huge orange hulk of the recovery vehicle was stood ready and waiting. Not long now, he thought. Soon the stolen Transit van would be winging its way back to a police compound and clawed over with a fine toothbrush. Tom Hedley's team would make short work of it. Information was currency, and the sooner the truth emerged, the faster he could make an arrest.

Mason stretched his legs and tried to get some mobility into his limbs. For the first time in days, he felt upbeat. The team had done well. Tired perhaps, but good preparations would undoubtedly make the difference.

'Coffee?' said Stan Johnson, the duty SOCO present.

'Love a cup,' Mason replied, blowing on cold hands.

The SOCO peered up at him. 'Not wanting to disturb our traveller friends, I've deliberately held back on the dog teams.'

'How considerate of you, Stan.'

'I'm like that, Jack.'

Mason smiled. Johnson was eccentric. He bred budgerigars for show and was honorary president of the local Morris Dancers' society. They'd worked together many times, and Mason always found him amicable. When it came to problematic crime scenes such as this one, Johnson was a stickler for detail.

They sat silent for a moment as more police officers scrambled up a small bank on the opposite side of the river. A lean wiry sergeant in his late twenties, carrying a long wooden pole gave out some instructions. Seconds later they moved in single file along a sharp sweeping bend in the footpath before disappearing from view.

'How's the missus?' Mason asked casually. 'Still working at the nursery school?'

'Betty loves kids, especially toddlers. Apart from a few arthritis aches and pains, she's in her element.' Johnson sighed. 'Not like some of us, Jack.'

'No. I suppose not. If you can wake up in the morning to find nothing has fallen off, then everything else is a bonus.'

'Too damn right,' Johnson smiled.

The sun peeping over the horizon, the chief inspector watched as three lines of heavily armed police officers moved into their respective positions. One skirting the riverbank, another heading north to block potential escape routes on the eastern side of the woods, and a third covering the lane to the travellers' camp. It had just turned 05:00 and as Mason picked up the pace, detectives Carrington and Savage followed. Neither spoke. Each deep in thought, he sensed their anticipation. Both were capable, and he could not have chosen a better pair of officers.

Mason stopped abruptly.

So much for the element of surprise. They'd barely turned the corner when the man with the thinning jet-black hair confronted them. The chief inspector stepped forward.

'You asked for a search warrant, and I have one,' Mason announced, in his best authoritative voice.

He waved the court papers under the man's nose.

'What the hell is this. This isn't right. There's women and kids here.'

No sooner had the words left the man's mouth than dozens of heavily armed police officers streamed past in single file.

'Put your hands where I can see them,' the lead officer demanded.

As sleepy heads poked out from caravan windows and doors, armed officers flooded the area. Shouting broke out, but the search teams were determined and swift. The moment Mason moved towards the white Transit van; the hulk of the huge recovery truck appeared on the scene. Headlights switched on, within minutes the driver had reversed into position ready to winch the stolen vehicle onto the back of his trailer.

'Did you hear me?' the man, still standing there, shouted.

Mason ignored him and continued to give out instructions.

'Who do you people think you are?'

As the chief inspector stepped aside to let more officers through, he caught movement out of the corner of his eye. The youth running towards him had a baseball bat in his hand. Mason swallowed hard, just as a quick-thinking officer stuck his foot out and brought him to ground. It was then Stan Johnson emerged.

'Any more news?' Mason asked eagerly.

'The dog teams are out searching,' the SOCO confirmed. 'If Walker's out there, they'll find him.'

'Good man.'

Johnson pointed to the handcuffed miscreant still making his mouth go.

'Who rattled his cage?'

'He thought he was Superman.'

The SOCO laughed.

The clunk of winching gear starting up brought everyone's attention back to the task in hand. As the last of the transporter straps were secured in position, the driver of the recovery truck locked his ramps into place. Jumping down from his vehicle, he checked everything was secure and in order before turning to face them.

'Will that be all, sir?' the driver asked dutifully.

'Yes, for now,' Mason replied. 'Tell Tom Hedley I'll catch up with him as soon as I'm done here.'

'Will do.'

Mason stood thinking. These situations had a nasty habit of kicking off, and the sooner they were away from here the better. He watched as the recovery truck wound its way back down the narrow lane and could see it was a tight squeeze. Branches snapped under the strain, and one fell to earth with a thunderous crash. Never a dull moment, Mason mused.

Then, out of nowhere, a thin-faced man with a gawky look appeared. Wearing a baggy camouflage jacket and unfashionable blue jeans, he walked with a stoop as if he had lead weights in his pockets.

'Jim Strainer,' he announced. 'I run things around here.'

Mason held up his warrant card.

'You left it a bit late, Mr. Strainer. We've got what we came for.'

'You can't just walk in and take what you want. It's not right.'

'We're police. That's what we're supposed to do.'

'Are you fucking serious?'

'Had you people cooperated, I doubt it would have come to this.' Mason shrugged.

The man glowered. 'It's bollocks.'

'Really?'

'It's utter bollocks. You know it is.'

'I take it you're responsible for these people's actions?' Mason said, forcefully.

'So, I am.'

'In which case there's a few important questions we need answers to.'

The so-called camp spokesperson glared at him incredulously. Despite his age, he was playing to the crowd and making a damn good job of it. Mason stepped closer and tried to curb his emotions. Eager to impose his authority, polite conversation was the last thing on his mind.

'Who gave you people authorisation to set up camp here?'

'Why. Is there a problem?'

'I take it you do have permission?'

The camp spokesperson fell silent.

'Okay. Let's try another approach. Which one of you lot stole the Transit van?'

'No one stole anything, mister.'

Having read out the charges to him, the young halfwit who had lain claim to the Transit van, had become docile and was led away for questioning. Knowing travellers had a nasty habit of striking back, the chief inspector decided to let Rob Savage deal with the man's attitude problem.

Despite all his setbacks, Mason was more than happy with his overall findings. What had started as a fruitless adventure, had ended in a victory of sorts. It wasn't much, but it was enough to justify his heavy-handed approach.

'Let's hope he talks,' said Johnson, removing his riot helmet and wiping the sweat from his brow.

'I doubt it, Stan. These people never do.'

'No. I suppose not. With any luck forensics might trump up a few answers.'

Mason turned sharply. 'God help these people if they're involved in a kidnapping. I'll throw the bloody book at them.'

'Let's hope it sticks,' Johnson chuckled.

With that, the SOCO strolled back to the major incident vehicle.

CHAPTER TWENTY

Not all was unwelcome news, thought Jack Mason as he fired up his laptop. Soil sample found in the white Transit van's tyre treads were consistent with that found in the surrounding regions of Amsterdam. They now had a clear link. Something to get their teeth into at last. Although none of Walker's fingerprints or DNA were found in the vehicle, the short answer was they were working on it. Tom Headley believed the van had been steam cleaned, confirming that this had been a professional job.

Fired up by the latest developments, Mason was having to restrain himself. First, he shared what news he had with the team, then asked if they had anything to add. On a more positive note, Rob Savage had managed to interview the man, Mark Rigg, who had tried to knock Mason's head off the previous day. Rigg was a crass, tactless chauvinist pig who lived with his Uncle Thomas. Not a stable relationship, the sergeant believed the two of them were involved in major crime. From what he could gather, according to the Hampshire police, Rigg had been on the run for several months. Wanted for questioning by three separate forces in connection with burglary, grievous bodily harm, and numerous theft offences, Rigg was facing a long prison sentence. Even longer if he had anything to do with a kidnapping. The man had form, but not all was bad news. Rigg's claim he'd found the Transit van abandoned on open waste ground in Wallsend only fuelled Mason's suspicions. Uniforms were out canvassing, and he was hoping to get to the bottom of it.

From his study of the evidence so far, it seemed a straight forward case. The only remaining question was Ed Coleman. Did he have a hand in this? At first, he thought he did. Furious, he was now having doubts.

Mason was tucking into a steak and ale pie when DC Carrington knocked on his office door. Eager to hear what the detective had to say, he wiped the crumbs from his mouth and sat back in anticipation.

'What can I do for you, Sue?'

'I've finally finished those vehicle checks you requested, boss.'

'Find anything?'

The detective laid out a series of monochrome images on the table in front of him.

'What am I looking at exactly?'

'Take a look at the scrape marks running along the side panels of this vehicle,' Carrington began. 'Here, here, and here. These images were taken at the campsite shortly before the Transit van was taken away for forensic examination.' The young detective smiled wryly. 'Now compare them to these images taken shortly before it boarded the overnight ferry in Amsterdam.'

Mason stared at the images trying to get his head around it.

'They look identical.'

'They are,' she smiled. 'Now compare the vehicle registration plates.'

'Goddammit,' Mason replied, 'they're different.'

Carrington's eyebrows rose. 'The thing is, we've been concentrating our efforts on facial recognition and never given the Transit van a second thought.'

Mason picked up the images and began to study them.

'What made you think the plates had been switched a second time?'

'Mistrust,' she replied. 'People who TWOC vehicles for a living always change the number plates no matter what. It's the first thing they do.'

Mason's grin broadened, confirming just how razor-sharp the detective was.

'The question is, did Rigg steal the vehicle, or was it left abandoned on waste ground as he said it was?'

'Hard to say,' Carrington shrugged. 'It's my guess he stole it.'

Mason checked his notes. If the van was stolen in Wallsend, did it mean that Ellis Walker was being held captive there? Chuffed with his detective's efforts, it was an astute piece of work which meant they could now backtrack the vehicle's full movements.

After a few minutes tapping at the keyboard, Mason lifted his head.

'Have we checked with Road Traffic?'

'We have.'

'Find anything?'

'No, unfortunately.'

'What about Rigg? Did you find anything more when you ran his name through the system?'

'No. There's nothing we didn't already know.'

'Rigg's not exactly the perfect role model, that's for sure.' Mason took another bite out of his steak pie and considered this. 'There's always the possibility that Rigg was paid to get rid of it, of course.'

Carrington screwed her face up. 'I doubt it, boss.'

'Oh, and why not? Every police force in the land is out looking for it.'

'It's more likely that Ed Coleman had a hand in this.'

Mason's ears pricked up at the mere mention of Coleman's name. Whoever killed Terrence Baxter surely had a hand in Ellis Walker's kidnapping too. The two crimes were intrinsically linked, and it was time to put Coleman under the microscope.

'Okay,' Mason said, still scrutinizing the images. 'Let's see what Tom Hedley's team make of it. Who knows, they might send a few hares running.'

Carrington stared at him. 'What about Rigg?'

'He's up to his neck in trouble and isn't to be trusted. That said, if we can get Rigg to confess where he nicked the vehicle, it may lead us to Walker.'

Mason's desk phone rang.

It was the area commander looking for updates. *God!* he groaned. Did Gregory expect the answers to fall on his lap. It didn't work like that. Not down at street level it didn't. Every scrap of information was hard fought.

Dispensing of pleasantries, Gregory cut him short.

'Have you read the Chief Constable's latest financial budget report?' he asked in a tone more demanding than enquiring.

'No sir, I haven't. I am in the middle of—'

'I think you should, Chief Inspector.'

Mason tried to curb his emotions.

'Why. Is there an issue?'

'We need to discuss this in more detail. Meet me in my office in fifteen minutes.'

Mason slammed the receiver down and shuffled a few papers around on an untidy desk. His wasn't the most glamorous job in the building, but he was aware of the dangers of being complacent. Murder investigations were intense, and the burnout rate amongst senior officers in charge of major crime was scarily high. That worried him, but there was no simple answer – apart from a backseat desk job and the downward spiral of being buried alive under a mountain of paperwork.

Blimey! What a prospect.

'Him upstairs?' Carrington giggled.

Mason shot her a glance.

'Get your sorry arse out of here,' he groaned.

Chapter Twenty-One

It was late Friday morning, and Jack Mason was sitting inside Gregory's office drinking coffee and discussing the state of play. The atmosphere was strained although things were moving along nicely now. Later that afternoon, Tom Hedley the senior forensic scientist was due to carry out further tests on the white Transit van. Combined with the previous soil findings, it firmly placed the vehicle in Amsterdam around the time of Baxter's murder. It was a huge breakthrough.

As expected, nothing new had transpired regarding the Schiphol diamond heist, so there was little to discuss. There was one piece of good news though: Special Branch were putting a list of potential ringleaders together which might throw up a few useful names. Hopefully, they would produce something before the weekend.

Still very much in their thoughts, the team were seeing far less of Ed Coleman these days. Whatever the gangster was up to, it was obviously not good. Mason would need an absolute slam-dunk case to get a conviction. If not the man's smart lawyer would keep him at arm's length. It was an unnecessary setback, and one that was being poorly managed by the area commander.

As for Ellis Walker's captors, his boss did agree with Mason that all three men belonged to an international crime syndicate even though none of them was on Interpol's wanted list. The description of the men was vague. One was tall with big feet, another stocky and middle aged, a third Middle Eastern with a thick gold choker around his neck.

At least it was a start. And yes, Mason had been spending far too much time at work lately and not enough time with Barbara. A weekend in Scotland might do the trick. They could go walking together, take in the sights, and the local pubs around Loch Lomond always served decent food. Barbara loved visiting castles, and there were plenty of those in the Scottish Highlands. Fortunately, his partner was different from the rest, more mature, more understanding, and less demanding than the dozens of women he had known and had met after his divorce. He'd been fortunate, of course. His partner was very understanding about the long unsociable working hours that most senior police officers had to put up with, which meant he had his own space and wasn't tied down.

As he let his mind drift, a weekend in Scotland seemed the perfect answer.

'This stolen white Transit van we recovered from the traveller's camp,' said Gregory, breaking Mason's thoughts. 'Do we know who it was registered to?'

'It belonged to a meat wholesaler in Aberystwyth and was sold at auction ten months ago. I've done a few checks, and the man who bought it has since passed away.'

'That's unfortunate. Any connections to the Northeast?'

'None whatsoever.'

The sun streaming in through the office window, Gregory lifted his head. 'Mark Rigg. What charges have we brought against him?'

'The Bail Act for starters,' Mason replied. 'Once Tom Hedley's team have concluded their findings, I'm hoping more will follow.'

'Do we know what part Rigg played in Walker's kidnapping, if any?'

'Not at this stage we don't, but we know the Transit van is a vital link.'

Gregory eyed him warily. 'I'm told Rigg attacked you with a baseball bat.'

'More a damp squib than anything,' Mason grinned.

'He's obviously a troublemaker. If I'm not mistaken, he's wanted by every police force up and down the country.'

'I've not spoken to him yet, but I'm aware Hampshire police would like a word with him.' Mason allowed himself a brief, smug smile. 'The question remains, was the vehicle abandoned as Rigg claimed, or was he paid to get rid of it.'

Gregory's eyebrows raised as if another option had suddenly crossed his mind.

'What's your take on it, Chief Inspector? Is our undercover officer being held captive in Wallsend, do you think?'

'It's possible, but my money's on Ed Coleman.'

'Ah, Ed Coleman. I was wondering when you'd mention him.'

'Sir—'

'What makes you think Coleman is involved? It's my understanding he's been keeping his nose clean lately and mixing with a lot of horse racing people.'

Mason eased forward in his seat.

'The man's a menace, and we know he was in bed with Terrence Baxter.'

The uneasy silence indicated more disagreement.

'You're not suggesting this racehorse adventure is a smokescreen, are you?'

'Of course it is.'

Gregory shook his head in contempt. 'Your obsession that Coleman is the brains behind the Schiphol diamond robbery is wearing a little thin.'

'Really?'

'I suspect you haven't a scrap of evidence to support such a claim, and frustration is ruling your head. I know you're angry with the way Coleman's lawyers handle his affairs, but you seem to forget sometimes that not every charge against him will stick.'

Mason stared at Gregory incredulously.

'It's my view Coleman knew Baxter had survived the Istanbul terrorist attack. If not, then why send Ellis Walker over to Amsterdam to meet him?'

Gregory leaned back and regarded Mason through narrow eyes.

'So, who killed Baxter?'

'The same people who abducted Ellis Walker.'

'And you think Coleman is responsible for this?'

Mason laughed. 'Anything's possible knowing him.'

'That's preposterous.'

'But is it?'

'What, you think an undercover police officer engages in homicide? Surely not.'

Mason tried his best to stay calm. 'All roads lead to Coleman, and it wouldn't surprise me to find these gypsies are also in his pocket.'

Gregory opened his notebook and jotted something down.

'Why would Coleman kidnap his own man? Your reasoning doesn't make sense.'

'Why don't we bring him in and ask him that very question?'

Gregory's frown lines tightened. 'On what grounds?'

'Surely we don't need a reason to question a notorious felon.'

'I'm not convinced,' said Gregory, putting down his pen. 'If I'm honest with you, Head of Control, Alison Jefferson, is far from happy with the way you conducted your stakeout operation on Coleman's property. It was a bit over the top, don't you think?'

'We wouldn't have found the Transit van had we not,' Mason insisted.

Gregory looked taken aback.

'Are you aware the Metropolitan police are keeping an eye on Coleman?'

'That doesn't surprise me in the least.'

'Meaning?'

Mason looked at his boss quizzically. 'Perhaps you'd explain why all of the Coleman case files have recently been redacted. It's as if someone is trying to protect the man. Why would someone do that, I keep asking myself?'

Gregory raised his hand as if to command attention.

'As far as Alison Jefferson is concerned, your remit is to establish Walker's whereabouts and relay that information back to Special Branch.'

Gregory gave Mason a stern look. 'You're good at what you do, and that's why you were chosen for the job. The one thing you've not picked up on, not yet at least, is that Coleman is in bed with Specialist Crime Directorate 7.'

Mason flopped back in his seat as if he'd been struck a hammer blow.

'What?'

He watched as the area commander slid a large brown envelope towards him stamped "Classified." Inside were several images, along with a few handwritten notes.

'Things are never what they appear to be, particularly where Special Branch are concerned. You of all people should know that, as you've worked with them often enough.' Gregory gave him another sombre look before continuing. 'Take these images for instance. These people's identities are fake. None of them are who they say they are – every one of them is an imposter.'

'Holy shit,' Mason swore.

The AC shook his head despairingly. 'Once SCD7 get involved, everything's thrown up in the air. It's the way these people operate.'

'Are you saying Coleman is now working for us?'

'It would appear so.'

'In what capacity may I ask?'

For a moment, the area commander looked wistful. 'According to Special Branch,

THE POACHER'S POCKET

Coleman's involvement in the Schiphol diamond heist was minimal. SCD7 have a much bigger fish to fry and are using every trick in the book to get to the mastermind.'

Mason could hardly believe his ears.

Gregory's smile broadened. 'That's the thing about this type of operation, you never know which side of the fence you're sitting on. But rest assured, as far as Ed Coleman is concerned, Special Branch are well aware of his dodgy background. That's why they coerced him in the first place.'

'Are you saying he's turned Queen's Evidence? Surely not.'

Gregory raised an eyebrow. 'I couldn't have put it better myself, Chief Inspector.'

'Holy shit,' said Mason, flopping back in his seat, 'and here's me thinking I was onto something.'

'You may well be, but now Special Branch have Coleman in their back pocket, we have a lead into the criminal underworld.'

It figured. Annoyed with himself for not having thought this through, he'd been barking up the wrong tree as usual. If counterintelligence were manipulating Ed Coleman behind closed doors, there was neither rhyme nor reason he'd want to abduct his own man. It was far too obvious. Besides, SCD7 would have been onto him. It all made sense suddenly, and the faceless grey people who protected our national interests had undoubtedly fooled everyone. Including him. The landscape had changed; from now on he would need to tread carefully.

His mind running amok, Mason stared at his notes.

'Does Coleman know Ellis Walker is an undercover officer?'

'I doubt it.'

'So, Shaun Quinn is still operating as aka Ellis Walker?'

'This operation has been going round in circles for weeks now. If we knew everything, then we'd know what SCD7 were up to. We don't unfortunately. As I've already pointed out nothing is black and white.'

Mason sat quietly for a moment.

'What's to say Ellis Walker hasn't defected to the other side?'

'I doubt it, but there's nothing wrong in keeping an open mind about these things.'

Mason glanced up.

'Why wasn't I informed about this before now, sir?'

'Your remit is to find Ellis Walker. Once you accomplish that, you can ask him all the questions you like.'

Having got over the initial shock, Mason was beginning to think differently. Things made sense suddenly, no wonder everyone had been keeping tight lipped.

'Do we know who these kidnappers are working for?'

The AC drew back in his seat. 'There's a top-level meeting tomorrow morning – 07:30 in the Chief Constable's command room. In the meantime, may I suggest you talk to your counterpart in Amsterdam. Find out where they are with their investigations.' Gregory looked at him gravely. 'Coleman still remains of major interest to us, but unless you're told otherwise, he's not to be brought in for questioning. Do I make myself clear?'

'Yes, sir.'

Crikey, Mason thought. He hated Coleman, vehemently. Just when he thought he had the gangster in his sights, he'd slipped through the net again. Still, he thought, there were many ways to skin a cat. But information transfer wasn't good. Everything about this case was cloaked in secrecy, including his dealings with the Dutch police.

Leaving the AC's office with mixed emotions, Mason felt there was no simple answer. It was time to work on a plan, and one that would lead him to Ellis Walker.

Chapter Twenty-Two

Jack Mason's meeting with Head of Control, Alison Jefferson, had thrown up very little in the way of fresh leads. What was of interest, though, was SCD7's grip on Ed Coleman's activities. The gangster was a prisoner in his own mansion, according to Jefferson. No wonder Mason's surveillance operation had been treated with such contempt: one mistake and a national intelligence operation could have gone up in smoke.

It was shortly after midday when his meeting with the team closed, and he set off to Wallsend. There was still enough time to set a few plans in motion, but motive was an issue. According to the latest reports, Terrence Baxter had been followed. The details were incomplete, but at least four people were now involved in Baxter's murder according to Special Branch. The one thing that struck Mason as odd, was the lack of cooperation from the Dutch police. Whatever their motive, it wasn't the best way to conduct a murder investigation. If so, why hadn't Head of Control, Alison Jefferson picked up on this? Yes, there was some classified information that could never be shared, he realised that, but this latest cloak-and-dagger approach to all things Terrence Baxter was beginning to wear thin.

As he swung the unmarked police car onto the slip road heading towards the Tyne, the suburbs of Wallsend came into view. Not everyone's cup of tea, row upon row of late Victorian terraced buildings reminded him of his childhood, and a misspent youth in the backstreets of London's East End. The shipyards had long gone, but the neighbourhood still maintained its closely knit communal spirit which pleased him no end. Not for the first time the area around the docklands had been of great interest to the team. It was time to dig deeper. Find out what was really going on.

'What do you think?' the chief inspector asked Carlisle, sitting next to him.

The profiler gave him a disparaging look. 'Hard to tell, Jack. Just because a white Transit van was found in the nearby vicinity, doesn't mean Ellis Walker is held here.'

'If you have an alternative hypothesis, I'd love to hear it, my friend.'

'I know what you're thinking, but the simple answer is why here?'

Mason pulled in behind a rusty Ford Cortina and switched off the car's engine. For once door-to-door enquiries had paid dividends, which gave him some confidence. There were three possibilities as to Walker's whereabouts, and this building was of particular interest to him. With his lifetime experience, this was a no brainer for Mason.

He sat motionless for a moment, thinking.

There was nothing in the world he would have preferred doing right now other than this. He loved his job, but to be told his plans had been a waste of time had pushed all the wrong buttons. Okay, his posturing had been aggressive lately, he would agree with that. But Gregory wasn't the nicest person to deal with at the moment, and he was furious at the way he was handling the case. Nothing seemed straightforward anymore, everything was fragmented and shrouded in secrecy.

His car radio crackled.

'I've got good vibes about this place,' Mason said, suppressing a grin. 'If that ain't proof enough, I don't know what is.'

'I'm not getting the same feeling, Jack.'

'Oh. What then?'

'To me it looks like a perfect drug den.'

'Nah. When something dubious is going on, it always gives me the creeps.'

'Any women seen entering the premises?'

'It's not a brothel, if that's what you think.'

Mason noticed junk mail sticking out of the letter box. Whoever occupied the property hadn't bothered with that. Whatever was going on behind closed doors wasn't an everyday occurrence. It was time to throw a spanner in the works.

'We're being watched,' Mason said, pointing to a chink in some upstairs curtains. 'If Walker is held here, I want him out of there. It's as simple as that.'

'What, just the two of us?'

The chief inspector tapped his forehead as he picked up the car's radio handset. Seconds later the voice of Ops-1 belted out.

'Delta Zero-Six.'

'Delta Zero-Six,' the chief inspector repeated aloud, 'activate Snake Bite.'

Mason knew the area well, but not this particular row of terraced houses. Within minutes dozens of police officers had piled out of two large, unmarked police vans which had been positioned at the bottom of the street.

'Blimey! You kept that one quiet,' the profiler gasped.

'Like I said. No stones unturned.'

As the chief inspector slid from the unmarked vehicle, he arched his back and walked dutifully towards the approaching officers. Now kitted out in full riot gear, they looked eager. Still without the facts, Mason was beginning to feel upbeat. Privately, though, he wished he had organised this raid much earlier.

It had just turned three o'clock when the property's front door caved inwards with a bang, but it was the heat that grabbed them. Along with a strong whiff of cannabis. Seconds later, they were inside and clearing rooms as they went. It was a slick operation, and over in minutes.

Mason heard shouting coming from the basement, followed by the clump of heavy police boots. Not what he was expecting, they'd broken into a large-scale professionally run cannabis farm. He watched as two bedraggled figures appeared at the top of the cellar stairwell. A wizened old Asian man in his late sixties, and a boy no older than ten.

'Who are you?' Mason demanded.

They watched as the boy cowered behind the wizen old man, who didn't speak a word of English. The moment they handcuffed him, the pair were led away to a waiting police van.

Carlisle pointed to a side door, and Mason followed.

The room was rectangular in shape, brightly lit; the walls and ceilings painted stark white. Mason felt uneasy in the place, as if stepping into a graveyard full of lost souls. As his eyes adjusted to the light, growing equipment filled every corner of the room. The heat was unbearable, with grow lights, heaters, oscillating fans, filters, and hundreds of plant trays aligned to extraction scrubbers in long neat rows. Illegally tapped into an electrical power source that looked decidedly dodgy if not downright dangerous, there were well over a hundred suspect cannabis plants on view. All in an advanced stage of growth, they still had two more floors to execute.

It was a sophisticated operation, complex, and the people responsible would be difficult to track down. He realised that. People like the Riley twins who had an army of legal advisors only too willing to accuse them of wrongful arrest.

'Pity,' Mason said. 'It's not what I was expecting to find.'

'No doubt the Area Commander will be pleased.'

'Anything for an easy life,' Mason groaned. 'The old sod wouldn't know what the inside of a cannabis farm looked like.'

The profiler scratched his head. 'Probably not.'

Mason knew from experience that raids such as this would set off a chain reaction. If Ellis Walker were being held close by, he'd have been moved by now. He felt sorry for the man, but if you allowed it to get to you, you were sunk.

He looked at his watch.

'This is exactly the type of building I'd expect them to be holding Walker in. I'm convinced of it.'

As the profiler's eyes toured the room, Mason sensed what was coming next.

'If we've spooked them, we may have endangered his life.'

'Let's not go there, my friend. I've enough on my plate without having to worry about another officers welfare.'

'But you can't just hide from the fact.'

Mason felt uneasy.

'No, maybe not.'

The profiler wiped the sweat from his eyes as he spoke. 'What concerns me is the lack of threatening ransom notes or video tapes from his captors. This isn't a stereotype kidnapping; this is more an interrogation exercise.'

'You don't pull any punches, my friend. What about the note they pinned to Baxter's chest. What's the significance of that?'

Carlisle drew back. 'Baxter was the sacrificial lamb, and that's why they killed him. Your officer's abduction is more about what he knows than anything.'

Mason's mobile buzzed in his pocket. He checked the screen. Three new messages, and none of them important. He hurriedly switched it off again.

'Sorry about that. Like I was saying, what about the note pinned to Baxter's chest?'

'More a promise than a threat I would imagine.'

'What, you think these people have rumbled Ellis Walker's true identity?'

'If they have, then Walker's a dead man.'

The profiler looked at him with concern. 'We're missing a trick here, Jack. Whatever it is that Special Branch are holding back from us, is a vital part of the puzzle. You were right about one thing, though. Where are the Schiphol diamonds in all of this?'

Whatever his suspicions, the profiler was not openly sharing them. His colleague could be extremely frustrating at times, but that's how profilers worked. They were methodical and concise in their approach.

Outside on the street, neighbours were gathering. Word had got out, and before long every Tom, Dick, and Harry would know of their presence. For now, further raids were out of the question. As for the two frightened occupants, or gardeners as Mason liked to call them, they were mere pawns. Slave labour brought in from the continent to monitor and tend to the crops.

Still, Mason thought. The chief constable would be pleased with his findings. It was all about statistics these days. The more successful drug raids you carried out, the higher up the national credibility stakes you rose. Gregory lived and breathed adulation.

Particularly from high office. The man was a menace and should have retired years ago.

God, what a thought.

Chapter Twenty-Three

It was late afternoon when Jack Mason pulled onto the house drive and parked alongside Barbara's VW Up. Pocketing his phone, he sat for a moment and stared at the garden's opposite. Meadow Lane was a quiet part of the estate, a mixture of three-bedroom semi-detached houses and elegant bungalows. At the far end of the lane was a corner shop, and behind that a primary school with a small recreation field and fenced-in playgrounds. He'd found the house by chance; according to local estate agents it had been on the market for several years. Grossly overpriced, the previous owners were trying to recoup lost savings having spent a fortune on doing it up. Ready to move, even Mason was surprised when the owners accepted his audacious offer. He later discovered the occupants were living in Spain and had got into financial difficulties over a tourist adventure they were involved in. Mason was fortunate and thanked his lucky stars.

Barbara was busy making dinner when he poked his head in through the open kitchen doorway. It smelt good, halibut, his favourite dish. Exhausted, he could not remember the last time he had finished work this early. As a rule, something unexpected would crop up and ruin his plans. Not tonight, he hoped, as he was feeling horny and could not wait to dim the lights.

'You're home early, darling. I wasn't expecting to see you so soon.'

Mason felt a ripple of excitement as he sidled up to his partner.

'All my little songbirds are safely tucked up in their cages,' he smiled, 'and I couldn't get away from them fast enough thinking about you.'

'Be off with you,' Barbara giggled.

'It smells delicious. Dare I crack open a bottle of wine?'

'That sounds like a good idea.'

Mason reached into one of the kitchen cabinets and grabbed a couple of wine glasses. God, he was excited, and could hardly contain himself. All he wanted was to rip off her apron and ravage her on the kitchen table.

Calm down, Jack. Don't rush it.

'Red or white?' he asked.

'It's fish my lovely.'

'Better make it Sauvignon Blanc then.'

Barbara moved in closer and gave him a peck on the cheek. An extremely attractive woman, she was exceptionally talented and a caring person. Having gone through a difficult divorce, he was slowly getting back to some sort of normality. One step at a time, he'd promised, and not to rush into things. Police work could be extremely demanding, and these past few months had been manic with a high workload. Worse still, according to the latest feedback the raid on the Riley twin's drug gang had been a total disaster. The new man in charge, a recently appointed inspector, had cocked up big style. If there was any justice to be had, the streets of Gateshead would be quiet for a couple of weeks before it all kicked off again. The Riley twins weren't daft. Once the dust had settled it would be business as usual. Drug barons never gave up on illicit dealing. It wasn't in their DNA.

'That's what I love about you,' Barbara said, in a low and sexy whisper. 'You're a man of big decisions.'

Mason smiled as he squeezed Barbara's waist.

'So, how has your day been?' he asked lovingly.

'Not a lot's been happening, if I'm honest.'

'How is the young lad doing who fell off his bike? Any signs of improvement?'

'Not yet,' his partner sighed. 'He was back on the treatment table today, but it's going to be a long and slow recovery. His mum's biggest concern is his mental well-being. He's been missing an awful lot of his schooling lately, and it's affecting his confidence.'

That's how they'd met, in a hospital treatment room a few miles north of Newcastle. Barbara worked as a physiotherapist there, at a time when Mason's career was under threat after a near-fatal encounter with a manic serial killer. It was a critical period in his life, and he was facing only a twenty percent chance of recovery from life-threatening knife wounds. Barbara's dedication and tender loving care had nursed him back to fitness again. It was a miraculous turn of events, and one he was forever grateful.

'You look tired, my love. How is the new case going?'

'Can't complain.'

Mason was exhausted; both physically and mentally. No sooner had one problem resolved than another cropped up in its place. Ed Coleman wasn't helping either, the sooner he was brought to justice the greater the chance of solving the case. If they didn't get an arrest soon, God knows where this would end.

He waited for Barbara to finish chopping some onions before moving in closer to feel her supple skin. He fancied the pants off this woman. Dating her was the best decision he had ever made.

'I need to spend a few days over in Amsterdam,' he said.

'Oh. I thought you'd finished with that side of the operation.'

'No. There's still a few loose ends we need to tie up.'

There was a look in her eyes that he had not seen before. Inviting and sensual, which instantly took his breath away. The moment she slid her free hand inside his shirt, he felt his heart race.

'You poor thing,' Barbara said, pouting her lips, 'have those nasty little men been up to no good again?'

'They're not all bad, my love. There are still a few good apples in the cart.'

'Yes, there's good in everyone, Jack,' she said chinking glasses. 'Now be off with you, I'm extremely busy here.'

God, he loved her to bits. Elevated to new heights, he moved into the living room and flicked the TV remote button to find one of the local news channels. Not that he was interested in regional affairs, but sometimes it threw up some interesting news. Crime mainly. Robberies, murder, and rape were never far from the media's attention these days. Still, he smiled. These were the people who paid the bills.

'So, what happens now?' Barbara shouted through.

'Regarding what, my love?'

'This Amsterdam trip. Has this got anything to do with the murder investigation you're involved in?'

'How did you guess.'

'Why can't the Dutch police manage it themselves?'

'I wish it were that easy, but a murder on Dutch soil involves a UK citizen and now the British Consulate are involved.'

'It all sounds complicated to me.'

Barbara was right. It was complicated, and he would be mad to think otherwise. There were dozens of new avenues to investigate, but where to begin was the problem. The more he thought about it, the more he wished he'd challenged the area commander instead of taking it on the chin. Coleman was a menace, if anyone knew who the Schiphol mastermind was, it was him. But his hands had been tied, and people in high places were making life difficult. Still seething at the lack of feedback from Allison Jefferson, he felt isolated and tired of constantly being pushed around.

Now deep in thought, Mason took another sip of his wine and began to ponder his options. Aware of the precarious position Ellis Walker was in, if he didn't find him soon, his captors would lose patience and kill him. That worried him. A fellow police officer in serious danger was never a good situation to be faced with. The trouble was, Tom Hedley had thrown up little in the way of fresh leads, which was disappointing to say the least. Apart from a few fibre strands found in the back of the Transit van, he had little else to go on. Mason wished the vehicle had been torched. At least that would have saved them a lot of leg work, which was always a major plus. Whoever was holding Walker, knew what they were doing. He was certain of that.

Then there was Mark Rigg. A born liar, who had led them up the garden path on more than one occasion. How Rigg had obtained the transit van was still a matter of conjecture. The man was a nuisance, and no two stories were ever the same. Even Rob Savage was agreed on that. The only person able to get inside the traveller's head was the profiler. Even he had been noticeably absent of late. But that's how profilers worked, nothing was ever straightforward.

'Have you changed into something more comfortable, my love?'

'Not yet, darling.'

'In which case you can pour me another drink; my hands are tied at the moment.'

Mason caught the look in his partner's eye. When Barbara knocked her wine back at this rate, it could only mean one thing.

'How long before dinner is ready?'

'Why, do you have something in mind?'

He gave her a steamy look. 'I could have.'

'Do I have time to change into something a little more comfortable?'

'That depends on what you're planning to wear.'

She returned his gaze.

'Not a lot…'

'Sounds good to me,' Mason grinned.

No sooner had they drained their glasses than they raced each other up the stairs.

Chapter Twenty-Four

It seemed a lifetime since the Poacher's last interrogation, and these past few hours had been a living hell. Pain in Walker's arm was unbearable. Infection had set in, and he felt physically sick. He knew he had an increased temperature, and there was a burning sensation in his hand where they'd amputated his finger. Sensing death wasn't far away, he tried to stay focused.

It had taken three of them to drag him here. The driver of the van, the man who spoke little English, and the Poacher. Blindfolded and gagged, day two had unquestionably been the evillest. Waterboarding it was called. One of those nasty tortures where water is poured over a cloth covering your face and breathing passages. It triggered a gag reflex, as if fighting for every breath. There were times when he thought he was drowning. A slow suffocating sensation that took him to the depths of despair. The Poacher's evil was unparalleled, and nobody deserved to suffer such insane punishment. Nobody.

He heard footsteps approaching. Then sliding bolts. The moment the gaffer tape was ripped from his mouth, Walker felt the trickle of warm blood. The evil bastard was back, only this time more furious.

'Where are they?' his captor demanded.

Walker struggled with his bonds.

'Last chance motherfucker. Talk, or I'll cut your tongue out.'

Walker tried to speak, but his badly torn lips were preventing him from doing so. The Poacher didn't do empathy, there wasn't an ounce of compassion in his veins. How much more could he take? How much longer could this go on?

'You know why I'm here,' the Poacher said, glaring down at him.

Walker shook his head as if not knowing.

'Where are the documents you dumb bastards stole from us?'

With the knife pressed hard against his throat, the officer's eyes narrowed. The moment the saline drip was yanked from his arm, he felt a burning sensation running through his chest. It was time, and Walker had thought long and hard about this moment. Too long. Ensnared in the Poacher's pocket, his was a bottomless pit full of misery and the first level of hell.

Walker felt the cold steel moving slowly across his jugular. He froze. Was this how it was meant to end? Left to die with the rats?

He'd never wanted to end up a poster boy hero. All Walker ever wanted was to see his wife and kids again. As fear ripped through him like never before, he felt his life was slowly ebbing away.

A door slammed, followed by more sliding bolts.

Very still, the undercover officer held his breath and listened.

Legs locked tightly together, body bolt upright, he began the chair rocking motion. Not twenty feet away, close to the rear cellar wall, lay a table full of instruments of torture. Some had sharp edges, others were blunt, but all had been used against him with devastating effect.

His mind spinning in a vortex, Walker inched his way forward and sensed the gap to the table was closing. He was close. Another few feet and he could physically reach out and touch them. Caught in a race against time, he pushed hard on his heels. Fail now, and it would all end here. He knew that, as if his life depended on it.

As he let his mind drift, he knew nothing of any documents. Then he remembered. The night he met Terrence Baxter his phone rang. It was pitch black and Baxter's voice was barely audible. Fearing the worst, he'd tried to level with the man, but the mood he was in, and the threats he was under, he knew it was futile.

The rage inside him building, Walker was angry with Coleman for having sent him to Amsterdam in the first place. Even angrier with Baxter, whom he now knew had double-crossed them. He then turned his resentment on the priest. It wasn't the best laid plans in his life, he realised that. Having arrived at the church of Our Gracious Lady Amsterdam, Father Jagaar knew nothing of Judas's arrangements. Nor of the package he was to hand to him. The priest was vague. Vain. Tormenting his already troubled mind.

Walker stiffened. *Was the priest an imposter?*

No, he argued. If he couldn't trust a man of God, who else could he trust?

He heard scraping and craned his neck.

Nerve-ends pinched, Walker began the chair rocking motion again. Progress was slow, but he felt the table of torment was drawing ever closer. Then, in the darkest corners of uncertainty, his head struck the concrete beam. Rocked sideways suddenly, he toppled over and fell in an unconscious heap on the floor.

How long he had lain there, he had no idea. When he opened his eyes, the Poacher was standing over him and drooling.

Walker froze.

Nothing had prepared him for this. Nothing

Chapter Twenty-Five

The two detectives were beavering away in MIR-1 when there was a knock at the door. The clock on the wall had just turned 11:30, and Sue Carrington was busily working her way through a pile of witness statements. Rob Savage, meanwhile, was looking at CCTV footage captured from a local petrol station. As the meeting room door swung open, a small, plump woman with a rounded face and dark inquisitive eyes entered. She wore a blue button down skirt, pink blouse, matching flat canvas shoes, and carried a large bundle of case files tucked under her arm.

'How can we help, Dorothy?' asked Detective Carrington.

'Sorry to disturb you, ma'am,' said an anxious looking liaison officer as she turned to face them, 'we're getting reports of a house disturbance over in the Bensham area where a large cash of stolen goods has turned up.'

Both detectives looked at one another. It was Carrington who spoke first.

'What has this got to do with us, Dorothy?'

The liaison officer looked across at Savage who had pushed back in his seat with a puzzled expression on his face. 'I know it's none of my business, but the officer in charge believes it's connected to one of the cases you are currently investigating.'

'Where are they now?' asked Savage.

'The last I heard the male suspect had been brought in for processing.'

Savage turned to Carrington. 'I wonder if it has anything to do with this recent spate of shoplifting over at the Metro Centre.'

'It's possible.'

'Thank you, Dorothy, you did right to inform us.'

No sooner had the door closed than Carrington's thoughts immediately flashed to another case. 'We'd better warn the desk sergeant of our interest,' she said.

As the two officers made their way towards the reception area, they stopped at the vending machine to grab a coffee. It was rarely the big leads that sparked detectives into action, more the unexpected snippets of information that sent their adrenaline racing. Despite all the horrors she'd encountered in her short but eventful career, Sue Carrington loved her job. Life had been good to her, unlike her sister Claire who seemed to move from one crisis to another. Going through a bad patch in her life, her younger sister was facing the dreaded downward spiral with nowhere to call home. It was a sorry state of affairs, but Carrington had never trusted her sister's boyfriend. She thought him too pushy, as if every woman were fair game. Some men didn't have an ounce of morals in their bodies and her family was suffering because of it.

Carrington stood silent for a moment. It was obvious that Clair's boyfriend had a big ego. Naturally attracted to other women, these days the internet had made it far too easy for men to live out their fantasies. Not all relationships stood the test of time. Many failed, as her younger sister had unfortunately discovered.

The front desk was busy, but the sergeant in charge waved them forward with a flurry. 'What can I do for you?' the officer asked.

'What's the latest on this house disturbance over in the Bensham area?' asked Savage. 'What do we know about the suspects?'

'They're booked into Suite Two,' the custody sergeant announced, poking her head around the tall Perspex safety screen. 'Colin Dobson's your man, and the duty solicitor is currently in attendance.'

'That wouldn't be Dipper Dobson?' said Savage, despondently.

The custody sergeant shrugged. 'I'm afraid so. Wanted for murder, is he?'

'I doubt it,' Savage replied.

'No. I wouldn't have thought so.'

'What's Dipper Dobson been up to this time?' asked Carrington.

The desk sergeant checked her computer screen. A fastidious police officer, her fingernails were beautifully manicured, and her makeup lightly applied.

She turned to face them. 'The initial call out is down as a house disturbance in Alexandra Road, which according to the officers in attendance is an Aladdin's cave full of stolen goods.' She waved her hand as if to emphasise a point. 'Dobson's partner can't agree about anything, it seems. Especially after a drink. This is the second time this week we've been called to the property.'

Colin Dobson and partner Kelly Rooney were well known to Gateshead police, having spent time in prison for theft and numerous shop lifting offences. They operated together, one to distract their victim, the other to fleece them of wallets, phones, and anything they could lay their grubby hands on. Known amongst station staff as "Dipper and Diver," they'd been aptly named according to Rob Savage. Technology had moved on, and the moment the pair set foot anywhere near a shopping precinct, security was onto them in a flash.

Carrington mulled over the facts. How many people drunk alcohol before nine in the morning? Few, she wagered. Fuelled by drugs and alcohol, these people were more of a public nuisance than anything. No matter how small or insignificant it may appear, every lead had to be followed up. That's how the majority of crimes were solved; small pieces of a jig-saw puzzle coming together. Nothing was cast in stone, and some leads would open up a whole new line of enquiry.

'These reprobates are in no way involved with gypsies, I take it,' asked Savage.

'I wouldn't have thought so,' the custody sergeant replied. 'Why do you ask?'

'Just curious, that's all.'

The desk sergeant smiled as her fingers tapped the computer keyboard.

'Someone's obviously got their wires crossed, but I can certainly put the question to them if you wish.'

'Yes. That would be useful,' Savage nodded dutifully.

They walked back to MIR-1, as determined as anyone to find Walker. He was out there somewhere, but where was the million-dollar question.

Savage sighed. 'It's not our day, Sue.'

'No, I guess not.'

'Every new lead sends us down another blind alley these days. I'm beginning to wonder if Walker is still alive.'

Carrington shook her head as she checked her phone for messages. There was one. *Get a grip*, she thought. A fellow police officer's life was at stake, and here she was checking to see what time her hair appointment was.

Savage closed the door behind them and moved towards the window.

'Back to the grindstone again.'

'Let's hope the boss has a plan up his sleeve.'

The sergeant looked wistfully across at her and frowned.

'I wouldn't hang my hat on it, Sue.'

Chapter Twenty-Six

It was 09:15, and after another fruitless night spent searching run-down properties looking for Ellis Walker, dozens of tired police officers climbed into their vehicles looking decidedly despondent. Now fearing the worst, Mason pondered his options. Seven long days had passed since the undercover officer's abduction, a heck of a long time. He wished he had done things differently, followed his instincts instead of sticking to police protocol. The profiler was right, there had to be a logical explanation to all of this.

Had Rigg lied to them about the abandoned white Transit van? More importantly, if Special Branch had Coleman in their back pocket, why the lack of feedback? So many unanswered questions, so many avenues to go down, and no fresh leads to drive them forward. Was Shaun Quinn aka Ellis Walker alive? The area commander thought so, but his opinion counted for nothing these days. The man was a menace and so far removed from the real world that Mason was beginning to lose faith in the command structure. He felt let down by it all, and being in charge of a murder investigation was a heavy burden of responsibility to carry.

He was about to move off when he spotted DC Carrington leaving the command vehicle. Dressed in a pair of tight denim jeans, casual blouse and flat shoes, the detective looked totally disheartened. He wound the driver's window down to speak.

'Heard anything?' the detective asked.

'Not a lot.'

'I know it's a longshot, but what about checking on industrial factory units? Who knows what might abound inside?'

'Not today, Sue,' Mason replied, screwing his face up. 'If Ellis Walker were in the vicinity, they'd have moved him long before now. These people aren't daft.'

'No. I guess you're right.'

Mason's phone pinged, and he answered it. Reports of a homicide were filtering through, and his presence was requested in Howden. The details were sketchy, but knowing Tom Hedley was already in attendance meant it was serious.

He finished the call and hung up.

'I'm wanted over in Howden.'

She stared at him. 'What about our street search? We still have a team out looking.'

'Give it an hour. If you haven't found anything by then, simply call it off.'

'Will do,' she replied.

There was still a mountain of legwork to get through. Door-to-door enquiries took time, but he was conscious of not getting involved. Murder was no respecter; it took precedence over everything. He was also mindful that if Walker were alive, he would now be in grave danger. He sat for a moment, thinking. No calls from the undercover officer's mobile, no payments from his credit cards; he'd vanished without trace.

'Just out of interest,' the chief inspector said, as he turned the ignition key. 'What are you doing tonight?'

Carrington stared at him oddly.

'I'm meeting someone for dinner. Why?'

'Just curious, that's all.'

'If there is a problem, I can cancel.'

'No,' Mason replied dejectedly. 'That won't be necessary.'

He left Carrington in charge of the mop-up operation and pulled out of the street. The only thing in his favour was that Howden wasn't far away. It was Tuesday, quiz night, and one of his team had cancelled at short notice. He would have asked Barbara to join them, but his partner had made other arrangements. Still, he mused, it was just as well that Carrington didn't step in at such short notice, as they'd only end up talking about work.

***

Mason drove up a steep hill, squeezed in behind a marked police car, and sat for a moment. No matter how many homicide callouts he had attended over the years, they always had the same impact on him. Death came in many guises, but violent deaths shocked even the most hardened police officers.

From the outside, the house looked a dump. Unkempt gardens, grey pebbledash walls: there was nothing to suggest he'd want to live here. Parked at the end of the street and slightly set back from the rest, he could see the square hulk of the major incident vehicle sticking out. Surprised to see so many police officers in attendance, he struggled into his forensic suit, and moved through the media throng.

Some murder scenes spoke volumes, but this one felt different. He remembered the buzz he got from attending his first murder as a young fledgling detective. Not anymore. It was the fear of what you might walk into that held him back. He always cared deeply about a victim's grieving family and friends; it was never easy trying to explain, and many a person's life would be ruined by it all. Mason had had a belly full of homicide over the years, but the day he didn't care anymore would be the day to call time.

He signed the crime scene log and walked towards the open doorway. Beyond the police cordon tape was a hive of business-like activity. Known as a RED ZONE in the force, this part of the city had a high rating on the crime score chart. The last time he'd attended the area, was to an all-night house party in the early hours of the morning. A young lad, stark naked, strung up behind a bedroom door with a leather belt wrapped around his neck. It was an open and shut case of suicide, but no one gave a damn as to why he'd done it. They just wanted his body removed. And quick. Life in these parts was cheap, and never ceased to amaze.

The moment he walked through the open front door, Mason heard the familiar whir of a digital flashlight popping. He knew then into what he was walking. No two crime scenes were ever the same, but speed was key to solving most homicides. As his eyes toured the room, he could see the body had slumped forward slightly, and the tongue forced out of the mouth. At first, he thought it was Ellis Walker, but on closer inspection saw it wasn't. Blood everywhere, ceilings and walls, it felt as though he had stepped into a slaughterhouse at the end of a hard day's graft.

'Jesus!' Mason gasped.

'They didn't mess about, Jack. That's for sure.'

'Do we know who he is?'

Dr Colin Brown, a lean long-backed, balding man, stretched as he stood. 'He's male, mid-forties, around five-ten with dark brown eyes, and has "Janice" tattooed on his left forearm.'

'What's he done to deserve this, Colin?'

'Quite a bit by the looks.' The doctor gestured towards the body. 'Whoever killed him certainly made an excellent job of it. Stab wounds to the abdomen, neck, back and chest, the carotid artery has been severed as if to make sure of it.'

'Who's the Crime Scene Manager?' asked Mason.

'Peter Cox.'

Cox was good at his job and would protect a crime scene with his life if necessary. Mason peered at the corpse. It was still early days, but the note pinned to the dead man's chest had a familiar ring about it.

He knelt down to take a closer look.

Who are you, my friend?

The frenzied attack bore all the hallmarks of Terrence Baxter's violent death, but it was far too soon to make a judgement. Dr Brown was spot on. Whoever had killed this young man definitely meant business.

'Just the person,' said Cox, as he peered in through the open living room doorway.

'What have you got for me, Peter?'

'Not much, I'm afraid. What he was doing here and why, we have yet to establish. The house has been empty for months. It's up for auction according to the local estate agents, but I doubt it will sell. Not in this estate.'

'No. It's not a nice area.'

'You can say that again.'

Mason sighed as he stood. 'Time of death?'

Dr Brown spun to face the chief inspector.

'I cannot be precise, but judging by the body temperature, I'd say he's been dead at least seven hours. Although rigor has started, it isn't complete yet.' Brown looked at his watch. 'That puts the time of death between two to three in the morning.'

'What about neighbours?' asked Mason submissively. 'Did anyone hear or see anything?'

'Nobody heard a thing. Knowing this neighbourhood, the majority of residents would have been smacked out of their minds that time of night.'

The chief inspector patted the dead man's pockets. Nothing. It was a funny old world, Mason mused. Having left an unsuccessful search and rescue operation for a missing police officer, he'd now walked into a full-blown murder enquiry.

'Anything found on him? A mobile phone, wallet, a payment slip perhaps?'

'No. Nothing. He's been stripped clean. Whoever killed him also had a good hunt around the property.'

'Searching for something do you think?'

'It would appear so.'

Mason pointed to the corner of the room where the floorboards had been lifted.

'You're right about them looking for something. If not, then this estate has some bloody big mice.'

Cox smiled. 'Forensics will tell us more.'

He studied the body. Dressed in blue tracksuit bottoms, green sweatshirt and matching trainers tied loose, the victim looked at odds with his world. Apart from the horrific injuries, nothing untoward sprang to mind. Once they'd established who he was, one of his family would be summoned to identify the body and all of them questioned and eliminated.

'Who found him, Peter?' asked Mason quizzically.

'A local community officer shortly before seven o'clock.' Cox turned as he spoke. 'The front door was wide open, and that's when he became suspicious.'

'Has he said anything to us?'

'Not to me he hasn't.'

Mason's eyes toured the room. Once Tom Hedley got his teeth into the case, the enquiry would be invasive. No stones unturned, everything done to the book. That's how the senior forensics scientist worked. Hedley was good at his job, a stickler for detail.

The master bedroom was modest in size, with a small sash window overlooking the street. He could see the place had been turned upside down. Loose floorboards strewn everywhere, drawers thrown open, and heating ventilators ripped from their mountings. There was something else that had caught Mason's attention, something that didn't sit right. Whoever killed this man had been looking for something, that much was obvious. But why would they want him dead?

His mind stuck, he'd thought about giving Inspector Jansen a call. If this man's killing was linked to Terrence Baxter's murder, it might save them a lot of legwork. Abandoning the idea, he would wait for the coroner's report. If there were clues to be had, the pathologist would uncover them. He pocketed his phone and descended the stairs to the hallway.

'Find anything of interest?' asked Cox, looking up.

'No. Nothing. Let's see what forensics makes of it.'

Cox stared at him hesitantly.

'More likely drugs related. It's rife in the area.'

Mason pointed to the corpse. 'Why not ask him?'

'Sod off. I've far better things to do with my time.'

Mason waved an annoying blow fly away. It was impossible to keep them from decaying flesh, as blow flies could smell a corpse a million miles away. To him, their only purpose in life was to tell them how long a person had been dead.

As thoughts turned back to Baxter's murder, he smiled resignedly. The minute the news broke, no doubt the area commander would be on the blower. The notion of another mafia style killing on the outskirts of Newcastle wouldn't go down well. A decade ago he would have rushed to tell everyone, not anymore. Whoever killed this man had yet to be determined, but it wasn't looking good. No, Mason thought. His report would come later. No doubt the handwriting experts would scrutinize the note pinned to the victim's chest. Hopefully, they'd find a match. If not, he'd sleep on it.

Mason stared at his watch.

It was eleven-thirty, and he could murder a coffee. Avoiding the press, he thanked Peter Cox and Dr Brown for their assistance and left via the back door.

All in a day's work, he smiled grimly.

Chapter Twenty-Seven

Logged into the web, David Carlisle leaned back in MIR-1 and stared long and hard at the crime board. Positively identified as Ed Coleman's nephew, this unexpected turn in events had certainly put a new slant on their investigation. The profiler could think of no plausible reason why Gregory would refuse Mason an interview with Coleman now. Once they'd established what Samuel Jackson was doing in Howden shortly before he was murdered, then things would fall into place.

Now onto his second cup of coffee, Mason ran through the latest pathology report. Having stopped out drinking most of the night, the chief inspector was in no fit state to watch an autopsy. That task had fallen to Rob Savage. The sight of replacing all the internal organs, stitching the body up and applying make-up to ensure they looked presentable for formal identification, simply horrified the sergeant. Despite his protests, Mason seemed unphased by it all.

Having read Doctor Julien King's initial findings, the team sat thinking. The general consensus of opinion was that Coleman's nephew had been lured to his death just as Baxter had. Proving it was a different matter. Apart from the victim's carotid artery being severed, no less than twenty-seven puncture wounds had been recorded to Jackson's upper body. Four to the neck, twelve to the upper chest, and the rest to the back, arms, and legs. In what had been another brutal attack, the effect on morale was palpable.

What was of particular interest to Carlisle was the nature of the wounds. In his mind, the length of each entry wound was always a good indicator as to the width of the blade, and a symmetrical wound with two sharp ends implied a double-edged knife had been used. Whereas, if only one end of the wound was clean, it meant the knife had a single sharp edge. Depth of penetration was another useful factor and a clear indication as to the length of blade. In most frenzied attacks he'd come across, the assailant would persistently drive the blade home at least ninety-five percent of the time. It was a psychological thing, the more blood, the more gratification the perpetrator got from his attack. It was all about control and domination.

From what Carlisle could deduce, a double-edged boot knife had been used. Popular with the mafia and hired killers, if confirmed, then gang warfare could not be ruled out. That worried him, as death would be a never-ending circle of retribution killings.

The profiler tapped the timeline with the back of his hand. 'Two separate murders, one kidnapping, and all by the same hand.'

'Any idea of motive?' asked Carrington.

Carlisle had thought long and hard about this. Being a profiler meant a lot of pressure was placed on you, even though you didn't have all the answers. Lack of preparation was the problem, along with Jack Mason's mother of all hangovers.

The profiler turned sharply to face them. 'The message pinned to Samuel Jackson's chest; is not by the same hand according to the experts.'

'But it is the same pen,' Carrington added.

Mason glowered.

'Think diamonds, those sparkly things that dangle on pretty women's fingers. Just because Ed Coleman is untouchable, doesn't mean he's not privy to knowing who the mastermind is.'

Carrington looked confused.

'Hang on a minute, boss. You're not suggesting that someone's cottoned on that Coleman is working for Special Branch? Surely not?'

'If they have, Coleman's a dead man,' Carlisle said, grimly.

'What makes you say that?'

'Crime families don't think highly of informants, and don't mess about.'

Mason drummed his fingers but said nothing.

'Why take Walker prisoner?' asked Carrington. 'Why not kill him?'

'How do we know he isn't already dead?' Savage chipped in.

The profiler studied their faces as Mason squinted his eyes at the crime board. He was agitated about something, and the veins in his neck were standing out like a road map. Sometimes it was easier to say nothing, as he could be quite overpowering at times.

'So, where's Walker now?' Mason demanded.

'A part of me agrees with David's theory,' Carrington replied calmly. 'Whatever these people are after, they're desperate to get their hands on it.'

'Cats do that,' Mason shrugged.

'Do what, boss?'

'Leave trophies on your doorstep to let you know what they're capable of.'

'True, but I don't see any kidnappers' demands. Apart from a note pinned to the victim's chest, that's the only contact these people have made.'

Mason looked annoyed. 'Who's to say they aren't already in contact with Coleman? It seems pretty obvious to me. Let's face it, it's too close to home in my opinion.'

The room fell silent.

'If it's not diamonds, then what else could they be looking for?' queried Savage.

'We're merely the bottom feeders,' Carrington acknowledged. 'That's why SCD7 and Special Branch are involved as they've a much bigger fish to fry. It's my view they are holding back on something, and whatever it is, they're not willing to share it.'

Mason hunched his shoulders. 'I agree. Everything's shrouded in secrecy. It's like sitting in a nuclear submarine and waiting for the order to push the button. It's never going to happen.'

Carlisle recognised the frustration but ignored the reasoning behind it. Mason was a creature of habit; he never liked bad vibes. It wasn't good, and the angry look on his colleagues face told him he was about to go off on a rant.

'We're making all the wrong noises,' Carlisle said calmly.

'What's on your mind, my friend?'

The profiler put his hands behind his head. 'Everyone present agrees the Schiphol diamond heist was a well-planned operation. What if the gang didn't have a clue which shipment package the diamonds were hidden in? All the airline requires is an accurate description of the contents on their documentation, but no indication of what the contents are, or its value must appear on the outer packaging.'

Savage drew a long intake of breath and then said, 'In which case I'd take them all, and search for the diamonds later.'

'Exactly.'

Mason folded his arms in an aggressive stance. 'And?'

'What if one of the packages contained something of national importance. Something so valuable you had to kill for it?'

'Like what?' Mason frowned.

'If I knew the answer to that, I'd know what they were looking for.'

It was Carrington who came to Carlisle's rescue.

'David has a point. And a good one at that. Burglars don't rummage around your property looking for valuables. They tip everything into a heap and search for the good stuff later.'

'What are you suggesting?'

Mason's reaction was brusque. They would need more time, but time was precious, and the chief inspector was pushing for answers. Fresh leads had a habit of vanishing quickly; he knew that. Now that they had Mason's attention, Carlisle could sense the almost vulture-like air of anticipation in the room. They were running out of ideas, and if they didn't find Walker soon his captors would finish it.

Carrington leaned forward, the strain showing. 'With barely a fifteen-minute window before take-off, it's my guess the gang would grab every security box from the hold and search for the diamonds later.'

'Isn't that what the reports are suggesting?' added Savage.

Mason sat in stunned silence. The frustration showing, Carlisle could see the blood draining from every artery in the chief inspector's body. He was clutching at straws, too quick to blame Coleman for everything. It was an all too familiar tactic. This was the twentieth team briefing of Operation Wizard, and they'd finally reached stalemate.

The moment a pot of fresh coffee arrived, the chief inspector perked up. 'Okay, if we can't bring Ed Coleman in for questioning, does anyone have any bright ideas?'

'Let's sleep on it,' said Savage. 'Something will crop up.'

As the meeting broke up, Mason gave out some instructions and took off towards the canteen.

What a shambles, the profiler mused.

Chapter Twenty-Eight

Hands in pockets, head stooped slightly forward, Jack Mason watched as two burly officers lifted the manhole cover whilst a third climbed into the bowels of the city's sewage system. Dressed in blue overalls, gum boots and hard hats, they appeared determined. Not the best environment to go searching for a missing fellow police officer on a busy Friday afternoon, but they had no other option.

Having stayed up most of the night searching through old sewer plans, the chief inspector did his best to assemble his thoughts. Close to Northumberland Street in the centre of Newcastle, his quest made a mockery of covert operations. Wall-to-wall shoppers, bars heaving with people, the city was alive and kicking. Mason was desperate for good news, something to lift his spirits. He could delegate, of course. That thought had already crossed his mind. But Mason never felt comfortable with delegation. This was a team effort, and to be seen leading from the front meant an awful lot to him.

THE POACHER'S POCKET

His phone pinged.

'What's up, boss?'

'I've had better days, Rob. What can I do for you?'

'Keeping you busy, is he?'

'If you must know, I'm up to my eyeballs in shite and could murder a cup of coffee.'

'Sounds about right,' Savage chuckled in his usual gruff Geordie accent. 'Some better news,' the sergeant said.

'Like what?'

'Ed Coleman's lawyer has just landed at the station's front desk.'

'Really! What does Sandy Witherspoon want now?'

'God knows, but she'll only speak to you.'

'Do you know what it's about?'

'Something to do with a pregnancy test and a night back at her flat after the Christmas party.'

'Sod off!'

Like most senior officers in charge of major crime investigations, Jack Mason didn't like the legal profession. Whilst police officers were breaking their necks trying to keep Joe public safe from maniacs with bad intentions, these people were making a good living at trying to get them off.

'What's she after, Rob?'

'God knows. I can't stand the woman.' There was a long pause on the other end of the line.

'Sue Carrington is currently talking to her, so maybe she might get some answers.'

'I doubt it. Not with Witherspoon's vitreous tongue. She's a pain in the arse.'

'You can say that again.'

Mason thought for a moment.

'Something's afoot, Witherspoon wouldn't have turned up unannounced.'

'Who knows what she's up to.'

He watched as the officer opposite poked his head above the manhole cover and gave him a despondent thumbs down. His overalls thick with slime, he felt they were fighting a losing battle. Beginning to lose heart, he thought it was a simple matter of searching beneath the streets of Newcastle. He was wrong. There were thousands of secret passages to hold a person captive, and none of them had come up trumps.

'I don't like the sound of this, Rob.'

There was another long pause on the other end of the line.

'Shall I tell her to come back in the morning, boss?'

'No. Her client obviously wants to get a foothold in the door, and we need to know why.'

'So, what shall I tell her?'

Mason quickly made his mind up. There was a small interview suite at the station which they used to talk to vulnerable witnesses; it could be monitored by fellow police officers via a camera from an adjoining room. It was ideal, and in the comfort of a classy environment it was more likely a person could relax and talk more openly. If nothing else, the videotapes might come in useful at a later date.

'I'm all but finished here, just keep her occupied until I get back.'

'Christ! It's hard enough trying to keep my head above water, let alone talk to a smart-arsed lawyer.'

'Not your type, eh?'

'Definitely not. She gives me the creeps.'

'What else have you heard?'

'Nowt much. Mind, Samuel Jackson's murder has gone viral. It's playing out on all the media channels. Could this be the reason of her visit?'

Mason stopped in his tracks.

'And here's me searching the bloody sewers.'

'It was your call, boss,' Savage chuckled.

'My call?'

'It's you who's been beating the drum that informants are the eyes and ears of the city.'

'Yes, but—'

The line went dead.

Chapter Twenty-Nine

Five-foot two and pitifully thin, Sandy Witherspoon wasn't liked. Not that she was dishonest, but if your case against her client wasn't watertight you had no chance. One of the brightest legal minds in the business, what Witherspoon lacked in looks she oozed in intellect. Mason couldn't stand the woman but admired her tenacity.

The private interview suite was occupied when Mason checked in at the station's front desk. Not wishing to use his own office, he had to make do with suite two. Not the best environment to conduct sensitive business in, he was eager to know what this dreadful woman had to say. Feeling stressed out, he grabbed a quick coffee from the dispensing machine and entered the interview room with trepidation.

Dressed in a blue polka-dot skirt, white blouse, and high heeled shoes, Witherspoon looked sharply at Mason. They'd had dozens of run-ins over the years: Crown Court prosecutions mainly. Not to be taken lightly,

Witherspoon was as devious outside the courtroom as she was inside. Apart from speaking four languages fluently, never once had she failed to obtain her client bail. Good at what she did, Mason always thought she could have done much better for herself regardless of the notoriety she'd built up in the criminal world. Well, he thought. If Witherspoon was willing to engage in another slugging match, then so be it.

He glanced at his notes.

'I was under the impression that diamond smuggling was illegal,' Mason began.

'It is, and you of all people must know that.'

'In which case, perhaps you might tell me what your client's involvement was in the Schiphol airport heist?'

Witherspoon leaned closer. 'My client was acquitted on all charges against him, and I bluntly refuse to go back over old ground. If you must know, he recently signed a sworn affidavit to that effect. So, unless you have further charges, I'm here on other matters.'

'Strange,' Mason grimaced. 'I thought we might get off to a better start.'

'Don't push me,' Witherspoon replied.

God, he thought. Surely there were much better ways of making a living. He was hoping for a calm approach, but this felt far from relaxed. Not wishing to enter into another slugging contest, he tried to think positively.

'I was merely asking if your client knew anything about fifty-million dollars' worth of uncut diamonds that have gone missing. Nothing wrong with that.'

'I doubt I'd discuss such matters, and you know it.'

'No, I suppose not.'

Witherspoon uncrossed her legs as she sat bolt upright in her seat.

'Lots of things are illegal, Chief Inspector. Like speeding in a police vehicle when you're off duty. No doubt you'll have done that on more than one occasion over the years.'

'Where are you going with this, Sandy?'

'When Jack-shit gets a speeding ticket and loses his licence, he can't drive his vehicle. When he loses his job and can't pay the mortgage, he finds he's out on the street. No roof over his head, a wife, and kids to support, they are living in temporary accommodation. His life in ruins, and all because of a speeding ticket. So, what's illegal and okay for some, is a nightmare for others, if you get my drift.'

'Okay,' Mason said, shaking his head, 'You've made your point. What can I do for you?'

Finding it difficult to understand her line of attack, Mason had planned to keep his answers short and tight. But she was far too good for that. Unnerved, he watched as she flicked a long strand of hair from her face and eased forward in her seat.

'I'm told you're looking for Ellis Walker?'

'Could be. Then again, I'm looking for a lot of people at the moment. Including anyone connected with Samuel Jackson.'

'Sad affair,' Witherspoon said, lowering her eyes. 'Who'd wish such a terrible fate on such a law-abiding citizen.'

'I was led to believe he was your client's nephew, was he not?'

'He was, and that's one of the reasons for my visit here today.'

'Really?' Mason was hoping for some better news. 'So, what is it you're itching to ask me?'

'It's more a request,' Witherspoon said, resentfully.

'Ah. A request.'

'I'm not sure if you're aware of this, but my client is suffering ill health after undergoing a triple by-pass heart operation in Switzerland. This latest news has come as a terrible shock, and his doctors are genuinely concerned about his well-being.'

'I wasn't aware of any heart surgery,' Mason lied. 'The last I'd heard, your client had returned from Ireland having purchased a couple of thoroughbred racehorses. Quite a stressful pastime I would imagine. Not the sort of thing to go delving into if you've got a dodgy ticker.'

The lawyer's expression gave little away. Witherspoon's connections with the criminal underworld had not exactly done her career any harm. She knew how to work the system, whom to speak to, and more importantly, when to open her mouth. He also knew he was skating on thin ice. This woman was good. One fraudulent slip and she'd make his life a misery.

'My client's an extremely sick man,' she continued. 'Any undue stress and his doctors have warned it could have serious consequences. He needs rest, Chief Inspector. Whatever else you've heard is nothing more than street talk. Those are the facts; you can rest assured.'

'I presume you're referring to an interview I need to conduct with your client?'

'I am,' she acknowledged.

'If your client has nothing to hide, then I'm sure we can come to an arrangement regarding his nephew's unfortunate demise.'

'Good. I was hoping you would see it that way.'

Bullshit, Mason thought.

At first, he assumed Witherspoon was here to tell him something he didn't already know. Not dictate the terms and conditions for future interviews. If Coleman couldn't face the criminal justice system head on, he should have spared a thought for the poor unfortunate bastards he'd sent to an early grave.

'The problem I'm faced with is this,' said Mason, lifting his head, 'we need to eliminate your client from our murder enquiries. It's the law of the land.'

'I'm familiar with the law, Chief Inspector.'

'Yes, I believe you are,' he answered, sarcastically.

'I was rather hoping you'd show a little more compassion, that's all.' Her expression hardened as she wagged a finger at him. 'In exchange for all the help he's given you people over the past few months.'

'What are you suggesting I do?'

'I'm looking for sympathy towards my client's ill-health.'

'I see.'

'What would you say to a written statement?'

Her tone had hardened, and Mason had picked up on it. 'I've not heard any mention of that before,' he lied. 'Enlighten me, what does that entail?'

'I'm sure you know where I'm coming from.'

'I don't if I'm honest.'

'Why don't we talk this over with high office,' she said.

'Regarding what, may I ask?'

'About the help my client has given you people these past few months.'

Curious as to where this was heading, Mason took stock. He knew what she was up to, and Ed Coleman's untimely agreement with counterintelligence was now at the forefront of her mind. But he wanted her to spell it out for him. Tell him her client was a twofaced shit who was snitching on fellow criminals in an attempt to save his own neck.

She opened her notepad and flicked through the pages.

'Ellis Walker, what do you know about him?'

'I'm aware he was recently released from Liverpool prison and has a string of serious offences against him. Why, am I missing something?'

'Let's cut to the chase, Chief Inspector. I'm told you're looking for him.'

'Could be.'

She was fishing. Having played her trump card, was Witherspoon aware that Ellis Walker was an undercover police officer working for SCD7? If not, then what else was she unaware of? So far, she'd told him nothing he didn't know already. What was she playing at? He tried to stay composed, contain his temper, but the irritating tone in her voice and the overpowering stench of her perfume was starting to get to him.

Witherspoon drew on her reserves.

'I'm a little concerned about the press nowadays, especially when they're vying for headlines.' She stared at him hard. 'We all know what underhand tactics those people can get up to.'

He put down his pen.

'If you must know, I'm looking for Ellis Walker in connection with a recent murder case we're investigating.'

'Which murder is this? There have been so many lately.'

'You obviously don't read the newspapers, Sandy.'

'You're forgetting, Chief Inspector. My client may be in poor health, but he's still connected to some very influential people.'

Mason trod cautiously, not wishing to halt her flow. 'How do I know I can trust you?'

'You have my word on that.'

Mason laughed. 'You and I have been down that avenue before.'

'What if I told you this kidnapping was nothing more than a media hoax?'

Mason gave her a withering look. 'You don't expect me to believe that crap, surely not.'

The lawyer pursed her lips in anticipation. 'You'd be surprised where that information came from. Rest assured, it comes from a reliable source. This kidnapping is simply meant to drum up newspaper sales. It's pure fantasy.'

Mason raised an eyebrow. She was lying. Trying to fob him off with a bullshit story which made a mockery of the whole justice system. Her client wasn't ill either. But now wasn't the time to throw the gauntlet down. Do that and she'd walk away and make his life a living hell. No, Mason thought. He would sleep on it, work on a private interview no matter what anyone else might think. It would be difficult, as neither Gregory nor the chief constable would be keen to cut across a counterintelligence operation. Witherspoon had gained the upper hand. Even so, she wasn't off the hook yet. He still had a murder on his hands, and Samuel Jackson was Coleman's nephew.

'It seems I've been barking up the wrong tree,' Mason shrugged with a smile. 'How was I to know about your client's ill health?'

'Perhaps a compromise is in order.'

'Compromise?'

'A cessation of protocol in exchange for information regarding Ellis Walker.'

'What kind of information?'

'I take it you *are* looking for Ellis Walker?'

'I am.'

'Do we have a deal?'

'Not unless you have something of worth,' Mason smiled.

Coleman's lawyer slid an envelope towards him, and he opened it. Inside he found a dog-eared image that looked as though it had been dragged through the gutter. On closer inspection he could see Ellis Walker was standing in woodlands somewhere. But that didn't mean a thing. Not when the image had been doctored. He could have this verified within minutes, of course. It was a dumb move, and Witherspoon was trying to manipulate him into a trap.

They faced each other in silence.

'Where's Walker now?'

'I'm a lawyer, not a clairvoyant.'

'Indeed you are,' Mason begrudgingly replied.

Witherspoon turned sharply to face him. 'One thing I can assure you of is this. My client has struck a deal with the Metropolitan Police, and I have a signed declaration to that effect.'

There it was, straight from the horse's mouth.

'In which case it's out of my hands, Sandy.'

'You asked for proof and now you have it.'

'Yes, and I've made a note of it.'

'I don't envy your task, Jack.' Witherspoon stood to leave. 'Let's hope the media don't get hold of the Ellis Walker story or we'll never hear the last of it.'

'Meaning?'

'You know how these things work; everything has a price.'

'Including trust,' Mason acknowledged.

'Indeed. Including trust.'

The devious bastard, Mason thought. Scaring him with the press was flagrant extortion. But she was good, extremely good. Threatening to disclose information about Ellis Walker's disappearance had backed him into a corner. Refuse to cooperate, and she'd trample all over him. No, he thought. It was time to gather the troops. Bring Gregory back into the fold and convince him that Coleman wasn't above the law.

Mason heard the ping of an incoming text.

He checked the screen.

"Just eliminated Rigg from our enquiries. We now have the CCTV evidence to prove it – Roy."

'Shit,' Mason cursed. As if he hadn't enough on his plate right now.

Chapter Thirty

Shortly after five o'clock, David Carlisle drove his P4 100 Rover into an empty parking space and switched off the engine. He knew the area well, and the Queen's Head in North Shields was the perfect venue to meet with Jack Mason.

He sat for a moment, then checked his voicemail for messages. There was none. Keen to set up a meeting with a client, a pharmacist with marital problems whose Thai wife had been salting his life's savings away to her family in Thailand, he rang the office. It was a sorry state of affairs, but fortunately no children were involved, just a wife's pushy brother-in-law who seemed intent on taking every penny his client had stashed in the bank. Some cases he wished he'd never taken on, and this was one of them.

He found the chief inspector sitting in a corner seat overlooking the main road. Apart from a man with heavily tattooed arms talking to a chatty barman, the pub was empty.

'Took your time,' the chief inspector said, looking up.

'The Tyne Tunnel's manic this time of day, Jack.'

'I've told you before, my friend. You're living on the wrong side of the water.'

'Nothing wrong with South Shields.'

'It's full of ice cream parlours and screaming kids, as I remember,' Mason chuckled. 'Who'd want to live there.'

Carlisle unzipped his jacket and took up a seat opposite. After years spent delving into other people's minds, it was only second nature to watch for emotional signals in a person's behavioural patterns. A nervous twitch, an uncharacteristic smile, even a hurried conversation was enough. But Jack Mason was thick skinned and difficult to decipher.

'What's new at the zoo?' the profiler asked.

Mason took a sip of his beer and wiped the froth from his mouth.

'I've just come from a meeting with Coleman's lawyer, Sandy Witherspoon.'

'Oh, and what did she have to say?'

'According to her, Ed Coleman's recovering from a triple heart by-pass operation and is in no fit state to be interviewed over Samuel Jackson's murder.'

'I thought Witherspoon told you her client was in good health?'

'She did. Now she's changed her mind.'

'So, what's the alternative?'

'It's a difficult one. I suspect she's playing the sympathy card.'

'What else did she tell you?'

Mason slid a grainy image across the table towards him. 'She handed me this and swore Walker's kidnapping was a media stunt.'

Carlisle looked at the battered image and smiled. 'It's fake, Jack. Even a ten-year-old could tell you that.'

'I know.'

'What then?'

Mason shook his head. 'Witherspoon's obviously concerned about this latest murder leaking out. Once the press get a hold of it, she fears her client will be put under the spotlight. She's asking for a compromise and talking about a written statement in lieu of a police interview.'

'Why would you do that?'

'If not, she's threatened to go to the press over Ellis Walker.'

Carlisle sat back. 'Does she know he's an undercover officer?'

'I doubt it, but I cannot take that risk.'

'It's outright extortion. The minute you submit to her demands, she'll put two and two together.'

'I know, and that's why I'm seeking your advice.'

The profiler shifted in his seat.

'I'm not a police officer, Jack. Besides, this is a law enforcement issue.'

'But you're not tarred with the same brush, my friend.'

Carlisle examined the photograph and tried to get to grips with it. He understood his colleagues dilemma, but this was a police matter. In many ways he wished he could have attended Witherspoon's interview, but that wasn't possible. If Ed Coleman had turned Queen's Evidence, then events could turn ugly.

'What else did you tell her?'

'Not a lot. Why?'

'Did you agree to any of her demands?'

'Not in as many words. I told her I'd sleep on it.'

He looked at him quizzically. 'Did she say where Ellis Walker was?'

'Not to me, she didn't.'

Carlisle sat thinking.

'I thought Ellis Walker was Ed's number one sidekick?'

'He was. But that all changed the moment he went missing. She's worried about a backlash, and Samuel Jackson's murder isn't helping either.'

'I smell a rat, Jack.'

'Tell me about it.'

'Coleman's not daft; whoever's holding Walker captive is of major interest to him.'

'I would have thought so,' Mason agreed.

The profiler took another sip of beer and watched the kaleidoscope of lights on the fruit machine change colours. Three hours from now and the pub would be heaving with revellers. This was a student's hangout, a place to connect with friends.

Carlisle turned to face Mason. 'If Walker met Baxter under Coleman's instructions, he'll want to know who killed Baxter. On the other hand, he may feel he's been double crossed.'

'Why would he think that?'

Carlisle considered the facts, and his reply was brusque. 'Something doesn't sit right. An undercover officer is missing, and the man he linked up with is now dead. If Special Branch have eyes on Coleman, they'll pounce the minute he shows up.'

'Yeah, but nobody knows where he is.'

'That's my point.'

Mason drummed his fingers on the table. 'What's going on. Do you think Walker could be involved in a murder?'

'This isn't about diamonds anymore, there's more to it than that. Coleman's trying to pull a fast one, I'm convinced of it.'

'What, deceive Special Branch?'

'Would you trust him, Jack?'

'Like hell I would.'

The profiler pointed down at the photograph again. 'Was Walker fully briefed about his mission before leaving Liverpool prison?'

'That would be down to the Metropolitan police.'

'In which case they're not telling us everything.'

'Why would they. The least people who know about Walker's background the less risk of blowing his cover.'

Carlisle tapped the side of his nose. 'We're missing a trick here, Jack. Walker's a trained police officer and knows how to handle himself. If these people are trying to extract information through the use of torture, how much has he told them?'

Mason sighed despondently. 'The noose is tightening, my friend. Whatever went on in Amsterdam has spilled onto the streets of Newcastle. That worries me. There are too many obstacles being thrown in our path, and every one of them shrouded in secrecy. Witherspoon's not daft, she knows how to play the system. Something has to give, if not we'll end up with a pile of dead bodies on our hands and all-out gang war.'

The profiler turned to face Mason.

'Which brings us nicely onto why Special Branch recruited Ed Coleman. The pieces of the puzzle don't fit, and for whatever reason all roads lead us back to the Schiphol mastermind. But there lies another problem, as there were dozens of people involved in the raid and it only takes one lose tongue.'

Mason allowed himself a brief smug smile as he took another swig of his beer.

'I've been telling you that for weeks now.'

'You have, but according to the latest intelligence reports when the gang raided the Lufthansa jet, they took every security box from the hold.'

'Let's not go there,' Mason groaned.

Carlisle shuffled awkwardly.

'The trouble is, Mr. Big has become a persona, an assumed identity who craves anonymity at all costs. And yet his insecurities are beginning to catch up with him.'

Mason twiddled with his beermat, turning it over and over in his hand. Whatever was running through his mind, was causing him grave concern.

'I agree it's complicated, but there must be a simple answer to this.'

'Think about it, Jack. Why would Coleman arrange for Baxter to meet with these people in the first place?'

Mason screwed his face up. 'Did he?'

'We agree these people killed him.'

Mason put his glass down and tapped Walker's photograph. 'So, what are they looking for, do you think?'

'I'm no clairvoyant, but whatever it is it's obviously worth killing for.'

'Hang on a minute, I thought that's what special couriers did.'

'Did what?'

'Convey things of national importance around.'

'They do. Isn't that why SCD7 are involved?'

Mason mulled over the facts as though the cogs in his brain were finally slipping into gear. 'Is that why these people killed Baxter and Samuel Jackson, do you think?'

'I can't think of another reason.'

'What about Ellis Walker?'

Carlisle looked at Mason. 'Let's not forget Walker would know how to handle awkward situations. The minute he tells them all he knows, he's a dead man.'

'What if Walker knows nothing?'

'He may well do, and that's my point. The solution to solving their problem lies inside Walker's head – or so they believe.'

'Blimey. The man's a ticking time bomb,' Mason replied. 'What about his wife and kids?'

'That's why dozens of counterintelligence officers are out in the field. Walker's one of us, and we know the rules of engagement as well as anyone.'

Mason looked at Carlisle and frowned. 'What if we set up a meeting with Coleman? Throw him a lifeline in exchange for information.'

'That's not a bad idea.'

The chief inspector's face dropped. 'Nah! I doubt the area commander would agree to such a thing. Not without involving Special Branch.

The man's a pain in the arse and refuses to get involved. Let's face it, he'll turn his back on me the minute I mention Coleman's name.'

'You're right about one thing though. If you don't ask you don't get.'

Mason picked up his beer mat and began fiddling with it. 'It's strange you should say that, because that's what my ex-wife used to tell me.'

The profiler's stare intensified.

'Throwing Coleman a lifeline is a sound idea and we're only a small unit.'

'I know, but I'd prefer talking to the chief constable direct.'

'What! Go over Gregory's head?'

'The AC's fickle. He's too close to retirement to upset the apple cart.'

After Mason had brought him up to speed on other developments, including a future trip to Amsterdam, a bigger picture emerged. Even so, none of the uncut diamonds had ever been recovered, and not a single person had been arrested for the crime. The question was, why? Surely SCD7 knew who these people were. This wasn't a straightforward investigation anymore, and yet everyone involved was tight lipped and cloaked in secrecy.

As their conversation drifted into small talk, they finished their drinks and went their separate ways.

Chapter Thirty-One

Jack Mason drew the unmarked police car alongside a red Volkswagen Golf GTI and switched off the engine. His nerves frayed after another hard-fought day at the office, nothing seemed simple these days. Not all was bad news, though. DC Carrington had arranged an interview with Samuel Jackson's ex-partner and that was the purpose of their visit today.

He rang the doorbell, took a step back, and checked the downstairs windows for movement. Seconds later a studious woman in her mid-thirties appeared wearing a Peppa Pig T-shirt and paint-stained tracksuit bottoms.

'You police?'

Mason held up his warrant card.

'Janice Wainwright?' he asked.

'That's me.'

'This is DC Carrington, and I'm DCI Mason. May we come in?'

The house had a clinical feel, more functional than homely. The first thing he noticed, as she ushered them into a backroom conservatory, was the large bookcase that stood against the back wall. It was huge, crammed full of fascinating autobiographies and other well-known literary authors. Like most police officers he knew, Mason felt uncomfortable when discussing bad news, especially in a murder enquiry.

Wainwright steered them towards a large rattan settee scattered with throw cushions. 'Sorry about the mess, but I wasn't expecting to see you so soon.'

'We were passing the end of the street and saw your red car on the drive,' Carrington replied.

'As you can see, I'm studying for my final exams.'

'No time is ever convenient, Ms Wainwright.'

'No, I suppose not,' she replied, in a soft upper-class accent that had unexpectedly thrown Mason off balance. 'Sam's death came as such a terrible shock. Who would have dreamt that such a kind loving person could end up being murdered?'

Mason gave her a sympathetic look. 'I realise this is a difficult time, Ms Wainwright, but I promise you this won't take long. There's a few routine questions we need to ask regarding Samuel Jackson.'

'Like what?' She put her hand up to her mouth and abruptly drew back. 'How silly of me, can I offer you a drink?'

'Coffee for me,' Mason nodded. 'Milk, no sugar please.'

'White, one sugar,' Carrington added.

No sooner had Wainwright disappeared into the kitchen, than Mason walked over to the sideboard and picked up a silver framed photograph. An elderly couple, standing on the back of a cruise ship somewhere in the Caribbean, he assumed. They were distinguished looking, well-to-do people. On closer inspection, the elderly woman, wearing a beautiful pink halter dress bore a striking resemblance to Janice Wainwright.

Carrington glanced up as he placed it back down again.

'Who's that?' she whispered.

'Her parents, I assume.'

Wainwright returned carrying a small oval wooden tray with three large mugs, and a plate of assorted biscuits. This was the moment Mason dreaded most in a murder enquiry – eliminating the victim's close relatives and friends.

Now operating in police mode, it was Carrington who broke the silence.

'I believe you and Samuel were in a relationship?'

'Oh, my God,' Wainwright burst out, visibly shaken. Her eyes were tearful, and her skin was pale and sallow. 'Please tell me Sam didn't suffer.'

'We believe not,' Mason said, trying his best to avoid eye contact. 'We're treating this as a murder enquiry and doing our utmost to bring the perpetrators to justice.'

'What, there was more than one person involved?' she gasped.

'We believe so,' Mason replied, realising his mistake.

There was a prolonged silence.

'Tell me,' said Carrington. 'How long were you and Sam living together?'

'For almost a year. Why do you ask?'

'And how did the two of you meet?'

Wainwright appeared anxious and her demeanour had stiffened. 'In a pub in Newcastle of all places. The Busy Bee. They do live music there, and I would go there every Thursday night with friends. That's when I first met Sam, he was sitting on the next table.'

'And how long ago was this?'

'Two years ago.'

'You're right,' Mason suddenly cut in. 'It's a great venue.'

Wainwright stared at him.

'Do you go there too, Chief Inspector?'

'Occasionally. Sunday nights mainly. Heavy metal night. They serve a cracking pint, and the atmosphere is always terrific.'

'It's funny because that's what Sam used to say.'

'It's owned by his Uncle Edward, I believe?'

Wainwright levelled her eyes at him. 'Do you know Mr. Coleman?'

'Let's just say we've met on several occasions.'

If only she knew the other half of it, Mason groaned inwardly.

'What about Sam's friends,' asked Carrington. 'What can you tell me about them?'

'Most of Sam's mates are married with children nowadays. That's what we were planning to do. Get married and raise a family of our own. It wasn't to be, not after we drifted apart.'

Mason leaned back in his seat and cradled his chin on his hands.

'Oh, and why did you separate, Ms Wainwright?'

She sounded hesitant, informing them her boyfriend had a bedsit over in Gosforth High Street where they'd spent most of their spare time together. Nothing flash, just somewhere to hunker down and get away from it all.

Her face dropped suddenly; Mason picked up on it.

'Take your time, Ms Wainwright, I know this must be difficult.'

'Not all was plain sailing. There were so many ups and downs. Good times and bad.' She wiped the tears from her eyes and took a sip of her drink. 'You know how these things go, the wretched arguments, the fights over nothing. It was unbearable at times. We tried our best to hold it together, but nothing ever worked.'

'Any reason?' asked Mason.

'That's how things were with Sam and me, we had nothing in common. Sam spent most of his time drinking with his mates, and as for me, I was wrapped up with the local parish council trying to get things done.' Wainwright fidgeted with her button as if trying to compose herself. 'We were both to blame if I'm honest. We just didn't love each other anymore, and that's when I decided to move out.'

'Were you still on speaking terms?'

'Yes, we were. There were never any hard feelings between us, Chief Inspector. The truth is I still like him, and we occasionally meet from time to time. Nothing serious, of course. But we would never get back to living together again.'

Carrington stared at her notes.

'What did Sam do for a living, Ms Wainwright?'

She looked at them through shallow eyes. 'Sam was part owner in a local scrap metal merchant's yard over in Howden. He was involved in the recycling side of the business. Waste metal, metallic material, that sort of thing.'

Wainright went on to tell them about the breakdown in their relationship, and about

Sam's business plans. No doubt his uncle would have had a hand in all of it.

'This scrap metal merchants that Sam ran,' Mason said, raising his voice a little. 'It sounds quite involved. Was it?'

'It was,' Wainwright acknowledged. 'The thing was, Sam was never happier than when he was up to his eyes in muck. He loved to fiddle with things, take them apart to see how they worked. It would drive me crazy at times, and for the life of me I could never understand why someone would want to do that.'

'It's a man's thing,' Carrington smiled.

Mason shook his head in disdain.

'Can you think of anyone who would want to harm Sam?' asked Carrington.

'No,' Wainwright whispered. 'Sam wasn't an aggressive person, far from it. Selfish, yes, but never one for causing any bother. I still cannot believe that someone would want to kill him.'

'And you can't think of anyone who would want to do that?'

'No. Definitely not.'

Mason thought for some moments.

'What about his uncle, Edward. Did Samuel ever mention his name to you?'

'All the time,' Wainwright replied. 'Especially after Sam's mother passed away. The two of them were inseparable. Mind, his uncle never had any children of his own and treated Sam like a son.'

Carrington looked at Mason, then down at her notes.

'What about his uncle's pub business. Did Sam ever get involved?'

'Yes, he did, especially when they were short staffed. He served behind the bar and dealt with the cellars, that sort of stuff.'

'A busy man by the sounds.'

'Sam was always good like that. Mind, his uncle did work away a lot of the time, and that's when Sam would step in to help.' Wainwright was silent for some moments, then turned to face them and asked, 'Will I be able to see him, Chief Inspector? I know he would have liked that.'

'There's still a few details we need to sort out, Ms Wainwright. Once the coroner's office has completed their business, I'm sure someone will be in contact.'

Wainwright did not press the matter. Only after the body had been formally identified could it be released to an undertaker. And that was another ace up Mason's sleeve, as he could think of no better person to formally identify his nephew other than the man himself. Edward Coleman. Sometimes, staring at a body could make a man look at life differently, and a friendly chat might even throw up a few responses.

Wainwright looked at Mason as tears welled in her eyes. 'It all happened so quickly, and to think Sam and I only visited the mansion last weekend. It was—'

'Last weekend?' Mason said, the surprise showing in his voice.

'Sam was never away from the place. He loved it there.'

'Any particular reason?'

'It was this new venture the two of them were involved in. Sam was so excited he could never stop talking about it.'

Pen poised, Mason looked up with great expectation. 'And what venture might that be?' he asked.

'Horses,' she replied. 'His uncle had bought a couple of thoroughbred racehorses from Ireland and was intending to race them during Race Week.'

'Sounds like fun.'

'It was typical of Sam, and you never knew whether to believe him or not.'

'Tell me about Sam,' said Carrington quietly. 'Was he ever into drugs?'

Wainwright looked at them warily. 'What makes you think he was?'

'It's purely a routine question,' Mason lied. 'It can save the coroner's office an awful lot of unnecessary time.'

'Umm – oh – yes, I see,' she replied hesitantly. 'Sam did dabble in them from time to time. Never in a big way, more for recreational use than anything. He had problems with his hands, rheumatoid arthritis, and swore that heroine worked far better than anything his doctors could prescribe.'

Mason watched as Carrington's eyebrows fluttered at the mere mention at the word "dabble." Had Jackson been wrongfully targeted, he wondered.

His impression of Jennifer Wainwright was that of a studious young woman, someone who played around the fringes and not the sort of person to get into a serious relationship with a scrap metal dealer like Samuel Jackson. Surely, she must have known about his underhand rogue business deals. The people he spent time with, and the type of business he ran. Buying scrap metal "no questions asked" had helped to fuel a crime wave of copper thefts around the city. Not forgetting the lead stolen from church roofs, and the long lengths of signalling cabling that were nicked from railway sidings in the dead of night. His was a lucrative business, and anything that could be lifted into the back of a lorry, no questions asked, seemed fair game to some people.

It was all making sense suddenly, and Janice Wainwright had been by far their best witness. This wasn't about driving a murder enquiry forward anymore. This was a means of getting closer to his number one suspect.

After a while, the intervals between the sobs grew less but Mason could still detect the bitterness in her voice. He suspected Wainwright was trying to isolate herself from something, as if another side existed. They might never get to the bottom of it; he knew that, but sensed Coleman was involved somewhere down the line.

As he closed his notebook, the chief inspector felt another vital link in his murder investigation had been established.

'You've been most helpful,' the chief inspector said, in his usual uncompromising chirpy voice. 'We'll not keep you a minute longer.'

'Only too pleased to be of help.'

Mason turned sharply at the door.

'Good luck with your exams.'

As they pulled off the drive, Carrington fastened her seat belt and turned to face Mason. 'I get the feeling she knows more than she's letting on.'

'What gave you that impression, Sue?'

'Wainright's visits to Coleman's mansion for one, and Sam's recreational use of drugs. She was extremely liberal with her information. Maybe I'm reading this wrong.'

'One thing for sure,' Mason smiled. 'We need to keep an eye on Ms Wainwright, she's not out of the woods yet.'

Pleased with his findings, the chief inspector drove west towards the motorway before joining the heavy stream of traffic heading south. All things being equal, it wouldn't be long before word got out, but he'd deal with that later. After the dust had settled.

Chapter Thirty-Two

Only time separated pain. But time was meaningless. How much longer could this go on? Was darkness the new form of punishment? Dazzled by the light, the undercover officer squirmed against his bonds. Though there was little he could do to stop his torturer, he still reviled this man. Unnerved, Walker tried to push the vision to the back of his mind; rid himself of the nightmares. The torture. The relentless beatings in getting him to talk. Now nearing the end of his tether he was running on pure adrenaline and fear.

The rats were everywhere. The slightest hint of blood and they appeared in huge numbers. Thousands of them. A writhing mass of flesh eating vermin that scurried from the bowels of the earth to put the fear of God in him. Rage burning inside, loathing for these grotesque creatures was beginning to drag him down. How would it end? Would they eat him alive? Or simply wait till he was dead and strip his body of all flesh?

He shuddered at the thought.

THE POACHER'S POCKET

To one corner of the room he heard movement. He tried to open his eyes, but the light was preventing him from doing so. Blackness gave comfort. Not much, as the light was spreading and widening into unnerving forms. He could see shapes moving around. Lumbering patches of greater darkness. All around he heard the sound of scurrying feet. The rats had been disturbed, and Walker sensed a darker presence.

'You and I must talk.'

'I know nothing of any documents,' Walker argued.

The Poachers voice was gravelly and rasping, and his eyes blazing with fury.

'I know you do, but it's not that fucking simple.'

Walker flinched, not daring to move.

Would he die here without ever seeing his family again?

His head forced backwards, the Poacher pushed a water bottle into his mouth. In agony, the officer gulped its contents. At least they were keeping him alive. Only just. Even so, they had good reason to. He had told them nothing so far, and the Poacher was furious. There was no simple answer to this. He knew that. But the moment he broke his silence, he understood what the outcome would be.

As darkness closed in on all sides, Walker felt a sudden sinking sensation in the pit of his stomach. It had begun, and there was nothing he could do to stop them.

Nothing.

Chapter Thirty-Three

It was the sound of gunshot fire that caused Jack Mason to flinch. A short, sharp rap coming from nearby woods. Now close to race week, activities surrounding the equestrian facilities had begun. Set in seven-hundred acres of outstanding Northumbrian countryside, Coleman's handsome Georgian manor house was positioned centrally within a magnificent tiered, walled garden with an attractive courtyard of outstanding natural beauty.

Accompanied by DS Savage, the chief inspector fidgeted uncomfortably in his mud-spattered jeans, which were beginning to dry out and causing his leg muscles to tighten. Having trekked through dense woodlands for the past two hours, they were now climbing a steep knoll with open panoramic views overlooking the whole of the estate, including farmsteads and cottages beyond.

Easing his way forward through the thick undergrowth, Mason could see stable hands saddling up horses whilst others were busy mucking out stables and laying down fresh hay. Racehorses were athletes, schooled competitors, and any good trainer knew exactly which distance a horse was best placed to run. No expert himself, Mason knew enough to realise that these racehorses were at the top of their game. It was all about distance, as some thoroughbreds were fast over short courses whilst others were slower but kept on going indefinitely.

'Here we go,' said Savage, binoculars glued to his face.

'What have you spotted?'

'Over to your left by the training ring.'

At least twice a week, horses were being put through their paces using starting stalls, a machine employed to ensure a fair start at the beginning of a race. Most horses never flinched, but one particular horse, a huge black gelding was resisting. Stable hands were having to use two heavy duty pulling straps to force the blindfolded horse into the stall. It was fascinating to watch.

'Any new arrivals, Rob?'

'Nah, same old faces. Mind, that young filly you spotted earlier this morning does have a massive rump on her.'

Mason smiled but refrained from answering as he crawled on all fours to get a closer look. Still no sign of Ellis Walker; he was beginning to fear the worst. It was now 09:00, and the odds of the undercover officer turning up were diminishing by the hour. Mason hated uncertainty. Something was afoot, and whatever Coleman was involved in, he had yet to declare his hand.

Wary of being spotted, they moved forward together through tall grass until reaching a clump of thorny bushes. To the casual observer, this type of gathering might appear innocent enough, but not everyone present was a racing fan. Many were notorious felons, wannabe power freaks striving recognition amongst the criminal elite. Some faces he recognised, others he'd never seen before. Even so, only a handful would be law abiding citizens. And, just for the record, every one of them was being filmed on camera and fed into the facial recognition system for future reference.

'Over to your right,' whispered Savage.

As twenty or thirty new faces arrived, they huddled in small groups around one of the starting stalls. Eyes focused ahead, Mason zoomed in on a section of the paddock and felt almost vulture-like in his approach. It was surreal. With so many hardened criminals making an appearance, it didn't take a rocket scientist to realise that something important was taking place.

'Looks like the clay pigeon shoot is over.'

'For now, but they'll be back.'

'What's going on, Rob?'

'God knows,' the sergeant replied, 'but if I'm not mistaken isn't that Harry Naylor wearing the camouflage trousers?'

'If it is, he's piled on the beef since last leaving prison.'

'It's him okay, I can tell by the way he swaggers.'

Mason shuffled in his position and adjusted the focus on his binoculars.

'What's he doing here? I thought he'd buggered off to South Africa after his missus caught him in bed with his boyfriend.'

'She did, but he's back it would seem.'

'Are you sure it's Harry Naylor?'

'I'm positive.'

'If it's him, he's good with explosives as I remember.'

'Yeah, that's Harry all right.' Savage laughed. 'A few years ago, the lads tried to carry out a full strip search on him. The man went berserk and swore that if anyone so much as laid a finger on his private parts he'd blow their brains away. Harry likes to strut his stuff, but who wouldn't with half a kilo of coke stuffed into the abdominal cavity.'

Mason smiled as he panned the area.

'The guy in the mohair suit, what do you know about him?'

'Never seen him before. Who is he?'

'His face looks familiar, but I can't put my finger on him.' Mason made a mental note and then said, 'The scraggy-faced guy to his left, the one in the yellow T-shirt. Isn't that George Powell?'

'Can't say as I've heard his name mentioned before. Who is he?'

'Powell was involved in the Teams Warehouse robbery and served a ten-year stretch in Franklin prison for running down a security guard. After crushing him against a wall, he backed over him to ensure he was dead. He's a nasty piece of work, and not right in the head.' Mason turned away, still smiling. 'Powell's an electronics expert and good with security alarms.'

'Now that you mention it, I do remember the case.'

Mason fell silent.

'There's an awful lot of heavyweight muscle on parade.'

'Yeah. Somethings definitely afoot.'

The moment Ed Coleman swaggered into view Mason's whole body locked solid. Surrounded by a group of henchmen in immaculate grey suits, the gangster wore the obligatory horn-rimmed sunglasses associated with mafia don's. It suddenly felt like old times again, stepping back onto the streets of London's Soho and riding by the seat of his pants. Mason loved the thrill of the chase, but this gathering felt menacing.

The chief inspector zoomed in on the paddock building and watched as two broad-shouldered henchmen sauntered across the yard towards a black Range Rover. If ever there was a time for Walker to come forward, it was now.

'Where's our man?' asked Savage, eagerly shaking his head.

'Can't see him, Rob.'

'I could have sworn he'd make a grand appearance.'

'It's still a strong turnout, nevertheless. I've never seen so many hardened criminals gathered in one place.'

Mason checked the notes the profiler had given him earlier and found the information he was looking for. 'The guy in the blue blazer. That must be the Irish racehorse trainer Kerry Waterman.'

'If it is, he's much taller than I'd imagined.'

'He seems quite at home on the property, despite the controversy surrounding the gangster's shady past. Sandy Witherspoon reckons he's Coleman's new best friend, but for the life of me I can't understand why. Waterman's quite a celebrity amongst the racing fraternity and has met the Queen on several occasions.'

'What's he doing here?' asked Savage, looking curious. 'If he thinks Coleman's legit, he's off his fucking rocker.'

Twenty minutes later they were heading south towards Gateshead police station. Having captured enough video evidence to keep the tech boys busy for months, Mason was more than happy. All that remained now was to convince the area commander it was time to bring Ed Coleman in for questioning. He doubted that would happen, even with this amount of new evidence.

If only the old sod would get real,' the chief inspector mumbled to himself.

Chapter Thirty-Four

They were all a bit drunk, but that wasn't unusual in the Stag's Head on Thursday night. Tucked back on the High Street, close to the railway station, this was the in place to be if you were engaged in dodgy deals. It was remarkable for a town of its size how many names were already on the police computer system. Not that it bothered Rob Savage. He'd been wired, and two blocks away a team of surveillance experts were listening in on his every conversation. Not the only active detective involved in undercover operations that night, at least fifty officers were out searching for Ellis Walker. Twelve days had passed since the officer last touched base, and everyone was tetchy.

Now worse for drink, Savage was caught up in a game of poker with local punters. Masquerading as Samuel Jackson's distant relative, the sergeant was keen to tap into local gossip. High on the agenda was Jackson's last known movements. There was even talk he was one of Coleman's trusted henchmen, but the sergeant doubted it. Eager to establish if Jackson had anything to do with the diamond heist, he was looking for new leads.

The majority of customers drinking in the Stag's Head that night were law abiding citizens. But the man sitting opposite was shuffling the cards as if trying to rig it. Short, stocky and in his late fifties, "Ronnie the Gearstick" had a shady past which, among other things, involved dodgy dealings in the second-hand car market.

Nervous, the sergeant reached over and picked up a fresh card from the deck as he dropped another fiver into the kitty. Three hundred quid was resting on the outcome, and the stakes could not have been higher. Shielding his cards, he watched as the miscreant opposite reached over and exchanged one of his cards. The moment his brow corrugated; he knew then he had a bad hand.

'So,' Savage began, in a low gruff voice, 'was Sam a regular in here?'

'At least five days a week.'

'A drinker, was he?'

Ronnie gave the sergeant a guarded look. 'What makes you think he was?'

'Before Sam moved into the scrap business, we worked together on the building sites. He drank back then and would never pass on a pint.'

The man with a mouth full of yellow stained teeth spoke next.

'Is that so?'

'I'm family mate. I know these things.'

'Maybe, but Sam made it his rule never to talk about business.'

Savage shrugged before leaning closer. 'The trouble with Sam was, he could never stop making his mouth go when it came to family.'

'It's funny you should say that, as he was always a bit of a dark horse,' said the man with tattooed hands. His eyes were small behind framed glasses, and he bore the look of indifference.

Savage watched the rest of their faces, Ronnie's in particular.

'I take it you knew him?'

'He may have liked a drink, but he was never an ounce of trouble. Not like some of the clowns who get in here.' Ronnie shrugged, as he picked up another card from the deck. 'You should talk to the local casino owner.'

'Gambling man, was he?'

'I thought you were family,' said Ronnie peering warily across at him.

'I knew he liked the horses, but never once did he mention casinos.'

'Is that so...'

'Not to me he didn't.'

Ronnie fell silent, as if to weigh up his remarks. He leaned forward slightly, his fingers curled around his cards. Ronnie was different. Not like the other fools.

'What else do you know?' asked Ronnie.

'The last time I saw Sam he was on the bones of his arse, and his partner had walked out on him. If it hadn't been for the scrap metal business, he'd have ended up in the gutter.'

'Sounds about right,' the man with the swallowed tattooed hands answered.

Ronnie swung to face Savage.

'Had it not been for his partner, the casino would have taken him for every penny he owned. He never saw it coming. Trouble was, Sam had this crazy notion he'd win it all back again.'

Things had begun well enough, but the sergeant would need to tread carefully. Ronnie wasn't daft, he only portrayed himself to be dim. As for the other miscreants, they were mere pawns. He watched as Ronnie took another huge gulp of his beer and pulled up a creaking seat. It had just turned ten-thirty, and as tongues began to loosen, he felt more stories would emerge.

'What have you suckers got?' asked Ronnie.

'Two pair, queens and tens,' replied the man with the swallow tattooed hands. He made a point of laying his cards out face up on the table in front of them.

'Beats my three Jacks,' said Savage.

'Bollocks,' another cursed, throwing his cards onto the table in disgust.

Ronnie's eyebrows rose a fraction. 'A straight flush,' he announced.

The man with the swallow tattooed hands rolled his eyes in disgust.

'You suckers had enough?'

'Double or quits,' said Savage, cockily. 'Winner takes all.'

Ronnie drew on his cigar and blew out a long smoke trail in contempt of any smoking bans. The pub was a dive, but the sergeant felt somewhat at home here.

'There's something you should know,' said Ronnie.

'What's that?'

'A few months back Sam came into money, and I mean a lot of money. Nobody knows the exact amount. Some say it was over two-hundred thousand big ones.'

'Don't tell me he hit the jackpot,' Savage laughed.

'Who told you that?'

'They didn't, but that's how these stories pan out.'

Annoyed, Ronnie ignored him, but his newfound friends were keen to reveal more. Posh hotels, fast cars, and the night Coleman's nephew was caught with his trousers down giving the night club owner's daughter the thrill of her life.

'You're having a laugh,' Savage joked.

'It's true,' the man with swallow tattooed hands said smiling.

As more of their story began to unfold, heads huddled under a cloud of choking cigar smoke. It was then the miscreant sat opposite lowered his voice. Resisting the temptation to give him a piece of his mind, the sergeant allowed him to continue.

'Sam took on more than he could chew. Everyone knew that. The trouble was, he paid for it with his life.'

'You don't expect me to believe that crap? It's bollocks.'

'Are you calling me a liar?'

'No.'

'What then?'

'It's bollocks. The police would have been all over it the moment word got out.'

'You obviously don't know the police around here, mister. They're as thick as pig shit and couldn't solve a crime if it were handed to them on a plate.'

Savage blew through clenched teeth.

'You think this casino owner had Sam bumped off?'

'We didn't say he did,' Ronnie scowled, 'just that Sam took on more than he could chew.'

'So, who killed him?'

They stared at one another with tight lips.

The sergeant drew back thinking. They'd been making their mouths go for the best part of the evening, and most of it a load of rubbish. But another notion was telling him, there could be an element of truth in their narrative. This was a close-knit community, a place where gossip thrived.

'Great story, but I'm still awaiting the punchline.'

Ronnie the Gearstick tapped the tip of his nose.

'Like I say, mister. You need to speak to the casino owner.'

Savage stared at their faces and found they were serious for once. After finishing his drink, he staggered through the bar and out into the cool night air. Not all was a lost cause, and the notion that Coleman's nephew had been splashing huge sums of money about weighed heavily on his mind. Had he won it fairly at the casino table? Or was this, as he now believed, the proceeds of the Schiphol diamond heist.

Unsteady on his feet, he strolled awkwardly to where the surveillance vehicle was parked. Despite his drunken state, the sergeant stopped short before reaching it. Thinking with clarity, not all had gone to plan. Sometimes it was the little things that made the difference, like the casino manager and his daughter. What was of major interest to him though, was the huge sums of money that Jackson had come into. He would need to look into it, but that would come later. Once he'd sobered up.

Chapter Thirty-Five

The week had flown by without any significant progress. Walker was very much the centre of attention, but Mason was feeling the pressure. No thanks to Sandy Witherspoon and some sharp legal practices regarding her client's ill health, she'd managed to convince the courts that unless the police pressed charges against her client, he had nothing further to add. It was the kick in the teeth he'd been dreading, and Mason was furious.

Not the best day in his life. Far from it. Mason still had to endure a meeting with his nemesis Superintendent Albert Gregory, and he wasn't looking forward to that. There had been, not surprisingly, repercussions over his attempt to interview Edward Coleman. Bad move, he thought. His boss didn't give a damn about excuses, just that he wasn't implicated in the story.

It was Friday, and apart from Tom Hedley's meagre offerings regarding new blood sample found on Jackson's trainers, they were no further today than yesterday. What's more, his inquiries into Mark Rigg's whereabouts had ground to an abrupt halt. Having failed to show up at his court hearing, the man had vanished into thin air.

Down on his luck, Mason was hoping for some better news. It wasn't to be, and the sight of Rob Savage's weary face didn't help his mood either. One hundred and fifty pounds of hard-fought police funds had been transferred into the sergeant's expense account. It was a significant sum. But hopefully something good would come of it.

'Tell me about these new allegations regarding Samuel Jackson,' Mason said. 'What have you found out?'

The sergeant raised his head and there was something unconvincing in his smile. 'A lot of rumours have been slushing around about this two-hundred grand that Jackson won at the casino table. Whether it's true or not has yet to be established. I've done a few checks, but nothing has shown up so far. The problem is, he was using hard cash and none of it traceable. Mind, Coleman's nephew did have a bit of a reputation, especially amongst loose women.'

Carrington was quick to react. 'That's sexist, Rob. It takes two to tango.'

'No offence, Sue.'

Mason eyed Savage warily, wondering if another spat was about to kick off.

'What does your gut feeling tell you? Is there any truth in the rumours?'

Savage allowed himself a brief, smug smile as he flicked through the pages of his notebook. 'Well, he was definitely seen splashing a lot of money around before he was murdered.'

'Anything to do with the proceeds of a diamond heist, do you think?'

'Now there's the thing. Looking into Jackson's bank accounts, there's nothing to cause alarm,' the sergeant sighed. 'We've been over everything. Money transfers, purchases, debt settlement, you name it.'

'Sounds fishy to me.'

There was a momentary hush while the team absorbed this.

Mason's initial thoughts were that Jackson was involved in the heist. If not, where did the money come from? Cash was king, it was the key to success and got you into places where other people couldn't go. Then again, if Coleman's nephew had been throwing it around as if he had a money tree in his garden, there was no way it was legit.

'This casino owner, Mark Chambers? What do we know about him?'

'Chambers is well-liked. Apart from his being an active member of the local Labour party, he sits on the board of school governors at the local grammar school. Everyone speaks highly of him.'

'Anything on our criminal files?'

'No. Nothing,' Savage replied, shaking his head. 'Mind I could be asking the wrong people, of course.'

'It sounds like you are. Have you managed to talk to Mark Chambers at all?'

'Not in person I haven't.'

'It's time you did,' said Mason, forcefully. 'If Chambers is as squeaky clean as he professes to be, the man has nothing to hide. Ask him a few awkward questions. Put him under the spotlight. Better still, threaten to close his casino down.'

'On what grounds, boss?'

Mason smiled in a half-hearted way. Savage was old-school, methodical, and set in his ways. One of life's plodders, the detective sergeant had an awful knack of upsetting people for all the wrong reasons. He liked the man. He was dependable and could get results when you least expected them.

Carrington shot Mason a glance. 'Do you want me to get involved, boss? A woman's touch and all that.'

'No, Sue. I doubt this casino romp is kosher anyway. If you must know, I've had my fill of pub talk.'

Carrington nodded and jotted something down.

The moment Carlisle lifted his head and pointed to the crime board, anticipation hit the room. The profiler had arrived in a sullen mood that morning, complaining his cat had sparked off another neighbourhood war. Not one for showing his emotions, the profiler was normally placid, laid back. Not today. The casual leather jacket that he favoured had been replaced with a crumpled old grey suit, a white open neck shirt, and a pair of mud spattered trainers that looked distinctly out of place.

'We're veering off at a tangent,' the profiler said, grumpily.

'What makes you think that?' asked Mason.

The annoyance showing on the profiler's face, it looked as if he'd swallowed a wasp. 'Looking at the post-mortem report, the knife wounds found on Jackson's body are similar in size, shape, and form to those found in the Baxter report. Two separate pathologists – both reaching the same conclusion. What does that tell us?'

Mason took stock.

'Okay, so a similar weapon was used?'

'Considering the time, location, and method of Jackson's death, this smacks of a retribution killing. The question is, why here? Why this city? What's the connection with Newcastle?'

'Simple, this is about diamonds. Fifty million dollars' worth,' Mason said, 'and let's not rule out Ed Coleman.'

'It's time we revisited the facts.'

Mason's face stiffened. 'Regarding what?'

THE POACHER'S POCKET

Carlisle opened his case files and peered over the top of his spectacles as he spoke. 'Looking at the airport security transcripts, the diamonds were snatched from the hold of the Lufthansa jet barely fifteen minutes before take-off.'

'Okay, okay. We all knew it was tight.'

Carlisle lowered his gaze. 'Considering the gang had to break through a security cordon, overpower ground staff, and grapple with dozens of security boxes before making good their escape, it didn't leave much room for error.'

'So, what are you implying?'

Carlisle pointed to a grainy image pinned to the whiteboard. 'According to the airport security manager, the gang arrived at the airport gates dressed as security guards. These gates.' he said, pointing to another image.

Mason looked up doleful.

'And?'

'There lies your clue. Someone in airport security must be working for the gang.'

The room fell silent.

Carrington pursed her lips. 'Intelligence suggest otherwise, and we've been over this ground before. Let's face it, the airport authorities were slow in deciding who to question, which has led to ambiguities in the report.'

'I can agree with that, but something's not right.'

Mason thought carefully before replying. If Carlisle's theory was true, it was another urgent reason to find their fellow police officer. Walker held most of the answers to the Schiphol diamond robbery, he was convinced of that. Wasn't that the reason he was being held captive?

'It's another way of looking at it,' Mason reluctantly agreed, 'but why kill Samuel Jackson after they'd kidnapped Ellis Walker?'

'What if Walker is already dead?' Carrington conceded.

Carlisle stroked his chin. 'Then we may have a gang war on our hands.'

'Let's not go there,' Mason groaned.

Savage looked up. 'Why haven't counterintelligence told us more?'

Mason tapped the crime board with the back of his hand. 'Walker's mission was to find the Schiphol mastermind, the man behind the diamond heist. That's why counterintelligence recruited him. We know a second heist is in the planning, but that's as much as we know.' Mason turned sharply to face the profiler as he spoke, 'Or, is this about the contents of another stolen security box?'

'Isn't that the reason why SCD7 are involved?' replied Carlisle.

Mason took another swig of his coffee before answering. 'What if Walker's captors are holding him as a bargaining chip? If the two sides can't come to an agreement? It's another option.'

'In which case, why haven't these people made contact with anyone?' said Savage.

'Who knows, maybe they're dealing with Coleman direct?'

'It's possible. I wouldn't put it past him.'

Carrington shook her head looking confused. 'I'm not so sure.'

'What about the Lufthansa shipping list. Where are we on that?' asked Mason.

'Still working on it, boss,' said Savage.

'Why not run it past the area commander?' asked Carrington. 'If we can get him to agree it may give us some leverage.'

Mason's first reaction was not to rush into things. Do that and it could fall on deaf ears. Besides, the area commander was the last person he'd want to deal with. No, he thought. He would need to think of a better plan, and one involving the chief constable. How was the problem.

Feeling on edge, the chief inspector felt a disconcerting churning sensation in the pit of his stomach. It wasn't good, and it was slowly stripping away his confidence. His priority was to establish Walker's whereabouts, but that was proving difficult. Going over his boss's head could be problematic, and he knew the consequences of failure. Even so, he wouldn't be the first senior police officer to do so.

'Okay,' Mason said, realising the enormity of the task. 'Let's contact Lufthansa airlines and chase up the shipping list. Failing that, we need to look into insurance claims. If nothing else, it should give a clear indication as to what these people are looking for.'

'And our search for Ellis Walker?' quizzed Carrington.

'Coleman holds the key to that; I'm convinced of it. Besides, if these people went after his nephew, they're bound to go after him. It's the way their minds work – it's a predatory thing.'

'Unless...' Savage's voice tailed off.

'Yes, Rob?'

'Nah. It's nothing.'

Mason sat silent for some moments, then said quietly, 'It's time I had a private word with the chief constable and put our thoughts to him.'

Everyone sat gobsmacked.

It was then Mason realised he'd gone and put his foot in it again.

Chapter Thirty-Six

The drive back from Alnwick was a nightmare. All the way along the A1 they were stuck behind lorries churning up gallons of filthy spray. On reaching Cramlington, the rain had eased off slightly, but visibility was still poor with long tailbacks as far back as Scotswood Bridge. Earlier that morning, still grappling his emotions, Mason was hoping for some positive news regarding the undercover officer's whereabouts. Despite all his frustrations, Sue Carrington had managed to secure a list of insurance claims surrounding the Schiphol diamond heist. Now on her way to see him, he was keen to establish what she'd found.

He was eating a sandwich when his phone rang, and he let it ring out. Ever since joining the force as a young constable he'd learnt never to answer a call during lunchbreaks. He didn't mind eating and talking whilst answering but detested cold coffee. Most calls were small talk anyway.

His phone pinged again, but this time an unexpected impulse drove him to pick it up. 'Yes, Rob. What can I do for you?'

'It's about Coleman's nephew,' the sergeant replied hastily.

'What about him?'

'I've been following up on Jackson's movements around the time Baxter was murdered, only to find he was out of the country.'

'Anywhere nice?'

'Try Amsterdam.'

'You're joking!'

'It gets even better. I've been talking to border control, and both Walker and Jackson were on the overnight ferry crossing that day. I've done a few checks, and it was the same vehicle the Amsterdam police recovered after Walker's kidnapping.'

'Why wasn't this picked up earlier?'

'You might ask your counterpart in Amsterdam that.'

After he'd hung up, Mason drained the dregs of his coffee. He remembered how David Carlisle had told them that Baxter and Walker were inherently linked to Ed Coleman's criminal activities. Not only that, but he now knew why Samuel Jackson had been murdered after Walker's kidnapping. They'd been followed, just as Terrence Baxter had.

As he let his mind drift, Mason recalled walking into the empty council house where Jackson's body had been found. Slumped forward slightly, the tongue forced out of the mouth, Jackson's carotid artery had been severed after enduring multiple stab wounds to the back, neck, and chest. Blood everywhere, it was the same horrific fate that Terrence Baxter had suffered. Even down to the note pinned to his chest.

He glanced at his watch.

Things were shaping up, and with any luck something important might come of it. How much Ed Coleman knew about his nephew's murder, he was longing to find out. But red tape was preventing him from doing so. Feeling upbeat, he was striding along the corridor and heading for Major Incident Room 2 when he was stopped in his tracks.

'Ah! Chief Inspector Mason,' the Chief Constable called out.

Mason turned sharply.

'How can I help, sir?'

'Do you have a minute?'

'Certainly.'

'Alison Jefferson and I are just on our way back to police headquarters after an update briefing on Operation Wizard. Like everyone else in the building, we're keen to be kept in the loop, especially when one of our officers has gone missing.'

Eager to get his point across regarding Jackson's murder, Mason felt a beat of excitement. This was the perfect opportunity to go over the AC's head. How to approach it was the problem. Any errors of judgement and the old sod would haul him over the coals.

'I'm heading to a meeting, sir. Is my office okay?'

'Of course.'

The minute they stepped into his office, Mason's phone rang. Releasing his grip on a bundle of case files he was carrying; he checked the display. It was Rob Savage again. Knowing the importance, he decided to take the call.

'I'd almost forgot to mention it,' the sergeant said excitedly, 'the day Ellis Walker was kidnapped, Samuel Jackson was residing at the Holiday Inn Express in Amsterdam Centrum. He stayed on a few days before catching a flight back to Newcastle.'

'What was he doing there?'

'I've absolutely no idea, but it wasn't sightseeing I'd wager.'

'Good work, Rob. I'm currently with the Chief Constable and head of control, Alison Jefferson. As soon as I'm finished here I'll be straight back to you.'

He ended the call.

'Trouble in the camp,' the chief constable enquired.

'Quite the contrary, sir. There's been a new development regarding Samuel Jackson's murder, and I'm sure you'll be keen to hear about it.'

'Indeed, we are.'

Chapter Thirty-Seven

Ellis Walker woke with a start, with a searing temperature and badly in need of a pee. It was never this dark, and normally the stairwell light was on. He froze. Something wasn't right! Then it all came flooding back. The Poacher. The torture. The agony.

As a rule, Walker trusted no one, but he'd failed miserably, lowered his guard in a moment of unexplained uncertainty. He knew nothing of any documents, but these morons felt he did. Whatever was snatched from the hold of a Lufthansa jet was now in the hands of a priest. A man of God, whose life was now in grave danger.

Having lost all track of time, Walker was beginning to look at things differently. He still had his hearing and sensory buds. Although deep underground, he swore he could hear passing trains. And, if he listened carefully, the pealing of church bells. Not loud. Enough to know he wasn't imagining things.

Until recently, he'd almost given up on escape. Almost. Failure wasn't an option and his new technique with the chair rocking motion had given him a new sense of purpose. He could cover a lot of ground, and in a short space of time. No more jerky movements. No more cramping of legs. He'd learnt to adapt, stay clear of trouble, not like the last time he'd toppled over.

In what had been a terrible learning curve, the moment the Poacher had cottoned on to his exploits the cruel bastard had set about him as if he were a dog. He thought he was going to die, and for days his whole body was racked with pain from the merciless beatings. Beyond all that, he recalled the Poacher's parting words as he climbed the cellar stairs that day:

"*Try that again and I swear I'll slit your throat.*"

Slowly at first, Walker began the chair rocking motion. Heels hard to the floor, legs locked solid, he was able to gain some traction. He stopped after a while, then listened. Pain welled in his bladder, and he clenched his thighs together until unable to hold out any longer. The moment he relieved himself the rats scurried to investigate.

Those bastards were never far away from the smell of death.

Walker never felt comfortable in confined spaces, not since he was a little boy. It all began when his big sister locked him inside the bathroom cupboard. He'd hated the dark ever since. The not knowing. Now imprisoned with the rats, it was playing havoc with his emotions. If they didn't eat him alive, they would feast on his body once he was dead. The mere thought sent shivers down his spine.

He started the rocking motion again.

Please God, don't let me topple over.

As terror turned to fury, he arched his back as he transferred his weight to the balls of his feet. Somehow, and he didn't know how exactly, he was able to maintain balance. And one thing in his favour: the Poacher had forgotten to gaffer tape his mouth. He could breathe more freely now, conserve energy, and concentrate his mind on the task in hand.

Moving his head to one side, he rested his cheek on the table. It felt cold. Uninviting. The moment he arched his back, the pain in his shoulder returned. He thought he was going to pass out, but he didn't. Half twisting and turning, the instant his nose touched the knife blade, he twisted his head sideways.

Craning his neck, in one swift movement he flicked his tongue towards the knife and clenched his teeth around the handle. The next thing he felt, after crashing to the floor, was the trickle of warm blood down his face. Not daring to move, he lay perfectly still and listened.

Nothing.

Only the sound of scampering feet.

Incited by the smell of fresh blood, the rats were everywhere. Thousands of them. A writhing mass of feverish chaos that sickened him to the core.

He moved for the knife.

Not daring to breathe, at first he thought he was hallucinating. It was then he realised the weight of his fall had shattered the chair back and his arms were free.

Assume nothing. Think positively.

Slowly at first, Walker began to cut through his leg restraints. First the left leg, and then the right. His heart beating as a drum, no matter how hard he tried to cut the bindings they reluctantly refused to yield. Then circulation returned. An agonising pain that caused him to cry out. He felt dizzy suddenly. Physically sick.

Half crouching on one knee, Walker grabbed the table with both hands and precariously heaved himself up. As his eyes cut through the darkness, there was only one thing on his mind.

It was the driving force above everything else.

Chapter Thirty-Eight

In a field, and up to his eyes in mud, Jack Mason was soaked to the skin. It had rained incessantly these past twenty-four hours, and there seemed no end to it. He paused and stared at the hand now lying palm up. As always when attending crime scenes, his mood was a mixture of fear and unease. Having all but given up in trying to look macho these days, it was no longer part of his makeup. Mason hated murder scenes, as most perpetrators showed little or no remorse for their victims. Nor for the unimaginable mayhem they left behind.

Beyond the yellow barrier tape marked: CRIME SCENE – DO NOT CROSS, Mason spotted the slightly built figure of Peter Davenport. Camera poised at the ready, the scene of crime photographer was busily capturing everything and anything of forensic interest. Nothing could be taken for granted. Further afield, he noticed a group of forensic officers stood huddled around a black plastic bag. Motionless, as if each daring the other to peep inside, its edges were flapping in the breeze. On the surface their mood appeared relaxed, but Mason knew otherwise.

The whole area now swarming with police, dozens of officers had been drafted in from outlying districts to bolster numbers. It was a remote location, secluded, and well off the tourist track. Close to a gate, beyond the long line of police vehicles, he picked out the huge hulk of the major incident truck. No matter how large or small a task may appear, everything would be controlled from there. The focal point of every police officer in attendance, it was the hive of activity where policies and plans were formulated, and fingers kept on the pulse. If nothing else, he might scrounge a welcome mug of hot coffee and catch up on any new developments.

Beginning to feel sorry for himself, Mason felt his legs chilling as his shoes let in water. The wind in this neighbourhood was relentless, which wasn't helping either. It was then he caught the cluster of yellow evidence flags fluttering on the breeze. Each carried a number, each an important piece in the forensic jigsaw puzzle. Still looking for answers, he trudged through the mud and moved cautiously towards the black plastic bag. Not the best day in his life, Mason groaned. He could have sorely done without this.

Despite his setbacks, the arrival of Stan Johnson at least brought a calming effect to proceedings. If there were nasty surprises to be had, the scene of crime manager would know of them. Stan was dependable, and never shirked responsibility.

'Morning, Jack,' Johnson said, in a low commanding voice. 'Welcome to sunny Morpeth.'

'Not exactly deck chair weather, Stan.'

'No. It comes with the territory, I'm afraid.'

Mason drew back. 'What do we know so far?'

Johnson knelt down in front of the black plastic bag and drew back the outer flap. In all his years of investigating serious crime, not much shocked Mason. But the moment the contents of this killer's handy work were revealed, his stomach lurched.

'Crikey!' he said, blowing through clenched teeth.

'I know,' said Johnson, in a low respectful whisper. 'There's still a few sick bastards around.'

A well-built male in his late thirties, the corpse had a wax like appearance. The eyes wide open were staring into space. The hair had been cropped short at the sides, and he had a small birthmark behind his left ear and scar above his left eye. From what Mason could gather, the back of the head had been blown away and both hands had been severed above the wrists. What other injuries the victim had sustained were not clearly visible.

'Someone's called for a pathologist, I presume?'

'They're on their way,' Johnson nodded, staring at his watch.

'Good man.'

There were a few decent Home Office pathologists Mason knew who would attend such a murder scene, and he was hoping one of them might show. His favourite was Jillian King, a dignified middle-aged woman, who he always got on well with. Married with two grown up girls, King had a bubbly personality which always cheered him up on such morbid occasions. Mason hated mortuaries, vehemently.

'He doesn't look familiar, Stan.'

Johnson sighed. 'Whoever they are, they didn't mess about.'

'An execution, do you think?'

'Low muzzle gunshot wound to the forehead by the look. It would be swift, decisive, and hopefully he didn't suffer.'

'Any notes pinned to his chest?'

'If there were, we haven't come across any. This weather isn't helping any. It's rained incessantly these past twenty-four hours and if it continues like this, we can expect to see flooding.' Johnson gave a wry smile. 'Tom

Hedley will have a fit when he sees the state of ground play.'

True, Mason thought. Clues were fast draining away before their very eyes. Ballistics would be his safest line of enquiry. At least they'd tell him what type of weapon was used, calibre, bullet type, size of entry and exit wound. Looking at the body, what range the gun was fired was anyone's guess.

'Who found him, Stan?'

'A local farmhand taking a shortcut to work. The moment Morpeth police were alerted, they cordoned the area off and that's when they found the hand.'

'What time was this?'

'Just after five o'clock.'

'And we've no idea who he is?'

'No doubt the pathologists will tell us more.'

'Let's hope he's known to us. If not, until someone realises he's missing, it could take a lot longer.'

Mason weighed up the facts. This was a pretty remote spot, so either the victim's body had been brought here and dumped, or this was his place of execution. What puzzled him more than anything, was why both hands had been removed.

Mason turned to Johnson. 'Did he die here, do you think?'

'It's my guess they came through the village in the dead of night, so a house-to-house is vital. You never know, these places may seem isolated and remote to us, but the locals know exactly what's going on.'

Mason squelched the mud from under his feet.

'You've been watching too many Miss Marple movies, Stan.'

'It's the missus,' Johnson laughed. 'She loves those programmes.'

'Tell me about it. Barbara can't get enough of Police Interceptors these days. Sirens blaring in your living room, road traffic officers chasing after the bad guys, it's as if we don't get enough of it at work.'

'I'm not alone then,' Johnson chuckled.

Having seen all they wanted to see, they made their way towards the major incident truck. Mason had witnessed dozens of crime scenes like this one before, and most of them drugs related. Turf wars mainly, or the odd execution over non-payment of drugs. It was a never-ending cycle of death. Once Tom Hedley's team got stuck into the case, they would paint a clearer picture. Until then, he could only assume what had taken place here.

He watched as forensic officers erected a white incident tent over the body, then placed more yellow evidence markers in the ground. Much to his relief, the man lying dead in a rain sodden field wasn't the missing officer he was looking for. Still a full-blown murder enquiry, once he'd completed his findings here he would hand the case over to another team.

'Why here, Stan?'

Johnson gave a little shrug. 'Difficult to say. Once the coroner establishes the time of death, we'll be able to work on a timeline. Which is always crucial in this type of investigation.'

Mason caught movement towards the edge of the perimeter fence. Seconds later a mud-spattered black Range Rover parked up behind one of the police dog handlers vans and a man got out. It was time to grab a hot drink, dry out, and bring some circulation back to his legs. It was then he clocked Christopher Sykes. What the hell, he groaned. Where Sykes got his information from beggared belief, but that's how journalists worked. They had a way of finding these things out.

Mason took a deep breath and tried to stay calm.

'What can I do for you?'

Pen poised at the ready, Sykes turned his collar against the driving rain.

'Not the sort of place to be out in this kind of weather, Chief Inspector.'

Mason nodded stiffly.

'A little bird tells me you've found another body. Mind telling me who he is?'

Mason pretended to act dumb. The last time he'd spoken with Sykes, he'd ended up complaining to the independent press standards organisation about running what he claimed were inaccurate stories on a major crime case he was working on. He got nowhere, of course. Apart from causing more grief, he received a stiff rollocking from the acting chief constable. *Stay calm*, he thought.

'Have you checked with the local constabulary?'

'I already have. I just wanted to know what your views were, that's all.'

Sykes was weird, and not to be trusted. Rumour had it he'd been caught messing around with teenage girls in one of the local park toilets. Nobody could pin a thing on him, and that was the problem. The chief inspector hated him with a vengeance.

'We've yet to establish the actual time of death,' Mason said, begrudgingly. 'What I can confirm is, he's male, around five-ten, with short, cropped hair, and has a small birthmark behind his left ear.'

'How did he die, Chief Inspector?'

'No doubt a Home Office pathologist will tell you more about that.'

'That's odd. I'd heard he'd been shot through the head.'

'What else have you heard?' asked Mason, swivelling on heels.

'He was found by a local farmhand early this morning,' Sykes dribbled. 'You know me, Jack. I do like to keep my readers informed.'

Like hell, Mason thought. Sykes only interest lay in selling headline stories, no matter how many people's toes he trod on. It's what sold newspapers, what made scumbags like Christopher Sykes such an enemy of the police.

'Okay,' Mason began, 'I'm holding a press conference in the morning. If you care to give me a call around six-thirty, I could make it worth your while.'

Sykes gave him a wry smile of approval as he pushed off towards the line of parked vehicles. Nice one, Mason thought. Feed a scumbag with shit, and they'll think they've got an exclusive. If only.

Chapter Thirty-Nine

A wind-swept Poppy Field Farm just north of Morpeth did not constitute ideal conditions for a pathologist to carry out his homework. Dr Brown, however, had managed to extract enough fibres lodged in the victim's flesh and clothing to establish he'd been shot through the head at point blank range using a low-calibre handgun. A Glock. Smuggled in from Eastern Europe and converted here in the UK to a 9mm weapon. Sold on the black market for an extortionate price, all it took was a four-quid plastic switch imported from Pakistan to convert it to a devastating weapon. He'd seen it done before. Many times. Convinced that's how hardened criminals preferred to convert low-calibre weapons into automatic guns, Mason was confident that's what they were dealing with.

'What do you reckon?' he asked, turning to Carlisle.

The profiler looked at Mason quizzically. 'Mode of death is completely different from the others, Jack. This one was swift and decisive.

A killing more in line with an execution than anything.'

'No letter pinned to the victim's chest either.'

'Which you'd expect to find if it were connected.'

Mason shielded his eyes against the early morning sunlight. What a difference twenty-four hours made. Although the ground underfoot was beginning to dry out, a cabbage field had been turned into a quagmire. Still cordoned off, much of the forensic work had been scaled down, but a few uniformed police officers were still out searching for clues. Hedgerows and outlying buildings mainly. Not that he was expecting them to find much, but it still had to be done, nevertheless.

'What puzzles me,' said Mason, thoughtfully, 'Is why here? Why Morpeth?'

'How much do we know about the victim?'

'Not a lot. He's been stripped clean of identity, and we now await the Home Office findings. Looking at the facts, it's my view he crossed a red line at some point and has been made an example of.'

The profiler thought before answering, and Mason swore he could hear the cogs in his brain ticking. Carlisle could be difficult to read at times, but he was hoping to be thrown a lifeline.

'Any other significant injuries?'

'Apart from gunshot wounds to the head, the duty doctor found burn marks to the back, shoulders, and neck. It all points to a hot domestic steam iron being used. As for the hands, he believes they were removed using a power saw. More a botch job I would have thought.'

'Sounds like the victim was tortured before he was killed.'

Mason nodded. 'A full post-mortem is arranged for two o'clock, so we'll get a better understanding of what took place here.'

'What about DNA?'

'Nothing back so far. A few scraps of interest have been recovered, but it doesn't amount to much.'

'Like what?'

'A zip lighter, a local betting slip, and a few discarded cigarette butts.'

The profiler's boots squelched in the mud as he turned. 'How close to the body were they found?'

'Fifty yards. Along one of the hedgerows,' Mason replied.

They strolled along a muddy footpath, sliding as they went before turning into a large open farmyard. Poppy Field Farm was a handsome 18th century grade II listed Georgian property which sat on an elevated and secluded position overlooking rural Northumberland, or a significant part of it, at least. Set back in 200 acres of arable farmland, the farmhouse was enclosed on three sides by stone barns, stables, and several outbuildings. To one corner stood a large modern combine harvester alongside other expensive machinery. These people had money, there was no doubting that.

Their main witness, John Smith, had a rectangular face with a defined, slightly pointed chin and sturdy jaw line. His eyes were small and sitting below trimmed eyebrows that were permanently stuck in a raised position. The jacket he wore over broad shoulders was threadbare at the elbows, and his baggy work-worn trousers were tucked into a pair of mud-spattered green Wellington boots. Having spent his whole working life on the farm, Smith's intimate knowledge of the area was of major interest to them.

During questioning, Smith came across as a hardworking, conscientious man, who kept to himself. Far from talkative, Mason gathered he'd unwittingly stumbled into a murder enquiry. Not the best way to start your day, he thought.

'Thank you,' the chief inspector said, pocketing his notebook. 'I appreciate your honesty but having discovered the body, these type of questions need to be asked.'

'Any idea who he is?' asked Smith.

'Not at this stage, we don't.'

'No, I guess not.'

Mason handed Smith one of his business cards, and he stared at it.

'If you do think of anything else, you can ring that number.'

'Yes, of course. Will that be all, Chief Inspector?'

'For now,' Mason nodded.

Smith gave a wry smile as he took off towards one of the large stone outbuildings. Now one-thirty, Mason stared across the cobbled farmyard and considered his options. The victim had died of gunshot wounds to the head, the muzzle of the gun having been pressed hard to the forehead at the moment of discharge. Known as a hard contact technique, it was used to minimise the sound, powder, and blood spread. Dumped in a cabbage field in the dead of night, gave all the indications of a professional job. No one in the vicinity had heard or seen anything, and their door-to-door enquiries in the village had drawn a blank.

Thinking this through, it meant the victim must have been executed elsewhere, as Mason could think of no other logical explanation. He would need to involve the tech team, get them to trawl through hundreds of hours of CCTV footage. It would be painstaking work, but necessary.

It was something the profiler had said that was still niggling away in the back of the chief inspectors mind – *had Walker been held captive here?* Anything was possible, no matter how large or small that notion may be. This place wasn't plucked out of thin air as an afterthought, so there had to be a logical explanation as to why the body had been dumped in the middle of a field.

'What do you think?' Mason asked.

'Hard to say,' the profiler replied. 'The manner of execution may appear different, but whoever executed this man was working under orders.'

'Same people you think?'

'No. The person who killed the others is sexually aroused by the power and domination of watching his victims die slowly. This killing was more direct, the work of a hardened professional. Let's not forget there was torture, which is always a good indicator as to the type of people involved.'

'Not the same hand then?'

'I doubt it, and there's no physical connection to the others. We need to understand what some people are capable of. What makes them tick.'

'So, what makes you think this killing is different from the rest?'

The profiler looked at him oddly.

'What does a knife sound like when it cuts through human flesh?'

'How the hell would I know.'

'Because the person who killed Baxter certainly understands those fantasies, and that's what makes him so different. The volume of stab wounds and the pleasure he derives from seeing his victims suffer is all part of his makeup.'

'So, it's not the same hand?'

'Not this time, Jack.'

Damn profilers, Mason cursed. Uncovering the truth was like watching paint dry. Why couldn't they tell it as it was instead of drooling over a killer's fantasies. If this were a professional assassination it meant they could have a gang war on their hands.

'Are we looking at a hired professional here, or is this something else?'

'Hired hands, assassins, call them what you will. The person who killed Baxter suffers from a paranoid delusional disorder, and this killer doesn't.'

Mason turned sharply to face the profiler and said, 'Sometimes you scare the living shit out of me with all this psychological dribble.'

'It's why you hired me, Jack. To get inside these people's minds.'

When Mason was training to be a detective, his mentor had advised never to underestimate the criminal mind. It was sound advice, and one that had stuck with him ever since. His wasn't a good position to be in right now. What with another murder on his hands, a shit load of awkward questions to answer, he was staring down the barrel of another dressing down.

As thoughts drifted back to Sandy Witherspoon, Mason wondered how much truth lay in her story. According to her, Walker's kidnapping was pure pantomime intended to drum up newspaper sales. Apart from an undercover officer failing to report into central command, no one in the criminal fraternity had seen Coleman's right hand man in weeks. Was he alive, or better still, was Witherspoon's story a means of deflecting police attention away from the truth? If so, what part did her client play in all of this, and why were these people specifically targeting his organisation? Still keeping an open mind, he was feeling far from optimistic of ever finding Walker.

His phone rang.

It was Rob Savage, enquiring whether he'd be attending the post-mortem that afternoon. Mason grinned. No way. Standing in a cabbage field up to his eyeballs in mud was far better fun than watching a victim's body being dissected. Instructing the sergeant to stand in for him, he ended the call.

God loves a trier, he mused.

Chapter Forty

Jack Mason wasn't keen on the idea of widening his search around Poppy Field Farm. To cover every inch of the crime scene would achieve nothing other than a waste of valuable police time. His main focus of attention was to establish who the victim was, but that was proving more difficult.

After grabbing a bacon butty and mug of black coffee from Starbucks, his plans for an early night with Barbara was a nonstarter. Disheartened, the pathologist's findings had placed the time of death around 15:00; later than first anticipated. Doctor Julien King's examination had been thorough and comprehensive according to Rob Savage, but they still awaited toxicology reports. Once they had those, they could establish if any substances were present in the victim's body and whether he had taken drugs.

Other than a zip lighter, a betting slip, and a few discarded cigarette butts, nothing important had emerged from the crime scene.

Although it looked like a planned execution, he was still keeping an open mind.

It was late afternoon when Mason peered in through the betting shop window. The place looked deserted. Some clues were easily come by, others more challenging. Even so, he had yet to contact the Amsterdam police and bring them up to speed on the latest developments. Information exchange was vital, but he'd fallen behind on his workload and was now having to play catch-up. Gregory wasn't helpful either, or his ridiculous refusal to allow him to interview Coleman. His boss was a total train crash, and it was making life difficult.

The betting shop manager, a woman in her late forties, had a long-hooked nose and short curly brown hair. Dressed in a white cotton blouse, neck scarf, and emerald, green skirt that clung to her waistline three sizes too small, she seemed friendly enough. Escorted into a backroom full of old computer parts, she seemed ill at ease.

'I'm sorry about the mess,' she said turning to face him. 'How can we help?'

'I'm looking for the person who placed this bet with you,' Mason began, holding up a plastic forensic bag with a grubby bookmaker's slip inside. 'We believe he's one of your customers.'

'What's this one been up to?'

'A name would be useful,' Mason grinned.

She looked at him oddly. 'That could be difficult.'

'Any reason?'

'Yes. There's thousands of bets placed here every day.'

'Really. It doesn't look busy to me.'

She smiled, showing uneven teeth.

'Most of our clients are mid-morning regulars. Apart from its close proximity to four regular bus stops, there are three public houses within easy walking distance.'

None the wiser, Mason handed her the betting slip and she glanced at it.

'It's definitely one of ours, but this one's not traceable.'

'A regular, do you think?'

'I have absolutely no idea.'

Mason pressed harder. 'What I do know is, that on Saturday afternoon around 14:30, someone placed this bet with you. That's a fact. So, who placed it?'

'I'm sorry,' she said, shaking her head. 'I wish I could be of help.'

'Pity. I was hoping for some better news.' Mason spun on heels. 'I noticed you operate CCTV cameras. I assume they are operational.'

'Yes, they are.'

'Any objections to me looking at the footage?'

She appeared anxious, as though uncertain how to deal with the situation. 'I would need to clear that with head office first – but I can't see it being a problem.'

'Good, at least that clears one issue up.'

'And the others?'

'I'm not a betting man,' Mason admitted, 'but fifty-quid on a total outsider is an awful lot of money to be throwing around wouldn't you say?'

'You'd be surprised. That's peanuts to some people around here.' She looked at him awkwardly. 'If it helps, I know most of our regulars and they're a decent bunch.'

'I'm not questioning your clients integrity,' Mason argued. 'I'm merely asking if this is an unusual amount.'

She stared at him sternly. 'Would you mind telling me what this is all about?'

'Certainly,' the chief inspector replied. 'I'm investigating a murder, and this betting slip was found in the vicinity of the crime scene. It may have nothing to do with the case, but we need to eliminate it from our enquiries.'

'Goodness. I was…' she stuttered, her voice tailing off at the last syllable.

'Good. That ticks another box off my list.'

She stared at him.

'Is there anything else, Chief Inspector?'

'Just the CCTV footage if you would.' He handed her one of his business cards and she took it. 'Any problems, and you're to ring that number. In the meantime, one of my officers will be along to collect the footage.'

'Yes, of course.'

Her face like thunder, they moved into the front of the shop. She was right. The place was a tip, and the whole building was desperately in need of a makeover.

'Will that be all?'

'For now,' Mason replied. 'If I do think of anything, I'll get back to you.'

Her face dropped. 'I don't doubt it.'

Outside on the street, Mason soon stumbled across The Four Ladies public house. It was directly opposite – close to the first of the four bus stops she'd told him about. He made a mental note and sauntered along the high street in search of the other two pubs. Then it struck him. Judging by where the betting slip was found, he doubted it had anything to do with the case.

His phone rang.

'What can I do for you, Sue?'

'These Lufthansa insurance claims you asked me to follow up on. I've managed to whittle it down to two packages without claims against them. Both are valued around $500,000 and are listed as sensitive data. According to the insurance assessors, the contents could be virtually anything.'

'Do we know who they belonged to?'

'It's definitely the same client, but that's as far as the system will allow me to go.'

'Why? Is there a problem?'

She hesitated. 'They are registered to a Turkish holding company which is covered by some sort of diplomatic immunity. I've tried several searches, but the system keeps locking me out.'

'Have you run it past the computer experts?'

'It's not that easy.'

'Sounds to me like you need some technical assistance.'

'I'm already on it, boss.'

'Let's talk it over at tomorrow's briefing.'

As he ended the call, he peered in through the baker's shop window at the large assortment of mouth-watering cakes on display. It was then his eye caught the raspberry cream buns. They looked delicious, and Barbara would sell her soul for one.

How could he possibly resist?

Chapter Forty-One

Mason had not felt this low in a long time. Other than the post-mortem findings, he had nothing more to report to the area commander. Coleman was a free man, and unless he gathered enough evidence to put him away for good, there was little point in raising the issue.

Feeling as a schoolboy when summoned to see the headmaster, Mason entered Gregory's office with unease. His worst nightmare realised, he now had another murder on his hands. It wasn't looking good, and Walker's whereabouts was a complete mystery. Someone out there knew where he was. Surely? The trouble was no one was willing to come forward for fear of reprisals. He knew that. But what else could he do?

'Have you read the PM report?' the area commander began.

'I have, sir.'

'Do we know who he is?'

'Not yet, but we're working on it.'

'What about motive. Any thoughts?'

Mason braced himself. As usual he'd not been invited to sit down. A technique used to make him feel inferior – another way of keeping their meeting short.

'A few possibilities spring to mind. It's either a gangland killing, drug related, or an opportunist at work.'

'What about this diamond heist? Any thoughts on that?'

Gregory's phone rang but he ignored it.

Not since his first reprimand as a young constable had Mason felt this deflated. First the chief constable, and now this dickhead who dared to call himself his boss.

Gregory stared at him hard.

'I realise the pressures you're under, but every twist and turn in the case cannot be put down to Edward Coleman. It's poor judgement, and it's affecting your team's performance.'

'With all due respect, this isn't a personal grudge. Besides, Samuel Jackson was Coleman's nephew with links to Terrence Baxter and dozens of other associates in the crime syndicate.'

'What are you suggesting?'

'This latest victim was found within a short walking distance of Coleman's property. That's a fact.'

'And yet you have no proof it was linked to a diamond heist?'

Frustrated, Mason took a step back. This meeting was orchestrated. He knew that, and it angered him. But more puzzling was Gregory's persistence to defend Coleman. It didn't add up. Why would he do that, he was a police officer God dammit.

'For what it's worth, I believe this was another gangland killing,' Mason argued.

'That may be so, but it doesn't mean Coleman's responsible for every murder that takes place. You've said yourself; you don't have a scrap of evidence to support such a claim.'

'True.'

'The fact is, only last week your name was being bounded around police HQ regarding Ellis Walker's kidnapping, and now we have another murder on our hands.'

'Coleman needs to be brought in for questioning. Isn't that how the system works?'

Gregory took stock.

'I've been asked to reconsider your current position.'

'Regarding what?'

'Need I spell it out to you?'

'You cannot expect me to run a murder enquiry when I'm constantly being kept in the dark. It doesn't work like that.'

The area commander fiddled with his pen. He was dithering. Weak. Full of bluster and indecision. He knew what the old sod was up to, but there was nothing he could do.

Gregory stared at him.

'I'm expecting another backlash from the press, and it's not good enough.'

'Those maggots never have anything nice to say.'

'It's all well and good, but police operations aren't run by the press. We need to be seen leading from the front.'

Still fuming, Mason realised that whatever he said it was falling on deaf ears. The man was so entrenched in a personal blame culture that he couldn't face up to the reality. He should have retired long ago.

Gregory gave Mason a guarded look. 'The Chief Constable is nervous about the damage being done to police reputation. This was supposed to be a low-key operation, and I can't turn my head without someone asking me what's going on.'

'That's a bit steep.'

The AC nervously fiddled with his pen, as if choosing his next words carefully. 'The truth of the matter is, we're no further forward in finding Ellis Walker than we were three weeks ago. What's going on, Jack?'

Mason was livid.

'How do you expect me to run a murder investigation when I'm denied an interview with my number one suspect?' Mason flung his arms in the air in despair. 'And another thing, all the important case documents have mysteriously gone missing from the system and those that remain have been redacted. That's what's going on.'

'You're missing the point. It's not me who's in charge.'

'Who is then?'

Gregory was clearly taken aback.

'I've been asked to take over tomorrow's press briefing – bring some semblance of order to proceedings. This is an extremely sensitive operation, and we cannot afford to fail. You know it. I know it, and the whole damn building knows it.'

Mason shook his head.

'Is there any good reason why I'm being denied an interview with Coleman?'

Gregory narrowed his eyes.

'Are you questioning my authority, Chief Inspector?'

'No. But you don't expect me to turn a blind eye knowing we're dealing with a dangerous criminal.'

'I'd advise you not to make a bad situation worse.'

'Meaning?'

'If you're thinking of bringing my name into this, it won't serve you well. I can assure you of that.' Gregory fell silent for a moment. 'Your remit is to find Ellis Walker, and you're not making a very good job of it, Jack.'

There it was again. Jack. No longer chief inspector. It was incidents like these that were indelibly etched in his mind. This wasn't a dressing down; this had all the makings of a hierarchy blame culture. Was Gregory hiding behind his rank to cover his own inefficiencies?

Then out of nowhere the red mist emerged. 'What do you think I'm doing all day? Sitting on my arse and twiddling my thumbs.'

'Whatever you're trying to do, you're not making a very good job of it.'

'What do you expect when I'm...'

'This isn't about personalities,' Gregory insisted. 'Reliable sources tell me you've been trying to undermine an agreement with Coleman's lawyers.'

'Who told you that crap?'

'It's time you dropped this personal grudge against Coleman. As well as causing a lot of unnecessary friction amongst senior staff, it doesn't serve any purpose.'

Gregory was furious. Mason could see that, but he wasn't giving in to double standards.

'Friction with whom?' Mason asked.

'In case you haven't noticed, there's no institutionalised corruption in this police force. You can rest assured on that.'

Mason was incensed. This wasn't about his lack of progress, nor his justifiable persistence in bringing Coleman to justice. This was about Gregory's lack of involvement in the case. His inability to get things done. He'd been caught out, and someone in high office was beginning to tighten the screw. The more he thought about it the more he felt Sandy Witherspoon was the instigator. She'd been threatening him with the press if he didn't cooperate with her client. Like the fool he was, Gregory had fallen for it.

'One further question if I may.'

Gregory waved a dismissive hand and remained silent.

'Whoever unwittingly stole from these people, is now their number one target.'

'What are you inferring?'

'If it isn't Coleman's lawyer whose been spreading these rumours, then we must have a mole in our ranks.'

'That's absurd.'

'But is it?'

'You know it is, Chief Inspector.'

'Who told you I've been making secret deals behind people's backs?'

Gregory lowered his voice. 'I'm not at liberty to say.'

'In which case we do have a mole in our midst.'

Determined to have the last word, Mason stormed out of the office slamming the door behind him. All those years in the force and it had come down to this.

Chapter Forty-Two

Fighting his demons, Ellis Walker would need to act swiftly as there was little room for error. The Poacher would lunge out at him at the first opportunity. He knew that. The man was a narcissist and more than a formidable match. Standing six-foot-two and in excess of one hundred kilos, the Poacher was no fool. His back pressed hard against the wall, the undercover officer struggled to curb his emotions. There would be no better opportunity. No second chance.

Stand firm, remember your police training.

As the rectangle of light through the gaps in the cellar door swelled stronger, the echoes of approaching footsteps grew louder. Groping his way forward, the officer found what he was looking for. It wasn't fear that was dragging him down, it was the thought of what failure might bring.

Light flooding into the darkest corners of the room, he was half expecting to see the flash from a gun barrel. It never came. Instead, the moment the cellar door burst open a new figure emerged.

Was this his executioner?

As Walker's grip on the knife handle tightened, a new surge of adrenaline coursed through his veins. It would need to be decisive, and he was close. Now within easy striking distance, he still refused to rush it. Unsure of what he'd walked into, his assailant spun sharply to face him.

Now's your opportunity!

Lifting the steel tray in his good hand, Walker flung it hard against the cellar wall. The sound it made was deafening. Startled, his assailant ducked and instinctively protected his face.

'You bastard!' he screamed.

As Walker's body uncoiled, he lunged out at him with the knife. It was his sole line of defence. His only chance of survival. As darkness came and went, the two men were locked in mortal combat. Then, through the mist of uncertainty, his assailant lashed out with his fist. Walker was beyond caring now, and the moment the blade sank deep into the man's face, his opponent lurched back in agony.

'Fuck yoooou—'

Still keeping his distance, Walker dropped to his knees. The pain in his arm was excruciating, and his body felt on fire. Half expecting his assailant to rise again, he caught the glint of the knife. Embedded into the man's eye socket, he was clawing at his face and screaming in a desperate attempt to stem the blood flow.

It wasn't over yet.

Staggering to his feet, it was then Walker caught movement. Slight at first, then more predominant. It felt as though the whole floor was shifting, a rolling sea of motion. The noise was deafening, and the heat generated caused Walker to panic. Then down to his right, he saw what the movement was.

A conveyor belt of rats.

Thousands of them, frantically gnawing at one another in an effort to get to the bad guy. Having picked up the scent of fresh blood, nothing could stop them now.

Keep calm.

Legs like jelly, Walker drew on his reserves. Sweat pouring from his brow, he heaved on the cellar door. First the top, and then the bottom bolt slid into place. As the door sealed firmly shut, all the while the pitiful screams of his assailant could be heard. Lashing out in a hopeless attempt to stave off the inevitable was futile. As more rats joined in the melee, the sound they made was terrifying. Thousands of them, gorging at flesh and eating him alive.

Then silence.

Only the scurrying of tiny feet.

Exhausted, Walker tried to think positively. In what had been a fight to the death, he'd somehow managed to survive. But it was close. Too close, and as fear gnawed at the pit of his stomach, he stared at the trek ahead. There were twenty-nine steps to the cellar landing. He'd counted them. Every single one. He also knew, in the back of his mind, that his captors had a nasty habit of springing surprises. They were good at it, and the end if it came would be decisive and swift.

Now perfectly still, he felt movement around his legs.

A bumping sensation.

Peering down, he discovered that several rats had followed him through the open cellar door. Teeth punctured his thigh, and he lashed out at them with both hands. As the small, confined chamber exploded into a violent frenzy, the high-pitched squealing slowly began to subside. The risks he'd taken were enormous, and his thoughts were all over the place.

Gaining in confidence, he began the long, arduous ascent up the long flight of stairs. His lungs spurting their protest, the slightest mistake and he would pay for it with his life.

He was aware of that too.

On reaching the cellar landing, he grabbed the door handle and gave it a gentle twist. It creaked, then opened. Holding his breath, he peered into the black abyss.

Six doors. Only one would lead to freedom!

Chapter Forty-Three

He thought he could smell burning, then caught the stubbed-out cigarette butt lying in an open ashtray. The hallway felt damp, draughty, an uninviting place of uncertainty. Now running on adrenalin and fear, Walker checked the first door he came to.

It was locked.

Not daring to breathe, he tiptoed along a dimly lit hallway. Cringing at every step, the sound of creaking floorboards sent shivers down his spine. He wasn't alone. That much he knew. There were others, and they would kill him without hesitation.

The next door opened, and he warily poked his head inside.

The room had an eerie feel, high ceilings, oak panelled walls, and a smattering of Persian rugs closely scattered around the floor. The air stank of cheap aftershave, and a strong whiff of stale garlic that clung to his throat like a million bad nightmares. Above a large open fireplace hung Salvador Dali's surrealist masterpiece *The Persistence of Memory*.

Instantly drawn to it, he stared at the melting clocks as if time had stood still. It was strange how the mind worked, as he imagined himself standing in the painting. Like the handles of the clocks, everything was dreamlike.

Slowly at first, and keeping his eyes peeled, he inched his way forward. The next room he came across was spacious and rectangular. It had small and multi-paned windows at the rear emanating a claustrophobic atmosphere. Unsure of where he was, or which part of the building he was in, Walker vaguely remembered being dragged here in the middle of the night. Injected with drugs, the abuse and punishment they'd meted out to him was indescribable. He would never forget the face of the man who had beaten him to within an inch of his life. A cruel and brutal individual who was void of all feeling.

There were four of them in total, and all of them evil. Apart from the Poacher, he feared the Albanian more than anything. A puny man in his mid-thirties, with a detestable cocksure manner he loathed vehemently. He always dressed snappily and walked with an invincibility as if fear wasn't part of his vocabulary.

Two more doors?

Walker crept forward with grim determination and pushed on the penultimate door. It opened, and he went through. His eyes adjusting to the dark, like some frightened nocturnal animal, he found he was standing in a room full of medical supplies. Strange, he thought. These morons were inhuman, they did not do empathy.

He heard a floorboard creak followed by voices. It was coming from another part of the building. To his left somewhere. Walker took a deep breath before moving along a passageway – a dark satanic tunnel which appeared to lead to nowhere. The next thing he felt, as he pushed through the exit, was the blast of cold air in his face. It felt pure, comforting, a feeling he'd never experienced before.

Above the rooftops and beyond an open courtyard, he made out the distinct orange glow of city lights. There was a remarkable unnerving familiarity about his new surroundings. Unsettling, which caused him to panic.

Slowly at first, he clawed his way along a dimly lit alleyway. As darkness slid away on two sides, at the end of a long narrow underpass he could see his path to freedom.

It couldn't be. Surely not?

As the terrifying truth emerged, Walker found himself standing in the middle of Gosforth High Street – a place he dared to call home.

Physically and mentally shaken, nothing seemed real anymore. Uncertainty gripped him, and the thought that he was stepping into another nightmare was difficult to dismiss. Everything was jumbled up. Even his mere presence here seemed in question. As thoughts drifted back to a deeper sense of horror, he relived the terrifying sounds of the cellar's feeding frenzy. Tears welled in his eyes, and he wanted to cry out and tell the whole damn world that he was a free man.

Walker pushed on. Towards the shaft of light.

His breathing now shallow, his heart was racing so fast that he thought it was about to explode. Then he noticed the stationary marked patrol car. Tucked back in one of the side streets, he imagined the officers were asleep. They weren't, of course. The moment they spotted him standing in the middle of the road, they were out of their vehicle in a flash. Nothing had prepared Walker for this, and for the first time in weeks it felt as if God was finally looking down on him.

With barely an ounce of strength left in his body, he tried to move his feet. They were stuck, solid, and he could not find the energy to lift them. The next thing he noticed, after opening his eyes, he was lying in the back of an ambulance with paramedics standing over him. Everything was a blur, but Walker was beyond caring now. As he drifted into a false sense of security, he suddenly sat bolt upright.

Was this a dream?
Had his captors taken on a different guise?

Chapter Forty-Four

Jack Mason was sitting in his kitchen watching TV and eating breakfast cereal when the news of Ellis Walker's escape came through. Picking up his car keys, he closed the front door and could barely contain his emotions.

First, he phoned Rob Savage and instructed him to organise a rapid response team and meet him at the Freeman Hospital. Next, he rang David Carlisle, and brought him up to speed. He knew it was a longshot, but if Ellis Walker did have anything to say he wanted to be the first to hear it.

Squinting against the low sun, Mason put his foot down and joined the steady stream of southbound traffic. How many people would know about Ellis Walker's reemergence? Few, he imagined. From what he could gather, in the early hours of the morning the undercover officer was found wandering the streets of Gosforth after being held captive in a four-story gable end property there. Picked up by two fellow police officers, he'd been rushed to Freeman Hospital. The details were incomplete, but more importantly, Mason knew that Walker's life was now in grave danger. These were dangerous times, and the first mistake could be their last.

Keeping Ellis Walker alive was Mason's number one priority, and there were two trains of thought running through his mind. Either Walker had come in from the cold or he was trying to link up with Edward Coleman again. There were other possibilities, of course, but he quickly dispensed them from his thoughts.

On reaching the outskirts of Newcastle, the traffic was moving at a crawl. As he swung onto City Road, it was now at a standstill. Speed was essential, and switching on his blues and twos he watched as the traffic pulled over. He loved this city but driving like a maniac was always fraught with dangers.

His car speaker crackled, and he turned the volume up.

'Yes, Sue.'

'Ellis Walker has been transferred to intensive care. Ward 18,' Carrington said.

'Roger that. Do we have any more details as to what happened exactly?'

'The two officers who picked him up say he was running a feverish temperature. The hospital suspects blood poisoning.'

The line went quiet.

'Who's with him now?' Mason asked.

'The same two officers who went with him to the hospital. Fingers crossed he pulls through, but I'm told it's not looking good.'

'Blimey. That's all I need to know.'

'Anything I can do, boss?'

'Yes. I've instructed Rob Savage to throw a protection screen around the hospital grounds and to check all visitors. You might wish to talk to hospital security. See what plans they've put in place, and check with central control. If the press gets hold of this, it will be blown out of all proportion.'

Mason swerved as he narrowly missed a crazed cyclist who seemed intent on getting himself killed.

'You okay, boss?'

Mason swore, 'Just some brainless idiot.'

'You were saying?'

'Ah, yes. This needs to be managed discretely. If it ever leaks out that Walker is an undercover officer, then the whole operation will be blown into the stratosphere. Let's get Sandy Witherspoon involved. Once she gets her teeth into the story, she's bound to make her mouth go.'

'What should I tell her, boss?'

'Inform her we're holding Walker on a murder charge. It needs to sound convincing, so tell her he's refusing to talk.'

'I'm on it.'

'And another thing,' Mason said, as he turned into the hospital grounds. 'These people won't give up on Walker now. Once they find out where he is, they'll want to finish it. Whatever you do, make sure security is watertight.'

'How do you propose to stop them?'

'Once we get the OK from his doctors, he'll be moved to a secure ward.'

'And Ed Coleman, what are we doing about him?'

'No doubt counterintelligence will deal with that side. Before we go rushing into things let's see what the state of play is at the hospital. Then we can formulate a plan.'

The moment the chief inspector stepped into the hospital reception; he held his warrant card up against the Perspex screen.

'DCI Mason, I'm looking for Ward 18.'

'Intensive Care is straight along the corridor, sir. Second turning on your right.'

He pocketed his warrant card and took off at haste. It wasn't far, and he soon spotted the two police officers standing guard. Both unarmed, they still looked a formidable presence.

Seconds later, a doctor appeared from a side door carrying a stethoscope slung loosely around his neck.

'I'm here to see Ellis Walker,' Mason announced, in a well-practiced authoritative voice.

'And you are?'

'DCI Mason, Northumbria Police.'

'I'm afraid Mr. Walker is in no fit condition to see anyone right now. Is there anything I can do?'

'Is Walker conscious?'

'Unfortunately, not. He is heavily sedated.'

'The minute he pulls round, I'll need to speak to him. It's important. In the meantime, I must warn you that Mr. Walker is a dangerous criminal and must be treated as such. Are you people aware of the "bed watch" procedures?'

'Yes, we are.'

'Good. Your patient will be put under twenty-four-seven police supervision from now on. I'm sorry for any inconvenience, but we need to consider your patient's and staff's welfare.'

The doctor looked tentative.

'Yes, of course. Mr. Walker is currently in a side ward, so I'll pass that information on to hospital security. I'm sure they'll want to get involved.'

'They already are.' Mason handed him a business card as he weighed up his options. 'If Walker pulls round, you're to contact that number.'

'May I ask what Mr. Walker has done?'

'We need to question him about a murder enquiry we're investigating. That's as much as I can tell you.'

His phone pinged and Mason checked the display.

It was Rob Savage confirming the heavy brigade were sitting in the hospital carpark and awaiting further instructions. The sergeant sounded anxious, as if ready to jump into action.

Turning his collar up, Mason went with his gut reaction hoping the rest of the pieces would fall into place.

Chapter Forty-Five

Jack Mason had left the house a little later than usual that morning, having arranged to call in on the forensics team. After days spent trying to establish who the latest victim was, he was hoping to hand the case over to another murder squad. It wasn't to be. Hair and fibre found from the recent murder scene, were a perfect match to those found on Samuel Jackson's body.

Now facing an uphill struggle, it was shortly after 10:30 when DCI Jack Mason walked through the station's reception. With barely enough time to grab a coffee before addressing his team, he was feeling the pressure. He read a summary of his latest findings and answered questions. Everyone present was now up to speed, but it would be some time before they knew who the victim was.

'What's the latest on Ellis Walker?' asked DC Carrington.

'He's stabilised, I'm told, which in hospital speak means he's critical. Having tortured him to within an inch of his life, Walker is suffering from septicemia. It's a serious bloodstream infection and can become life-threatening if not properly treated.'

The young detective screwed her face up in disgust.

'What kind of monsters would do that?'

'Make no mistake,' Mason countered, 'these people will stop at nothing.'

'It would seem so,' said Carrington, shaking her head in revulsion.

'Any more news on the four-story property in Gosforth?' the chief inspector asked.

'Forensics' are still over there, boss,' replied Savage. 'It could take a while.'

'What about CCTV footage?'

'From what we've recovered so far, two men are of particular interest to us. Both were spotted hanging around the property, but the images are grainy so we can't make a positive identity. The problem is there's hundreds of hours of footage to get through, so it could take a while.'

'If the timing fits, these could be prime suspects,' Mason acknowledged.

'True,' Savage murmured.

Mason watched as Carlisle studied the timeline and jotted something down. Wearing a casual white open neck shirt, jeans, and Nike black trainers, he looked more like a premier football star than a criminal profiler. But outward appearances could be deceptive, and this cool cookie was extremely good at climbing into other people's minds.

'Whoever's responsible for this latest killing clearly has a Jekyll and Hyde mentality,' the profiler began in his usual laid-back manner. 'Most psychopaths are ruthless manipulators who will go to extreme measures to get what they want. But there's a distinct pattern about this latest killing that demonstrates a clear-cut ruthlessness.'

As the room hung onto the profilers every word, Mason paused in thought. If he felt his protection operation was going to solve his problem with Ellis Walker, he had another think coming. He'd seen it before. Over, and over on the dead victims' faces.

The profiler drew breath.

'The person who killed this man has a deep sense of gratification in conducting their punishment, and that is worth keeping in mind. As for Ellis Walker, the challenge of torture and interrogation is to obtain precise and credible information.'

Mason mulled over the facts.

'What's their next move, do you think?'

'I'm sticking with my original theory. Whatever these people are looking for is of the utmost importance to them, and Ellis Walker holds the key.'

'Hence SCD7's involvement,' said Savage.

'I would say so.'

'In which case how come SCD7 haven't paid Walker a visit?'

'They have, besides adding another layer of security to the hospital grounds. Make no mistake, the next twenty-four hours are critical.'

The room fell quiet again.

'Where does that leave us now?'

The profiler looked at Mason quizzically. 'You've lost me, Jack.'

The chief inspector stretched his legs as he stood. 'Now that Walker is back on terra ferma, isn't it up to counterintelligence to sort out the rest of the operation?'

'I'm still not with you.'

Mason turned sharply to face them. 'Nine months ago, Special Branch received a tip off that an audacious diamond heist had taken place, and their number one priority was to find the mastermind involved. Given an elaborate cover story, a little-known undercover officer was able to earn himself a prominent position inside Ed Coleman's camp. Now here's my problem,' Mason said, tapping the crime board with his pen. 'When the Dutch police found Terrence Baxter's body in an Amsterdam flat, Walker's fingerprints were all over it.'

'You're not suggesting that Baxter's murder is down to Walker, surely not?'

Mason sucked in the air through clenched teeth. 'Our sole purpose was to find Walker and bring him in for questioning. Now in safe hands, it puts a whole new slant on the operation.'

Savage leaned over as he spoke. 'Yeah, but we still have three murders to resolve.'

'That's true.'

Carrington looked at Mason, her face full of unease.

'It's my guess this case will run in parallel, boss. Besides, we've yet to establish if Walker has uncovered the Schiphol mastermind's identity.'

'Sue's right,' Carlisle chipped in. 'This case has a long way to run. Had it not, the Metropolitan police would have made dozens of arrests by now.'

'Okay,' Mason shrugged. 'Maybe I'm reading this all wrong.'

Coffee and biscuits arrived, and the chief inspector made a beeline for the plate before Rob Savage got his grubby hands on them. Thinking this through, he could not have picked a more resolute team; it felt as if a huge weight had lifted from his head as everyone around the table rallied round.

'What's the latest intelligence on these insurance claims, Sue?' asked Mason.

'I've been doing some digging around and found two more boxes still without claims. Initially I thought there were two, but after comparing them against the Lufthansa flight manifest, I discovered four were registered to the same company.'

'And the name?'

'It's an address in Switzerland, but that's as far as the system will allow me to search.'

Savage leaned over and grabbed a fistful of biscuits, just as Mason predicted he would. The man wasn't greedy, he just never ate breakfast.

'It's my guess that valuables were not in every box, and three of them are dummies.'

'Do we know who the end receiver was?' asked Carlisle.

'A safe storage lockup in Istanbul.'

Everyone looked at one another.

'Coincidence or what?' said Savage, slumping down in his seat. 'If we can't trace the box owners, and security arrangements won't allow us to uncover their contents, we're pissing against the wind.'

Carlisle raised an eyebrow as he glanced across at Mason. 'In which case, how come the Schiphol mastermind knew which flight the diamonds were on?'

'There you go,' said Savage, pointing to the timeline. 'Which means the gang had an insider working for them. Surely the Dutch police must have known that too?'

Mason rounded on him. 'Unless counterintelligence is withholding vital information then someone else must have known what's inside the boxes. If not, we have a mole in our midst.'

As the meeting wore on, they had covered a lot of ground, which pleased Mason immensely. Hopefully, he'd get his interview with Ellis Walker and establish how much the undercover officer knew about Baxter's murder. Above all else, he was keen to establish why Samuel Jackson had boarded the same overnight North Sea ferry as Ellis Walker, and if they were working together under Coleman's instructions. If so, why did Samuel Jackson stopover in Amsterdam and not return home with Ellis Walker? No doubt Sandy Witherspoon would want to make her mouth go, but he'd deal with that later. Once he had more facts.

As the meeting ended, Mason's phone buzzed in his pocket.

It was the doctor he'd spoken with at the Freeman Hospital. It wasn't good news.

Chapter Forty-Six

Jack Mason had kept his media statement short that morning. All the national television networks were present, many of them running live bulletins. Having spoken earlier with Christopher Sykes, the chief inspector was hoping the sleazebag journalist might stir up a hornet's nest. As usual, Mason gave little away. Confident the public's insatiable demand for answers might offer a response on his latest victims movements, he was hoping for better news. It was a big ask but sometimes you got lucky.

Wearing a black mohair suit, white button-down shirt, and red polka dot tie, he entered the operational command room at Police Headquarters in Ponteland and felt a cold shudder of excitement. Along with the chief constable, there were fifteen senior officers present that morning. Many he knew, others he'd never seen before. He presumed at least one of them was Special Branch but could not be certain.

Taking up the last available seat, he opened his briefing notes and placed them on the table in front of him. Having spent most of the previous evening going back over the case files, he'd done his research.

Prepared for every eventuality, he lifted his head. 'Apologies for the lateness. I've just come from a press meeting on Operation Wizard.'

The chief constable smiled at him. 'You might explain why Ellis Walker has been charged on suspicion of murder?'

Mason scooted his chair up and readied himself.

'Certainly, sir. I'm keen to protect the officer's identity.'

'You've certainly achieved that. The latest feedback suggests you've been overly enthusiastic.'

Crikey, Mason thought. Was another stiff rollocking coming his way?

'Until Walker recovers, treating him any different to other murder suspects might raise suspicion,' Mason continued. 'Besides, we are able to run a twenty-four-seven protection operation around the officer, which has allowed us to take back control.'

'You did the right thing, and without your quick thinking I doubt this operation could have continued.'

Strong praise, Mason thought. Especially coming from a member of Special Branch. At least he had one ally, which was more than he'd bargained for.

The moment the room lights dimmed, Alison Jefferson, Head of Control, and power-dressed for the occasion, moved towards a large dropdown screen covering the rear wall. A brief silence followed as Jefferson fiddled with her laptop.

'Good morning,' Jefferson said, her voice even more cordial than her smile. 'For the purpose of this briefing, if anyone does have any questions, could you please raise them at the end of the session. So, without further ado, I'm pleased to hand you over to Officer Robert who is to give a brief update.'

Right first time, Mason thought. Intelligence officer was a working title not a rank. Not only that, but Robert also wasn't his real name, just a fictitious nom de plume to safeguard his identity. He watched as the officer turned sharply to confront them.

'Thank you, Alison. Just for the record, according to his doctors I'm pleased to confirm that agent Walker has had a restful night.'

As the room fell silent anticipating more, none was forthcoming. Instead, an image popped up on the screen, and the officer pointed to it. 'For the purpose of the session, image 26G on the screen is of Terrence Baxter. Known to law enforcement agencies throughout Europe for his connections with the Turkish Mafia, up until recently Baxter was part of a large international diamond smuggling organisation. Trading in uncut gemstones across six known continents, they are stolen in Africa and smuggled into China for cutting and polishing. It's a slick operation; once in their finished state, the diamonds are then shipped to the Middle East through a network of middlemen and sold in the high-end jewellery market.'

As Mason took notes, a second image flashed across the screen.

'Image 21G on the screen is of Mustafa Davala, a notorious member of the Asif family with strong connections to corrupt politicians in the Grand National Assembly of Turkey. Earlier this year, both he and Terrence Baxter had arranged to meet in the departures lounge at Istanbul's International Airport in connection with a large catchment of uncut diamonds which had been stolen in the Schiphol Airport heist. Unbeknown to them, Turkish intelligence had managed to access Encrochat, an encrypted platform used by the smuggling gang, and were listening in. As many of you will know, on the day of their meeting Baxter was allegedly killed in a Jihadi suicide attack and declared dead at the scene.' The officer paused for effect. 'Having pulled Baxter from the airport carnage, the Turkish Mafia did an exceptionally good job of faking Baxter's death. Within weeks of the incident, he was back up and running again. Only this time operating out of a safe house in Amsterdam's world diamond centre.'

A third image now popped up on the screen.

'Prior to his meeting with Mustafa Davala, we now know that Baxter was involved with this man: Halil Altintop, a multi-millionaire arms dealer living in Oman with strong criminal links to Europe. Altintop is now of major interest to us. Well-known in the Middle East and throughout the African continent for his illegal arms dealings, particularly with small right wing opposition groups, Altintop has more recently been in discussions with Boko Haram. The group is a ruthless Islamic terrorist organisation with tentacles spreading into other global terrorist factions.'

The noise levels heightened, but the officer was in no hurry. Concise in his deliberation, his authoritative voice seemed to resonate around the room. As another new image popped up on the screen, this time a monochrome silhouette, an unexpected intensity hit the room.

'We are keen to speak with this man who is known only to us as G47.' Robert paused to take another sip of water before continuing. 'G47 has an interesting background, and travels under many guises. Known at the ABN bank in Amsterdam as Thomas Hector Williams, he poses as a successful businessman who frequents the bank at least once every year. Described as mid-fifties, of average height, he brandishes a US passport and speaks with an American accent. We also know that both Baxter and Mustafa Davala were in secret discussions with G47 over the same shipment of uncut diamonds stolen during the Schiphol heist. But that's only half of the story as we now believe that G47 is the mastermind behind the whole operation.'

It was a lot to take in, and Mason was frantically scribbling down notes as fast as Officer Robert was delivering them.

'Where is this heading?' said Robert, pointing to a new image on the screen. 'Seven months ago, Covert Human Intelligence Sources (CHIS) uncovered that top secret government documents were going missing from an undisclosed government research lab. As part of a joint operation with the Dutch Intelligence people, we now know that Halil Altintop was heavily involved. Shipped to Turkey in the holds of airline jets, when the Schiphol diamond robbery took place, we believe a number of security boxes containing key military documents were also stolen in the raid. Believing them to be rightfully his, Altintop wants them back. The problem is, we now know that Baxter's arranged meeting with Halil Altintop may have cost Baxter his life.' As the noise levels heightened, Roberts moved towards the whiteboard.

The officer continued. 'In his quest to recover the stolen documents, Altintop is using a team of professional hitmen which centres around this man. Anton Sericov. The fact remains, the stolen documents are still out there. Should Sericov and his team succeed in their mission, I fear it could have devastating consequences on our current Western defence capabilities.'

As more of the plot began to unravel, Mason felt he was travelling back in time – to his days with the Metropolitan police. But this was far more serious than anything he'd encountered before.

Within seconds of the room lights coming on, Officer Roberts slipped discretely from the room leaving everyone in no doubt as to the seriousness of the situation. There would be no Q & A session: counterintelligence were not in the business of discussing matters of national importance. That much was clear.

After coffee and biscuits, it was obvious to Mason that the chief constable had already been in discussions with counterintelligence over the stolen plans. Even so, there was a new buzz in the air, and for once Jack Mason felt an integral part of it.

'What do we know about this professional hitman called Anton Sericov, sir?' asked one of the senior officers.

The chief constable pointed to the whiteboard as he spoke. 'Anton Sericov goes under several aliases and is regarded by the Home Office as extremely dangerous.'

'Sericov's background, what do we know about that?' another asked.

'Code-named *The Poacher*, we believe Sericov may have links to these damned Russians.' The chief constable pointed to one of the bullet points outlined. 'This obviously shifts the emphasis from an operation of protection, to one of seek and destroy.'

'How do we intend to go about it, sir?' asked Mason.

'Our part in the operation is threefold. To assist in uncovering G47's identity, recover the stolen diamonds, and bring these wretched perpetrators to justice. Our secondary mission is to assist Special Branch in recovering the stolen documents, and in doing so prevent a dangerous international arms dealer from weakening our Western defences.'

'Do we know what these plans entail exactly?'

'All I can say is they involve a new type of sophisticated intelligence computer system which is aimed at combating long-range military satellite-controlled drone attacks.'

'A dangerous outcome if in the wrong hands.'

'Indeed. But that's CDS7's main concern. Ours is to stop Sericov and his associates from continuing with their current reign of terror.'

'Is there an outlined strategy, sir?'

'I was coming to that,' the Chief Constable replied with a smile. 'These people already form a major part of a murder investigation, but the way we go about our daily business will be vastly different from now on. The rules of engagement have changed, and as such we are now covered by the Anti-terrorism, Crime and Security Act 2001 – and I'm sure everyone's aware of what that entails.'

'What about our links with Special Branch, sir?' asked Superintendent Collins from the counter terrorist division. 'How is that going to work?'

Alison Jefferson explained. 'A joint committee at top government level is currently looking into home security. This means the main thrust of our operations will be channelled through Special Branch. However, owing to recent events surrounding agent Ellis Walker, we intend to set up a small specialist enforcement team spearheaded by DCI Mason.'

'That's understandable. What about support and back up?' another asked.

'Good point, Roger. For that we'll need to organise two rapid response units, each to be provided and run by Area Commander Gregory and Dick Black from 'C' Division. Naturally, we'll need to work in collaboration with our Dutch counterparts in Amsterdam. In other words, all future communications will need to be channelled through either me or DCI Mason.'

'One further question, if I may,' said Area Commander Dick Black from 'C' Division. 'Does that mean all temporary leave will be suspended?'

'I'm afraid so,' the Chief Constable replied. 'We need to be fully committed in our approach. Not only that, but I'm also keen to expand our enquires into this goddam mole who seems to have infiltrated our ranks – but more on that later.'

Fired up by his new role, Jack Mason could hardly contain himself. In a nutshell he was proud to be working alongside British Intelligence officers again. This whole operation had turned on its head, including three gangland murders. Carlisle had been right all along, having deduced it wasn't diamond's these people were after. No wonder SCD7 were involved.

He left the meeting with a new spring in his step. His first port of call would be to arrange an interview with Ed Coleman, and he was looking forward to that. No doubt the area commander would be displeased, to say the least, but there was nothing the old sod could do about it anymore.

Chapter Forty-Seven

Shortly before 06:00, Jack Mason and a small team of armed officers had surrounded a holiday chalet five miles northwest of Warkworth. Working on a tip-off that a male fitting the description of the latest victim had been spotted in the vicinity, he was here to follow it up. Not only that, but a red Nissan now standing on the holiday chalet driveway had been captured on camera hanging around Samuel Jackson's council estate.

Having conducted a cursory sweep of the area, from the outside, the chalet looked deserted. If someone was lying low behind closed doors, they were in for a massive surprise. Through the general hum of anticipation, Mason heard Rob Savage's voice as he gave out instructions to cover the rear of the property.

The moment the lead officer stood back from the front door and shouted, "POLICE!" Mason's nerves were on edge. Keen to secure the property as quickly as possible, if there were clues to be had then contamination was a crucial factor. Touch nothing, he had instructed everyone. Secure the building and nothing else.

Seconds later they were inside and going through every room. The air smelt stale, made worse by all the windows being shut. Whoever had occupied the property had walked out as if they had no intentions of ever coming back.

'Building and rooms secure,' the lead officer reported.

Mason nodded as he studied the chalet layout, a spacious timber-built building more akin to a logger cabin than anything. Not wanting to disturb a potential crime scene, he ordered the teams to stand down and join him outside on the veranda. Met by George Cohen, the senior forensic officer present, he was fully kitted out in his white forensic suit, gloves, and overshoes.

'Anything of interest?'

'No bodies, George,' Mason jested, 'just a sink full of dirty dishes.'

'Left in a hurry then.'

'It would appear so.'

'They'll have left something behind; they usually do.'

Mason turned sharply to face Cohen. 'I'm looking for a name, George. Something to get my teeth into instead of this "Cabbage Field Man" the press is calling him.'

'Bloody nicknames,' Cohen protested petulantly. 'Whoever dreams them up must be sick in the head.'

'At least it tells you where the body was found.'

The officer's stare hardened. 'The name smacks of a character out of a children's book. It's enough to scare the living daylights out of your kids.'

He looked at Cohen and smiled. The senior forensic officer had a dry sense of humour, unlike Tom Hedley who could be taciturn at times. A newcomer to the team, Cohen was proving to be a good officer. Well over six feet, his hair had a mixture of grey and black, swept back at the sides and accentuating a high forehead.

Mason grumbled, arched his back, and stretched his legs from the cold damp morning air. He hoped the lab team would be able to produce a DNA match. If not, something that would lead them to the victim's identity. He walked over to Peter Davenport the forensic photographer, who was busily snapping away at the interior of the red Nissan Note.

Davenport lifted his head as he spoke. 'What date is it, Jack?'

'Twenty-fifth. Why?'

'That is interesting. There's a petrol slip here for the twenty-second. Whitehall service station. That's near Bradford if I'm not mistaken, close to the M62.'

'Could be, it certainly needs bagging and tagging as evidence. Has anyone checked the reg?'

Davenport gave him a look as though his intellect had been challenged. 'According to DVLA the owner died six months ago. The vehicle was sold at auction to a secondhand car dealer in Rotherham three weeks back; there is a team out talking to them.'

'Riding on false plates, was it?'

'Not this one. It's legit.'

Mason grimaced. 'That makes a change.'

'I know, but whoever drove it here isn't around to tell us how he acquired it.'

'We need to get Road Traffic involved.'

Still without a name, Mason was hoping the public might come up trumps. His latest victim's movements had not gone unnoticed by one eagle-eyed Channel 5 viewer, who had directed them to the property. It wasn't a million miles from Ed Coleman's mansion, he thought. He suspected foul play. No doubt the Newcastle mobster had his stamp on it but proving it would be difficult.

He examined the Nissan's boot, then checked the front wheel tyre treads. There was evidence of wear to the outer edge, suggesting the alignment of the vehicle was off. He made a note of it and peered at the back passenger seats. Sold at auction to a secondhand car dealer in Rotherham three weeks ago, whoever had driven it here would not be difficult to trace.

He turned to face Davenport.

'Instruct the South Yorkshire police they are dealing with a potential murder case. I want this Rotherham secondhand car dealer gone over with a fine toothcomb. We also need any ANPR sightings of the vehicle.'

'Will do, boss.'

As he strolled to the front of the vehicle, Roy Savage joined him looking decidedly upbeat.

'Found anything?' asked Mason.

'I've just been talking to a guy who thinks he may have spoken to our victim.'

'Oh. And what did he tell you?'

Savage shook his head dismissively. 'Turns out he's curious as to the large police presence and asked what we were doing here.'

'And what did you tell him?'

'That we are working on a murder enquiry and trying to establish the victim's identity. Could be a coincidence, but the man who was residing here had enquired about Ed Coleman in the local village pub.'

Mason's ears pricked up.

'When was this?'

'A few days ago.'

'How far is Coleman's place from here?'

'Not more than twenty minutes away.' Savage gave him a hapless look. 'I know what you're thinking, but it has nothing to do with this Anton Sericov fella.'

'Really?'

Savage screwed his face up. 'Once we know who the victim is, we'll know which way the wind blows.'

Mason smiled fleetingly. Everything was up in the air. They were close. He sensed it, and it wouldn't take much for all the pieces to fall into place.

The sergeant gave him a puzzled look. 'If he was staying here, how come he ended up at Poppy Field Farm with his brains blown out?'

'Whoever killed him obviously knew where to find him. Why, is there a problem?'

'Nah.' Savage shrugged. 'Just trying to get my head around it, that's all.'

There was nothing more to be done here, not until forensics had finished their sweep of the area. As the two detectives sauntered back to the incident truck, Mason's attention was drawn to the **red Nissan Note**. Their latest victim had been followed; that much was obvious. Taken to a place of execution and dumped in a cabbage field in the middle of the night. But why Poppy Field Farm?

Chapter Forty-Eight

He could not explain why, but David Carlisle's instincts were telling him that something fishy was going on. Either Ed Coleman was committed to assisting Special Branch in uncovering the Schiphol mastermind's identity, or he was participating in a massive cover up. Jack Mason thought he was but had no evidence to support it. What Ellis Walker knew about G47's identity was also a matter of conjecture. Ordinarily, the profiler would have made his mind up long before now, but far too many obstacles were muddying the water. Whoever the mastermind was, he was able to move in and out of society at will.

Another theory was that Terrence Baxter was in bed with the Russians. Not everyone believed that story, not after counterintelligence had confirmed a contract killer handled at least two of the recent murders. Moreover, Carlisle had always claimed that diamonds were not the real motive behind these senseless killings, and his theory had been proven correct. But never would he have imagined that sensitive military plans were at the bottom of this. That thought had not crossed his mind. It was obvious that Terrence Baxter had brought about his own downfall and had paid for his treachery with his life.

Carlisle put his mug down and sat back. What had started on the tarmac at Schiphol airport had spilled onto the streets of Newcastle. This wasn't cold-blooded murder anymore; this was an international showdown.

'Any luck with your Swiss investigations?' the profiler asked Carrington.

She shook her head in disappointment.

'No. Nothing. Even the computer experts aren't having any success. The key to cracking the problem lies in a fifteen-digit encrypted code, without which there is no way of accessing the system.'

'I suspect we may never know who the end receiver was.'

The detective glanced up at him and frowned. 'So, where are the documents?'

Carlisle smiled. 'Walker holds the key to that, I'm positive. What is going on in his mind and how he's coping with his recent ordeal is another matter. I'd imagine he needs counseling once he pulls through.'

'There's an awful lot resting on this officer's shoulders,' said Carrington, 'which is scary when you think about it. What happens once SCD7 have finished debriefing him?'

'I doubt Walker knows everything, Sue.'

'Yes, but these people obviously believe he does, or they would never have kidnapped him.'

'It's my guess that if he makes a full recovery and he's mentally up to it, Special Branch will want him back in the field again.'

'What! After all he has gone through?'

'That's what makes undercover operatives tick. They thrive off the adrenaline rush. It's like a drug to them, and they're always on the lookout for their next fix.'

'There's a bit of that in all of us, I suppose.'

Carlisle smiled, but for once remained silent.

'What does your gut feeling tell you?' she asked.

He lifted his head as he spoke. 'When I worked for the special crime unit many years ago, I could not get enough of it. But age creeps up on us and you're no longer the person you once used to be. Reflexes become sluggish, minds less sharp, and you're constantly putting yourself in danger because of it. It's an undercover officer's nightmare. The longer you continue to fight it, the more vulnerable you become. It's a fact. The older we get the harder it is to stave off the inevitable, I'm afraid.'

'Jesus,' Carrington laughed, 'you're beginning to sound like an old man.'

'Less of the old,' Carlisle countered.

Despite their age difference, Carlisle still felt butterflies in his stomach every time he was close to her. Carrington was a strikingly attractive woman, and they got on well together. They'd spent a romantic weekend away together several months ago, but after that...nothing. He'd thought about it often enough, but the risks were enormous, and your professionalism could quickly be called into question. Forming a close relationship with a fellow member on the team was a no-no as far as Carlisle was concerned. He wished he could be together with Carrington, as he found her incredibly sexy. But that meant losing other people's trust, which was the last thing he wanted. After all, he was Jack Mason's consultant.

He leaned over and tapped the keyboard, calling up a group of video files.

'What are you looking for?' asked Carrington, quizzically.

He pointed to the screen. 'This so-called "Cabbage Field Man." I've been studying the video clips taken in Amsterdam. If I'm not mistaken, the facial images are an uncanny match to the stills from Border Control.' He turned to Carrington. 'What's your opinion, Sue?'

The detective leaned over to take a closer look.

'It certainly looks like him. Same height and build, and his facial features are remarkably similar. We should run it through our facial recognition system.'

'I already have, and it's not coming up.'

She looked at him oddly. 'Whoever he is, Coleman must know him.'

'I would imagine so.'

'Have you talked to the Chief Inspector at all?'

'Not yet I haven't, as I was looking for a second opinion.'

Carrington looked at him through narrow eyes and gave him an affectionate smile. 'That's terribly noble of you, David.'

He put his mug down and sensed his sexual desires surfacing.

'What else do we know about him?'

Carrington smiled coyly. Eyes alert, fingers flicking through the pages of her case notes, she stopped at the desired page.

'We know Baxter struck a private deal with the arms dealer Halil Altintop to buy the stolen drone documents back. But something obviously went wrong, and Baxter ended up with his throat cut.'

'I was thinking more along the lines of Baxter's meeting with Ellis Walker at the Bovenkerk flat.'

'What about it?'

Carlisle looked at her guardedly. 'Could Baxter have double-crossed them? After all, we are dealing with notorious criminals here including the Turkish Mafia.'

'Now that you mention it, after killing Baxter, they quickly went after Walker and Jackson.'

'Those were my thoughts.'

'If true, then it suggests they were already on these people's radar.'

'Exactly. The only odd ball is the cabbage field man.'

'He's obviously part of the plot. Which part I've no idea.'

'If this is him, we know he was in Amsterdam at the time of Baxter's death.'

She swung to face him. 'Jack Mason believes the man responsible for their killings is working for the Russian Federation. If not, then the Chechen Republic. Wanted for murder by the German authorities in Berlin, Anton Sericov is believed to be a former commander of the Chechen separatist force whom the Russian state describe as terrorists. It's a cover up, of course. But what else would you expect from the Kremlin?'

'Whoever hired Sericov's services could certainly afford a million dollars.'

'So, where does this leave G47?'

Carlisle made a little hand gesture as he replied. 'I suspect our latest victim is one of Sericov's men. Executed in retaliation can only mean one thing. Whoever was in charge of the Schiphol diamond heist has finally cottoned on to these people.'

'I'm not liking the sound of that.'

'Sericov's not the sort to be messed with. Known as the Poacher, his infamous reputation amongst many crime syndicates leaves a lot to be desired.'

'You think G47 is starting to fight back?'

'I believe so. The cuffs are off, and it's my view Sericov will stop at nothing.'

'What! This is all out gang war?'

'It's looking that way.'

'Perhaps you should talk to DCI Mason about this?'

'It's only my thoughts at this stage, Sue.'

'We may never get a better opportunity than this,' said Carrington pensively. 'If G47 is striking back, it means Coleman could be working to orders. If not, he knows where the stolen documents are and that's why Sericov is at war with him.'

'That's a good point.'

She looked at him oddly. 'Who the hell is G47?'

'If Coleman's working to orders, then he must know who he is.'

Chapter Forty-Nine

Thirty minutes after the morning briefing, Jack Mason was travelling north towards the Warkworth turnoff with Detectives Savage and Carrington. As thoughts turned to Barbara, he was really looking forward to celebrating their first anniversary of living together. Having bought a bottle of her favourite red wine, Chateauneuf-du-Pape, he'd ordered flowers and planned to arrive home before the rush hour traffic build up. Never in a million years had he believed he would fall in love again. He adored everything about her. She was the perfect English rose, and her beauty belonged to a different world.

As he swung off the A1 slip road marked Warkworth, he thought about the task ahead. Most murder victims in the UK were either killed by a family member or someone they knew. But this case was different. The man he was about to interview had reluctantly turned Queen's Evidence in an operation that was causing havoc across five continents. That alone was a credible reason for Anton Sericov's team wanting him dead.

At the end of a long sweeping bend, they turned left passing many expensive properties tucked back in the tree line. Cruising slowly, he had often wondered what type of people lived here and what they did for a living. They would be lawyers, bankers, doctors, professional people with public influence; nothing like the scumbag he was about to meet. After weeks of legal wrangling with Coleman's lawyers, he'd finally been given the go-ahead, and he was prepared for every eventuality.

Turning right at the bottom of a steep hill, they were travelling in convoy now along a rutted driveway with trees on either side. Mindful of being watched, this was the closest he had ever come to the gangster's property. What sort of reception they would receive was debatable, but there would be no welcoming party.

At the end of a long driveway were two ornate wrought-iron gates. It was then he spotted the cyclops eye of the security camera as it pointed down at them from the top of the gatehouse roof. To his right, and set back in the wall, was an intercom panel. Alighting his vehicle, he pressed the speaker button and stood back.

'Yes,' the voice crackled out.

'Police,' Mason replied, flashing his warrant card towards the eye of the security camera.

Moments later the gates swung open, and they drove through in convoy.

From the outside the mansion looked enormous. Commissioned by Thomas Wessington at the turn of the 19th century, the grand entrance faced east, and included a balustraded, three storey, four-bayed central stone building. Extended at the turn of the twentieth century with flanking two-story, three bay pavilions linked by pedimented passages, he dreaded to think what the upkeep of such a building would cost.

Who said crime doesn't pay, he thought.

After a short three-minute drive he pulled up behind a silver Alfa Romeo 4C and switched off the unmarked BMW's engine. Only in rare moments like these did he question his own achievements, or lack of them. God, this was ridiculous. If he worked his bollocks off for the rest of his living days, he would never achieve this kind of lifestyle.

The man who approached them from the grand hall was a few inches taller than Mason. Built like a brick, he had a craggy face, and thinning grey hair cut short at the sides. Not a man to be messed with, Joe Angelini wore a dark cashmere suit, white open-necked shirt, and black slip-on shoes with gold studs running along their sides.

The DCI took his warrant card out and the gorilla glared at it.

'I presume you people have an appointment?' Angelini said, in gruff broken English.

'We have. We're here to see Mr. Coleman.'

'He's unavailable today.'

'I was told he was expecting us.'

Joined by Savage and Carrington, the three detectives now glared at Angelini.

'Mr. Coleman is too ill to see anyone,' the gorilla replied.

Mason looked at the others and was tempted to lay the law down but refrained from doing so. Instead, he politely said, 'I suspect your boss would prefer that he sees us now rather than cause a lot of unnecessary fuss.'

The gorilla mouthed something and pointed for Mason to follow, leaving detectives Savage and Carrington standing speechless on the forecourt. Entering the grand hall with its amazing, marbled flooring and beautiful ornate circular staircase, Mason was ushered into a palatial, beautifully furnished drawing room. The furniture was antique, Georgian, the kind only seen in stately homes. A scattering of expensive Persian rugs littered the floor, and a large bay window overlooked magnificent, cultured gardens.

'What brings you here this time, Chief Inspector?'

Startled, Mason swivelled on his heels towards the commanding voice.

Dressed in pink tracksuit bottoms, emerald, glitzy green top and matching expensive trainers, Amanda Coleman was seated at the far end of the room staring at him over the top of a glossy fashion magazine. Her eyes were clouded hazel, and her thinly plucked eyebrows were manicured into a perfectly shaped arch. From what he could see, Amanda had put on weight since the last time he saw her. Even so, she'd lost none of her vitriolic tongue.

'Your husband. I would like a word with him if I may.'

She threw her head back.

'What about?'

'We have reason to believe that one of your husband's associates is involved in a recent murder we're investigating.'

'Why not talk to him directly instead of bothering my husband?'

'That's not possible, I'm afraid. We also need to speak with your husband about it.'

Her pupils were dilating, but her tongue had lost none of its sharpness.

'You're fucking kidding me,' she screamed. 'How many times must I tell you people. If you wish to speak to Ed, you're to go through his lawyers.'

Mason stepped forward.

'I was rather hoping we didn't have to go through the official channels.'

'Tell me you're joking—'

'Not this time, Amanda.'

Still smarting, Mason felt she was giving him the full hairdryer treatment. Not a dislikeable woman, she sat in silence for a moment, staring into space and refusing to cooperate. As his eyes toured the room, the smell of her perfume was overpowering. A strong stench of lavender and rosehips.

'Don't tell me it takes three of you to deliver a simple message,' she suddenly burst out. 'What kind of police force are we fucking running nowadays?'

There was no simple answer to that.

'Is your husband at home, Amanda?'

'No, he isn't. If you must know, Ed's not been in the best of health lately and you people aren't helping either.'

Like hell, Mason thought. Having spent the past ten days planning for a race meeting in Newcastle, Ed Coleman was in far better shape than she was letting on. Not only was she quick on the uptake, but her mind was as sharp as a steel trap. Annoyed, Mason was hoping he could have managed this differently instead of having to go through this lawyer nonsense.

She glared at him again.

'Are you done here?'

'For now,' Mason replied, dejectedly.

'Good. You know where the door is.'

Angry, the chief inspector spun to squarely face her. 'There is one other thing. Do you happen to keep a guestbook by any chance?'

She flicked a strand of hair from her face. 'What is it with you people? This is a family home not a frigging knocking shop.'

'No, I suppose not,' Mason shrugged.

Half expecting her to throw another wobbler, the moment he stepped into the grand hall Joe Angelini met him. He was peeling an apple with a long-bladed flick knife as if daring him to question him over it.

Best not today, Mason thought.

Chapter Fifty

The major focus that morning was damage limitation. The story had made all the headlines and no thanks to Sandy Witherspoon, their suspect had arrived outside Gateshead police station propped up in an enormous black wheelchair. On reaching the top entrance ramp, Coleman's lawyer addressed the large media gathering and was at once showered in a blaze of camera flashlights. It was pure theatre, and the press were loving every minute.

His coffee cold, Jack Mason peered out of the office window and could hardly believe what he was witnessing. Witherspoon was making his blood boil, milking this press opportunity for every penny she was worth. Gathering his notes, the chief inspector had already decided against bringing Rob Savage into the interview room with him. The sergeant was pugnacious, and certainly no match for Coleman's quick-thinking lawyer. His best course of action was the profiler. With any luck he would bring a calming effect to proceedings besides reading into the gangster's mind.

As he left his office, Mason felt the adrenaline kicking in. The thought that the whole damned world would be watching this Oscar-winning charade had thrown him off balance. *'God help us,'* he cursed. What was she up to?

The moment Coleman entered the police station, expectation levels heightened. Wearing black Ray-Ban sunglasses, hoodie pulled low, and a large fleece blanket covering his legs, the North East's most feared gangster looked more like some star-studded celebrity than the notorious troublemaker he was.

Still making her mouth go, Witherspoon was claiming the room temperature was far too high and causing her client unnecessary anxiety. It wasn't looking good, and having been made to look a fool in front of the whole goddam police station, Mason was furious.

There was an awkward silence between them, a coming together of minds. Known as the Don, the undisputed leader of Newcastle's West End, Coleman was well respected and widely feared by his subordinates. An extremely wealthy man, having amassed vast fortunes from unlawful gambling dens spread across the region, his recent exploits into racehorses seemed the perfect fit for this mobster's palatial lifestyle. What puzzled

Mason more than anything, was the man had turned Queen's Evidence. Considering the organisation's "Omerta" – the "code of silence" never to talk to the authorities, did this mean the head of the Coleman family had finally turned his back on the criminal society? Or, as Mason suspected, was something more sinister going on.

'It's been a long time, Ed,' Mason began, trying his utmost to stay calm.

'Yeah. I've enjoyed the break.'

'I hear you've got a dodgy ticker?'

The gangster shifted awkwardly.

'They say you put Jack Henry down for life.'

Mason sat for some moments, wondering where to start. 'If you confess to killing this cabbage field man, I'll tell you all about it.'

'I don't deal in vegetables, Jack. And before you ask, I ain't got no frigging diamonds either.'

Mason held eye contact. 'It's strange you should mention diamonds, as we've recovered fifty grands worth from a flat in De Wallen. It's a red-light district in Amsterdam.'

'They were uncut I presume. If not, that's your first problem.'

'We also found fingerprints in a flat where Terrence Baxter was murdered. They belong to one of your henchmen.'

'So, what. I don't own real estate in Amsterdam.'

'We know who was involved in the Schiphol airport raid, as we have it on camera.'

The gangster said nothing, just shrugged. His eagle-eyed lawyer, meanwhile, was hanging on Mason's every word. It was all about trust, building a rapport and trying to strike an even balance. At least her client was talking, which was more than many had expected.

It was Carlisle who spoke next.

'I've been looking into your nephew's murder,' the profiler began. 'Quite a messy affair. Died from asphyxia and loss of blood. They say he was—'

'Who the fuck is this?' Coleman said, thumping the table with his fist.

Carlisle held eye contact. 'I'm sorry.'

'Who are you, I asked?'

'I'm here to make sure you don't overstep the mark.'

Eyes cold and piercing, the gangster's gaze was intense. If nothing else, Carlisle's clever ruse had certainly left the gangster pondering.

'You must be intelligence then.'

'I could be a lot of things, Ed.'

Witherspoon intervened.

'Perhaps you might tell us who you are, Mr. Carlisle.'

'Think of me as a good Samaritan,' the profiler insisted. 'I'm here to help you find Samuel Jackson's killer.'

Coleman's eyes remained expressionless, staring across at him as though still undecided. The gangster drummed the table with his fingernails as he spoke. 'Let's be clear about one thing here. Whoever killed Sam is not fit to walk the streets of Newcastle. That's how I see it, and unless you people can convince me otherwise the man will get his comeuppance.'

A stony silence befell the room. Only the sound of the heater fan clicking.

'Whoever killed Sam also murdered Terrence Baxter,' Mason said quietly.

'Hold it right there,' Coleman's lawyer demanded, as she wagged a finger at Mason. 'I thought we'd agreed to talk about Samuel Jackson?'

'We are, and I was coming to that.'

'So, why bring Baxter into this?'

Carlisle leaned forward and lowered his voice. 'These killings are far closer to home than you think. I'm no gambling man, but it's my guess it won't be long before these people come knocking on your client's door.'

'Which people are these?'

Mason felt his throat tighten. 'I thought Ed might tell us that.'

The gangster's posture stiffened.

There was no easy approach, and Mason was struggling to impose his authority. But there were some situations, like the one he was taking part in, where an opponent's reaction was the giveaway.

'Don't frig me,' Coleman replied. 'If anyone dares so much as to put a foot across my doorstep, I'll blow their fucking brains away.'

'Which people are these?' Mason asked, repeating the lawyers question.

'What the fuck?' Coleman grunted.

The chief inspector smiled as he watched the gangster's every twitch. Seconds later the profiler leaned over and slid a monochrome image towards Coleman as he spoke. 'We're interested in this man, Ed. Do you know who he is?'

'No comment.'

'Strangely enough, the day before yesterday he turned up at the coroner's building.'

'Why not talk to him direct?'

'We would if we could,' the profiler answered, 'but he was there for his own post-mortem.'

'That's your fucking problem, not mine.'

'But is it?' Mason said, sliding another monochrome image across the table towards Coleman. 'This is him again, only this time much closer to home. Do you recognise him now?'

Coleman drew back, unease showing in his glances.

'No comment.'

Mason shrugged. 'If I'm not mistaken your nephew was in Amsterdam around the time this photograph was taken.'

'No comment.'

'Well,' Mason frowned, determined to turn the screws even tighter. 'Look carefully and you will see he has a birth mark behind his left ear and a scar above his left eye. The funny thing is the day before yesterday someone took a dislike to him and put a 9mm slug in his head. The word on the street is these people are stepping up their game.'

Witherspoon lifted her eyebrows a fraction.

'That's preposterous and you know it. My client has nothing to hide, nor any information on these people. Perhaps you should start by telling me how you came by these images?'

There was much to talk about, many unanswered questions, and here they were on the backfoot. Not a good start, Mason thought. They were digging a bloody big hole for themselves, and Coleman's lawyer was enjoying every minute of it.

'This works both ways,' Carlisle said, pointing at the images. 'We're concerned for your client's safety, and without a name that makes our job much harder.'

Witherspoon threw him a guarded look. 'Who are you working for, Mr. Carlisle?'

'Whoever these people are, they're not welcome in our country.'

'I'll ask you again,' Witherspoon insisted. More forcefully this time. 'Who are you working for?'

She was good. Too good, Mason thought.

The profiler drew back in his seat and clasped his hands on the table in front of him. Annoyed, Mason caught the anger in his colleague's stare. He knew what he was trying to achieve; it was all about getting under the suspect's skin. It was a battle of wits, and Witherspoon was playing devil's advocate at every opportunity.

Carlisle sucked in the air. 'I can't force you to name these people, but what I can say is, your client's life is now in grave danger.' The profiler tapped his finger on the table as if to emphasize his point. 'This isn't a game these people are playing, rest assured. They're working their way through a list. One at a time. They'll not stop now until they get what they rightfully believe is theirs.'

'And what might that be?'

'Who knows. You tell me.'

Witherspoon's brow corrugated. 'That's not relevant, as I still don't know what your role really is.'

The profiler drew back in his seat.

'In which case I've nothing more to add.'

Blimey, Mason thought. What was Carlisle thinking of? Then, out of the corner of his eye he caught the hesitation in Witherspoon's glances.

'Hold it right there,' Coleman said, wavering his lawyer aside. 'What's in this for me?'

'Your life,' Mason bluntly replied.

Coleman sat stunned. 'Don't fuck with me. What is it with you people?'

'It's not a threat Ed,' the profiler said calmly. 'It's a fact.'

The Newcastle gangster managed a wry smile as he leaned forward in his wheelchair. 'You're so full of crap. Talks cheap. Me... I'm all for a simple life.'

'I don't doubt it,' Mason cut in, 'but your inner circle isn't exactly choir boy material. We have it on record, and in any court of law the evidence will be hard to swallow.'

'Are you calling me a liar?'

'It's your call, Ed.'

Coleman stared at them petulantly. 'What assurances do I have?'

'There is another reason we don't believe you, but right now we're not willing to share that information.' Mason stared at Coleman hard. 'It's not looking good.'

'What are you implying?'

'There are those who think you're snitching on them. Shitting on their nest to cover your own back.'

'Yeah, but it's all down to this crap agreement I signed with you people. It ain't worth the paper it's written on. Let's not beat around here, what is it you people want?'

'A name, Ed.'

Witherspoon put her pen down. 'Meeting over,' she said, angrily.

'Any reason?' asked Mason, looking directly across at her.

'Not until I know who your friend here is.'

Once the chief inspector had revealed Carlisle's role, things calmed down a tad. In what had been a tense standoff, Coleman leaned over and whispered something in his lawyer's ear.

'My client wishes to know why you think he knows who these people are?'

'The fact is three murders have been committed, and they all point to your client's doorstep. These people have a bee in their bonnet, and that worries me. The odds of them walking away empty-handed is zero, and no copper works with those odds.'

'What are you suggesting, Chief Inspector?'

There was mistrust in her eyes. But that's all it took with Witherspoon; the slightest doubt and the long knives were out. That's how criminal lawyers worked. Unless you had all the facts, they'd turn the screws on you.

It was Carlisle who reacted next.

'There's two ways of looking at this. If you do not know this man's identity, then we've no further business here. If you do, a deal can be struck.'

All eyes turned to Coleman, and silence fell upon the room.

'It's simple,' the gangster replied. 'The guy overstepped the mark. That's as much as I'm willing to tell you.'

Mason steadied himself.

'Is this the same guy who killed Terrence Baxter?'

'How the fuck would I know? I wasn't there. Baxter was a shit. You of all people should know that.'

'Double-crossed you, did he?'

'Who said he did?'

Not wishing to press the matter, Mason felt a surge of relief. Convinced it was one of Sericov's men whose body had been found dumped at Poppy Fields Farm, was Coleman locked in a gang war? With no further mention of Ellis Walker, the chief inspector wasn't keen on the idea of pressing the matter. Knowing Walker may wish to work for the gangster at a later stage, there was always the risk of endangering his cover story. It was a strange old world. Had Rob Savage been present, then things may have turned out differently. The profiler had done an excellent job. They'd opened a few new possibilities and uncovered a potential killer.

Witherspoon peered down at the pile of documents on the desk in front of them. Avoiding eye contact, she spoke in a low whisper.

'You know my client's position.'

'Indeed, we do.'

'Good. At least we understand each other perfectly.'

Mason sat back thinking, but not saying. *Really? We're not finished with this little shit yet!*

Chapter Fifty-One

They were seated at a corner table in Sambuca's, an Italian restaurant in the Watergate Building on Newcastle's Quayside. There were much trendier, upmarket, restaurants they could have gone to that night, but this was where they'd spent their first evening together after Barbara had moved in with him. Besides, the food was fabulous, and the staff were always friendly, especially Thomas, who had found them a great corner seat overlooking the River Tyne and the bridges.

It was now nine o'clock. The restaurant was lively and every table in the house was occupied. He recognised the regulars, but the majority were total strangers. City people, Friday night revelers out for an enjoyable time. Who could blame them? The food was reasonably priced, and the Peroni amongst the finest kept lagers in town.

'I'd like a pink gin and tonic please,' Barbara said.

The floor waiter turned to Mason.

'The usual for me, Thomas.'

After another hard-fought day at the office, Mason was looking forward to a relaxing night with Barbara. It had been ages since they'd last had a meal out together, and he'd thought about this moment for days. Having agreed not to mix work with pleasure, they'd settled for a night of fun and frivolity – whatever frivolity entailed.

Barely a mile from Gateshead police station, trying to ignore work was impossible these days. He'd tried it before, but it never worked. Picking up the menu, Mason's mind drifted back to the five o'clock team briefing.

He'd tasked Sue Carrington to investigate the seedier side of Anton Sericov's background. He knew she was deft with computers. Intelligence gathering was the team's lifeblood, and without it they were nothing. What had intrigued him more than anything, was execution-style killings. Particularly close-range shootings. This latest slaying certainly fitted that category – death in a warehouse with a single bullet to the head. But who pulled the trigger? Believing Ed Coleman was solely responsible, he'd asked David Carlisle to check through his private database in the hope it might throw up a name.

Rob Savage was a completely different animal, of course. Tasked with trawling through every public house in Warkworth was right up the sergeant's street. Bars always hosted a different type of clientele at night, and those within a five-mile radius of the holiday chalet might unearth a few useful nuggets of interest. Not that he was expecting any, but the sergeant had an uncanny knack of uncovering the impossible.

Mason glanced at the menu and asked Thomas to give them a few more minutes. Still undecided, he didn't fancy the Calzone pizza and was erring more towards the Spaghetti alle Vongole. A dessert was out of the question, not whilst drinking lager. Besides, they always rested heavy on his stomach and indigestion was the last thing he needed tonight.

God, he felt racy, and Barbara was looking simply stunning. Dressed in a low-cut silk blouse and Gucci black trousers, she appeared far too upmarket to be working as a physiotherapist. The most beautiful woman in Sambuca's that evening, his partner was blowing his mind.

'What do you fancy, Jack?'

'Later, my love,' he winked.

She laughed. 'Is that all you can think about?'

'It is when you are around, my love.'

She pretended to huff, but he guessed she was as excited as he was.

'I'm stuck between the Cannelloni and Spaghetti alle Vongole.'

'Snap,' Mason chuckled. 'I was thinking of ordering that too.'

'Which one?'

'The Spaghetti alle Vongole.'

Barbara swirled her drink in her glass. 'Why don't we share darling?'

Having made their minds up, they skipped starters and went straight for the main course. Every available table was full, and the queue at the door was steadily growing. Even so, he knew they would not be giving up their seats in a hurry. Not tonight, as they were far too relaxed and content with their surroundings.

'A year to the day,' Mason said, clinking glasses, 'Where does time go?'

Fixing her eyes on him, Barbara smiled and then replied, 'I couldn't have picked a better man to drag out of the gutter had I tried.'

Mason loved Barbara's subtle humour, her cute little smile, and sweet, dimpled chin. He couldn't think of a single thing he didn't like about her. He'd been lucky, of course. Had it not been for a deranged serial killer intent on taking his life, they would never have met. After four long months of painful suffering, Barbara had nursed him back to fitness again and he was forever grateful.

Thinking back, never once had Mason dreamt his partner would have agreed to them taking a long weekend break away together. Italy, Florence, where they took in the sights and got to know one another better. Nothing serious, as their first few months together had been more a lasting friendship than real love. But they had so much in common, so much to talk about and share. They'd now reached that point in their relationship when past secrets had begun to unfurl. They both carried baggage for sure; Mason having suffered far more than his fair share of problems over the years. Barbara was a good listener, though, and that's what had made all the difference.

He finished his lager, hailed the floor waiter, and ordered another round of drinks. He was beginning to relax and enjoy himself when his phone buzzed. He let it ring out; if they wanted to find him that would not be too difficult. All this cloak-and-dagger stuff was supposed to have been gone long ago, but it was slowly creeping back.

Fresh drinks arrived, and Mason checked his phone. When he didn't recognise the missed caller's number, he chose to ignore it.

'Is that the new dating site?' Barbara joked.

'You wish,' Mason replied. 'Scam mail more like.'

Barbara locked eyes with him. 'Strange you should say that, as I had a call from Amazon the other day claiming there was an issue with my account.'

'I hope you didn't give any details away.'

'Of course not. I told them my partner was a big strapping police officer and if there were any problems with my bank details, they should talk to him.'

Mason burst out laughing.

***

The two of them were the last to leave the restaurant that night and were so caught up in each other's company that neither realised that everyone else had left. Mason had lost count of the number of drinks they'd had, but as he stumbled into the back of the waiting taxi his wallet was a hundred and twenty pounds lighter.

It was still warm outside, and for one brief inextricable moment the world was moving in slow motion. Not that he cared that three Barbaras were sitting beside him in the back of the taxi that night, he loved every one of them to bits. The moment he felt the warmth of her body snuggle up to him, his heart raced. He kissed her soft tender lips, touched the graceful curve of her neck, and drowned in her beautiful dark blue piercing eyes. This wasn't a dream: this was right now.

As the taxi pulled away from the Quayside, thoughts slowly drifted to a warm king size bed. Barbara was lying naked beside him, and a night of mind-blowing sex was about to kick off. *God, he wanted Barbara so much.*

How much longer was this journey going to take?

Chapter Fifty-Two

Mason listened to a voicemail that had come in earlier. It was the chief constable, and he seemed in good mood by the sound. According to the latest feedback, Ellis Walker was planning another trip to Amsterdam. It was the breakthrough they'd been waiting for, and confirmation their officer was now back in the business of intelligence gathering. Things would be different this time. Vastly different. There was a mole in their midst, and they were determined to weed them out.

He was about to give Inspector Jansen a call when there was a sharp rap on the door, and Rob Savage sauntered in.

'Tried to contact you last night, boss.'

'Oh, what time was this?'

'Around eleven.'

Mason lifted a heavy head. 'What can I do for you, Rob?'

'This holiday chalet geezer you asked me to investigate. He was seen sniffing around Coleman's property shortly before he was bumped off.'

'Spying on the place, do you think?'

'It would appear so.'

Mason thought about it. 'What else did you find out?'

'He's Middle Eastern by the sound.'

Mason took another sip of his coffee and tried to shake off a stiff head. Savage loved to exaggerate and given half the chance would have made a great children's author. There would be some truth in his reporting, but most would be bar talk. Hunches were an important part of police work, but it had its drawbacks. People jumped to conclusions without bothering to examine the facts. It was a common mistake, and before they knew it, they'd subconsciously selected the evidence that best fitted their hunch.

'Not just hearsay?'

'Nah, he was definitely caught sniffing around Coleman's property.'

Mason frowned. 'It sounds like the gangster may have the documents. If not, then why go after him?'

'I can't stop thinking about this holiday chalet the perp rented. Why there? Why so close to the gangster's property? He was asking for trouble if you ask me.'

Mason thought for a moment.

'There's been a new development. Ellis Walker is about to head over to Amsterdam on Ed Coleman's instructions.'

Savage perched on the edge of Mason's desk as he spoke. 'Don't tell me Inspector Jansen has finally woken up? I've never met anyone like her.'

Mason filled him in about a counterintelligence sting to trap the mole, along with Ellis Walker's latest feedback. Things were moving along nicely.

'What about this G47 guy? Has Walker mentioned anything?'

'No, but this Amsterdam trip could have something to do with it.'

'Let's hope you're right.'

'Who knows, it could lead us to the documents.'

'It's a pity we didn't interview Walker before Special Branch got involved. Whoever this G47 is, he certainly knows how to cover his tracks.'

'The trouble is, he's still out there.'

The sergeant scratched his head. 'Yeah, and trying to organise another diamond heist, no doubt?'

'If he is, then SCD7 will be onto it.'

'You're right, they don't miss much.' Savage drifted into thought. 'Why's Coleman sending Ellis Walker to Amsterdam? Is it to link up with G47, do you think? The last time he was there he was kidnapped, so there must be good reason for him going there.'

'I'll talk to you later about that, Rob.'

'When?'

'After my meeting with the area commander.'

Savage looked at him oddly. 'Mind, ever since Gregory was put in charge of an armed response team, he spends most of his time running around like a headless chicken.'

'Out of sight, out of harm,' Mason chuckled.

'The man's a bloody menace if you ask me.'

'Now, now.'

Savage screwed his face up. 'What's the profiler's views on this Amsterdam trip. Has he said anything yet?'

'He believes it has something to do with unfinished business.'

'Nah. He may be good at profiling, but he knows naff all about how crime organisations work.'

Mason raised an eyebrow as he stared back at him. 'He did say diamonds wasn't what these people were after. You must give him credit for that.'

'Nah. He's far too laid back. He gives me the creeps every time he stares at me.'

'I'd be careful,' said Mason in enigmatic tones. 'He could be reading your mind...'

'Sod off.'

Mason laughed.

'I know he comes across as reserved at times, but he's as solid as a rock.'

The moment the sergeant left the room, Mason opened his laptop to check on Amsterdam flights. If Ellis Walker were booked on tomorrows overnight ferry, the chief inspector would need to team up with Inspector Jansen. It was time to put aside their differences. If the undercover officer were back in the fray, no doubt counterintelligence would be keeping a watchful eye on proceedings.

He heard the familiar connection, then a solid click.

'Inspector Jansen, how can I help?'

'You sound bright and cheerful this morning,' Mason jested. 'How are things over in clog city?'

'Everything is fine. What times your flight in the morning?'

Mason sat bolt upright in his seat. 'Who told you I was coming?'

'We're not a Mickey Mouse outfit, Chief Inspector. We know Ellis Walker is due to land here the day after tomorrow, and plans are being put in place.'

Mason looked at his laptop as he spoke, 'I'm on the first flight out of Newcastle.'

'Easy Jet or KLM?'

'KLM. Why?'

'Good. I'll be in the arrivals lounge to pick you up.'

She ended the call, and Mason gathered a few papers in preparation for his meeting with the area commander. He still had a lot of catching up to do, including a summary report on his recent meeting with Ed Coleman. If the gangster was engaged in a tit-for-tat killing, he had a lot of explaining to do. But that would come later, once he had established the purpose of Walker's visit to Amsterdam.

Chapter Fifty-Three

As the cabin crew prepared the aircraft for landing, Mason gathered his personal belongings. Knowing Ellis Walker was booked on an overnight ferry that night, it meant the undercover officer would dock at the Ferry Terminal in the early hours of the following morning. No doubt his every movement would be monitored, even down to the equipment interface and contact calls he made. He knew also that covert human intelligence sources (CHIS) were engaged in gathering potential external threats, whilst SCD7 were monitoring the gang's encrypted chatter lines for the latest updates. No stones unturned, he mused.

As the plane docked with a bump, Mason waited for the seatbelt signs to switch off before moving towards the exit door. His mind on the task ahead, he ran back over the key elements again – Walker's safety, surveillance updates, and any potential hot spots.

The moment the cabin doors opened, he instinctively moved into detective mode. The weather seemed mixed, but that was the least of his worries.

***

An hour later Mason was standing in a large open briefing room inside the main Crime Division building in Amsterdam Centrum. A few officers he knew, including Peter van der Vleuten the SOCO who he had met at the Bovenkerk flat. The team had grown considerably, and Inspector Jansen was eager to introduce them to him.

The moment Commissioner Cruyff entered the room, everyone stood to attention. Dressed in a smart police uniform and carrying a baton under his arm, he signalled them to be seated before taking up position behind a tall Perspex lectern. Not the easiest man to deal with according to fellow officers, Cruyff had an abrupt manner and could be annoyingly obnoxious when it suited him.

'Good morning, ladies and gentlemen,' the commissioner announced, in a gruff authoritative voice that resonated around the room. 'After months spent monitoring Charlie Alpha's chatter lines, I'm pleased to announce that we are finally ready to strike at the heart of the Altintop crime organisation. People who threaten our national security understand their illicit activities may attract attention. To thwart anyone intercepting our highly sensitive plans, we are working closely with our friends at the Dutch intelligence services.'

The Commissioner paused to take a drink of water, and you could have heard a pin drop. It was a strong turnout. And many of those present were senior officers from specialist national crime units, which meant the operation had stepped up a level.

Cruyff turned to a flip chart and pointed to it.

'Thanks to British Intelligence and their current dealings with rogue splinter groups, I'm pleased to confirm that "Operation Morning Breeze" will commence at 05:00 tomorrow morning. With that in mind, could you please break into your respective groups to finalise your individual strategies.'

Every crime puzzle required thousands of pieces of information, but once the green light was given, there would be no turning back. This type of operation was fine-tuned and required precise timing. It was all in the detail, choosing the right moment and employing the element of surprise.

Mason continued to watch their reactions. Only a select few were aware that a mole was in their midst – a dangerous double agent who SCD7 were eager to take out. It was a no brainer as far as the chief inspector was concerned, and the longer this person was free to go about their business, the more operations would come under threat.

Gathering his thoughts, Mason mulled over the facts. What had started in a Bovenkerk flat had suddenly turned into potentially one of the biggest international operations he and the Northumbria police were likely to experience. The atmosphere was strained, and every seat in the hall was taken up. The moment he was introduced to a small select group of people he'd be working with, he swiftly felt part of it. It was a huge operation and as a bigger picture emerged, his excitement levels heightened. Outwardly he was keen to get going, but inwardly he still had a few reservations.

Jansen explained in more detail.

'We've recently acquired some interesting feedback from Alison Jefferson who is Head of Control at Northumbria police headquarters. It concerns CCTV footage we've obtained from a GoPro camera which confirms Sericov, and his so-called associates are here in Amsterdam.'

'Are you aware of this man?' another officer asked Mason politely.

'Yes, we know all about him,' he dutifully replied, 'and that Sericov's sole mission is to recover stolen military documents for a man called Halil Altintop.'

'Good.' Steven Brinkman nodded, a stocky, clean-cut, red-faced detective sergeant from

Amsterdam's special ops division. 'What about Alison Jefferson, do you know her?'

'Not personally, but we've met on several occasions,' Mason acknowledged. 'She runs an intelligence unit at police headquarters in Northumberland which deals with the more serious crime.'

'Excellent. At least that clears another issue up.'

Mason was aware of the reputational risks of working alongside the Dutch special ops division, but also knew he was not the only UK representative present that morning. There were others, including British Intelligence officers – the faceless men in grey suits.

'Do we know where these people are residing?' asked Mason.

'They're here in De Wallen and currently booked into the Hotel Ambassade,' Brinkman acknowledged. 'We also know that late yesterday afternoon they hired two **rental cars**, and we've managed to attach satellite tracking devices to both of them. MIVD are currently monitoring their movements, so wherever they go we can keep a track of them.'

Jansen addressed the team.

'Ellis Walker is the only person who knows where the military documents are, and that's what our operation strategy is based on.' She lifted her head towards Mason as she spoke. 'It all makes sense when you think about it. Once

Walker lands on Dutch soil, it's up to us to keep abreast of the situation.'

'Sounds like a plan,' Mason smiled.

'It is,' Jansen acknowledged, 'and this time the bad guys have taken on more than they can chew.'

Brinkman shuffled awkwardly, and Mason noticed the change in his tone. 'We understand that British Intelligence are shadowing Walker as far as the ferry port terminal. That's when our group will take over. Knowing Walker's vehicle and phone are also fitted with tracking devices, it shouldn't be too difficult to keep tabs on him. If anything should go wrong on the ground, we do have a bird in the sky.'

'What could possibly go wrong?' Mason replied, wryly.

Jansen smiled. 'Over here in the Netherlands we have a saying. To stop a small problem from becoming a large one you keep your finger in the dyke.'

Still smiling, detective Brinkman turned to face Mason.

'Our task is to stay close to Ellis Walker. Once he leads us to his place of contact, only then do we move in.'

'Do we know when and where that is?'

'Nobody at ground level knows that, only central intelligence.'

Mason considered this. Was this part of the plan by British counterintelligence to catch the mole at their game? It seemed logical, and there would never be a better opportunity than this.

Mason looked at his watch. 'What time do we gather in the morning?'

'There's a team briefing at 04:30,' Inspector Jansen acknowledged. 'I'll be in your hotel reception lobby around 04:00. May I suggest you get your head down. Tomorrow is another long day, so we need to be on our game.'

Mason nodded in agreement, knowing full well that would be impossible.

Chapter Fifty-Four

Ellis Walker hesitated as he entered the church of Our Gracious Lady Amsterdam. Daylight breaking, fear clawed at his skin, and the mere thought of being taken prisoner sent shockwaves down his spine. It was 06:00, and the chaos inside his head was building. Firearms were ill advised, especially in a place of worship. But these were dangerous people they were dealing with, and there would be no room for error. The only thing that mattered to Walker was to recover the stolen documents. Once those were back in his possession, he could settle his account with the Poacher. It wasn't the best way to deal with this. He knew that. But it was the sole reason for his wanting to continue with the operation. Deep down, he had so much hatred towards this man that nothing would get in his way.

A door latch clicked, and a puny figure emerged from the nave. Something wasn't right. He sensed it. Forced on the backfoot, Walker watched as the priest clung to the shadows and took up a hostile stance. He stepped forwards and caught a whiff of his aftershave.

'What is it you want?' asked the priest.

'I'm here to see Father Jagaar.'

'About what may I ask?'

Walker considered this.

'It's a private matter.'

The priest appeared tense, as though he didn't belong in a church. Dressed in a long black cassock, the shoes were the giveaway, along with an expensive Omega watch that no priest could afford. Whoever this imposter was, he was no man of the church.

'That's not possible,' the priest replied. 'Father Jagaar is unwell. If you must speak with him, you can do that through me.'

There was something sinister about this man's appearance. Something that rested uncomfortably on his mind. Walker wasn't daft, and he'd mentally prepared himself for every eventuality.

'I'm here to partake in the Holy Sacrament,' Walker replied.

The man stared at him confused. 'Holy Sacrament?'

'That's when you and I both pray in total abstinence.'

'Ah. Yes. But first we must talk.'

Walker drew back as he stepped from the shadows towards him.

'Who are you?'

'I'm new here,' the phony priest stammered. 'Father Jagaar did warn me to expect you, and I knew you were coming,'

'Did he now?'

'He did. He said you were here to collect a package.'

The silence was more frightening than any reply. He was lying. He'd never once contacted Father Jaager, nor had he seen the priest since the night he was kidnapped. Who was this man who dare call himself a man of God. Anger welled in Walker. This was no priest, this was his Albanian jailer. A man he loathed vehemently.

'Where's Father Jagaar?' Walker demanded, reaching for his gun.

The Albanian made a desperate lunge at him. But the undercover officer was quick. Too quick, and swiftly brought him to ground.

'Move another muscle and I'll blow your fucking brains out,' said Walker, pressing the gun barrel hard against the imposter's temple.

It all came flooding back. The relentless beatings. The waterboarding. The amputation. This miscreant had repeatedly set about him. The man was a monster.

As the rage inside him built, Walker pressed the cold steel barrel hard against the Albanian's temple. It was a tense moment, but Walker had been wired shortly before leaving the ferry terminal and knew they'd be listening to his every word. Soon backup would arrive, and that gave him some comfort.

Walker heard footsteps approaching and froze.

He recognised the shuffle. The distinct gargling sound he made in the back of his throat when about to mete out punishment. No more, he told himself. How dare this man think he could hide his identity and carry on as he did.

As the Poacher stood tall, there was nothing but rage in his eyes.

'It's over,' Walker shouted. 'This place is completely surrounded.'

'So what?'

'Take another step forward, and I swear I'll blow his brains out.'

'Go ahead,' the Poacher replied calmly. 'He's expendable.'

Walker drew on his inner reserves. He faltered as the Poacher mockingly stared across at him and slumped into the shadows. He was testing his resolve, whilst all the while the Albanian was desperately struggling to break free of his grip.

Show weakness and it will all end here.

Walker sucked in the air and prepared for the inevitable.

Two shots rang out, followed by silence.

Chapter Fifty-Five

The moment they heard gunshots, Inspector Jansen's team moved swiftly forward and into position. Whatever had erupted inside the church of Our Gracious Lady Amsterdam, the outside was surrounded by a solid cordon of steel. Jack Mason was worried: the sole purpose of his being here was to protect a fellow police officer.

Then three more shots rang out.

Annoyed at the lack of response, Mason put his shoulder against the door. Seconds later, he was inside with two Dutch police officers in close pursuit. Entering the gloom, the vestry had an eerie feel. To their left was a door, and their right an archway leading to another part of the building. Creeping forward, detective Brinkman signalled them to follow. Nerves jangling on edge, Mason flattened himself against the chapel wall. He waited for several seconds before moving down a long narrow aisle. It was dark inside, and the air stank of fresh cordite and a mixture of candle grease that hung in the back of his throat.

Was this a trap?

Mason took a deep breath as he prepared to unleash his own idea of hell. Not thirty metres away, a lone figure emerged from behind one of the large stone columns. There was resentment in his eyes, bitterness, and he was pointing an automatic rifle at them.

Mason ducked, instinctively, just as a hail of bullets tore over his right shoulder.

'POLICE!' Brinkman yelled. 'Drop your weapon, you're completely surrounded.'

Not a religious man, Mason never felt comfortable carrying a firearm in a church, let alone discharging one. As he peered towards the high altar, he reluctantly unclipped the holster strap and wrapped his fingers around the butt of his trusty 9mm Smith & Wesson. It felt good suddenly, like greeting a long-lost friend after months of separation.

'POLICE…' another armed officer called out.

The answer came in a hailstorm of bullets, this time sending fragments of sandstone dangerously close to his position. It was a tense standoff, a moment of sheer madness. Crawling forward on all fours, the chief inspector signalled his intentions to the other two officers. Now within firing range, barely ten metres in front of him he could hear spent cartridge cases pinging off the cold stone floor.

The next thing he saw, after changing his position, was fast flickering shadows coming from his left.

'He's heading for the belfry tower,' someone shouted.

For one brief moment in time, dozens of armed police officers flooded into the building from every conceivable direction. Still holding his nerve, Mason instinctively ran towards the open door with Brinkman hot on his heels.

The space felt hollow, uninviting, as if they shouldn't be there. To his front, and running from left to right, was a stone spiral staircase. Dimly lit, a heavy rope handrail was attached to the outer wall, as if offering added stability. Brinkman tugged hard on it as if to check the tension. Now working blind, together they climbed the stairwell. Eyes peeled ahead, and following in his footsteps, they moved through the gloom with caution. As his grip on the Smith & Wesson tightened, he turned to his fellow officer.

'Hear anything?'

'No. Nothing,' the Dutch detective acknowledged with a nod.

His back close to the wall, Mason continued to lead the way. The light wasn't good, but on reaching the upper floor a single shot rang out. He tensed, then eased the door open with his foot and caught sunlight pouring through stained glass leaded windows. There were dozens of places to hide, but still they pushed forward.

Cursing the light, together they worked their way through the belfry tower. Creeping forward, the minute he stepped onto the wooden trap door his pulse quickened. Peering through gaps in the joints where the light was shining through, his mind was thrown into turmoil. *Crikey,* Mason thought. What was a sixty-foot sheer drop to the transept, he was staring death in the face. Not one for heights, he prayed to God it wouldn't give way. All those nights in the pub, an over-indulgence in fast food, thoughts turned to Barbara. If only he'd stuck to his diet as she'd advised him to do.

As another short burst of shots rang out, this time to his right, Mason caught the cry of pain. The next thing he saw was Brinkman dropping to the floor. Torn between halting and pressing forward, he was now caught in two minds.

Eyes rolling in sockets, blood gushing through fingers, Brinkman pointed towards the open rooftop door. It was then Mason caught movement. Thirty metres away, halfway along a narrow parapet, their adversary was working his way towards the lip of a steep overhang. There was nowhere back from there, apart from a sheer drop and the hard city streets below.

Surely this madman wasn't trying to escape.

Edging his way forward, the chief inspector moved out and onto the roof. Police running across street corners, sirens blazing below, he now found himself the centre of attention. *Don't rush it,* Mason kept telling himself, *you're good at this.*

Continuing to edge closer, not daring to look down, he soon found himself caught out in the open. Sweat pouring from his brow, the fear swirled in the pit of his stomach.

Not twenty meters away, his adversary was goading him to step closer. He froze, then watched as a police helicopter rose and fell from behind a tall building opposite. The noise it made was deafening, but that wasn't all. As the distance between them closed, it was then he realised who his assailant was. It was the man they feared most. Anton Sericov the notorious "Poacher."

Bold as brass, Sericov was perched on the end of a narrow ledge and beckoning him to step even closer. No way, Mason thought. **This was pure madness, and he shouldn't be here at all.** Looking down, he could see his trouser leg had snagged in the gutter, causing his whole body to lock solid.

What the hell are you doing here?

Slowly at first, he slid his leg backwards and unsnagged himself.

'Give yourself up,' he shouted.

The Poacher adjusted his position as he turned.

'Frightened of heights, are we?'

THE POACHER'S POCKET

In what seemed an eternity, Sericov lifted his automatic rifle and made a strange gurgling noise in the back of his throat. Mason froze. He knew then the game was up. All those years on the force, and it had all come down to this. Defiant to the last, he flinched as a single shot rang out. The noise it made was deafening, but he felt no pain. Confused, there was no way a trained assassin could miss from that range. No way!

As the sound of the helicopters clattering rotors intensified, his body swayed in its downdraft. Still grappling his emotions, he opened his eyes and could not believe what he was witnessing. Arms flailing the air, legs bent at crazy angles, Sericov was plummeting to earth at break-neck speed. He heard the curdling screams, the inevitable sickening thud, then silence.

Not daring to move, Mason felt a sickening sensation in the pit of his stomach. It was over, and the man who'd dragged him through the gates of hell lay dead on the pavement below.

Faint at first, then growing louder, a voice in his head called out to him. It was then he noticed the Dutch detectives extended friendly hand. Close to his side, and propped up against the open doorway, he could see detective Brinkman. Drawn tight at the cheeks, his face had a waxlike appearance.

At least he was alive, Mason thought.

Sweat stinging his eyes, the chief inspector slowly began to inch his way along the narrow ledge and ever closer to safety. *Take your time. Don't cock this up!*

Another step.

'Not much further to go,' the reassuring voice called out.

The moment he reached firmer ground, he let out a long sigh of relief. 'Did you see that?' Mason gasped.

'See what, sir?'

'That maniac jump to his death.'

'I doubt it,' the detective replied. 'He's more likely to have been taken out by a marksman's bullet.'

His heart beating like mad, Mason flopped on his haunches in a state of utter shock. In what had been a moment of sheer madness, he'd risked his own life for the sake of the job. What was he thinking of? He hated heights at the best of times.

Still shaking, in an attempt to stem the heavy blood flow the chief inspector pressed the vein in Brinkman's arm. A few centimetres more, and things could have ended differently. He'd been lucky, but that's what policing was about. When the call to duty came, you had to respond regardless of the risks involved.

Chapter Fifty-Six

The nave was a hive of activity when Jack Mason returned to it. Not all had gone to plan. Having secured the church against further attack, the Dutch police were now in the process of securing the surrounding area. It was a large operation, as several members of the gang were still in the vicinity.

Stepping back, Mason spotted Commissioner Beekhof, a rotund, balding officer who seemed intent on questioning him over his impulsive actions. Keen to steer clear of him, Mason walked slowly towards the pulpit. *Job done,* he thought. What the hell was Beekhof going on about. Yes, detective Brinkman had been unlucky, but it was a flesh wound, and not life threatening as Beekhof was making it out to be.

Minutes later he caught up with Inspector Jansen's team as they stood awaiting instructions. It was now ten o'clock and Mason could have murdered a coffee.

'Where's Ellis Walker?' he asked.

'Walker's been taken away for questioning.'

'Was he injured, do you know?'

It was Inspector Jansen who pulled him to one side, and her expression as black as thunder. 'No, strangely enough. It wasn't easy though, as he was holding a gun to one of the assailants' heads and took some overpowering.'

'All is not as it appears,' Mason confessed. 'You may wish to speak with British Intelligence before you go pressing charges.'

'They've already spoken to us,' she replied. 'What the hell is going on?'

Mason stood in numb silence as he stared at the number of spent cartridge cases littering the floor. At least Ellis Walker was safe. But equally, he assumed the undercover officer's part in the operation was over. Once Special Branch had debriefed him, he would be whisked away with his wife and kids and given a fresh start and lifelong anonymity. That's how the British justice system worked. Most police officers never had to go through such a process and were able to return back to normal duties. But there was a mole in their midst, and if they didn't get to them soon, it would lead to institutional paranoia and paralyse future operations.

Mason thought quietly for a moment.

'What about the priest?'

Jansen looked at him oddly. 'I doubt he knew much about what was going on. Besides, these people had threatened to burn the church down if he didn't cooperate.'

Still in shock, Mason didn't warm to her answer. What if Father Jagaar knew the Schiphol masterminds identity. What then?

He turned smugly to face her. 'It seems everything's under control here.'

'I wish it were,' Jansen shrugged, showing her annoyance. 'We still have a few loose ends, and we've yet to recover the Schiphol diamonds.'

'And the military documents... are they secure?'

'I'm informed British Intelligence have taken charge of that side of the operation.'

The notion that CDS7 had everything under control, intrigued Mason. It was as if that side of the operation had been concluded well in advance. Strange, he thought. Had **Operation Morning Breeze** been used as a lure? A ruse to trap a mole? There was more to this than first met the eye. No doubt Ellis Walker had been grilled regarding his part in the affair. That much was obvious.

Jansen's phone rang and she answered it.

'It's Special Ops,' she mouthed, 'they've positively identified Anton Sericov and one of his accomplice's.'

Mason reflected as she pocketed her phone.

'Halil Altintop's men, no doubt.'

'We suspect they are. At least one of them is being held in custody, so we may get to the bottom of it.'

'I was beginning to wonder when. . .'

Jansen cut him short and could hardly contain herself. 'I'd be careful what you write in your report, Chief Inspector. The Dutch police are strict on protocol – that's how it works over here. Rushing headlong into a live operation without informing the rest of the team could have serious repercussions.'

'In which case I'll keep my report short,' Mason nodded.

He could tell by her expression that she wasn't enthused by his reply.

'Do all British police officers do crazy stunts such as running across church rooftops, or was it a knee-jerk reaction?'

'Believe me I hate heights.'

She turned sharply to face him. 'Another few centimetres and it could have been you who was making all the headlines.'

'I doubt it.'

She scowled at him but said nothing.

'It's a funny old world,' said Mason, refusing to get bogged down in police protocol. 'The next time I'll remember to keep my finger in the dyke.'

Jansen saw the funnier side and smiled.

'Let's hope that's the end of the matter...but I doubt it.'

Mason felt a sharp, sinking sensation in the pit of his stomach. Jansen knew nothing about the mole in the camp, nor of Ellis Walker's identity as a British undercover police officer. That apart, she was efficient, effective, and he wouldn't think twice about selecting her on his team.

'Let's see what forensics have to say. Who knows what surprises lay in store?'

Inspector Jansen had calmed down a tad and gave him a smile. 'Once everything's closed down here, I'll be holding a debriefing. Perhaps you might join us and give us a true account of what actually took place after you broke ranks.'

Jansen spun on heels and took off towards a group of senior police officers. It was then Mason spotted commissioner Beekhof. He was moving towards him at pace and looked like he'd swallowed a wasp. Caught in two minds, all Mason could think about was the Poacher tumbling to earth. It was over. Their number one suspect lay dead, and that was the end of the matter. What the hell, he thought. He knew he'd acted impulsively, but that was the way of the world. Even so, it was an argument he knew he couldn't win.

'How can I help, sir?'

Chapter Fifty-Seven

Gateshead police station was in full swing when Jack Mason entered the main building that morning. Whilst diplomatic channels were hard at work behind the scenes, Mason had switched his attentions towards the next task in hand. The Schiphol diamonds.

Things were taking shape: and the assailant the Dutch police had detained in the Church of Our Gracious Lady Amsterdam was an Albanian gangster called Roan Lucaj. Wanted in Germany in connection with two murders, he was a nasty piece of work according to Interpol. But that wasn't all. Now that Anton Sericov had been taken out of the equation, SCD7 were keen to talk to the international arms dealer, Halil Altintop. Currently being held for questioning by the Belgian police, Altintop had been caught by border guards trying to leave the country. As for the military documents he'd purloined from an undisclosed military testing facility, he was now the centre of interest. No doubt European defence chiefs would be delighted with the result, but heads would roll, and many top-secret military establishments would be faced with rigorous security reviews.

Although the evidence against Edward Coleman was overwhelming, the gangster's defence lawyers argued that having turned Queen's Evidence the case against him wasn't as straightforward as the police were making out. There were far too many loopholes for Mason's liking, and smart lawyers like Sandy Witherspoon would drive a herd of elephants through it if ever it was brought before the courts. Even so, the chief inspector was adamant the gangster had a hand in the execution of one of Sericov's gang and was determined to bring him to justice. If nothing else, at least his days as an international diamond smuggling don were over. Special Branch had made sure of that.

The moment Mason sat down with the rest of the team, his phone warbled in his pocket. It was Inspector Jansen. Father Jagaar had skipped his court hearing and was nowhere to be seen. Was there a more sinister side to the priest, he wondered. It appeared so, as the church authorities had no record that a Father Jagaar ever belonged to the church of Our Gracious Lady Amsterdam. As for the man they called Judas, nobody knew who he was.

It was beginning to sound as if another conspiracy was taking place, and the Dutch authorities were continuing to withhold vital information from them. Everyone had turned inwards on themselves, and no doubt the chief constable would have something to say about it. After ending the call, he relayed his findings to the team and sat back thinking.

When coffee and biscuits arrived, there was a strange but comfortable silence between them. DC Carrington's biggest concern was how the mafia don, Mustafa Davala would react now that Anton Sericov had been written out of the script. She'd always had her suspicions about Davala and had never wavered in her judgement. As the head of the notorious Asif family, Davala had far-reaching connections to dozens of corrupt Turkish politicians which made him an ideal candidate for the Schiphol mastermind.

'What's your take on Terrence Baxter,' asked DS Savage. 'Was he our man?'

There was an awkward silence between them, then Mason said, 'I doubt it, Rob. From what the Dutch police are telling us, they'd never considered him to be the architect. Baxter was more a go-between than anything, he knew how to shift stolen gemstones. The danger was, he had far reaching connections in Asia which is always a valuable asset to an international crime smuggling syndicate. Looking at the files, it seems Baxter upset too many people and paid for it with his life.'

'The way I see it,' said Savage, wriggling in his seat, 'when the Turkish Mafia faked Baxter's death, they were willing to set him up in the backstreets of Amsterdam. Whichever way you dress this up, if the Asif family considered him to be that high up on the diamond smuggling chain, it's worth a second look.'

'True, but we're talking fifty-million dollars' worth of stolen uncut diamonds here. Baxter was a mover and shaker; he was never mastermind material.'

Savage deflected the comment with a smile. 'So why fake Baxter's death and set him up in the backstreets of Amsterdam?'

'You raise a valid point, but it's not Terrence Baxter.'

'Then why was he murdered?'

'He was in bed with Altintop for one. As to the purchase of the stolen documents, no money ever changed hands.'

'What about the diamonds?'

'It's my view they were shipped out to China for cutting and polishing. We know Baxter visited there, and we have bank statements to that effect. Where they are now is anyone's guess, but I wouldn't rule out Coleman.'

'Nah, I'm still not convinced.'

Mason tapped the table with his pen. 'What's on your mind, Rob?'

'It's not just the stolen documents. It's my belief that someone else knew exactly what was inside the other security boxes, and it wasn't just Halil Altintop.'

'Plans in exchange for cash I would imagine,' Mason argued. 'That's why Coleman sent Walker to Amsterdam with them.'

'It's all a bit complicated if you ask me,' said Savage, dejectedly.

Mason gave Savage a sympathetic look. 'Guys like Halil Altintop have no scruples and would pay good money to get their hands on important military secrets – especially those concerning a new type of intelligence system involving drone attacks.'

'Is that why you believe G47 is Coleman?'

'Who else is in the frame, if not the gangster?' Savage flopped back in his seat.

'So, why did Anton Sericov murder Coleman's nephew?' Carlisle cut in.

Mason looked hard at the profiler. 'Something obviously went wrong the night Terrence Baxter was murdered, and neither Coleman nor Baxter could be trusted. That's why Special Branch were involved.'

Savage sat thinking. 'Do you know what, that's a bloody good point, and SCD7 would never get involved unless it concerned our national interest.'

'It makes sense,' Carrington agreed. 'But this was all about stolen military documents and had nothing to do with diamonds.'

'Not directly,' the profiler replied.

'What do you mean by that?'

'Not everyone had interests in the military plans, Sue. There are those out there who still have the Schiphol diamonds in their sights, including this so called G47.'

'The military documents are only one side of the coin,' Mason agreed, 'which is why Sericov was working for the rogue arms dealer.'

'Or the Russians,' said Carlisle.

Mason leaned overlooking anxious. 'So, who is G47?'

All eyes now turned to the profiler.

'It's not Coleman, I can assure you of that. Had it been, then Counterintelligence would have charged him long before now. So, that rules out Terrence Baxter, who we now know was sitting on both sides of the fence.'

'Who else is in the frame?' demanded Savage.

'What if G47 never existed in the first place?'

The room fell silent.

'That's a ridiculous statement,' Mason replied angrily.

'But is it?'

The chief inspector looked confused. Seldom did he question his own judgement, but the profiler was up to something, and whatever it was it had unsettled him.

'What's on your mind, my friend?'

Carlisle drew back in his seat.

'Terrence Baxter's murder was no accident, and we're all agreed on that. Which poses another question, who set the Bovenkerk flat meeting up in the first place... and more importantly, why?' The profiler turned to the crime board as he spoke. 'What else do we know about G47? Well, according to the ABN bank in Amsterdam he's known to them as Thomas Hector Williams, a successful businessman described as a grey-haired man in his mid-fifties who speaks with an American accent.' The profiler tapped the rogues gallery with the back of his hand. 'Tell me, which one of these people fits that description?'

'None of them do,' said Savage, with a shake of a head.

Mason considered this.

'So, what are we missing here?'

'What about this man?' the profiler said.

'What, the priest?'

'Tell me why not?'

'Nah,' Savage shrugged. 'It's a no brainer. The priest's no mastermind. From what I can gather, the church was being used as a safe house.'

'Rob's right,' Mason agreed. 'If it was the priest, the Dutch police would have arrested him long before now.'

'Just a thought,' the profiler shrugged.

'And a poor one at that,' said Savage, grumpily.

The profiler rallied quickly. 'But nobody knows where he is, or his network of cronies. The one thing we can all agree on is, Father Jagaar is no priest.'

Savage gave Carlisle a hard stare. 'If the priest was the mastermind, Ellis Walker would have sussed that out long ago.'

Carrington, meanwhile, had opened her case files having sat quietly listening to their exchange of opinions. Still undecided, she now drew their attention back to the rogues gallery.

'The Albanian they arrested at the church, Roan Lucaj. He certainly has an interesting history,' she said, reading from notes. 'I know he's no mastermind but having returned to Albania after spending several years in a Greek prison, within weeks of his release he was known to have played an active role in illegal arms shipments to East Asia. He's a bit of a hot head according to his prison governor and could be Baxter and Jackson's executioner.'

'Do you have any proof?' Mason asked.

'Oh yes,' she replied. 'Having checked with forensics just before the meeting, it turns out the knife wounds found on both Baxter and

Jackson's bodies are a perfect match to the knife found on Roan Lucaj during the raid on the church.'

'Can you be sure?'

'One hundred percent.'

'So, it must be Altintop's men who killed them.'

'Nice one, Sue,' the profiler said excitedly. 'It fits perfectly. The Albanian Roan Lucaj obviously gets his kicks from carving his victims up.'

Mason's interest levels heightened suddenly. 'Hang on a minute, if I'm not mistaken Halil Altintop was in talks with Ed Coleman, was he not?'

'He was,' Carrington nodded, 'and that's what got me thinking.'

Mason sat back digesting this.

'Could Coleman and Altintop have fallen out at some stage. Reneged on a deal?'

Carlisle shook his head. 'That's the most likely scenario, and we know Altintop was in bed with known terrorist organisations concerning arms deals to East Asia.'

'That's another good point, and we also know that Anton Sericov only targeted Coleman's gang.'

'You're right, and we now have that proof.'

'Well, it certainly puts Coleman back in the mix,' the profiler admitted.

'Do you know what,' said Savage pushing back in his seat, 'Nothing surprises me about Coleman anymore.'

Carrington inhaled deeply. 'Yes, but did Coleman and Altintop fall out over these stolen military documents, or has someone else cottoned on the gangster has turned Queen's Evidence and is now working for Special Branch?'

Mason mulled over the facts. And yes, there was no disputing that Ed Coleman was back in the frame, but was he the architect behind the Schiphol diamond heist? Carrington had made a strong point, and they could not ignore the fact. The only odd ball was the mole in the camp. How much influence did they play in all of this? Quite a bit, he would imagine. The last he'd heard was that someone at police headquarters had been suspended from duties pending further investigations. It was all very hush-hush, but God help anyone who fell into SCD7's trap. They'd never see the light of day again.

Mason took notes, then turned to face the team.

'There's some brilliant teamwork going on here, but it still leaves us with that all-important question – who is the Schiphol mastermind? And more importantly, where are the diamonds?'

The profiler leaned over and took an image out of his case files and pinned it to the rogues gallery. 'Let's not rule this man out,' he said, with an air of confidence.

No one spoke, but the look on their faces said it all.

Chapter Fifty-Eight

Feeling upbeat, DCI Mason slid from the unmarked police car and stood for a moment. The forecast wasn't good, but that was the least of his worries. The whole area now swarming with police, he watched as a team of handpicked armed officers prepared to move on Coleman's property. They were in no hurry. Two miles east, protecting the rear entrance roads, a small group of officers were now in position. Further south and guarding the western flank, snatch teams were covering potential escape routes.

Looks good, Mason thought. If that wasn't enough, the mansion's carpark was full to overflowing. They'd never seen so many luxury cars assembled in one place, and many of them belonging to gangsters. Was this the gathering of the clans, the meeting of all meetings? Something was afoot, and whatever had drawn so many hardened criminals to Coleman's estate was now the focus of attention.

Joined by Sue Carrington and Rob Savage, they were met in the grand hall by Coleman's gorilla, Joe Angelini. Having flashed his warrant card under the pompous prat's nose, Mason breezed past him as though he'd never existed. Gangsters were fickle and easily provoked, which meant they would need to stay vigilant.

'Where do you think you're going?' a familiar voice called out.

Mason turned sharply.

Swaying on her feet, Amanda Coleman was staring at him and trying her utmost to stay upright. What a clip, he thought. Her hair was straggled, and the front of her dress was covered in vomit. Not the prettiest sight in town, Amanda could still pack a formidable punch, nevertheless.

'I'm here for your husband,' Mason said, firmly.

'You know the rules,' she slurred, slopping more wine down the front of her dress. 'Go through the proper channels.'

'Not this time, Amanda. I have a warrant for your husband's arrest.'

'Pieces of paper,' she scoffed.

'Is Edward at home?'

'Stuff you. It's none of my concern.'

The moment marked police vans pulled onto the forecourt, she struggled to come to terms with it. He knew she could be a handful, but as dozens of armed officers formed up in front of the grand entrance, she let fly with her venomous tongue.

'Who invited you lot?' she screamed.

Standing shoulder to shoulder in two ranks, the officers continued to stare straight ahead. Amanda wasn't finished yet. Furious, she staggered drunkenly towards them and fell flat on her face to howls of laughter.

'You bastards,' she shrieked.

Mason had seen enough. 'Where's your boss,' he said, turning to Joe Angelini, 'or do I tear this place apart looking for him?'

Following in the gorilla's wake, they entered in force into a palatial high-ceilinged drawing room. Walls crammed full of art, rooms dripping with expensive antiques, the place smacked of money laundering and the proceeds of major crime.

Then, through a secret side door, they moved at speed along a dimly lit corridor. Mason could hear music blasting, and it was coming from the rear of the building. As if in slow motion, the moment the room's doors slid inwards to the sounds of American hard rock band Guns N' Roses, everyone froze in their tracks.

Mason drew breath. In front of them, and in various stages of undress, dozens of gangsters were cavorting in a room full of scantily dressed young women. People were out of their heads, none of them in a fit state to think straight. His brain in overdrive, Mason stood perfectly still.

Many of these troublemakers would have weapons nearby, and it would only take a second. Fearing a mass shoot-out, the moment he turned the music down, a strange calm befell the room.

Not for long.

Stoned out of his mind, and seated in a large leather armchair, was a man in his late fifties involved in a sexual activity that left little to the imagination. Tension filled the air, as all eyes now centered on Jack Mason.

'What the fuck?' Coleman protested.

As armed police officers fanned out in silence, the chief inspector stepped forward and made his presence felt. 'Edward Coleman. I am here with a warrant for your arrest.'

The gangster gave him a weak smile as he pushed the startled young blonde from his lap. Apart from the Texan hat he was wearing, the gangster was stark naked.

'What are the charges,' he screamed. 'Screwing a dumb blonde in my own house? She's a consenting adult, God dammit.'

Mason rounded on him. 'Try murder.'

'Who let you bastards in here?'

Puzzled, the gangster glared dumbfounded across at Joe Angelini. It was a tense moment, and as more armed police officers flooded into the room, Mason moved in for the kill.

'You don't have to say anything...'

'Don't shit me,' Coleman screamed, angrily. 'You need to speak to my lawyers.'

'We already have.'

'That's bullshit!'

The stench of cannabis and sweat catching his nostrils, he was finding it difficult to breathe. As he turned sharply away, it was then Mason clocked the racehorse trainer, Kerry Waterman. Wearing a blue polo neck shirt, grey chinos around his ankles, he was desperately trying to excuse himself from the compromising position he now found himself in.

Amidst the confusion, one of the officers close by stepped forward and slipped handcuffs on Waterman's wrists. Taken aback, the racehorse trainer looked at him in stunned silence. There was more to this man than Mason first thought. Detained in an illicit drug den wasn't good, but what else was Waterman involved in? He'd lost count of the number of surprise arrests like this one. The lucky breaks. Alibies and stories unravelling after numerous interviews. Having spent months trying to uncover the whereabouts of a missing police officer, what other gems were about to unfold?

Then out of nowhere Amanda Coleman appeared.

This woman was in crazy mood, unpredictable, and could set off a chain reaction. It was a tense impasse, and before

Mason had time to warn Rob Savage, she'd already clapped eyes on her naked husband.

The gangster's face drained of all colour.

'You dumb scumbag,' she yelled. 'Who invited this piece of shit to the party?'

'Leave her out of it,' Coleman protested.

'Jesus!' Amanda screamed, picking up a heavy ash tray and throwing it hard against the wall. 'You're old enough to be her fucking granddad.'

A young female police officer stood opposite ducked as another expensive ornament whizzed past her head and smashed into an ornate mirror. Glass everywhere, this was turning into a full-on domestic dispute.

Coleman was furious.

'That was Georgian, bitch. It cost me an arm and leg.'

'Oh, yeah,' Amanda shrieked. 'Take that you little two-faced shit.'

As another expensive vase flew in the gangster's direction, it smashed into a thousand pieces. This was kicking off big style, and all Mason could do was watch.

Stepping into his underpants, Coleman was having none of it.

'Get that bitch out of here before I damage her skull.'

Right on cue, Joe Angelini grabbed Amanda by the arm and yanked her kicking and screaming towards the door.

'She's out of her fucking mind,' Coleman screamed.

The friction mounting, Rob Savage brushed past Mason and handcuffed Coleman's wrists. The gangster stared at the sergeant speechless. No match for a woman scorned, his lips were quivering as if the words were stuck in his throat.

Savage took the gangster by the arm and led him to one side.

'What the hell is going on?'

'You're under arrest for murder,' said Savage, 'you do not have to say anything that––'

'Don't spout that crap to me, talk to my fucking lawyers.'

'We already have,' Mason gloated.

'Stuff you too.'

As they led Coleman away kicking and screaming, he pulled up suddenly. Having turned Queen's Evidence, the slightest sniff he was working for the Metropolitan police, his friends would tear him apart. Coleman knew that, and so did every police officer present. But that wasn't all, Amanda was still waiting in the wings and ready to kick off again.

'Poxy pervert,' she screamed.

'Stuff you. Bitch.'

'Good riddance,' Amanda shrieked. 'I hope you get life.'

Not wishing to escalate matters further, Amanda was led away for questioning. As more gang members were rounded up, a semblance of order returned. It was a massive undertaking and would take all day to clear the backlog.

Still buzzing with excitement, the chief inspector was having to pinch himself to stay focused. All he needed was a conviction, and he had plenty of those in his back pocket. He'd been here before, of course, but this time felt different. More rewarding, more gratifying.

Mason made a circuit of the room.

Kerry Waterman appeared chirpy enough, but once they'd processed him through the system everything would change. Taken to Gateshead police station, he'd be thrown into a cell to appear before a magistrate's court to answer for his crimes. It was a great feeling, and for once Mason recognised the importance of what a close-knit murder team really meant. Tom Hedley would have a field day. Once his team had turned the mansion upside down, they'd gather enough evidence to convince a thousand juries. God, it felt good.

Mason pondered his options.

The moment the press got hold of the story, Waterman's celebrity status would plummet to earth like a lead balloon in free-fall. No doubt Special Branch would want to talk to Ed Coleman, as would every other Tom, Dick, and Harry in the land. Fifty million dollars' worth of uncut diamonds had gone missing, and the gangster had a lot to answer for.

He watched as another helicopter swooped low over the mansion's rooftops. Flying in a southerly direction towards Cramlington, he was pleased with his findings. It had been a good day, the best in years, and for once he was feeling cocker hoop. As more ruthless criminals were being led away, the streets of Newcastle would be a much safer place to move around in.

On reaching the grand entrance his phone pinged.

It was Barbara, and she was bubbling with excitement.

'How's your day going?' Mason asked.

'I'm out shopping with friends. What are you up to, my love?'

He frowned. 'I've not stopped all morning and could murder a coffee.'

'You need a break, my love. I've told you often enough.'

'You're right. Let's talk it over at dinner tonight.'

'Sounds good to me.'

Ending the call, he watched the police van as it pulled off the forecourt with Ed Coleman and Kerry Waterman inside.

'Who says crime doesn't pay,' he chuckled.

Chapter Fifty-Nine

It had just turned nine o'clock when Jack Mason pulled into the carpark at Gateshead police station, in what had been the first warm day in weeks. Hoping the weather would hold up, he was looking forward to some quality time with Barbara. It was race week, and she was so hyped up about the occasion, she'd gone out and bought a new outfit. His wallet close on two-hundred quid lighter, he wasn't sure about the new headgear. Cream, with loads of feathers sticking out, and a fancy mesh that fluttered when she walked. It must be a woman's thing, he reasoned. Whatever she wore, he still loved her to bits.

He locked the car and smiled resignedly to himself.

The main office was busy when he entered it, a continuous warbling of landlines and mobile phones. Barely twenty-four-hours had passed since Kerry Waterman had been moved to a high-security wing at Durham prison, and the media were loving it. Not that he was anticipating problems, he wasn't. He still had a few interviews to complete before finalising his written report. Now that Special Branch had taken back control, he was mindful not to tread on other people's toes. It was never easy, as there was always someone willing to criticise your handling of events.

MIR-1 had trumped up all the usual faces that morning, and all except David Carlisle were in remarkably good spirits. After weeks spent trying to convince neighbours it wasn't his cat who was digging up their lawns, things had turned ugly. Having called in the help of the local pest control services, the evidence was conclusive. It was moles. But some people could never be convinced, and that was another problem the profiler faced.

'Okay,' Mason began. 'What's the latest feedback on Ed Coleman's property? Any signs of the diamonds showing?'

'No nothing,' Savage replied.

Mason smiled. The sergeant was dressed more for a round of golf than a team briefing. He would have liked a game himself, but there wasn't the time.

'They're not at the mansion?' he asked.

'No, boss. Forensics have pulled the place apart and found bugger all.'

Sue Carrington raised her hand to speak. Wearing a short sleeve blouse, trousers, and flat shoes, she too was dressed more for comfort than work.

'It's not all bad news,' the detective acknowledged.

'Oh. What have you heard, Sue?'

'The lab technicians have run scans on Coleman's computers and found a boat load of condemning new evidence. Apart from the criminal activities we already knew about, they've recovered a list of candidates involved in the Schiphol airport raid.'

Mason stiffened, ready to lay more charges at the gangster's door.

'Care to explain?'

'It's to do with initial payments made out to people prior to the diamond heist.'

'As in bank transfers?'

'No. As in payments for equipment used in the raid.'

'That could be useful, but how do we know these people were connected to the robbery?'

'We don't, but we do know the fraud squad are involved and it's now down to them to sort out. No doubt they'll trawl through everyone's bank accounts and check for spurious money transfers.'

Mason shot Carrington a glance.

'What about Coleman's personal banking details?'

'All of his assets have been frozen. As for his so-called accounting books, they've been handed to the financial conduct authority for scrutiny.'

'Sounds like Ed is about to be stripped of all of his ill-gotten gains.'

Savage smiled pensively. 'Not quite, boss.'

'Meaning?'

'Sandy Witherspoon is now involved.'

'I thought as much,' Mason huffed. 'What is she whittering on about now?'

'The usual crap. But whoever runs with the case can expect a fight on their hands.'

Mason nodded. 'Having turned Queen's Evidence, I suspect that's down to the Metropolitan police to sort out.'

'Knowing Witherspoon, she'll want this kept local, especially when five of her clients have been charged with taking part in the heist. Rumour has it she's already started the ball rolling, so we can expect to see appeals before we even press charges.'

'That's not how it works. It will probably be dealt with in London.'

'I doubt it,' Savage replied, in his usual thick Geordie accent.

'God,' Mason groaned. 'Will this woman ever get out of my hair?'

'What hair is this, boss?'

Mason grinned and gave the sergeant a mock-stern look.

'On a more serious note,' said Carrington. 'Is there any news on this mole?'

Mason lifted his head and spoke in a low determined voice. 'I'm advised that someone in high office is to be charged with breach of the Official Secrets Act and one breach of the Regulation of Investigatory Powers Act. The details are sketchy, but it's all very hush-hush at the moment.'

'The conniving bastard,' said Savage. 'Do we know who it is?'

'All I can say at this stage is that counterintelligence are dealing with it. The Chief Constable's involved, so I suspect it's someone who works at the police headquarters in Ponteland.'

'Sounds like they've thrown the book at them.'

'If the charges stick, it's my view they'll be serving a long prison sentence.'

'They should bring back hanging,' Savage said, with a little shake of the head.

Mason realised their involvement in the case was fast ending. They still had a few loose ends to sort out, but the bulk of their investigations would be handled by the Metropolitan and Amsterdam police. Apart from Shaun Quinn aka Ellis Walker, who had since been offered a new role with an undisclosed police force, things had turned out far better than he'd anticipated.

As Mason closed his case notes there was a strange but comfortable silence between them. They'd got lucky for once and had come out of it unscathed.

'What now?' asked Savage.

Mason smiled as he sucked in the air. 'I always said Coleman was a shit, and now we have the evidence to prove it. You people did a great job. Not only did you achieve the impossible, you managed it under difficult circumstances. I'm proud of every one of you, but don't take that as a compliment as I expect the best from anyone who works on my team.'

Savage swung to face Mason.

'Sounds a bit over the top if you ask me, boss.'

Everyone burst out laughing.

After a few minutes, Carrington leaned over and asked. 'What happens to Coleman's racehorses now?'

The profiler sat back as if trying to do the math.

'They'll be scratched from the race card; isn't that how the system works?'

Mason's grin broadened. 'If you lot don't know what's happening around here, it's time I looked for another team.'

'Chance would be a fine thing,' Carrington frowned. 'Who'd want to work for you, boss?'

Mason's shrugged. 'Amanda Coleman has taken over ownership, and both horses are running in Thursday's three-thirty handicap.'

'Shit. What are their chances?'

'I was hoping you might tell us that, Rob. Especially after all the bar expenses you've run up lately.'

Everyone fell about laughing.

As the meeting ended, Mason pulled Carlisle to one side.

'What now, my friend?' he asked.

'Somewhere in the sun, Jack. Far away from the dregs of city life. And you?'

'Barbara fancies a week in France, but I'm not overly keen.'

'Oh, and why not?'

'I was hoping for somewhere further afield. India, or East Asia. There are some great package deals on offer at the moment. People are spoilt for choice.'

'A group tour perhaps? Visiting the major sights?'

'Something along those lines.'

Mason waited for Sue Carrington to close the door before he spoke again.

'I'm not usually one to worry about close contact situations, but when I was up on that church roof, I really thought I would meet my maker.'

'You were lucky, Jack. Assassins don't usually hesitate in the kill zone.'

'I know. But what I keep asking myself is, why didn't he shoot me when he had the opportunity?'

THE POACHER'S POCKET

The profiler dug his hands deep into his trouser pockets as he spoke, 'It's the way these people's brains work, I'm afraid. They're unpredictable. Most assassins are usually politically or ideologically motivated whereas hitmen or contract killers are more decisive in their approach. Which one was Sericov you might ask? Who knows, but if he thought he was spending the rest of his life behind bars he would have ended it there and then.'

'But why hesitate? It still doesn't answer my question.'

'Who knows what was going on inside Sericov's head. Capture would have meant failure in his mind. His was all about control, the power of overseeing his own destiny.'

'Is that how you see it?'

'That amongst other things.'

'Maybe I just got lucky for once.'

'One thing for sure, you can never say the Poacher didn't try to kill you.'

'That's true.'

They caught each other's eye, and Mason knew then what the profiler was thinking. It had been ages since they'd last had a serious conversation. Things had been hectic these past few months; everyone was exhausted and seriously in need of a break. Employing Carlisle was the best move he'd made. There were times, and he could think of many, that without his lateral thinking the case would have dragged on for months.

Mason gave a little shrug.

'I still don't understand why he hesitated.'

The profiler shot him a glance. 'Perhaps we'll never know. A psychopath's mental behaviour is never easy to decipher. Out on the roof with nowhere to hide, the Poacher would never have given himself up. It wasn't in his nature – failure would be the last thing on his mind. Could that have been his downfall?'

'Who knows, you tell me.'

Carlisle chewed the end of his pen. 'There comes a point in every killer's mind when they think they're invincible.'

'That's a bloody good point.'

'I know, and most killers without a conscience believe that. It's part of their DNA, it's what makes them tick.'

Mason considered this.

'At first I thought he'd jumped, finished it there and then.'

'If you thought that, then you must have seen the hesitation in his eyes.'

'Maybe I did.'

'Try not to dwell on it, Jack. It's over.'

Satisfied with the profiler's explanation, Mason felt much better. Even so, Commander Cruyff thought his actions gung-ho. Fortunately for him the chief constable was delighted with the outcome, and apart from

G47's ability to slip through the net undetected, he was singing everyone's praises. Now the crime syndicates illicit diamond smuggling network had been dismantled, many of its members were behind bars.

Some things never change, Mason mused.

Chapter Sixty

Jack Mason stood in awe at the number of people who had turned up for the area commander's retirement presentation. Still undecided whether it was out of respect for the old sod's thirty-two years in the force, or finally seeing the back of him. Presented with a beautiful carriage clock and a full set of expensive gardening tools to while away his days, the chief constable gave a glowing speech covering Gregory's achievements.

Mason was surprised to learn his boss had grown up on a rough council estate and risen through the ranks to reach area commander. It was quite an achievement in many people's eyes. Had he misjudged the man – been a bit harsh? Had Gregory gained some respect? Nah, Mason thought. The old sod should have taken voluntary retirement years ago instead of making his life a total misery. It was Gregory's one big mistake, and if ever he found himself in a similar situation, he'd pack in his job without the slightest hesitation.

When the chief constable pulled him to one side, Mason was expecting another glowing commendation. After all the hard work that he and his team had put in over these past six months, he was hoping for some recognition. It wasn't to be. The moment the chief constable levelled with him, Mason stood gobsmacked.

'What? Kerry Waterman is to appeal?'

'He's not implicated in the Schiphol diamond heist. His lawyers are adamant. Waterman swears he doesn't know who the mastermind is and has never had any dealings with him.'

'Whose representing him, sir?' asked Mason.

'Witherspoon and Co.'

Blimey, Mason groaned. Sandy Witherspoon would be the last person he'd want to face in a courtroom. He thought for a moment.

'If Waterman's not the man at the top of the crime syndicate, then who is?'

'If we knew the answer to that, I'd be telling you a different story.'

'Surely SCD7 must have an inkling?'

Mason was beginning to feel deflated. Sure, they'd covered a lot of ground, but the Schiphol mastermind was still of major interest to everyone on the team.

'Don't lose heart, Chief Inspector. Your job was to protect Ellis Walker and you got there in the end. At least everyone can sleep safely in their beds knowing they are safe from drone attacks. As for the Schiphol mastermind, it was never part of your remit. That's down to the Metropolitan police to sort out. They naturally have their suspicions.' The chief constable smiled as another police officer brushed past him. He turned to face Mason again. 'Some say it's the priest, whilst others believe Halil Altintop is the brains behind all of this. When you put all the facts together, it's highly feasible. If you're looking for my professional opinion, then my money's on the man they call Judas.'

Mason looked on in surprise. 'Judas?'

'Yes, and why not?'

'But his name has never cropped up before, sir.'

'All the more reason to suspect an outsider.' The chief constable gave him one of his penetrating stares. 'The more you look into the facts, everything fits perfectly. We still haven't recovered the diamonds and Judas walks free and is able to live a good life.'

Mason began to wonder about his own future commitment on the case. Dozens of arrests had been made, three murders had been resolved, and an undercover detective had been spared from certain death. Not bad when you think about it, he reasoned. Apart from that, yes, the mastermind was still out there along with a bag full of diamonds.

'You look puzzled, Chief Inspector.'

'I am, sir.'

'The truth is never what it appears. My father taught me that many years ago. Besides, many a scholar believes that Judas Iscariot was a fictitious character. Make of it what you will, but he is the man we should be going after.'

As the buzz of conversation hit the room, officers behind them broke out in light hearted laughter. Gregory wouldn't be missed, not like some of the brilliant senior officers who'd retired over the years.

The chief constable swung to face him. 'This case still has some way to run, I can assure you of that. Talking to my Dutch counterpart, it appears the Asif family are literally being torn apart as we speak.'

'What about, Mustapha Davala?'

'The mafia don is facing a life sentence by all accounts, but that's another story.'

'Perish the thought.'

The chief constable nodded his agreement. 'We're holding a washup conference back at HQ tomorrow at 11:30. I'd like you to attend.'

'Yes, of course, sir.'

'On a more serious note, this damn mole who has plagued us for the past few months has turned out to be one of my senior officers...'

'Really?'

'I'm afraid so. Alison Jefferson of all people.'

Mason stood stunned. 'What! Head of Control?'

'Twenty-five years' service down the drain, and all because of an affair. It was a set-up, of course. The crime syndicate had filmed everything. When they threatened to post it on Facebook, that's when she cracked.'

'Good God,' the chief inspector gasped. 'Alison Jefferson would be the last person I'd expect to turn rogue.'

'It shocked quite a few of us, as you can well imagine.'

Mason considered this. 'How did counterintelligence catch her out?'

'Special Branch had been monitoring her movements for weeks. These people have ways of finding things out. They're good at it. When they let slip that Edward Coleman was about to send one of his gang members over to Amsterdam and pick up the stolen military documents, SCD7 were monitoring the crime syndicates encrypted chatter lines. Apart from a priest, Shaun Quinn, and Alison Jefferson, nobody knew where the documents were.'

Still dumbfounded, Mason looked at the chief constable confused. 'It's funny you should mention that, as I found it odd that nobody on Operation Morning Breeze knew where the documents were hidden. Our only instructions were to shadow Shaun Quinn aka Ellis Walker once he'd landed at the Amsterdam ferry terminal. That might explain why Anton

Sericov and his gang were already at the church. Jefferson had tipped them off.'

'Nothing stranger than folk, Chief Inspector. When you consider that Jefferson was Shaun Quinn's boss before Special Branch recruited him into their fold, it explains quite a lot in my opinion.'

'Is that why Coleman's files were either removed from the system or redacted?'

'I'm not sure about that,' the chief constable said, guardedly, 'but no doubt SCD7 may have had a hand in it at some point.'

Mason thought about this. 'What about the priest. Father Jagaar. I thought he was on the crime syndicates books?'

'No. Father Jagaar is working for us.'

'Really?'

The chief constable smiled as he turned to face the rest of the room. 'Like I say, there's nothing stranger than folk. That's why my money's on Judas being the mastermind.'

With that, the chief constable disappeared into the throng.

Crikey, Mason thought. Whoever the Schiphol mastermind was, they were leading them a merry dance. So, who was this person who had so much influence in the diamond smuggling trade that nobody could lay a finger on? At first, he thought it was Coleman, then changed his mind when he learnt about Mustafa Davala's mafia connections. When it wasn't him, and after some serious soul searching about Terrence Baxter, he'd turned his attentions to the arms dealer Halil Altintop. After that theory had been blown out of the water, things became trickier. Still unsure about Waterman, all thoughts had turned to the priest.

Judas, Mason grinned. Now that was one for the book. Maybe the chief constable knew more than he was letting on.

As he slipped from the reception, thoughts turned to Barbara. It was another pleasant day, and the long-range forecast was looking good. Thursday was race day, and he was really looking forward to that. As for Barbara's new outfit, he could hardly wait to see her all dressed up in her fine new regalia. Gosh, she was stunning, and never once had he imagined he could have loved another woman so much. She was such a calming influence on his life.

As he slid into the undercover vehicle, he stopped dead in his tracks.

Hang on a minute! If nobody knew Father Jagaar was working for counterintelligence, then the minute agent Quinn handed him the stolen secret documents they were already back in safe hands. Then he remembered his meeting with Officer Robert. SCD7 had fooled everyone, it seemed. Including the Northumbria police.

Cloaked in secrecy, the only logical explanation Mason could produce was the need to eradicate the mole. The more he thought about it, the more he realised the risks that Alison Jefferson had posed to national security. Until the head of control had been taken out of the equation, every future operation was under threat.

Blimey, Mason thought. The chief constable was right.

There was nothing stranger than folk.

THE END

MICHAEL K. FOSTER

You've turned the last page, but it doesn't have to end there . . .

If you are looking for more action-packed reading in the Jack Mason crime thriller series, there's a whole new series in store.

'Once again, the author has delivered another gripping tale of murders that leaves the reader wanting more. Very believable, gruesome, well-written and engaging to the end.' ***Dan Brown.***

Want to know more about DCI Jack Mason?

Why not subscribe to my monthly newsletter and receive your copy of **"Hackney Central"** FREE.

You can pick up your eBook copy at:
www.michealkfoster.com

Printed in Great Britain
by Amazon